By the same author

The Man of the House
The Easy Way Out
The Object of My Affection

Stephen McCauley

true
_____

enough

Simon & Schuster
New York   London   Toronto   Sydney   Singapore

SIMON & SCHUSTER
Rockefeller Center
1230 Avenue of the Americas
New York, NY 10020

SIMON & SCHUSTER and colophon are registered
trademarks of Simon & Schuster, Inc.

Designed by Deirdre C. Amthor

Manufactured in the United States of America

1   3   5   7   9   10   8   6   4   2

Library of Congress Cataloging-in-Publication Data
McCauley, Stephen.
True enough / Stephen McCauley.
p. cm.
1. Gay men—Fiction.   2. Married women—Fiction.
3. Boston (Mass.)—Fiction.   I. Title.
PS3563.C33757 T7 2001
813'.54—dc21   00-066177
ISBN 0-684-81054-9

For *Sebastian Stuart* and Lesli Gordon

true

_____

enough

One
Things to Do

In the course of one week, Anderton went from unknown lounge singer to Decca recording artist. "One morning me and the kids are having coffee," she told Look *magazine in 1961, "and a record producer calls and says he wants to cut a demo. That phone call gave me a whole new life, even though nothing changed."*

From *Cry Me a River:*
The Lives of Pauline Anderton by Desmond Sullivan

1.

Jane Cody kept lists—Things To Do, Things To Buy, Bills To Pay, Appointments To Keep—but because she knew they provided the kind of irrefutable paper trail that almost always got people into trouble at tawdry junctures in their lives, her lists weren't the literal truth. Some inaccuracies were alibis in case the reminders fell into the wrong hands, while others were there to mislead the people she practically forced to read them. It was a simple system that caused her problems only when she confused the code and started missing dental appointments and showing up at restaurants for imaginary lunches, both of which had happened in the past three weeks. Obviously, she'd been working too hard, unless maybe she hadn't been working enough.

She was sitting at her desk poring over tomorrow's notes to herself to stave off the anxiety attack she could feel brewing in the back of her brain, building in strength like one of the many tropical storms currently approaching adulthood somewhere in the South Atlantic. (The topic of a recent doomladen conversation on the show she produced: *Another* Storm of the Century?) It had been a bad morning—an argument with her son and a volleyball game of passive-aggressive selflessness with her husband—and then the chocolates one of her co-workers had brought in proved disappointing and the carefully arranged plans for this afternoon's taping of the show had started to unravel. At moments like these, she wished she hadn't tried to impress her shrink by agreeing with him that tranquilizers and antidepressants were grossly overprescribed. She was tired of going out of her way to impress Dr. Berman. She was paying him $130 an hour, which ought to be enough to buy his approval, no matter what her opinions.

It was one of those hot, irritating late-August days with the kind of filthy air you wanted to push out of the way. She actually could see—or thought she could—particles of dust and lead and pollen suspended in the fuzzy air, banging against her window, trying to get in. The Charles River was low and slow-moving there on the other side of Soldiers Field Road, and even the muscular rowing crews pulling their way through the murky green water looked sluggish. When she turned forty last year, Jane finally had been released from envying the physical perfection of youth, an unexpected birthday present and a useful one, too, if you had the misfortune of living in Boston, a city cluttered with colleges and private schools. Throughout her thirties, she'd been plagued by the conviction that she could be as fit and healthy and firm as all those running, rowing twenty-year-olds, if only she put her mind to it. Now she could hide comfortably behind that pathetic but irresistible slogan of defeat: "I think I look pretty good for my age."

Jane's office was on the third floor of the studios of WGTB, one of Boston's public television stations. She was a producer of a thrice-weekly show called *Dinner Conversation,* a newsy program considered cutting-edge because it was so low-tech retro, and successful because no one had figured out what to put on in its place. The concept couldn't have been more simple: six people were assembled at a round table in a studio made to look like a dining room and asked to discuss a topic in the news. Plates of nicely prepared food and glasses of respectable wine—both donated—were placed in front of them. The camera was turned on unobtrusively about ten minutes into the conversation and turned off thirty minutes later. There was no host, no moderator, no overarching point of view, and, most important of all, there were no expenses. The key was getting the right six people, something Jane had a special talent for, despite the fact that her at-home dinner parties were often disasters. It had been her inspiration to have an even mix of experts and man-on-the-street types. Half the viewers tuned in to find out what the biochemist from MIT had to say about global warming, and half tuned in to watch the biochemist from MIT get talked into a corner by an amateur weather watcher from one of the area's shabbier suburbs. As long as someone sounded brilliant and someone was made to look foolish, the show played well. Reasonably well. Lately, rumors that *Dinner Conversation* had reached the end of its life cycle swirled around the studio daily. If you could believe the mean-spirited gossip, some of the interns spent half their time coming up with cute headlines to announce its demise: "The *Dinner* Party's Over," "*Conversation* Grinds to a Halt," "Will That Be All?"

The office was eerily quiet this afternoon as it usually was when they were in the middle of a crisis. In two hours they were taping a conversation about a recent plane crash, and one of the guests, a flight attendant, had canceled earlier in the day. Then at noon, a pilot who had agreed to appear and would serve as the authority figure and centerpiece of the discussion called to say he was delayed in Dallas indefinitely. They were left with a couple of windbag travel agents, a friend of one of the other producers whose entire identity revolved around his refusal to fly, and a New Hampshire housewife who claimed to have "died briefly" in an airline disaster several years earlier. As far as Jane was concerned, going on to write best-selling religious tracts—in this case, *I Met God*—was ample evidence that death, no matter how short-lived, had not occurred, but as a nervous flier herself, she didn't want to tempt fate by calling the woman's bluff.

There was a faint knock on Jane's door and Chloe Barnes tentatively stuck her head into the office and gave Jane one of her trembly looks of empathic concern.

"Everything's under control, Chloe. I have several people lined up, I'm just waiting for them to call and confirm."

"You're sure there's nothing I can do?"

"Very sure."

Chloe bit down on her lower lip and raised her eyebrows, as if to say, "Poor you." Jane had fallen for this wide-eyed, lip-biting expression for the first few weeks Chloe worked at the station. Then she saw Chloe staring at her with the exact same mixture of worry and pain while Jane was combing her hair in the bathroom mirror and realized it was a young, beautiful woman's pity of a forty-year-old she considered past the point of sexual relevance. Jane would have laughed it off if she hadn't been worrying about the sexual relevance question herself.

Half an hour earlier, Jane had phoned Rosemary Boyle, an old college friend who was in Boston to teach a couple of courses at BU. Rosemary was a self-involved poet, usually a conversational black hole, but last year she'd written a memoir about being a widow, so she could provide an expert opinion on loss, or something equally pertinent and unspecific. Since the publication of *Dead Husband,* Rosemary was prepared to provide an expert opinion on anything, as long as it helped promote the book. The only thing she wasn't prepared to talk about was the $1.5 million poor Charlie had left her when he died or committed suicide or *whatever,* and how her wrenching description of intolerable privation had added another few hundred grand to her coffers. Jane still hadn't heard back from her. They could easily do the show with five guests, but four was out of the question.

"David's getting a little worried," Chloe said. "He's wondering if we should get some Harvard people lined up."

"Definitely not!" Jane snapped. "*I'm* handling this."

Chloe tugged at her lower lip, a sign that Jane had sounded annoyed rather than authoritative, thereby further undercutting herself.

David Trask was the show's executive producer and saw "Harvard people" as the solution to every problem, as if having an endowed chair, whatever that was, was enough to make up for being pretentious and phlegmatic. Why David was communicating through Chloe, instead of talking to her directly, was a question she'd have to ask when she had a free moment. Chloe had come to the station straight out of Wellesley College four months earlier and was, in Jane's opinion, making too much progress too quickly. She was intelligent—you couldn't deny her that—and so full of energy and ideas you wanted to cap her, like a well, to control the flow.

Chloe was wearing a black suit with a Mandarin collar and bell-bottomed pants, all made out of a tastefully shiny material that probably contained rubber or some other unwholesome, impractical material. No doubt her monthly wardrobe allowance exceeded Jane's mortgage. Her shoes were big lumpy things with immense soles that made her walk with a heavy-footed gait, as if she were about to slap on a pair of skis and hit the slopes, but even they didn't detract from an overall appearance of gorgeous malnourishment that had men throughout the building finding reasons to pass by her desk several times a day. Genetic engineering eventually would produce human beings very much like Chloe: satiny blends of the best physical features of every race with perfectly proportioned faces and figures, human beings with such a scrambled background that racial biases, stereotypes, and quotas were rendered irrelevant in their presence. Her father was a Korean, African-American, Italian lawyer who worked as a diversity consultant for a multinational, and her mother was a former model or dancer or something show-offy, part Colombian, part Chinese, part Native American. Despite all of the advantages wrought by her looks and her upper-middle-class upbringing, Chloe saw the world entirely in terms of villains and victims, and seemed to have equated victimhood with strength and moral superiority in a manner Jane found incoherent, infuriating, and increasingly common among the young people, male and female, who came to the station. The fact that she'd risen to assistant producer in four months didn't seem to register as evidence of her own good fortune. Jane suspected that Chloe, like most college grads of her generation, was bulimic, but there were bloated, premenstrual, post-lunch moments when she envied her even this messy but efficient affliction.

"I can't believe that airline pilot canceled," Chloe said. "We should do a show on people whose lives were ruined by flight cancellations—missing job interviews, weddings, important deaths."

"I hate missing important deaths," Jane said. "It ruins your day."

Jane would have gone into a defensive rage if someone had responded to an idea of hers with this kind of sarcasm, but Chloe took it in and decided to make the best of it. "Bad idea?" she asked.

"It needs fine-tuning."

Jane could see Chloe adjusting the knobs already, sharpening the focus and heightening the contrast. She could deal with Chloe's beauty and youth, write them off as superficial advantages which would fade in time, but there was no way to compete with someone willing and eager to actually learn from her own mistakes. She felt like saying, here, take my desk, my office, let's just get this over with right now.

2.

When Chloe left, Jane went back to her lists. Reading through the orderly arrangement of words on paper—true, false, and everything in between—made her feel more in control of her destiny.

Gerald's gymnastics class—3pm, halfway down the To Do list, was code for taking her six-year-old son to his shrink. She had no hesitation in admitting Gerald was seeing a shrink—if anything, telling her friends made her feel like a better, more attentive mother than she quietly feared herself to be—but her mother-in-law, who was temporarily installed in their carriage house, would have been horrified at the idea, even though she routinely told Jane, in her oblique way, that she thought Gerald was a peculiar child. In Sarah's view of the world, having a problem was *life* and attempting to do something about it was *self-indulgence*. The stoic put up with their God-given afflictions and addictions; the moral weaklings caved in and tried to do something about them.

So to avoid Sarah's scorn, Gerald was dragged off to his gymnastics instructor, Dr. Rose Garitty, M.D., every Wednesday. Poor pudgy, peculiar Gerald. The mere thought of him trying to do somersaults was enough to rend Jane's heart.

"Let's just tell her the truth," Thomas had suggested.

"The truth" was Thomas's solution for everything, which pretty much described her husband's optimistic, kindhearted, one-dimensional view of the world.

Facial—12:30 on the Appointments list was code for her own shrink. Not that she felt any shame about that either, but if Thomas got wind of the fact that she'd started seeing Dr. Berman again, he'd probably ask why, in that wounded way of his, and she might have to explain that for the past year she'd felt a thin crust of boredom forming over the top of their marriage. Or, to be more accurate, she'd begun to feel the thin crust of boredom that had always been over the top of their marriage thickening while she swam in the cold waters below trying to find a hole or an air pocket so she could catch her breath. She wasn't ready to talk openly about that with Dr. Berman, let alone with Thomas. After three months of twice-weekly sessions, she'd gone as far as explaining to the doctor her fears that her career was at a standstill, something she presented as neurotic insecurity, even though she had ample evidence it was true. Discussion of marital concerns would have to wait until she felt more solidly in control of them.

Finish reading Westerly biography. This referred to a book by someone named Desmond Sullivan, a soon-to-be colleague of Thomas's. She'd agreed to read and summarize the thing for her husband weeks ago. Thomas was too busy preparing his courses to read it himself, and too earnest to simply compliment the author with nebulous praise and then drop it. She'd had most of August, but thus far she hadn't done more than scan the index to find references to people who interested her more than the subject himself. The author would be showing up at Deerforth College any day now, and she'd written this little note to herself so Thomas would find it and be reassured that it was only minutes before she completed the tome and gave him her book report.

Up at the top of the Bills To Pay list was *Pay Roofer.* That stumped her. If she had to guess, she'd say it referred to some petty indulgence she wasn't interested in admitting to. Unless it meant that the person who'd reflashed their chimney six months ago still hadn't been paid. On a separate list, she made a note to look into that one.

When her direct line rang, she pushed the papers to the back of her desk and, assuming it was Rosemary Boyle calling about the show, grabbed the receiver on the first ring. But it wasn't Rosemary. It was Caroline Wade. Or, as Jane had come to think of her, Just Caroline.

"Hi, Jane, it's just me."

Jane appreciated self-deprecation as much as the next person, but only when it was clearly an attention-getting display of false modesty. Caroline's humble whimpers often pointed to actual flaws. But how nice that Dale Barsamian, Jane's ex-husband, had married Caroline instead of a fifteen-year-old beauty queen or a manic overachiever, someone who would have inspired crippling jealousy and made Jane wonder even more acutely if her own second marriage hadn't been a little hasty.

"I'm not getting you at a bad time, am I?" Caroline asked.

"I'm supposed to be doing damage control," Jane said, "so I'd much rather talk with you." Despite her annoying quirks, there was something relaxing about talking with Caroline; she was genuinely kind and thoughtful, and was so modest, you didn't have to engage in conversational one-upmanship with her. Jane often found herself bringing up boring topics she wouldn't dare discuss with someone she wanted to impress. "How are the cats?" she asked.

"All right, I guess. Willie kept me up last night. I don't know what's gotten into him. He's so talkative all of a sudden."

"Really? Has he got anything interesting to say about plane crashes?"

"I didn't mean it literally."

Caroline could be one of the most curiously dull intelligent people Jane had ever met, not counting everyone at Deerforth College. She had a Ph.D. in English Lit (from Yale, no less) and a law degree from NYU, but she didn't seem to know what to do with either of them. Since marrying Dale five years earlier, she'd devoted herself to studying Sufism. You'd think you could get her to make an interesting comment every once in a while, or at least recognize a joke when she heard one. The one time Jane had had her on the show, she'd made a few embarrassingly dim observations about George Eliot and then sat there eating, something most guests had the common sense to realize was out of the question, no matter how tempting the food looked.

And yet Dale was devoted to her. Jane didn't know whether to envy Caroline or pity her for that. At his worst, Dale was a cad, a liar, and a self-centered, uncommunicative brat. When their divorce had come through, Jane had felt a ripple of elation pass through her body, as if she'd just quit the worst job of her life. The problem was, as soon as she'd untied all the strings that had made Dale's bad qualities so maddening and confining, she was free to see all the good things that had made him so attractive in the first place: his intelligence, his spiky survival skills, and his languorous, louche sexual charms.

Caroline had been yammering on about the cats—they had three—in an overly detailed way that suggested she was using them to avoid talking about whatever it was that had made her call. When she finally grew silent and sighed wearily and sadly, Jane snapped back to attention, sensing that she was beginning to circle the field in preparation for landing. "Is everything all right, Caroline? You sound a little exhausted."

"Everything's fine. I don't even know why I called. I shouldn't be dragging you into this, it's not fair. I'm going to hang up. I'll call next week." She inhaled sharply, let out two short breaths, and, in a voice that sounded close to tears, said, "You don't have any idea how many times I sat here and dialed your number before I went through with the call. I know you're the last person I should be calling about this. You're the *last* person, but somehow . . ."

With anyone else, Jane might have said: What's he done now? But you had to be gentle with Just Caroline; she bruised easily. "If you've been running it through your head for days, it's probably not as bad as you think. I suppose it's about Dale."

"Oh, of course it's about Dale. Everything's about Dale, isn't it?"

"Certainly in his mind," Jane said, wondering why it was so satisfying to be thought of as an expert on the subject of her ex-husband.

"Well . . ." Caroline paused, and Jane heard her light a cigarette. Caroline had two saving graces: she smoked fiendishly and was insanely aggressive behind the wheel of her ancient Citroën. Without these steam vents, she probably would have blown someone's head off a long time ago, most likely her own. "I don't know why, I don't have any proof, but I'm almost certain Dale's having an affair. I don't know, Jane, maybe he isn't, but he's been acting so strangely these past few weeks. I know you're going to tell me to confront him, but I can't do that. I'm not like you. I wish I were."

Jane had begun to think of "I wish I could be more like you" as a frill people slipped over an insult to dress it up and try to pass it off as a compliment. You're a no-good lying thief. I wish I could be more like you. You're a hateful bitch. Oh, if only I were, too.

"Besides," Caroline went on, "I'm the kind of person people always lie to. I suppose it's something about my face."

No, it was something much deeper and more subtle than her blond, fine-boned beauty and her long-legged, Barbie doll figure, but now was not the time to bring it up. Chloe was pacing in her cinder block shoes just outside Jane's open door and unless Jane swung into action, any action, very soon, Chloe would probably do her the favor of finding a few guests ready to go on camera, making Jane look like a useless fossil.

Still, she couldn't hang up on Caroline until she had the full story. Jane had been married to Dale for six years and had incontrovertible proof of two infidelities and one all-out affair. What surprised her most about Caroline's worries was that they were coming so late into the marriage. "I think you need to take a deep breath and calm down," Jane said. "It sounds to me as if you're jumping ahead and assuming the worst. When you say he's been acting strangely, what do you mean?"

"Strangely. Distant, cut-off."

Jane was stung. Distant and cut-off had been the norm when she and Dale were paired up. Was he really that much more attentive and loving toward Just Caroline? An important part of putting the past in the past is believing that people really can change and that ex-husbands really can't.

"He's probably got too much going on," Jane said. "He's probably involved in some deal he believes the future of the planet depends upon." Dale was a developer, one of those real estate millionaires who destroyed whole neighborhoods with their buildings and then seduced a fawning reporter from the *Boston Globe* into writing laudatory stories about them because they included an affordable studio apartment for a Haitian family in one of their hundred-unit monstrosities. Now, in what Jane saw as a blatant attempt at acquiring a veneer of glamour, Dale was a principal investor in a grotesquely expensive restaurant set to open in downtown Boston sometime next year. She'd heard about this through her brother, an architect on the project, and had seen it as the first signs of a midlife crisis arriving right on schedule. Restaurant business today, cocaine habit tomorrow.

Caroline exhaled luxuriously. "It isn't his work," she said.

"I don't know what to tell you, Caroline. Somehow or other you have to ask him. If he admits to it, at least you'll know where you stand."

"And if he denies it?"

"Then you'll know he's lying."

There was a storm of hissing and yowling in the background, and Caroline squeaked out a halfhearted reproach: "Come on you two, cut it out." Jane could see her, pretty and puffy-eyed, sitting in their sunlit living room surrounded by stacks of books on some obscure, useless topic. Caroline had insisted they buy a modern house in Weston, a Gropius-style box that was ninety percent glass and looked out onto acres of conservation land. What an elegant, cheerful little refuge she'd made for herself, a perfect prison, cats and all, while Dale was off in the city carrying on like a middle-aged adolescent. She felt suddenly protective of Caroline, out there in her glass cage with the miserable cats taking swipes at her. Just Caroline with her degrees and her old-money family and, rumor had it, her barren womb. What a rotten deal for someone like that to be hitched to a cad like Dale. And worse still, what an absolutely wonderful deal for a cad like Dale, married to a trust-funded, well-bred, brainy beauty who was too timid to make him suffer the consequences of his actions.

Chloe stuck her head into Jane's office again and hooked a curtain of dark curls behind her ears. She'd been in the sun recently, and her skin had a wonderful glow, like polished copper; although she appeared to wear no makeup, her eyelids had a metallic shine that Jane found mesmerizing. She gestured toward her watch and then pointed up toward David's floor, not impatiently, but with that annoying pity of hers, as if she were warning Jane that she had ten minutes to save her career.

Jane covered the mouthpiece of the phone. "It's been settled. I'm speaking to our guest right now." Chloe's shoulders dropped with genuine, generous relief. "Close the door, will you?"

There was a satisfying whoosh of air as Chloe sealed her into her office. She'd have to get off and make a round of frantic calls. If Rosemary didn't come through, she'd try to get an air traffic controller they'd had on a couple of times, a bitter man who was full of horror-movie-quality statistics about catastrophes. "I wish there was something I could do for you, Caroline, but I've got so much going on now . . ."

"This is going to sound terrible, Jane, but I was hoping you might . . . talk with him."

"Me? Don't be ridiculous."

"Who else could I ask? It's too humiliating to even discuss it with anyone else. I knew you'd understand, having been through this. I know we haven't spent much time together recently, but somehow I've always felt close to you, almost as if you were extended family. Does that make any sense?"

In other words, Dale still talked about her; she'd never doubted it, but it was nice to have confirmation. Everyone wants to be remembered, especially by the people they'd most like to forget. "I'm going to need time to think this over, Caroline."

Not that the idea of calling her ex-husband on yet another round of infidelities didn't have its appeal. In the wake of their divorce, she'd picked up the pieces and made a successful second marriage; she had a child, a husband who was faithful to her, a legitimate career. He was still waist-deep in the same old rut. And here was fresh evidence, just in case either of them ever had had any doubts about it, that his disloyalties during their marriage were not owing to any of her inadequacies. Finally, it was the least she could do for Just Caroline. They'd been in a book group together two centuries ago and had been casual friends since; Jane had always felt partly responsible for introducing Caroline to Dale.

"There's just one thing," Caroline said. "If you do talk with him, I want you to tell me everything."

"Of course."

"Everything, Jane. Promise me."

"I promise you. Why wouldn't I?"

"You don't know how much this means to me. If there's anything I can do for you, please, just call me up and let me know. I have some extra time on my hands now."

It wasn't as if Jane would take her up on it, but she scanned down her lists even so. Caroline might feel better about the imposition and the embarrassment of the situation if she gave something back.

One item on one of the lists leapt out at her. Caroline was a close, fast reader, and it might do her self-esteem some good to put her academic credentials to use.

"I don't suppose you've read a biography of someone named Lewis Westerly by someone named Desmond Sullivan, have you?"

3.

Rosemary Boyle came through. Half an hour before taping was to start, she called the station. Predictably, she dominated the *Dinner Conversation* by making a series of vague comments that were basically meaningless, but gave the impression of being witty and profound. "Living is losing," she'd said at one point, a comment that silenced the other guests for a full five seconds.

As Jane was about to leave the office, she pulled out a pad of blank paper and started yet another list, this one for things she had to do as soon as she got in tomorrow morning. *Call Dale* she wrote. But then, thinking better of it, she attacked it with an eraser and changed it to the more ambiguous: *Call Roofer.*

Two
Going Away

Anderton claimed to hate going on the road and leaving her husband, Michael, her daughter, and her goldfish. "My family is the most important part of my life," she said during an appearance on The Mike Douglas Show. *"Aside from the booze. And I don't trust Michael with the fish."*

From *Cry Me a River:*
The Lives of Pauline Anderton by Desmond Sullivan

1.

The record dropped onto the turntable, and within seconds, the noise of the traffic on West End Avenue and the sound of the piano student practicing in a neighboring apartment and the deep rumble of a jet making its final approach toward La Guardia were drowned out by Pauline Anderton's big, grainy voice belting out the opening bars of "The Man I Love."

Desmond Sullivan sat back in his chair, the unfinished manuscript of his biography of Pauline Anderton spread out on the desk before him. That's singing, he thought. Not great singing—technically speaking, not even good singing—but sincere, unadulterated, and emotionally wrenching. There were no safety nets here, no studio filters or electronic tricks, just a beating heart, exposed nerves, and a tremendous amount of oxygen. "Some day he'll come a LOOOOONG." Every note Anderton sang went through your body, even when, clearly, it was the wrong note. Leave precision to brain surgeons and airplane mechanics; he'd take a singer willing to plow through a song with heartfelt inaccuracy any day.

He leaned his elbows on his desk, put his head in his hands, and stared out the bedroom window and across the air shaft. In less than a week he was headed to Boston for a four-month-long teaching job at Deerforth College. The offer had come through a mere three weeks ago, an indication that he wasn't the school's first choice and probably wasn't their second or third choice either. Well, guess what? Teaching hadn't been his first choice. He needed a salary and an airtight excuse for leaving New York for a little while, and Deerforth College was providing him with both. If the offer, with its aura of last-minute desperation, had been an insult, he'd thrown it right back in their faces by accepting it. With a little money and a little time away from Russell, he could finally fit all the pieces of this new book together and send it off to his publisher.

The song was approaching the bridge, the weakest part of Anderton's rocky performance. The pretentious way she pronounced Tuesday ("Ta-Youse-Day") always made Desmond cringe. One of Anderton's managers had tried to refine her diction by sending her to elocution lessons, and the result was this occasional lapse in honesty, especially when she'd been drinking before a show or a recording session.

Russell walked into the bedroom, his head cocked as if listening for a cue. He pushed his round yellow glasses against his nose and then, doing a nearly flawless imitation of Anderton, sang along with the record: "Maybe Ta-Youse-Day will be my good Na-Youse day." He left the room, laughing merrily at his own performance.

Depending on your mood, Russell's ability to mimic people could be an entertaining party trick or the emotional equivalent of psoriasis. This afternoon, it was a perfect example of why Desmond had to leave New York in order to figure out exactly what was missing from the book he'd been writing and researching for nearly four years. It wasn't that Russell was unsupportive of Desmond's project. It was hard to imagine how anyone could be more supportive. Russell owned a secondhand store on the Lower East Side. In scavenging for merchandise at yard sales and thrift shops, he'd unearthed: several records Desmond had given up hope of ever finding; a rare program from one of Anderton's rare performances at The Sands in the early 1960s; and a scrapbook of clippings kept by some obsessed fan that spanned the entire course of Anderton's career, from discovery by Walter Winchell to slide into obscurity fifteen years later. He was always willing to discuss Anderton or listen while Desmond trod the same ground over and over, trying to figure out what crucial piece of information or insight he was missing. The problem was that after nearly five years of cohabitation, Desmond was finding it increasingly difficult to make clear distinctions between his own thoughts about Anderton—along with everything else—and Russell's. Who had been the first to pick up on this grating quirk of pronunciation? He couldn't say for sure, nor could he say for sure why it mattered to him so much that he know, especially if it turned out he had picked up on it first.

Love was a strange, exhausting bit of human business. Based on the evidence of literature, torch songs, and the tattered fragments of his own experience, Desmond had come to the conclusion that all the beauty and wonder of the thing was wrapped up in the longing for it and the heartbreak after its demise. You couldn't say the same about much else in life. The pleasures of chocolate, coffee, and gambling, for example, were in the tasting and the doing.

The song was building to its climax, the orchestra swelling in the background. But instead of ending with the display of lung power you might expect, Anderton surprised the listener—here was her genius—by singing the final lines with a wistful, dissipated whisper. "I'm waiting for the man I love." It was enough to make you weep, assuming you'd had a few drinks and were melancholy with loneliness and longing instead of happily partnered off.

Desmond got up and shut off the record player. Russell was lying on the red velvet sofa in the living room, his head on one arm, his bare feet sunk into one of the cushions. His eyeglasses were resting on his forehead, and he had a book, a massive history of the Middle Ages he'd been reading for several days, spread open on his stomach. Russell Abrams came from a family of fire-breathing academics: an economist father who spent half his life delivering lectures in countries Desmond had never heard of and a child psychologist mother who'd written an infamous book arguing that play was the construct of frivolous adults and a complete waste of time. They lived in the Berkeley hills where Russell and his sister had grown up. Russell had rebelled against their intellectual snobbery by moving to New York and teaching art to special needs children in the public school system. Four years ago, he'd retired from teaching so that he and a friend could open the secondhand shop on the Lower East Side, an even more hostile gesture to his parents. Desmond, who'd initially taken Russell's anti-intellectual palaver at face value, had never escaped feeling betrayed by him for reading so eclectically and ravenously. All those tomes Russell foraged through on a weekly basis—dense volumes of history, art, and science, and last year *all* of Trollope—lay around the apartment like reminders of his own literary inadequacies. This was one of the challenges of being in a long-term relationship; sustaining necessary delusions about yourself when someone was always there to witness your limitations and exaggerations and malign you with the truth about yourself.

"I've been thinking," Russell said. "For your next book, you should write something that has a little more in it than a biography."

Desmond gave Russell's body a gentle push and lay beside him, their noses practically touching. The air conditioner in the window opposite them was blowing a chilly breeze in the general vicinity of their legs. "What more is there than the story of a whole life, sweetheart?"

"Less, for one thing. Less childhood and youth and old age, the whole dirge of time and the river. Lives are so unfocused and open to interpretation. I think you might do better with something clean and simple."

"For example?"

"Oh, I don't know. A murder, that's always good. You've got a background in law, so you'd be a natural."

Desmond was about to point out that this was basically criticism bordering on dismissal of the work he'd already done and a perhaps unconscious criticism of Desmond's intellectual abilities. But since he was about to leave town, it didn't seem worth the bother. He took Russell's yellow glasses off his forehead and put them on the end table, then reached his hands around and cupped his ass. Imminent departure had increased Desmond's libido, the way hunger is stoked by plans for a diet. Not that Desmond was necessarily planning a diet.

With the record player turned off, they once again could hear the neighbor in an apartment behind them practicing the piano. In the past three years, Desmond and Russell had listened to this mystery person advance from scales and five-finger folk tunes to Chopin etudes and jazz standards. Today he was playing in such a stop-and-start fashion, Desmond couldn't decipher a melodic line. Maybe more Gershwin. They called the enigmatic piano student Boris and had imagined an entire life for him, one which usually mirrored their own moods and emotions. "Boris sounds a little depressed," Russell would say when he was feeling down. Desmond already missed Boris. The tangled muddle of Russell's dark hair was crushed against the arm of the sofa. In the sunlight pouring in the window, he looked overheated and handsome. Someone should write a torch song about this, Desmond thought, letting go of Russell's behind and running a hand through his hair, this fleeting moment of exquisite tenderness that flares up once in a while to interrupt the long periods of jealousy, restlessness, submerged resentment, and boredom.

"If you hear of any worthwhile murders, keep me in mind. Are you devastated by the thought of me leaving?"

"Yes." He pressed his cheek against Desmond's. "But I won't give you the satisfaction of saying so."

"I don't blame you. I wouldn't either." The truth was, Desmond probably would have made more of a fuss if Russell had been the one leaving; of the two of them, Russell was the more trusting and, despite being three years younger, was, in his own way, more mature. Lately, Desmond had begun to worry that more trust was basically the same thing as less interest.

He slid his hands under Russell's T-shirt and up along the taut damp skin of his back. Russell was thirty-six, and although the skin around his eyes had started to wrinkle, his body still had the compact tightness of a man who hadn't yet bumped into the crisis of midlife. Aside from wearing his dark hair almost to his shoulders, Russell never displayed any vanity, which was, as far as Desmond was concerned, an indication of self-confidence about his looks that was the same thing as vanity. He had large brown eyes that were beautiful but nearsighted and made him look a good deal more vulnerable than he really was, and a narrow, dimpled chin. Desmond had his assets and he knew it, but he'd always felt awkwardly tall and skinny. Earlier in the summer when he and Russell were in a Wal-Mart in New Jersey looking for an air conditioner, someone had stopped him and said: "Excuse me, do you work here?" a comment that continued to echo in his brain like a reproach for a lack of physical grace and intellectual authority.

"I hope you're not trying to get something amorous going here," Russell said. He held his arm behind Desmond's head so he could read his watch. "We have to be at the party—at *your* party—in an hour."

"All the better." After living together for five years, having limited time to fuck was an aphrodisiac, while long, uninterrupted hours lying naked in bed tended to produce conversations about Madeleine Albright. He moved his body against Russell's. "We don't live here," he fantasized. "We're guests in someone's apartment, sleeping on their sofa, and they'll be home in ten minutes."

Russell closed his eyes, a sign he was beginning to respond. A faint smile came to his lips as he adjusted the scenario to suit himself. "You'd better hurry up," he said. "Your wife's my best friend, and I don't want her coming in and catching us."

Desmond kicked off his shoes and unbuckled his pants, feeling a mixture of relief, excitement, and jealousy at the thought that he was being written out of the movie now playing in Russell's head.

2.

It had been planned as a going-away party for Desmond, but shortly after arriving at their friends' apartment in Chelsea, Desmond sensed that something was wrong. They were met at the door by Velan, one of the two hosts. Velan and Peter had been a couple for sixteen years, far longer than almost anyone at this gathering had known either of them. Velan was the younger of the two men, an Indian beauty who had about him an aura of Dietrich-like haughty glamour, despite the thinning hair and little pouch of drooping chin. Like a lot of pretty boys who were still pretty but hadn't been boys for at least twenty-five years, Velan had a sluggishly leering attitude, intended, Desmond assumed, to trick you into thinking you'd just made a pass at him. Over the years, Desmond had made a number of passes at him, not because he was attracted but because it seemed like the polite thing to do. You wanted to be polite toward Velan, to court and appease him, because, like hollandaise sauce, he tended to curdle without warning.

"Ah, the guest of honor," Velan said languidly and then stood with his chin raised, waiting to be kissed. His black eyes were colder than usual, the first sign that something was amiss, although perhaps nothing more serious than an uncharacteristic bout of sobriety.

"Sorry we're a little late," Desmond said. "I've been trying to get things organized for the move." Aside from a few boxes of Important Books he'd been meaning to finish for a decade or more—*The Making of Americans, The Man Without Qualities, Forever Amber*, among others—he hadn't started to pack yet, mostly out of consideration for Russell. Lovers and pets get anxious at the sight of suitcases, and Desmond was afraid that his own preparations either would provoke a spell of heartfelt whimpering (making him feel like a louse) or would not (making him feel unappreciated).

"I'll bet you two were hoping to make an 'entrance.' The guests of honor, all dressed up—sort of. Don't apologize to me. It was *Peter's* idea to have this." Velan spit out his lover's name as if it were a rancid peanut. "Russell's looking flushed, Desmond. Is that the heat or did you do something to him in the cab?"

"We took the subway," Desmond said. "Where *is* Peter?"

"Somewhere," Velan said. "If you find him, don't bother telling me."

As they were walking down the hallway, Russell yanked off his eyeglasses and polished them on his shirt. "What was all that about?"

"Vintage Velan," Desmond said, trying to shrug off his blunt disdain for the party. After all, it hadn't been Desmond's idea to have this party and he'd even tried to discourage Peter when he first brought it up. Desmond hated going-away parties, almost as much as he hated birthday parties; it was embarrassing to be applauded for leaving town for a few months or for having been born, as if these were great personal accomplishments. "You can't pay too much attention to anything he says."

Velan was in charge of publicity for an intimidatingly trendy chain of Manhattan hotels. He drank too much, a prerequisite for his job, he maintained, and frequently made bitter, scathing comments you were supposed to appreciate as examples of his wit. It was Peter, a dour, portly lawyer, Desmond had originally befriended, but he and Velan had been together so long, it was impossible to think of either of them as entirely separate people.

"Unfortunately," Russell said, adjusting his glasses against his face, "you can't ignore what he says either. Not when he's wearing all that aftershave."

About thirty men and women, most of whom Desmond recognized, were crowded into the long, narrow living room, all holding glasses of wine and politely grabbing sticks of chicken satay from the waiter's tray. There was background music set at an appropriately low volume—poor Billie Holiday, Desmond thought, whose art had cost her so much pain and so many painkillers, now reduced to aural wallpaper for these kinds of gatherings—and the massive air conditioner in the front window had taken the bite out of August's most recent heat wave. It was after six, and the temperature outside was still hovering in the low nineties. Calm and cool though the apartment was, there was something slightly tentative in the way people were laughing and talking, as if a piece of bad news had started circulating moments before

Desmond and Russell had arrived. There was a disappointingly controlled murmur when Desmond entered—guest of honor, indeed; the only thing worse than being undeservedly applauded was not being applauded at all— and only a few people raised a glass toward him and then stood apprehensively, waiting, it seemed, for the sound of the other shoe hitting the floor. Sybil Gale, a former teaching colleague from Fordham, rushed up to him and grabbed his arm.

"I was afraid you weren't going to show," she said. "Hi, Russell."

In private, Sybil had let Desmond know she wasn't especially fond of Russell, had even hinted that she found him shallow. Desmond had mounted a full defense of Russell, but Sybil's admission had secretly thrilled him and had endeared her to him; everyone else, even old friends who should have known better, were so enamored of his charming lover, he often felt like a grumpy tag-along. He wanted his friends to accept his partner, but actually liking him was beyond the call of duty. Sybil's loyalty to Desmond, more than any interests or attitudes they had in common, made her feel like one of his most intimate friends.

"Is something going on here we should know about?" Russell asked.

"Well, yes, that's the question, isn't it?" Sybil had spent her childhood in Rhodesia and spoke in a clipped, breathless way that made her, at times, sound indignant.

"And the answer?" Desmond said.

She took a drink from a recklessly wide wineglass and shrugged. "No one knows, but we're all assuming the worst, even though we have no idea what that could be. Oh look, Russell," she said, "someone over by the window is waving at you."

One of Desmond's ex-boyfriends was beckoning Russell with his index finger. He was an attractive set designer with slicked-back blond hair who was always pawing at Russell—a cheap way of getting my attention, Desmond had convinced himself.

"He must be upset you're leaving," Sybil said, watching Russell make his way through groups of friends tossing promises of dinner invitations in his wake, setting up Russell as a victim of Desmond's ruthless abandonment. "One imagines him drifting aimlessly without you."

"Do you mean cruising?"

"Interesting you leapt to that association, but no, I mean wandering, unsure how to spend his time, drifting." And then, as if delivering the key to understanding a completely obscure sonnet, she said: "You're his anchor."

It amazed Desmond that this kind of criticism of Russell, which he knew to be not only incorrect, but precisely incorrect, could still make him feel better about himself. Russell was eager, energetic, and so unfamiliar with aimlessness, he didn't even recognize it in other people. Thank God. No doubt Sybil, who was dazzlingly astute and insightful about literature but always snatched at the most obvious conclusions when it came to flesh-and-blood people, was making assumptions based on the fact that Russell was a good four inches shorter than Desmond. As for the anchor comment, Desmond would take it as a compliment, even if anchor was just another way to describe a weight around your neck.

"I'm only leaving for one semester," Desmond said. "I'll be buried in students and he'll be buried in his work and then I'll be home. He'll barely know I've gone."

"Will you get some time to work on your book?"

"I'm hoping to squeeze in a few minutes once or twice a week, but I probably won't get even that."

Sybil nodded sympathetically and swirled her wine. She was a lean, fervid woman with pale eyebrows and pale thin hair she cut in a close-cropped style that made her look as if she were wearing a bathing cap. She had the sculpted beauty and adroitly undernourished body of an aging fashion model, but looking at the haircut and the pastel blue eye shadow (a signature of some kind), and an out-of season, nubby green pullover, you had to conclude that she objected to her own good looks on moral grounds. She'd been teaching in the English Department at Fordham for ten years, had been given tenure one month after an especially ugly divorce, and her devotion to her students was so unswerving it filled Desmond with a mixture of admiration, awe, and pity. She was an extraordinarily gifted and generous teacher, he thought, but surely she ought to have something better to do with her time. As a teacher, he always felt like a fraud in front of Sybil. He'd done a minimal amount of preparation for the two journalism courses he'd been hired to teach at Deerforth—he'd taught similar classes in and around Manhattan eight times—and had given serious consideration to passing out a trumped-up, dauntingly demanding syllabus the first class in the hopes of getting a handful of students to drop out. Pauline Anderton had spent her final days in a suburb of Boston, and Desmond was planning to arrange his schedule so he'd be able to spend the bulk of his time going over his notes and soaking up atmosphere.

"A lot can happen in one semester," Sybil said, but it wasn't clear from her tone if she meant it hopefully or as a warning. "I told you to look up Thomas Miller, didn't I?"

"You did. I have it written down somewhere," Desmond said.

"I haven't talked to him in years, but I always admired him in graduate school. I imagine he'd remember me. He was a big bore but terribly sweet, and he didn't push himself on you the way most bores do. I don't mind boring people as long as they're not self-confident along with it. I heard he married a TV producer or something. I suppose that can't be very significant in a town like Boston."

"I suppose not. I'll look him up if I have the time. Maybe his wife can get me an insignificant job in TV."

Sybil lowered her blue eyelids as she sipped. "There's a grim thought," she said. "I think I'll circulate for a few minutes and see if anyone knows what the problem is here."

When Sybil had disappeared into the crowd, Desmond leaned against the burgundy wall and surveyed the crowd. The guests were friends or acquaintances, former teaching colleagues, magazine editors he'd worked for, and two ex-boyfriends. He felt removed from most of them, as if he'd left town years ago and was viewing his friends from a different city and a different life than the one in which he'd met them. There was a vase of lilies on the table near him, and the sweet funereal stench of them was overpowering, making him feel even more dreamy and lost. It was hard to maintain close friendships when you were in a relationship; it seemed disloyal to discuss the intimate emotional details of your life, and besides, most people—even the ones who loved to gossip in lewd detail about their every anonymous sexual encounter—practically blushed at the particulars of domestic happiness or the mere hint of connubial sexual contentment.

After scanning the room several times, Desmond was certain his editor hadn't shown up after all. They'd been having some problems communicating lately, an optimistic way of saying she hadn't returned a couple of his calls, and he'd been hoping she'd put in an appearance. His biography of Pauline Anderton was significantly overdue. Whenever his editor mentioned this to him, Desmond longed to remind her that, given Anderton's slide into obscurity, it wasn't as if anyone was waiting for the book, but that hardly seemed to strengthen his case.

Several people came over to wish him well, and then quickly cast furtive glances around the room and asked if he knew what was going on. Speculation ran from a death in Velan's family to the possibility that the hotel chain had fired him. Most of the ideas seemed to boil down to revenge fantasies in which Velan was punished in one way or another for his smug beauty. Desmond couldn't help but feel a little cheated out of the attention he didn't want. Velan obviously hadn't planned the death of one of his relatives to steal his thunder, but it always worked out somehow that he became the center of attention. Velan was standing by the window berating a waiter for chatting with one of the guests (translation: for being twenty-five years old) in a smoldering voice that was halfway between insulting and flirtatious. It was a mystery how Peter put up with this outrageous behavior, most of which seemed to have been learned from the tail end of Joan Crawford's movie career. Maybe, Desmond thought, true love was an acute form of tolerance.

Kevin, a friend who was nearly as tall as Desmond, but a good deal fleshier and almost ferociously handsome, came and stood beside him and watched Velan's performance. Once the tirade had subsided, he said, "It must be awful to have so little impulse control."

"I guess," Desmond said. "Of course it could be wonderful, couldn't it?" That was what made Velan so irresistible; even if you found him hard to take, you couldn't help but want a little of his audacity for yourself.

"We may never know." Kevin turned and gazed at Desmond with his big green eyes, threatening him with his empathy and his chiseled good looks. "How *are* you, Desmond?" He asked so pointedly, it was as if he'd asked several times already but hadn't believed any of the other answers. He was wearing a dark suit and a very soft green tie, all nice, but so inappropriately formal, Desmond assumed he had someplace better to go following this gathering.

"I'm just fine."

"You are? Really? Not worried about leaving town?"

"It's only for a few months."

"I couldn't do it," Kevin said, shaking his long, narrow head and jutting out his jaw in an exaggerated gesture of disapproval. The problem with being as handsome as Kevin was that he looked so good in every light and expression, he always appeared to be posing, even when he was completely sincere. "I couldn't pack up and leave a lover for four months. I'm too much of a romantic."

Desmond said nothing. It was hard to figure out why everyone assumed that a separation was a threat to a couple when the evidence clearly indicates that spending time together is what usually kills a relationship.

Kevin worked at Smith Barney sixty hours a week and spent much of his free time attending to his aging parents in White Plains. He frequently made pronouncements about how romantic he was but never referred specifically to any romantic attachments. Friends were always trying to fix him up on blind dates, but nothing ever worked out. Desmond suspected that he had a secret life tucked away somewhere, one that revolved around slings and leather masks, or possibly women with penises, but he wasn't the type you could ask. He was studiously polite and evasive, which made him the perfect person to put beside a grinding bore at a dinner table. Desmond often felt reassured by his stoic diffidence; most of the time you knew more about a person than you cared to know, so Kevin was a refreshing change.

"I'll invite Russell out to dinner when you're gone," Kevin said. "If that's all right with you. Keep him out of trouble for you."

"I'm sure he'd like that," Desmond told him, comforted by the thought that Russell, who claimed to find Kevin "scary," wouldn't like it at all.

"Now I think I'm going to try to slip out of here. I have the feeling something's about to hit the fan and I'd rather not get the suit dirty."

"Another party?"

"Oh, I wouldn't call it *that.*" But of course, being Kevin, he wouldn't call it whatever it was, either.

After he'd departed, Desmond gazed across the room at Russell standing by the window, delivering an animated monologue to two bald, bearded men. Desmond could tell from his gestures and facial expressions that he was talking about his secondhand store, a bottomless source of material for anecdotes replete with characters he could mimic and merchandise he could describe in loving detail. Watching him run through his routine, Desmond felt unaccountably lonely. I wish he'd come stand beside me, he thought, and then he saw Russell excuse himself and cross the room. Maybe love was a form of telepathy. Desmond was always trying to find a chewable-vitamin-sized definition of love, one that justified the energy he'd invested in his relationship with Russell while reassuring himself that, in the blink of a jaundiced eye, he could live happily without it.

"You got a lot of attention over there, sweetheart," Desmond said, putting his arm around him. "Which story were you telling them?"

"The one about the $85 lunch box."

"I like that one. Did you put in the joke I gave you?"

"I was about to when you called me over."

"I didn't call you over."

"No? Well, it doesn't matter. Have you noticed that Peter isn't here?"

Desmond had noticed, but he'd assumed he was avoiding Velan's bad mood by hiding in the kitchen. Like a lot of people married to alcoholics, Peter spent vast amounts of time cooking and had become an expert chef.

"Apparently not. And rumor has it the bedroom door is closed. I think you should investigate."

Desmond liked opening bedroom doors, but at the moment, he didn't want to be separated from Russell. "Only if you come with me."

"One person looks concerned, two would look prurient. I'll keep watch out here."

"Maybe it's something as simple as an upset stomach."

"Possibly. But if it is, a lot of your friends here are going to be very disappointed."

3.

Desmond knocked lightly on the bedroom door. From inside, he could hear only the hum and rattle of an air conditioner and the distant sizzle of running water. "Peter?" When there was no response, he gave the door a noncommittal push.

It was a small room that looked out to an air shaft, but it had been given the movie set treatment made famous by Velan's hotel chain: an immense painting over the bed, long white sheets covering the windows, a few garish pieces of asymmetrical Italian furniture, all designed to trick the eye into zeroing in on individual corners of the room and thus missing the claustrophobic whole. There was a leather suitcase open on the bed. Desmond peered into it at the carefully packed shirts and pants, thinking for one loopy second that it had something to do with his own departure. Then the door to the bathroom swung open and Peter emerged, drying his hands on a big green towel. He was a heavy man who carried himself with calm self-confidence, the kind of man you'd call in an emergency, hoping Velan didn't pick up the phone. He had on a pair of khaki pants and a black T-shirt with a pad of graying hair sticking out of the neckline. He smiled wanly at Desmond, as if he'd been expecting him, and tossed the towel onto the bed.

"Going somewhere?" Desmond asked cheerfully.

"I'm afraid so." His voice was thick.

It was then that Desmond noticed he was unshaven and that his eyes were a bright, nearly alarming shade of red. Desmond felt the smile melt off his own face. "Peter," he said. "What's happened?"

"Velan's asked me to get out." Peter sat in one of the dark purple chairs and let his head fall into his hands. The chair, shaped more or less like a cupped hand, was far too whimsical a setting for this display of raw emotion. Suddenly, all the bright, pretty furnishings, the sound of the party in the other room, even the faint smell of Velan's sandalwood aftershave seemed inappropriate and poignant.

Desmond took a seat on the edge of the bed, his knees practically touching Peter's. Of all the people here tonight, it was Peter he respected the most. It took integrity to put up with the likes of Velan, and Peter got too little credit for that. Although almost everyone who knew them acknowledged that Peter was the more likable and sympathetic of the two men, the kinder and the more intelligent, Velan was still considered the catch, the one who'd been hooked by lucky and—it had to be, what other explanation was there for the loyalty of someone like Velan?—massively endowed Peter. Velan made frequent, humorless jokes about replacing Peter, which Desmond had taken to be verbal aphrodisiacs. But now, it had happened.

"I'm sorry this had to play itself out this afternoon, Desmond, just in time to ruin your party."

"Please, don't even mention that. It doesn't matter a bit. What happened?"

Peter shrugged. "We were talking about this party, about you, come to think of it. About you going away. Velan said something about the possibility of one of you meeting someone else, the kind of cutting remark you'd expect, the kind I've come to expect, anyway. You don't know how awful he can be. No one does. Everyone thinks he's such a joy to live with, so delightful."

Desmond had fallen for this trap before, leaping at the chance to tell a friend—at last—what he really thought of his partner at the first signs of trouble and then discovering a week later that his words had been repeated during a passionate reconciliation, thereby killing two friendships with one truth. "No one's delightful all the time," he said.

"We got talking about fidelity. Velan started going on and on about it, as if

38

there was something bothering him, something he wanted to tell me or ask me. Finally, I couldn't take it anymore, so I just asked him outright."

Peter stopped here, at what seemed like the most crucial point. "If he was seeing someone else?" Desmond prompted.

Peter let his hands hang between his knees. The backs of his hands and his fingers up to the second knuckles were covered in graying hair. Age, Desmond thought, was so unkind. Peter looked at him with a blank expression. "I asked him if he knew I've been having an affair."

"You?"

"For the past six months."

"Wow! Six months?" It shocked him to think that steady, reliable Peter had been carrying on behind Velan's back, but there was something undeniably impressive about the fact that he'd been able to keep it secret for so long. "That's quite a fling."

Peter looked out the window and started to rub his throat. "I think it may be more than a fling," he said. When he looked at Desmond again, he had a pleading expression in his eyes, as if, having made this confession of real emotion, he deserved understanding and sympathy. Who wouldn't understand cheating on poor impossible Velan? Desmond tried his best to nod sympathetically, but he found a curious kind of uneasiness and perhaps jealousy nipping at him, the way he'd felt last month when he went to Chicago to visit his father and learned that the woman sitting next to him on the plane had paid less than half of what he'd paid for his ticket. He looked away from Peter's hands, figuring he'd misread the tawdry hairiness of them a moment earlier; virility, not age.

"But, Peter," he said, "how did you think Velan was going to react?"

Peter squinted, pondering the question. "I don't know. Maybe I imagined that after being faithful to him all these years, I'd have a little room to wriggle."

Room to wriggle. That was what everyone wanted these days; not to wriggle out of contracts, vows, and legal obligations, but room to wriggle within them. Have it all, in other words; eat your potato chips without accruing fat grams. Certainly that was what Desmond wanted, but at least he had the good sense to keep quiet about it.

"So this is the first time you've . . . done something like this?"

"Yes, of course. I'm not saying it's been easy, but fidelity is a discipline, like everything else. You learn how to adapt. Like giving up cigarettes. When Velan started traveling for work, I found that if I went on a little bender while he was out of town, it relieved the pressure and I didn't need to fool around."

"A bender?"

"Oh, you know, call a few phone numbers, go to a couple of sex parties, line something up over the Internet. A couple days of debauchery to clear the pipes. I'm sure you've done the same thing"

"Russell doesn't travel much."

"When *you* travel then." Peter got up and started to sort a pile of clean laundry on the floor beside the bed. Some of the shirts and underwear he rolled up and tossed back onto the floor in disgust, others he carefully folded and laid in the suitcase. "I'll bet you've got a few things lined up in Boston already."

Desmond had spent two weeks negotiating with the Deerforth College housing office, trying to line up an apartment, but clearly this wasn't what Peter had in mind. He'd agreed to Russell's request for monogamy only when he had a guarantee that they'd keep that part of their relationship quiet; male couples who advertise their monogamy are usually tossed into the eunuch category and end up getting invited to dinner parties where people discuss dogs. Perhaps he'd misled Peter somewhere along the line about his own faithfulness to Russell, but probably not intentionally. As for Boston, he assumed the promise of monogamy would begin to grow fuzzy, like a radio signal, outside a hundred-mile radius of the broadcasting tower, but he'd barely had time to put together his courses, never mind organize a sex life. Admitting any of this in light of Peter's six months of extramarital bliss would sound too much like defeat. "Well, I've got some plans," he said vaguely. "A few things, you know . . . lined up."

"Exactly. It wouldn't be normal if you didn't."

"Exactly."

Peter finished packing the clothes, clicked shut the snaps on the leather suitcase, and set it beside the closet door where a fully loaded duffel bag was already waiting. He was making a temporary move to the extra bedroom of a recently divorced colleague at his law firm. It was a bad moment to be out pounding the Manhattan sidewalks in search of an apartment, but he'd manage. He was motivated, refreshed; he felt younger somehow.

He sat back in the hand-shaped chair, leaned forward, and said, "Is there anything you want to ask me, Desmond?"

It was an odd question, the kind of thing a veteran cancer patient might ask someone who'd recently been diagnosed. In fact, there were lots of things Desmond wanted to ask, but he was afraid most of the questions would sound voyeuristic: Where did you meet? How old is he? How did you find the time? Probably Peter just wanted what most people in his situation wanted—an excuse to speak his mistress's name aloud. "Who is this . . . person?" Best not to assume anything.

"His name's Sandy," Peter said proudly. "You don't know him." And then, draping his arms over the back of the chair, he began to rhapsodize about a stockbroker he'd met on the subway.

Three
Drinks with Dale

1.

The one thing you couldn't take away from Dale Barsamian was his looks. Time would do that sooner or later, but at least for the moment, his looks were there for everyone to enjoy, and for the most part, everyone did.

As Jane watched him walk into the cocktail lounge of the Boylston Hotel, she thought: Thank God I'm not married to him any longer. Handsome, sure of himself, oozing poised masculinity, Dale loosened his tie as he laughed with the maître d', and you could practically hear people sighing on all sides. Woe to any woman married to a man who was as effortlessly charming and seductive as Dale. If someone wasn't snarling at you for having snagged him, they were being nice to you in an effort to get closer to him. Men, women, it didn't matter. Just Caroline just wasn't up to this kind of rogue. Seeing him across the room, Jane was reminded of all the comforts of being married to a man like Thomas, someone solid and reliable, attractive but unexceptional, someone you could trust to be utterly steadfast, even when you didn't want him to be.

She hadn't seen Dale in more than six months, and she honestly couldn't remember the last time she'd been alone with him. It might even have been the warm January day of their divorce. After all the papers had been signed and she and he were officially free of each other, they'd gone to a diner near the courthouse and had a friendly, greasy lunch. They didn't mention the past or indulge in embarrassingly sloppy nostalgia. Instead, they talked about their plans in an open, effortless way that was completely without ulterior motives or hidden agendas—and therefore without precedent in the history of their relationship. They'd sat in their cramped booth for hours, and by the time they got up, a new weather system had blown in; the sky had gone gray and snow was falling. Out on the sidewalk with fat papery flakes floating past them, Dale had put his arms around her and kissed her goodbye. The next thing either of them knew, they were making out in an alley, leaning against a rusty Dumpster, their bodies pressed together, their shoulders covered with snow. Jane had finally let herself cry in front of him. "I'm not going to miss you," she'd said, her words slurred with emotion. "Janey," he'd whispered in her ear, "I'm going to miss you."

Now, all the doubts she'd had about this meeting melted away as she watched him make his entrance; she should have planned a get-together as soon as she felt the first stirrings of seriously icy discontent with Thomas. One look at Dale's craggy face and she was ready to rush back to her husband and smother him with affection, just for being his lovable, unlovely self.

The Boylston was one of the city's older hotels, but it had a convenient location and recently had become officially hip. Some ten-year-old entrepreneur had purchased it and turned the first three floors into a full-service day spa and health club where you could wallow in every form of self-improvement and body detoxification on the market. Salt rubs, high colonics, laser peels, sweatboxes—you name it. The entire health spa movement, with its mania for scrubbing the body, inside and out, was just a high-priced form of self-mutilation. The only thing left to implement was a treatment to gut the body completely and replace all those nasty internal organs with flax seeds soaked in perfumed almond oil. Self-improvement had become a matter of self-annihilation. Relaxation had become a competitive sport and inner peace a commodity.

But before you had the toxins drained from your liver, you could come to this cool pink cocktail lounge, smoke cigars, and drink yourself into a hazy stupor. Every itty-bitty table was equipped with a long-stemmed goblet with its own pink fish, swimming around in dizzying, pointless circles. Jane was sure it was meant to be soothing, and probably it was unless you had the misfortune of empathizing with the fish and seeing the whole going-nowhere tableau as a perfect metaphor for your life.

Dale spotted her and waved, all false modesty and apology. He was nearly half an hour late. She'd expected him to be late because he always was, and, hoping to give him a taste of his own medicine, she herself had arrived twenty minutes after the time they'd agreed upon. Obviously, she hadn't waited long enough.

He approached the table flashing a toothy, lopsided grin and held up his hands as if blocking a punch. "Before you get started on me, it couldn't be helped. There was an explosion down on Atlantic Avenue and that whole end of the city is in shambles. Three people were killed."

How convenient and how like him to come up with the kind of excuse that exonerated him and made you feel like a heartless scoundrel for having the audacity to care that he was late. "I'm sure I'll read about it in the papers," she said. "Anyway, I was held up myself. I got here two minutes ago."

"Oh good. Now I don't feel so guilty." He bent down and gave her a swift, sexless kiss on the mouth. Out in the real world—away from this flattering artificial light and cool maybe-marble floor—it was a hot afternoon. Dale was wearing a brown suit. As he straightened up, the scent of his warm body gasped out of his loosened collar, and Jane was enveloped in its acrid perfume, a blend of cedar, sweat, and Ivory soap that stirred memories of eroticism and anger. He examined her through squinted eyes, and then delivered his assessment. "You know something, Janey? You look spectacular. When did you start letting your hair grow out?"

"Third grade," she said. If he was beginning to flatter her already, there was a good chance Caroline had broken down and told him what this was all about. In that case, the best tactic was to let him think she was warming up to him, and then go for the jugular when he was least expecting it. The advantage of dealing with vain, self-confident men like Dale was that they couldn't imagine anyone being two steps ahead of them and so were always wonderfully vulnerable. Although he didn't look vulnerable. The suit brought out his tan and the light in his amber-colored eyes. You couldn't blame the man for dressing so well, but you certainly could resent him for always knowing exactly what piece of clothing would bring out his best features, especially if you had no instinct for clothes and accessories yourself and were therefore at the mercy of every avaricious salesclerk in the world with an advanced degree in fatuous flattery. To kill time this afternoon, she'd gone into a little jewelry shop on Newbury Street and bought a much too expensive pair of jade green earrings which the salesgirl had described as a great color and style for her. But as she was coming into the hotel, she caught a glimpse of herself in a wall-sized mirror. She saw freakishly big plastic triangles in a garish shade of lime with a graying head attached. She'd slipped them off and tossed them into her bag. Dale was good on details and would know immediately that they were brand-new and the purchase of them was somehow connected to seeing him.

The key to Dale's beauty was his ugliness. His face combined the worst elements of his father and his Irish mother, a punk's crooked nose, a fat mouth that was too large for his square, lean face, and those droopy Armenian eyes, all topped off by a thick brush of blue-black hair that refused to be tamed. Any one feature by itself was appalling, but they fell together in a way that made him look like a carefully sculpted ideal of rugged magnificence, not pretty, not perfect, just irresistible. Even his perfectly ordinary height worked to his advantage; taller men looked gawky and clumsy standing next to solid, compact Dale.

"I don't know what everyone sees in him," a friend of Jane's had once told her. "He looks like a prick to me." Which was, of course, exactly what he looked like to everyone else.

He was from one of those nondescript suburbs somewhere west of Boston—a shopping mall with a few cul-de-saced neighborhoods arranged around it. His father had died young, leaving Dale the head of a household of adoring women—two sisters and a flirtatious mother. He'd worked his way through Harvard, smoothing out his Boston accent so he'd be presentable and respected among Boston's Brahmin banking and business establishment. His real stroke of genius had been cultivating an aura of polite coarseness that made other men desperate for his approval, hoping, Jane supposed, that being liked by him would mean they were more like him. Jane had never understood why people didn't immediately spot the calculation behind his manner; it was too natural and unaffected to be real.

"You look pretty spectacular yourself," Jane said. "Just in case no one's told you in the last three minutes."

"I look like crap," he said. "Do you realize I've started sprouting hair in my ears?"

"It's the talk of the town. We're thinking about doing a segment on it next week."

Dale sat at the table sideways, one arm flung over the back of his chair, a friendly grin on his fat lips. He touched the rim of the water goblet and the fish swam to his side of the glass and gazed out at him adoringly.

"I saw the show when your friend Rosemary Boyle was on. I didn't realize poor old Charlie had died that way."

"It was horrible," Jane said, because you had to say it was horrible, even if you weren't so sure. "He was alone in Maine on a fishing trip, not that he fished. Rosemary was devastated."

Dale pushed the tiny aquarium to one side of the table, rested his elbow in the middle, and leaned toward her. "Between you and me, don't you think the whole thing is a little funny? I got a little spooked listening to her. To be honest, I started wondering if maybe she had something to do with it."

Jane laughed, as if he couldn't have meant the comment as anything other than a joke. "Talk about a vivid imagination," she said. Those were the words Thomas had used when she ran the exact same theory past him as soon as she heard about Charlie's conveniently lonely death.

Dale shrugged and sat back in his chair. "I'm not serious. But remember that weekend they came to visit us on Nantucket? She had him eating lobster every meal and was drowning his food in butter. She was running out to buy him cigarettes every five minutes."

Jane frowned. For the two nights Rosemary and Charlie visited, Jane and Dale lay curled up in bed, trying to muffle fits of hysterical laughter as they discussed what looked like Rosemary's attempt to induce a heart attack. She and Dale always got along best when there was someone else nearby to act as buffer, especially if it was someone neither of them liked. They *had* had good times, there was no point in trying to deny it, but anyone could have a good time if they let themselves get caught up in laughter and romantic outings that distract you from your basic unhappiness and incompatibility.

"I was thinking about having a Scotch on the rocks," Dale said. "Join me?"

It was 3:30 and there was no taping this afternoon, and in every practical sense, she'd finished working shortly after her morning coffee. She hadn't had a drink at this time of day for years, possibly not since those languid summer afternoons she and Dale had spent on Nantucket the first two years they were married, when she'd been dumb enough to trust him. These days she got a headache about half an hour after a few modest sips of liquor, went straight from the anticipation of the drink to the hangover, with no moment of release in between. But she knew that if she sat there nursing a coffee while Dale slugged back a Johnnie Walker, she'd feel like one of those priggish suburban mothers she despised. So when the waitress came over—a gaunt, pale girl with a boy's haircut; French, if you bought the accent—she decided to go for broke and ordered a martini.

"And would you mind taking the fish," Jane said.

"Oh. You don't find it relaxing?"

"I'd prefer something edible," Jane said.

Dale watched the girl's candlestick legs as she clicked away. "How's little Jerry?" he asked.

"Jerry's delightful," Jane said. Once, when he was three years old, Jane had made the mistake of calling her son Jerry. "My name is Gerald!" he'd screamed at her. "Gerald!" Fearing a major scene, neither Jane nor Thomas had made the mistake again. "He's been nothing but pleasure from the beginning. We got lucky with him."

"It's not luck, he just takes after you. How old is he? Five, six? I suppose he's into basketball."

What was that supposed to mean? "He's all caught up in gymnastics," she said. "We take him to lessons every week. The teacher thinks he's ready for the advanced class, but I don't want him getting competitive."

Gerald's doctor claimed the two of them were making progress, although it wasn't clear to Jane how they were progressing or in what area. Gerald was still surly, haughty, and frequently hostile to Jane, Thomas, and his grandmother. School had begun last week and it looked as if they were getting ready for the same round of problems they'd been having with him since the first day of day care. He wasn't a sociable boy, didn't get along with his peers, and scoffed at almost everything the teacher said. At the end of the third day of classes, the teacher had called up Jane and told her Gerald had mocked her during a drawing lesson and had complained that he'd given up playing with crayons years ago. "I'd prefer to work with pastels," he'd said. Where had he even heard the word? He was unusually bright for his age and astonishingly self-possessed, assets Jane supposed she should have been grateful for but which, in Gerald, seemed more like social liabilities.

"Is he on the parallel bars, all that?"

"Possibly," she said. Thinking about Dr. Garitty made her feel as if she'd talked herself into a corner, and she lost interest in elaborating on this gymnastics fiction. If she was going to brag, she should have bragged about his brains or his cooking skills, something real. In the end, it didn't matter what Dale thought.

The waitress came and set down their drinks. She batted her big, mascaraed eyes at Dale, playing up the gamine act. Hopefully the woman he was currently seeing was at least a couple of decades older than this one, someone who knew what she was getting into but was too old to care. "Anything else?" she lisped.

"Privacy," Jane said.

Dale clinked her glass. The first sip of her drink burned through her body and sent a warm flush to her cheeks. Maybe if she just gave in to the effects instead of trying to fight them, she'd avoid the instant headache. She was afraid of alcohol. This was the result of having grown up with high-functioning drunks for parents and was, she had to confess, the only long-term ill effect she could point to. She sometimes wondered why she harbored so much resentment toward her parents' drinking when they'd been successful and, in a sloppy, inconsistent way, cheerful. Initially, the resentment had to do with the fact that both parents had died of alcohol-related illnesses shortly after Jane graduated college, but after a few years of tending to her mother-in-law, she saw that there were worse things you could do to your children than die young.

"Do you watch our show regularly?" Jane asked.

"If I'm home at that time, which isn't very often. Caroline watches. It was just luck I caught Rosemary."

"What do you think of it, in general?"

"I don't know how you keep it so consistent."

"Ah. In other words, same old thing over and over?"

"That's not what I meant." He rattled his ice and stared off across the room, pulling his thick black eyebrows together. Jane tapped her glass, waiting for the qualification. "Although, to be honest, I have wondered how much longer you're planning to stay with it."

Here we go, she thought. "Funny, I wouldn't have imagined you spend a lot of time thinking about my career plans."

"I've always been interested in your career, you know that."

When they first met, Jane had been on the staff of a local weekly, writing news and features. To give him his due, Dale had been the one who encouraged her to get into TV and even provided the connection that got her her first job. (Harvard was basically a four-year networking seminar.) She'd earned her current position through hard work, but she knew she hadn't been aggressive enough about developing another project, something of her own, something that moved her career forward a few notches before *Dinner Conversation* was finally euthanatized. She resented Dale for bringing it up, almost as much as she resented Thomas for not taking her career worries more seriously. But to hell with him if he thought she was going to let him knock her down.

"I've been working on a big project for a while now," she said. "I don't know if anything's going to come of it, but it's looking good."

"I'm glad to hear it." He stirred his ice cubes, an excuse to draw attention to an expensive wristwatch. "What are the details?"

She wanted to think he was pumping her for information so he could catch her in a lie, but the way he asked, the way he leaned almost imperceptibly toward her across the tiny table, made her think it wasn't that at all, it was much worse: it was genuine interest. Any entrepreneurial endeavor got his blood pounding and he'd always encouraged her to be imaginative.

Just her luck that after all those years of Thomas encouraging her to relax and take time off, someone was finally grilling her about career advancement when she had nothing to haul out for show-and-tell. She'd let herself drift, had allowed herself to get distracted by motherhood. That had its own amazing rewards, but they weren't ones people like Dale—people who desperately wanted a child themselves but couldn't have one—would appreciate. She'd drifted further by convincing Thomas they needed a bigger house, with more space, and had ended up with a white elephant with endless space for hosting Sarah and all kinds of friends and relatives she'd rather not host. They should have bought an apartment on Beacon Hill. It wouldn't have been that much more expensive and they would have been within walking distance of Symphony Hall and theaters and museums, places that might have inspired her. What a grotesque miscalculation to think that they were doing the right thing for Gerald by moving to Brookline where they could have that most useless of American obsessions, a yard. Gerald hated the outdoors. Two minutes of direct sunlight and he broke out in bright, stinging rashes. As for sports, he sneered at all of them and had asked Thomas to take down the basketball net the previous owners had left because he hated looking at it from the window of his third-floor "apartment." Now they had a half acre of overgrown grass, flower beds gone to seed and weed, and bushes they couldn't identify covering up most of their windows. Thomas occasionally spent a Saturday morning shoving around a squeaky lawnmower, a practice that almost always produced a strained lower back and a circle of hacked up grass that looked as if a field animal had been chewing on it.

Never mind any of it. She wasn't about to let Dale get the best of her, make her feel bad about her own life when the entire purpose of this meeting was to make him feel bad about his. She smiled at him and finished off the rest of the martini. Yesterday, Caroline had faxed her a detailed outline of Desmond Sullivan's Lewis Westerly biography, and she'd scanned it into her computer and retyped bits of it so she could pass it along to Thomas as her own work. This morning, she'd read a couple of chapters, thinking she might find a topic for a dinner conversation and be able to use Desmond Sullivan as a guest.

"I've put together a proposal for a series of biographical documentaries," she said, amazed by the conviction in her own voice. "One-hour pieces, probably a series of six, although that depends on how successful it is. It easily could be expanded."

"Biographies." Dale nodded. "I thought cable had that all sewn up—Lifetime, A&E, no?"

Now he was showing his true colors, knocking down her work before she'd even explained it. "This is something that hasn't been done before. An entire series on lost or forgotten American artists—writers, performers, painters."

"Ah. The forgotten genius angle," he said. "That's always popular."

"The forgotten geniuses have all been remembered. People are sick of them. This is much more interesting and much more commercial. The whole culture is drifting away from geniuses and exceptional people who only make the rest of us feel inadequate. My series is about the true cultural influences: forgotten mediocrities."

Dale looked puzzled. He paused for a moment and said, "Who, for example?"

"Have you ever heard of a writer named Lewis Westerly? He wrote brilliantly so-so novels."

"The name sounds familiar."

Oh good, Jane thought, he's lying. She had him. She motioned for the waitress and ordered them another round of drinks. Jane was wearing a linen jacket, a boxy sand-colored thing that she'd never really liked but had thrown over her silk blouse this morning because she knew it would make her feel less exposed to her ex-husband's scrutiny. Now that he seemed so impressed with her project, she didn't care what he thought of her figure, which, after all, wasn't that much different from what it had been fifteen years ago when Dale had been so enthusiastic about it. Unlike the vast majority of heterosexual men she'd met, Dale actually liked women, and so wasn't repulsed by female fleshiness. Anyway, people generally take your lead in reacting to your appearance. Two thirds of Dale's attractiveness had to do with his narcissistic appreciation of himself. She slipped off the jacket, rested the back of her head against the banquette, and began free-associating, creating a brilliant plan right there while the silly, pretty fishes swam in circles in the goblets at the tables all around them.

2.

By the time both were on a third drink, the bar was more crowded, mostly with pompous, well-scrubbed young men with pink skin, no matter their race, and the boisterous good cheer that indicated a serious lack of life experience. Recent college grads working at Fidelity or Bank of Boston, so low down the corporate ladder they were still chummy with each other. Poor things, thinking that careers were ruled by logic and love was ruled by the heart. Thank God optimism like that dried up with age.

She'd laid out a whole theory behind her proposal for Dale, he'd bought it, told her it sounded wonderful, and in truth, it did. And why not? So what if she'd stumbled upon it at the last second, it was a hell of a lot more original than yet another fifteen-part series about the goddamned Monroe Doctrine or Westward Expansion, one of those showcases for someone's research skills and lack of imagination, the kinds of things people were so busy praising they didn't have time to watch. She'd arrange a meeting with Desmond Sullivan and pick his brains about it. Like most academics she knew, he could probably be bought out of academia with a few subway tokens and the promise of meeting a few third-rate TV personalities. The whole afternoon had been remarkably productive. So much so she'd forgotten why she was here until Dale brought it up himself.

"Tell me something, Janey," he said, leaning on the table, cupping his face in his hand and gazing at her with the limp focus she recognized as his stock look of seduction. "Why did you call me up and arrange this little meeting? After all this time?"

"Millennial fever," she said.

"I don't even know what that means."

"Neither do I," she said, "but I've heard it's contagious. I hope you realize you're making eyes at me."

"If I am, it's completely unconscious."

She mimicked his body language, chin in her hands, her face inches from his. "Puberty," she said, "was the last uncalculated move you made."

"Oh really? I thought it was falling in love with you."

"If you'd fallen in love with me, you never would have married me."

"You're so full of theories, Janey, you should have your own Web site. Why *did* I marry you?"

"How else were you going to have extramarital affairs?"

One of the big pink boys on the other side of the room dropped a cigar on the nearly marble floor and there was a stir of activity and laughter. Dale sat back in his seat and looked away from her, troubled now, and ran his hand through the dark brush of his hair. He had lovely, large hands, and Jane had always suspected he went for regular manicures. There was no other way to explain those perfectly shaped, shiny fingernails. "I have a suspicion," he said, "just a suspicion, Caroline's been talking to you. Am I right?"

"Caroline and I have friends in common. We were in a book group together before she married you, and we've been friends since. Why wouldn't she be talking to me?"

"I mean about me. She thinks I'm having an affair. And believe it or not, Janey, I'm innocent."

"I believe it not."

"I promise you."

"Oh. That's different."

"All right. There is someone I've been seeing, but it isn't like that. We've had dinner, we've gone for walks in the middle of the day, I've called her from the phone booth at the supermarket, but that's it. I don't want to fuck up my life again, Janey. I don't want to fuck up my marriage. I did that once and I've lived to regret it."

This outpouring sounded so heartfelt, she didn't know how to respond. The bitter envy she felt at learning that he just might have been faithful to Caroline all these years was tempered by his admission of regret over the mess he'd made of their marriage. "Well," she said, perhaps too quietly. "So have I. Regretted your fucking things up."

He put his heavy warm hand over hers, and she couldn't help looking down and admiring those pearly fingernails and his big fat wedding band.

"Tell Caroline not to worry. I'm not going to fuck up our marriage. Janey," he said, and she looked up into his eyes. "You can help, you know. You can help me through this. That's why I agreed to meet you here today. I knew what this was all about."

She felt a certain amount of sympathy for poor old Dale, who at this moment looked ridiculous. She'd always liked him best when he'd just made a fool of himself or had the flu. "I don't know how you expect me to stop you from sleeping with this girl."

"She's thirty-five. She's married. Her husband's a friend of mine. Tell me what's wrong with me?"

"You're a hopeless romantic and a shit. It's a deadly combination. You're over forty and getting restless. And your mick mother spoiled her darling prince rotten." She reached up and ran her hand down his rough face. Definitely showing the signs of too much sun. In five years, he'd look like luggage, the expensive kind, but old. She gave his face a sharp little slap.

He took her hand in his and pressed her palm to his lips. He murmured something into her hand, but she couldn't make out the words. Then he looked up at her and whispered, "You know me better than anyone."

"That's why I divorced you."

"You know how much I've missed you, don't you?"

"How much?"

He placed her hand against his chest, and through the thin, cool cotton of his shirt, she could feel the thump of his heart. "This much," he said.

She had to laugh. What else could you do? It was much too late in their lives for this kind of giddy flirting and already the afternoon had been much too long. She could see the reflected glare of the late sun, golden and vulgar, in a mirror near the entrance of the lounge. How could I possibly have spent six years buried under the weight of this louse? she thought.

But the truth was, she'd begun to feel a little golden and vulgar herself, and she was suddenly struck by the realization that he meant it, that somewhere in his heart, amidst the gridlock of self-absorption and sexual obsession, he did miss her. She felt something flare up inside her, not lust, but recklessness and power. If I were drunk and stupid and young and spiteful enough, she thought, something truly regrettable might happen here.

"Janey?" he said, so softly she could barely hear him. "Tell me the truth. You've missed me, haven't you?"

"Oh," she sighed. "Maybe a little, when I'm especially full of self-loathing."

"Will you see me again, later in the week?"

"For what? What possible reason could you have for wanting to meet me?"

"To talk. Who else am I going to talk to?"

"They have these wonderful things called shrinks," she said, "people who sit in little rooms and do nothing but listen to other people talk. You pay them by the hour so they're not allowed to participate or pass judgment. They're listed in the Yellow Pages under EARS." But as she said it, she was wondering how many of her carefully arranged plans she'd have to cancel to meet with him at whatever time and whatever place he wanted.

Four
Cry Me a River

1.

One of the more dubious advantages of being a homosexual is that people will tell you anything about themselves. You don't even have to ask. Show up at a dinner party with a companion of the same sex and by the end of the evening, you're almost certain to find yourself backed into a corner, listening to a whispered, alcohol-soaked confession of a love affair with a sister-in-law, a wedding day infidelity with the bridegroom's best friend, or a secret addiction to sedatives or cheesecake. When Desmond was younger—he suspected it was during that burst of optimism and self-confidence that burned brightly between the rush of revealing his secret sexual inclinations to the world and the disappointment of hearing that everyone already knew—he had a number of flattering explanations for this. Gay men are good listeners; gay men are sympathetic; gay men are trustworthy. More recently, he'd come to realize that people are eager to spill their darkest secrets because they assume that all homosexuals live in a swamp of moral ambiguity and are therefore in no position to pass judgment.

It was an assumption that baffled him. People whose lives are rife with moral contradictions are generally the first to pass judgment. Look at the Catholic clergy. Look at the whole of the American right wing, that strangely cherubic cast of haloed scoundrels, characters out of a Disney production of *Ubu Roi,* hurling insults and stones from their sloughs of hypocrisy. Still, Desmond wasn't one to correct anyone's suppositions, especially if doing so meant losing access to their dirty laundry. He was a voyeur by nature and he'd take whispered confessions whatever way they came. As for his own moral ambiguity, he wasn't sure. He liked to think he lived on the high ground of moral principles strictly adhered to, but he realized he'd chosen this absolutist path for what was undoubtedly the wrong reason: he found it easier to lead a productive life when his options were limited. Monogamy was a perfect example. For all its drawbacks, it certainly made it easier to find time to do the laundry.

It was his tendency toward voyeurism that had brought him around to writing his biography of Lewis Westerly, an act that changed his life on almost every front and was indirectly responsible for this pending move to Boston.

Desmond was living in Chicago when he became aware of Westerly. He was practicing law and was so desperately unhappy with his life, he was seriously considering taking up handball, the last stop on many a road to emotional ruin. He'd rushed into law school right out of college in a mad dash to follow in his father's footsteps, only to learn, on the day he graduated, that his father had secretly hoped he'd go into a more creative and loose-jointed profession. "If I hadn't had to support a family," his father had said, "I think I would have tried to put together a career as a songwriter. I used to write songs when I was in college. I'll show them to you sometime. What the hell, it's too late now, for both of us, probably."

Great, Desmond thought, I've gone through three years of law school to please a man who wishes he'd sired Kander and Ebb. The next time he planned his life around pleasing other people, he'd have to make sure he first knew what they wanted.

Lewis Westerly was the author of *Broadside, Ferocious Wind,* and *The Bright, Bold Beginning,* to mention only three of his twenty-three novels. He was one of a breed of writers that flourished in the early 1950s; burly, chain-smoking men who, in between drinking binges and divorces, churned out dozens of vast novels that attacked a variety of white-hot social concerns: Drug Addiction, Interracial Marriage, Juvenile Delinquency, Anti-Semitism. And they didn't just attack them, they sank their teeth into them and wrestled them to the ground, and made the reader feel he'd heard everything he ever needed to hear on the subject. On to Incest! Decades earlier, readers were in awe of these men and their massive, virile tomes. They couldn't get enough of them. The more rugged and verbose the better. Men had made the world safe for democracy, so they must be worth listening to. Before sensibilities were forever altered by feminism and LSD, these cartoonishly manly men were gods.

Desmond had first read *The Crowded Room,* one of Westerly's earliest novels, this one on the subject of schizophrenia. He'd come across the book on a sale table at a library and had bought it, feeling he was offering a last meal to an author whose work hadn't been checked out in nearly twenty years. By current standards, the psychology was laughable, and the happy ending, in which lobotomy is made to seem like a minor surgical procedure with fewer downsides than a nose job, was deplorable at best. Still, there were sections of the novel that were so stirring and powerful, Desmond had nearly wept reading them.

No one would accuse Westerly of being a brilliant stylist. He had a haphazard approach to sentences and an undisguised disdain for the logic of paragraphs. Out of my way! he bellows to the commonsense rules of grammar. I'm trying to make a point here! But he had the secret magic of a writer who could hold you to your chair and toss you into the middle of his imagined world, no matter how ludicrous or even offensive, and Desmond had been drawn to him immediately. As soon as he'd finished that first book, he haunted used bookstores trying to acquire the complete body of work.

As Desmond was purchasing a foxed copy of *The Hard Road to Hell* in an especially dilapidated shop off Halstead, the ancient owner glanced at it casually and said, while writing up a sales slip, "I didn't know we had any Lewis Westerly left in stock. We used to have shelves of him. I thought I'd cleared them all out."

"He's underrated," Desmond said. "Have you read him?"

"I skimmed a couple. He used to come in here sometimes. Kind of a sloppy old queen, usually drunk off his ass and slobbering on about some sixteen-year-old boy he was obsessed with. I wonder what happened to him?"

Desmond set off to find out, thinking he'd stumbled upon a hobby. Four years later he had a nearly completed manuscript, an advance from a publisher, and a new career.

After much consideration, he called his biography of Westerly *His Hard Road to Hell.* In ways that Desmond hadn't anticipated at the start, Westerly's life, like his novels, encompassed Big Social Issues, although not ones the author had written about at such exhausting length. In this case, it was Homosexuality, Domestic Violence (each of Westerly's four battered wives had divorced him, a fact which helped boost his macho image), Alcoholism, and Laxative Abuse. In the decades since his death, debunking the myth of the manly man had become as popular as sitting at his feet once had been, and the biography became a minor best-seller. In the wake of the publicity for Desmond's book, three of Westerly's novels had been reissued and had sold surprisingly well. Readers were no longer interested in hearing what he had to say about the world, but they examined the books closely, seeking authorial homoeroticism and unintended hints at pedophilia. Westerly's personal life was so vastly at odds with his public persona, Desmond's book was taken seriously by academics who saw some deconstructionist value in it. In a final coup, the book had been optioned by Paramount, although it looked to Desmond as if a film would never be made. Several screenwriters had attempted to come up with a script, but any movie star with enough clout to get the project made wanted to play an inspiring and heroic character, which meant doing away with every fact of Westerly's life that made it interesting.

Shortly after *His Hard Road to Hell* came out, Desmond had been offered a job teaching writing courses at Fordham. Since then, he'd accepted temporary teaching jobs around town when he needed money or formal structure in his life.

In his more grandiose moments—the ones in which he wasn't berating himself for a lack of talent, ambition, looks, and intelligence—Desmond saw teaching as a waste of his time and abilities. Paid headaches was how he'd started to think of it. Deerforth College promised to be more of the same, although rumor had it the campus was exceptionally beautiful. If things worked out as he had planned, this would be his swan song to teaching. The biography of Pauline Anderton had been his work in progress for four years and was, the last time he'd bothered to calculate, nineteen months behind schedule. Last year, his editor had stopped phoning him to inquire about it, and recently, the ominous communication problems. And yet, Desmond couldn't seem to pull together the material he had and draw it to a satisfying conclusion. He had enough facts, enough family history and social background, enough information about the recording industry in the 1950s and 1960s; he had two dozen chapters neatly typed, over a hundred interviews carefully recorded and transcribed, but Pauline Anderton, the long-dead woman herself, seemed to be swimming somewhere offshore, just out of his reach. I'm throwing you a life preserver, he wanted to tell her. Look what I did for Westerly. How many people get offered the chance for reincarnation? Her ghost wasn't having any of it.

There's a key to almost every life, a piece that holds the entire puzzle together and makes sense of all the disparate fragments: the ambitious mother, the clubfoot, the eye-opening journey to Spain. In the case of Westerly, it was the torment of his hidden sexuality. So far, Desmond had been unable to discover the piece that would bind together all the pages he'd written about Pauline Anderton, the essential truth or the essential lie that would bring her to life in his mind and, hopefully, on the page.

After her husband died, she moved to a suburb outside Boston to live with her sister and brother-in-law. Desmond hoped that by living in the area, turning over a few more stones, or simply soaking up the atmosphere, he'd find the elusive fragment he needed. That, he'd explained to Russell, was why he'd applied to six schools in the Boston area. The fact that they'd be temporarily separated was an unavoidable side effect.

2.

Since the disastrous party four days ago, Russell had been taking Desmond's pending departure badly. It was all loutish, sybaritic Peter's fault. The long-term couples in a circle of friends are like the big stores that hold down either end of a shopping mall. If one of them goes out of business, all the little folks in the middle start to panic that their world is falling apart; if Sears can't stay in business, what chance does Pot Pourri Palace have of surviving? Peter might not have felt he owed it to Velan to stay faithful, but he should have considered his friends' feelings. Russell had been cold and distant and had started spending long hours at the store while Desmond made desultory progress packing.

Boris wasn't helping matters. This afternoon, another humid day, he was practicing especially thunderous pieces—Bartok, unless Desmond was mistaken—with a good deal less skill than usual, music that was perfect accompaniment to the ongoing battle of Tina and Gary on the floor above. This young couple had moved in two years ago. In private, most of their communication was shouted insults and accusations, but Desmond had never seen them on the street or in the hallway when they weren't huddled together or holding hands, as if protecting each other from the hostile world. It was impossible to know which was the truth of their relationship, the private fighting or the public cleaving.

Desmond opened up a suitcase on the bed, put on a record (*Pauline Anderton Goes to the Movies*), and tried to drown out the sounds of Bartok and love, loathing, or whatever it was.

Desmond had always been wary of long-term relationships, perhaps wary of love itself. There was something about the enterprise of sealing yourself off in an isolation tank with another person that struck him as unwholesome. He didn't understand how it could be healthy for two people to sleep in the same bed every night, eat the same food at the same table, visit the same friends, have the same conversations, and, for all he knew, think the same thoughts. Friends crowed about the beauty of intimacy and the liberating joy of opening yourself up to another person, but when you pressed them for details, it always boiled down to being able to express your anger without inhibition or being comfortable leaving the bathroom door open in front of your significant other. They claimed long-term relationships brought out their best, but that usually translated into being unapologetic about their worst.

Desmond's own relationships had tended to be short-term tugging matches. If he met someone he was interested in, he worried they wouldn't find him attractive or interesting enough. But if they reciprocated his enthusiasm, he felt the bar had been raised on his own net worth and was plagued by thoughts that he could have done better. It was like shopping in Morocco; once your offer was accepted, you felt you should have driven a harder bargain. The best way to avoid this cycle of disappointment was to flirt with friends and fuck with strangers and thus keep yourself suspended in a safe no-man's-land somewhere between loneliness and suffocation. No soaring highs, but none of that get-me-out-of-here anxiety either. And after all, a comfortable emotional flatline was the Holy Grail half the population was seeking: How else do you explain the popularity of Prozac, hydroponic tomatoes, and Tom Hanks?

Then, six months after *His Hard Road to Hell* came out, he met Russell Abrams at a cocktail party, curled up in a chair in a quiet corner of the apartment, reading *Northwest Passage* by Kenneth Roberts, one of Lewis Westerly's great rivals. He invited Russell to dinner and, in one way or another, they'd been together since. Desmond found Russell a curious and appealing blend of arrogant confidence—passed down directly from his confident father and arrogant mother—and severe, occasionally crippling self-doubt, the B-side of the same inheritance. He was teaching art to special needs children when they met, a disarmingly noble profession, even if it was one he'd chosen because he knew it would meet with disapproval from his mother. ("Any child who's been properly toilet-trained," Gloria had written in her infamous first book, *Playing with Childhood*, "will be bored senseless by mucking around with finger paints.") Russell had the great virtue of wanting to take care of people and, at the same time, the unacknowledged but obvious need to be taken care of. Which made him, in Desmond's eyes, both lovable and easy to manipulate.

In the end, it probably wasn't productive or even possible to deconstruct attraction. One night, six months after they'd met, Desmond came out of a movie in the East Village and saw Russell walking along the street halfway up the block ahead of him. It was a warm, cloudy night and Russell was dressed in a white shirt and dark pants. From a distance, he looked short, young, and perhaps a little lost. Drifting, to use Sybil's word. Desmond was about to rush up to him, but instead decided to follow him, hoping to discover something about him he hadn't known before, a secret vice, perhaps, something he could use as a bargaining chip in the future—assuming they had a future together. Russell went into a greengrocer and bought flowers, paid for a magazine at a newsstand, stopped to talk briefly with a large middle-aged woman in an orange dress, picked up two coffee mugs and a small stack of books from a jittery sidewalk vendor. After twenty minutes of shadowing him, Desmond began to lose his sense of purpose. He turned and walked to the nearest subway. As he was standing on the hot platform, battered by the sound of a train approaching from the wrong direction, he realized he *had* discovered a secret vice; but it wasn't Russell's, it was his own. He'd been stalking someone for twenty minutes, stepping into doorways to avoid being seen. That had to mean something.

The next night, Russell showed up at Desmond's apartment carrying a vase filled with the flowers he'd bought at the grocer, and the mugs and books he'd bought from the street vendor. Later, as they lay in bed, Russell suggested he move into Desmond's apartment. "Oh, come on," he teased when Desmond hesitated. "You know you want me to." And lying in the dark with Russell's head against his chest, thinking about his behavior twenty-four hours earlier, he had to admit it was true, even if he wasn't sure why.

Pauline Anderton was singing the theme from *Goldfinger*. The whole album was more or less a disaster, an ill-conceived concept from the start. Anderton obviously had no feeling for the songs and took the movie motif as license to ham it up in a way that was frequently embarrassing. "His heart is *cold*," she sang in a nasal whine—a failed attempt at imitating Shirley Bassey—and then dug herself in deeper by forcing out an "evil" laugh. There were so many questions he wished he could ask Anderton. The main one, in relation to this album, was: "What the hell did you think you were doing?" He turned off the record player.

The bedroom he and Russell shared was too small for the king-sized bed Russell had insisted upon, and as he went from closet to suitcase, Desmond had to squeeze between the footboard and the bureau. Why were beds getting so big these days? Everyone he knew had enormous beds—no matter how small their apartment—with mattresses thicker than their walls. Everyone had such immense box springs under their mattresses and such deep sheepskin cushions on top of them, they practically ended up sleeping pressed against their ceiling. Everyone was saving to expand their bathrooms, install Jacuzzis, buy bath towels the size of blankets. Everyone wanted urinals, bidets, heat lamps over their sinks, and bathroom scales that carried on conversations. And then there were the cathedral-sized kitchens, even though no one cooked. It was all so primordial, in a sordid, indulgent way, this attempt to reconnect with the basic needs of the body through home improvement. The economic prosperity of the past decade had led to Welfare cuts and bigger bathtubs. It said something about the cultural moment, but he was too exhausted to articulate it clearly. He ought to write an op ed piece about it: The Flush Years.

But perhaps it wasn't the politics of the bed that bothered Desmond as much as it was the way it represented Russell's tendency to fill up space in the apartment. Like everything else in their relationship, Desmond had at first welcomed it. He'd never trusted his own taste in furniture and had equipped the apartment with functional chairs and tables and bookshelves. Russell brought color to the place and a cluttered style that made it look as if it had been decorated by some whacked-out grandmother addicted equally to overstuffed comfort, modernism, and irony. The Heywood Wakefield desk with a primitive, hand-embroidered portrait of Ike and Mamie hanging above it. The heads from three French dressmaker's dolls lined up on top of a glass-fronted bookcase.

Desmond had loved all of it, so much so that it wasn't until too late that he noticed almost everything he'd bought over the half dozen years he'd lived in the apartment alone had been moved into storage or exiled to the back of a closet door. It wasn't a stretch, not a great leap of faith, to recognize that his own thoughts and perceptions, his own solo identity, had probably been put on mothballs as well, and in a similarly insidious manner. His only real hope of finishing the Pauline Anderton book was to get away from it all, the books and the pottery, dolls' heads and doilies.

He closed up the suitcase and slid it under the bed with the other boxes and cases he'd already packed, not entirely sure if the undershirts and socks he'd packed had been his or Russell's.

3.

On moving day, Russell slept uncharacteristically late, and in order to make it to the store on time, he had to dash around the apartment pulling on his clothes and swiping at his hair as he brushed his teeth. He gave Desmond a distracted, passionless kiss as he hurried out the door. "Have a good trip," he called out as he ran down the hall to the elevator.

Desmond packed the car in the stifling midday humidity, bid farewell to the apartment, and got onto the West Side Highway. He made it only to 96th Street before hesitantly pulling off the road and driving back into the city. Desmond had been counting on Russell to initiate a big, sloppy goodbye, preferably with tears and a hint of anger and a fast hot fuck to finish it off properly. Instead, there had been all that emotionless rushing around. It wouldn't do to leave town like this. Among other things, it was unfair to Russell, who would regret having been brusque the minute he walked into the apartment that night and realized that Desmond wouldn't be living there for another four months.

He drove across the city in the dense haze of sick air, through the forest of Central Park where all the trees and the parched lawns seemed to be crying out for rain and a little privacy. They were predicting an active hurricane season this year, and after a summer of heat waves and drought and sub-tropical nights, Desmond was ready for it. Turn on the faucet, he thought. Drown me.

On Second Avenue, he slipped in a tape he'd made of some of Pauline An-derton's better-known recordings, and within seconds the car was filled with the overpowering sound of her amazing and awful voice singing "Cry Me a River." This was the first song on Pauline Anderton's first album, one of two recordings in her career to make the charts, and supposedly the song she'd been singing when Walter Winchell wandered into a dreary cocktail lounge—the Brown Room—on the outskirts of Tallahassee, Florida, and dis-covered her.

At a stoplight in Midtown, a passenger in a taxi glared at Desmond and rolled up her window. Desmond smiled at her and lowered the volume. Lis-tening to the tape and lane-hopping through the heavy traffic, Desmond felt a surge of enthusiasm for the project, something he hadn't felt in months. Perhaps it was a good thing he'd stalled as long as he had; by the time the book came out, Bette Midler would be exactly the right age to play Anderton in the middle years of her career.

He drove across Houston and wove through a maze of narrow, shadowy streets, finally turning onto Ludlow. Less than two blocks from Russell's store, he found something that would easily pass for a parking space and backed into it.

This ribald corner of the Lower East Side was changing so rapidly, stores and coffeehouses seemed to come and go within days. In June, Russell's store had been flanked by a gallery and a pet shop that had been converted into a café—cages and aquariums still in place. Both had disappeared. Rus-sell and Melanie had signed their lease when rents were still affordable. Desmond never would have guessed that theirs would become one of the most stable businesses on the block.

The store was called Morning in America and the theme was furniture, clothing, and memorabilia from the 1980s. When Russell had announced his plans to go in on the venture with his friend Melanie, Desmond had listened politely. Nineteen eighties style clothing and furniture? He had no idea there was such a thing. As far as Desmond was concerned, the entire decade had been a disaster socially and politically and a personal waste of time. Cele-brating it in any form, even acknowledging that it had given birth to a coher-ent aesthetic, struck him as counterintuitive and politically regressive. Russell's friend Melanie, a randy, gorgeous dyke from the Midwest, had inherited a basementful of Reagan memorabilia from the right-wing Christian father who'd tossed her out of the house at age seventeen. Russell had been trying to get out of teaching for several years and Melanie loved the idea of using her father's carefully hoarded junk to support herself in a life that would have made her old man shudder.

Four months after they opened, *New York* magazine had run a snide item about the shop and it was launched as a destination for out-of-town shoppers and jaded New Yorkers who thought they'd seen everything. A few 1980s icons occasionally stopped in to sign pictures and have their photos taken, Ron Reagan Jr., Shelley Long, and Bernhard Goetz among them.

Desmond walked into the artificial chill of the cavernous store and took off his sunglasses. Russell and Melanie were carrying a nondescript, vaguely industrial dining table to the back. Whenever he stopped in, the two of them were moving furniture from one end of the store to the other, trying to make the store seem less cluttered if they were overstocked or more cluttered if they were low on inventory. Presentation is everything, Russell had explained to Desmond, a statement Desmond wouldn't argue with, since the goods themselves were clearly nothing: nondescript, mass-produced furniture, nondescript cotton clothes Russell had labeled "early '80s Gap," Brooks Brothers suits representing the financial boom portion of the decade, lots of Tom Clancy novels. The store's big sellers were the Reagan memorabilia they had tucked into every corner—magazine covers, plates, framed photos of Ron and Nancy, political pins, even little diorama-type shrines—and assorted clutter relating to a variety of the decade's top television shows. Desmond was convinced that with the way things were going, American history courses would be using *TV Guide* as primary source material within a decade. Sooner or later, all cultural references seemed to circle back to *Cheers* or *Dallas*. Increasingly, students referred to television shows as the decisive factors in their spiritual and psychological development. They came to the store in droves buying up lunch boxes and dish sets and toys that reminded them of their very recent childhoods.

Russell and Melanie were about the same height and had similarly slight bodies. They were often mistaken for brother and sister, although at the moment, turning the table on end and maneuvering it into a sliver of empty space against a back wall, they looked more like husband and wife preparing their house for a natural disaster. They set down the table and Russell disappeared. Melanie—black work boots swimming around her skinny legs—clomped up to the front of the store, grabbed Desmond's hand, and shook it with the robust enthusiasm of a politician. "Big day, huh?" She pulled up a metal folding chair, motioned toward it, and held it for Desmond until he was seated. "Russell's all worked up about it, although suffering in silence." She shook her head with concern for her friend, lit up a cigarette, and plopped down on a sofa with her big feet up on a coffee table. Melanie had the gestures and vocal inflections of a three-hundred-pound truck driver, a bizarre juxtaposition to her wiry body. "It's going to be a rough few months."

"Just remember," Desmond said, "it is *only* a few months. Very few in the scheme of things." He shifted uncomfortably in the chair. "What's Russell up to now?"

"Just checking a couple of boxes in the basement. We're planning to open a '90s room down there, for all the shit we can't figure out what to do with up here. He'll be up in a minute." She tipped her pretty, angular face to the ceiling and blew out a lungful of smoke. "It's nice to talk to you, one on one. I hate when everything is about couples and you can't even talk to a person but you have to talk to some goddamned couple. Sometimes you look at this couple and you don't see two people sitting there, you see one behemoth with two mouths."

"Right." He hated to agree with Melanie, whose theories usually seemed crackpot, but sometimes he just had to.

"So, tell me about this school you're teaching at. What's it called?"

Desmond liked Melanie and had been infected with a smaller dose of Russell's desire to watch over her and take care of her. She claimed to be "well into" her thirties, but Desmond would have bet good money that she was no more than twenty-eight. Despite a disfiguring bleached crew cut and a recently acquired fondness for tattoos, she could look, in unguarded moments, like an abandoned child. She always wore white sleeveless T-shirts to display the bands of colorful design inked into her scrawny upper arms. She insisted upon pulling out chairs for Desmond, holding doors open for him, and hailing cabs, all of which he would have found unbearably emasculating if she hadn't been so blatantly vulnerable. Desmond started to tell her what he knew about Deerforth College, but after two sentences, she pulled a business card out of her shirt pocket and began to study it intently. Desmond let his words trail off.

"A friend of yours?" he asked, nodding toward the card.

"Not exactly. Maybe. I hope so. Let's just say gorgeous, whatever she is."

Melanie had the single most calamitous love life Desmond had ever heard of. She was always falling in love with lanky, glamorous women, the more audaciously blond, wealthy, and unavailable, the better. Most were Upper East Side types who popped into the store while slumming their way through the East Village with a friend. To prove her love and chivalry, Melanie showered these chilly goddesses with phone calls, flowers, and absurdly expensive gifts. Few, if any, of these entanglements blossomed into sexual relationships—a returned phone call was a major triumph—but that didn't seem to make them less powerful for Melanie. Eventually, they all ended with Melanie harassing her love objects and then retreating into a depression when she received threatening letters from lawyers. Legions of muscular plumbers and electricians who worked in the neighborhood pursued her, just dying, apparently, to show her what she was missing.

She put the card back into her shirt pocket and, a second later, pulled it out again. "You think I should call or wait a couple of days? Sometimes I scare people off. I'm too intense. That's my problem."

Desmond nodded. Everyone claimed they were too "intense," an amorphous term that usually indicated an obsessive-compulsive disorder they were trying to pass off as a surfeit of intelligence.

"I'm getting sick of this whole thing, Desmond, chasing after people. I'm too old for it. See if you can find me a nice wife up there in Boston."

Whose nice wife? he wanted to ask.

Russell strode up to the front of the store, and dropped down onto the sofa beside Melanie. He slipped the cigarette out of her hand and took a deep drag off it in a defiant way that seemed to be directed at Desmond. Russell was an occasional smoker. Desmond had felt obliged to discourage him from indulging although, in truth, he was turned on by the slutty way Russell held a cigarette between his middle and ring fingers and rolled the smoke around in his open mouth. "You didn't tell me you were coming down here," he said. "I don't guess you've changed your mind about leaving?"

"Surprise visit," Melanie said. "He wanted to see if you were shacked up with someone else already. Don't worry, Desmond, I'll keep my eyes on him for you. One of the guys working next door spends half his day in here, ogling him. Some nerve, huh?" She shoved herself off the sofa and gave Desmond a pat on the cheek. "I'm used to keeping him out of trouble."

She slipped outside, letting in a blast of ovenlike air. The store was quiet, except for the clicking and dripping of the air conditioner over the door, and the buzz of construction work from the neighboring building. Desmond felt suddenly nervous in Russell's presence, as if they'd already been apart for weeks and had begun the process of becoming strangers. Perhaps Russell was feeling the same way, for he stubbed out the cigarette and looked around the store shyly, as if he was trying to find busywork to distract him. "Did she tell you about this woman who came in here two days ago?" he asked.

"She mentioned someone."

"I hope you tried to discourage her. Whenever she starts talking like this, I can see the crisis brewing. 'I could tell she was interested by the way she was trying to avoid looking at me.' " Russell's imitation of Melanie was perfect, forced machismo, thrust-back shoulders and all.

"Maybe you shouldn't get so involved," Desmond suggested. "You're always out on a limb with her and she doesn't change. I worry she's too dependent upon you."

Russell stared at him for a moment. "Why are you so afraid of dependence, Desmond?"

"I didn't know I was."

"You are, trust me. People who rave about their independence are just lonely people who've given up hope." He pulled an Exacto knife out of his back pocket and slit through the masking tape on a carton on the floor. "Besides, I'm dependent on helping her. She's my friend. I love her." He went through the contents of the box—probably something Melanie had picked up at an auction—and held up a gray dinner plate that had no particular style or reference to period. "Quintessential '80s, don't you think?"

"Oh yes. I'd say so, sweetheart." One of the great virtues of the 1980s theme was that it was so undefined, anything could be passed off as belonging to the period. Russell admitted that he couldn't always tell by looking at it when a piece of furniture or clothing was from the 1980s, but as soon as he stuck a price tag on it, he *knew*. He had on a long-sleeved white dress shirt with the sleeves rolled up to his elbows and a pair of gray gabardine trousers that hung loosely off his legs. Desmond loved watching him go through all this junk—yellow eyeglasses on the end of his nose, long dark hair falling around his face—with the same studied concentration he had when he read Tolstoy. If I were a stranger, Desmond thought, and came into this store—not that he ever would—I'd fall in love with this little guy. Of course, the problem with being physically attracted to your lover was that you could imagine other people finding him equally attractive.

"You're looking especially handsome right now," Desmond said. "But then, you always look handsome . . ." He was about to say "to me," but after five years of living together, those little addenda had started to sound more like narrowing qualifications than compliments. "I like the way you look in that shirt" was now less flattering than "Mary (or Tom or Theresa or Rover) likes the way you look in that shirt."

"So that's why you came down here? To tell me you like the way I look?"

"I just wanted one more chance to say goodbye, that's all." And then, feeling a sudden urge to be completely honest about the small portion of the truth he wanted to discuss, he said, "Ever since that party, you've been so distant, I haven't known what's going on with you. I didn't want to leave town feeling there was something unspoken between us."

Russell muttered some kind of assent. "Well," he said, "you had to get a teaching job in Boston for the sake of the book."

"That's right."

"You need the money."

"At the moment, yes."

"Right, right," Russell said.

And yet there was an edge of hurt, doubt, or disappointment in his voice that troubled Desmond. Desmond had always believed that the only way to keep mystery—and therefore romance and mutual attraction—in a relationship was by lying about or keeping secret a good third of what you were feeling at any given moment. Russell had always insisted upon full disclosure, and over the years Desmond had become addicted to knowing everything, if not always telling everything. "What is it you're not telling me?" he asked.

Russell glanced up from his cardboard box of treasure and stared into Desmond's eyes as if trying to make a decision. He pushed the box away, sat back on the sofa, and used both hands to pull his hair off his face. "What I'm not telling you," he said, "is something I'm embarrassed about, but what the fuck, I'll tell you anyway. When you went to talk with Peter at that party, I hung around the living room for a while, trying to make conversation with some of your friends. Some sad little woman over in the corner bumped against a table and knocked over a vase of lilies, and Velan, who by this time had started to do some serious drinking, was about to make a scene. So I walked down the hallway to the bedroom—and here's the embarrassing part—and stood outside the door listening in on your conversation with Peter."

"Well, that's not so embarrassing. That's what I do for a living." And then, trying to remember if he'd said anything regrettable, he asked, "Which part of the conversation did you listen in on?"

"The part where you told Peter—bragged might be the better word—that you had some dates or tricks 'lined up' in Boston. I'm sure I heard other

things, but that's what kind of"—he gestured angrily toward his temple—
"*stuck* in my mind."

It was one of the few times Desmond felt tremendously relieved to have
been caught in a lie. If your lover was going to overhear you bragging to
someone about cheating on him, you couldn't ask for better luck than to have
the bragging be honest-to-God untrue. "But that was just something I said,"
he laughed. "Of course I don't have anything 'lined up.' "

Russell frowned at this comment, with annoyance, not doubt. "I'm not
sure I fully believed it to begin with," he said. "If I had, I probably would
have been a lot angrier. But what I've been left wondering for the past several days is *why* you'd go out of your way to say it."

The comment shattered the relief Desmond had been feeling a few seconds earlier. What had made him think it would be a good idea to drive all the
way down here instead of shooting straight north?

He doubted it would make Russell feel better about the entire incident if
he confessed that the comment had been part of his attempt to gain psychological distance from him. What would he say: Oh, I thought it might help
me pretend we're not a couple, just so I can get my mind back for a few
months? Surely that was an even graver betrayal than merely wanting back
his dick for a few months.

"I suppose," he said, tentatively, "I was bragging, although not about anything real. Peter had just confessed to his big conquest, and I didn't want him
to think I was—"

"You were what? Stuck in something as pathetic as a happy marriage?"

"Pathetic is a little harsh, sweetheart, but some variation on that thought
might have crossed my mind. Fleetingly."

Russell got up and went to the door. "It doesn't matter how long we've
been together, Desmond. I still think of you as a conquest, and I wish you
thought of me as one, instead of thinking of me as an embarrassing kid
brother you're forced to drag around to parties."

Calmly, without any particular animosity, Russell walked out.

An embarrassing kid brother. Had he really made Russell think of himself
that way? If so, he was undoubtedly a horrible person. Especially since there
was something in the "kid brother" business that turned him on. Desmond
looked around the store, at all the framed photos, amateur portraits, gaudy
posters, plates, and pillow of Ron and Nancy Reagan. It was like being surrounded by a horde of disapproving relatives, which pretty much summed
up the way he'd felt during most of the 1980s anyway.

By the time he got outside, Russell was halfway up the block, his baggy pants flapping against his legs. It didn't seem right to leave the store unattended, but without the price tags, most of the stock was worthless anyway. A workman stepped out of the doorway of the next building. "Russell!" he called out. "What are you doing for lunch?"

"He's busy," Desmond said, hurrying past. He was sweating heavily when he caught up with Russell. He grabbed his arm and spun him around. "Where are you going, sweetheart?"

"Coffee."

"But you don't drink coffee."

"Sur*prise.*"

"Maybe I should wait and leave tomorrow."

"The car is packed. Anyway, I've got dinner plans for tonight."

Standing on the sidewalk, surrounded by the smell of exhaust and the heat of the buildings, it crossed Desmond's mind, for the first time, that getting a little distance from Russell would mean that Russell had a little distance from him. Was that a good thing or bad? He glanced across the street. A police officer was standing behind a blue Volvo writing out a ticket. His car was next in line. "I'm sorry, sweetheart," he said. "I'm illegally parked."

"If you're illegally parked, you'd better go. I don't think you have much choice. Call me when you get to Boston."

He kissed Desmond on the mouth with what felt like a mixture of love and aggression. Desmond watched him walk into a coffee place on the corner. It was going to be much more difficult to go to Boston and feel comfortably released from his relationship with Russell if he didn't have the luxury of believing it was solid and utterly secure.

Five

Is This All Right?

1.

It was ten o'clock before Jane could convince Gerald to turn out the lights in his third-floor "apartment" and try to get some sleep. Earlier in the evening, they'd had an argument because she'd bought him a $5.99 Ace Hardware flashlight instead of the $15.99 Black & Decker version he'd requested. She'd expected there would be consequences for buying the cheaper model, but she'd vowed only two days ago that she wouldn't let him bully her anymore and she had to start somewhere.

Looking into his darkened room, she could see the big mound of his body under his sheet, his face turned away from her. "I hope you sleep well, sweetie," she said.

There was a sigh from the bed. "I intend to," he said.

Gerald had a phobia about sleeping with the windows open—another symptom Dr. Rose Garitty refused to discuss with her—and the room was stifling. "Are you sure you wouldn't like me to turn on the air conditioner?"

"I doubt that will be necessary, Jane. You know how I feel about that thing."

"All right, sweetie. Good night."

"Mmm hmm."

There were moments when Jane felt that Gerald was one of the most mysterious people on the planet. She didn't understand how he made decisions, where his strong likes and dislikes came from, how he'd developed such an adult sense of irony and outrage. Sometimes she looked at him with admiration—So independent! So intelligent!—but other times, most times, his independence was the source of free-floating anxiety and shame. Perhaps he was picking up on some subtle, unconscious message she was sending out, and that was what kept him so aloof and inaccessible. Thomas was amused by his behavior. The casual way he laughed off Gerald's opinionated outpourings and the ease with which he engaged him in serious discussions had created a bond between them that she envied. The one time she'd greeted Gerald's pretensions with a lighthearted, if slightly forced, laugh, her son had looked at her with disgust, as if she were foaming at the mouth.

As she made her way down the staircase, she reached into the pocket of her shorts, pulled out a rumpled piece of paper towel, and wiped sweat off her forehead. This humidity was beginning to make her feel claustrophobic, as if she were wrapped in a wet sheet and couldn't catch her breath. The other day, Dale had dismissed her environmental concerns and claimed the weather was just part of the natural cycle of things, a comment she'd interpreted to mean he'd become a Republican. Dale didn't have real political convictions and never had; he had social ambitions. When they'd met this afternoon, he'd described in detail the restaurant he'd invested in, using words like "tasteful" and "quality" about three hundred times. Caroline had obviously weaned him off "classy," but the echo of it was there in everything he said. If you didn't know better, you might find this eagerness to fit in almost touching.

She decided to unload the dishwasher, a mindless chore that was infinitely less odious at this hour than in the clear light of morning and always made her feel she'd accomplished something.

Since the day they moved into the house, Jane had hated the kitchen, the big rambling room facing the shady backyard with the tongue-and-groove wainscoting and the bleached pine cabinets and the long cool pantry with the worn butcher block countertops. Everyone who came into the house fell in love with the kitchen immediately, which was, in itself, enough to make her look at it with doubt. Loving a room like this was so obvious and easy, like a politician approving of tax cuts. Like the way people reacted to her friend

Rachel's' thirteen-year-old son. How unchallenging to love blond-haired, six foot, athletic, polite, brilliant Joshua. What about loving a person, or a room, whose virtues you had to hunt for a little bit?

For starters, she didn't like to cook. Not because she had any political objections to women slaving away over a stove—the lives of most of the women she knew revolved around food anyway, cooking it, eating it, or lusting after it through a fog of self-deprivation—but because it required too much patience and precision, qualities she'd never tried to nurture in herself. Thomas was the cook in their family, and a brilliant cook, too, although at times she found herself wondering if all the care he threw into cutting and slicing vegetables and reducing sauces wasn't just more passive-aggression.

She put away three plates and two glasses, decided it would be best to let them cool off for another hour or so, and headed to the refrigerator to check out the leftovers. As she was reaching for a plastic container of shrimp, she noticed that there was only a spoonful of Thomas's chocolate mousse concoction left in a bowl that had been half full two hours ago. That meant that Gerald had crept downstairs at some point and furtively gorged on it.

She took out a Tupperware container and sat at the kitchen table, poking through the broccoli and linguini until she found a plump shrimp. Gerald had always been heavy—he had Thomas's body type—but she hadn't given his weight much thought until the past year or so, when she started to worry about it. She didn't want to mention it and draw attention to what was a potentially explosive issue, not that all issues weren't potentially explosive where Gerald was concerned. On the other hand, it seemed irresponsible to turn a blind eye to what was a legitimate health concern. Dear old (young, really, and that might be part of the trouble) Dr. Garitty was maddeningly evasive on this subject and had looked at Jane with blatant disapproval the one time she'd mentioned it. As for talking about it with her own shrink, that was another lost cause. Dr. Berman was immense. In one session, she'd made a passing reference to Thomas's incipient potbelly and found herself blushing. To make matters more uncomfortable, she'd apologized to Berman.

As she was hoisting another dripping shrimp to her mouth, Thomas walked in the back door, fresh from a visit with his mother in the carriage house. He had on a pair of shorts and a T-shirt, both of which looked limp. Thomas himself looked a little limp, his light hair stuck to his wide forehead in strands. She felt a stab of almost unbearable poignancy, seeing him look so disheveled and overheated, the T-shirt stuck to his stomach with sweat. She had no illusions that she looked her best in this weather. Maybe people would finally become outraged over global warming when they realized how adversely it affects your appearance.

"How's Sarah?" she asked, popping the shrimp into her mouth.

Thomas shrugged and went to the refrigerator. "She seems fine. Cranky, but that's the norm." The kitchen was suddenly bright from the refrigerator bulb.

From time to time, Thomas offered Jane these mild criticisms of his mother, mostly as a way to appease her and show her that his allegiance was to his wife. One day, she'd love to hook him up to a lie detector and ask him which one of them he'd save first from a burning building. She heard his knees crack as he squatted down to forage. After a moment, he asked, "Any of that mousse left?"

"Gerald finished it off," Jane said.

"Oh good. I was afraid he didn't like it." He sat down at the table with a bowl of leftover salad and started to pick at the saturated leaves with his fingers.

"He claimed he didn't like it, but at some point, he sneaked down here and practically licked the bowl."

Thomas chuckled amiably as he sucked a limp lettuce leaf off his chin and into his mouth. "Healthy appetite," he said.

Healthy appetite, growing boy—haul out the usual clichés and lay the entire burden of concern about Gerald on her. Maybe if he took a bit more responsibility for his son's problems, she'd have time to enjoy his strengths. But she wasn't going to bring that up now. This unqualified approval of Gerald and refusal to look at any of his eccentricities and potential trouble spots was one of the many things about Thomas she'd come to expect and had learned to ignore. Hopefully, with a little more emotional growth, she'd stop seeing them altogether. Sometimes she worried that having a successful marriage to Thomas meant erasing him, trait by trait, feature by feature, until finally she'd find herself married to a completely invisible man.

"What did you do today, Jody?" Jody was an amalgam of her first and last names, a nickname she found inexplicably embarrassing.

She'd gone to work for a few hours, had an unproductive day, gone to see Dr. Berman, hauled Gerald to his shrink, then to his piano lesson. In the late afternoon, she'd met Dale at a coffee shop a few blocks from the house, ostensibly to discuss his ridiculous infatuation with his friend's wife, although most of it had been restaurant talk. Unfortunately, the conversation had taken place in a booth in a back corner that provided much too much intimacy for her taste, although not, obviously, for Dale's.

She nodded at Desmond Sullivan's biography of Lewis Westerly, propped up in the middle of the kitchen table. "Among other things," she said, "I took more notes on this book. I had an idea for using it in a proposal for a series, and I'm getting very excited about it. I'm indebted to you for insisting I read it. You'll have to invite the author for dinner when he gets here."

Thomas gave her one of his doe-eyed looks of sympathy. "You're always working," he said. "I wish you'd take a little more time for yourself."

She had another shrimp in her hand, but she felt her appetite dissipate and let it plop back in the Tupperware container. "This *is* for me," she said. "I wish you could see that."

"Don't take it that way, Jody. You know what I meant."

She did know what he meant and knew that, in his own irritating way, he did have her best interests in mind. She couldn't stay angry at Thomas for more than a few minutes without feeling guilty about something—not telling him she was seeing Dr. Berman again, not appreciating the amount of work he did around the house. "The dinner was wonderful tonight," she said. "One of your best."

"You thought so? I thought it was a little salty."

"No. It was perfect." Feeling light-headed and slightly nauseated, she snapped the lid on the container and put it back in the fridge. When she turned, Thomas was standing behind her, and he put his arms around her, tilted her chin up, and pecked at her mouth. "On you it tastes good," he said.

She could feel her breasts and her thighs pressed up against the sticky warmth of his body and tried to pull back from him enough to get some air without looking as if she was rebuffing him. "I'm a mess," she said. "I can't stop sweating."

"Horses sweat, women perspire, and you glow."

"Is that Tennessee Williams?"

"A paraphrase of Orson Welles on the subject of Rita Hayworth."

Oh please, she thought, please don't get libidinous, not now, not tonight, not in this heat, not after the week I've had. She immediately started to long for a small, harmless explosion somewhere in the house, a pipe bursting perhaps, something that would take hours to fix and would extinguish whatever ardor Thomas was feeling.

When they'd met, almost a year after her divorce from Dale, Jane had been comforted and warmed by Thomas's big, solid presence. He was every-thing Dale wasn't, a large lovable man who lavished attention and tenderness on her, a man who didn't hold back any of his emotions, a man who seemed to have been built for loyalty and fidelity. She'd had enough of fights and fire-works and the kind of overpowering sexual heat that had always been a part of her relationship with Dale. Thomas made love to her, soothed her with his clumsy hands, and even if, at times, she wished he wasn't quite so consider-ate, quite so eager to please, it was a relief to find herself on solid ground. With Dale, she'd always felt like one of those women you see identified as an "unidentified woman" on the arm of a movie star or business mogul. With Thomas, she was Jane Cody again. He'd lived with a woman for almost ten years, but they'd never married, and then she left him for a tenure track po-sition in Oregon and, eventually, another woman. Six months into casually dating Thomas for the peaceful pleasure of it, she found herself pregnant. There was never any question of what they'd do. After one tumultuous mar-riage, settling down and raising a child struck her as the practical, healthy choice. It didn't hurt that Thomas had a little inherited money, a cushion, like his big soft body. Marrying him felt like the sensible, adult thing to do. The way buying the house had seemed like a good investment.

But as with the house, she'd begun to think that she might have factored in the wrong criteria when making her decision.

Thomas pecked at her neck and then lapped at her ear, leaving behind a trail of saliva, and all she could think about were the slugs she'd seen crawl-ing along the walk all summer, marking their paths with ribbons of slime. What a way to think of her husband, the only man who'd been good to her, reliable, absolutely and unequivocally without qualification or hesitation.

Love in this marriage, she'd come to realize, was like the weather, coming and going in waves and seasons, blowing in strongly from one direction one moment, the opposite direction a few days later. Sometimes, the conditions were unbearable, like the heat and humidity tonight, sometimes they were so perfect and clear and invigorating, you almost couldn't believe they were ever anything else. It was a matter of staying calm and waiting. She had to re-mind herself that her feelings would change and that one day, hopefully soon, she'd wake up and a new system would have blown in and all her minor discontents and complaints and petty boredom would be a dim memory.

Thomas cupped her breasts in his big hands and delicately lifted them, as if he were admiring something she'd just brought out of the oven. He wasn't the type to talk about his desires directly, but she knew that the vast majority of his sexual interest in her was centered in her breasts. They were her best feature and she'd always been proud of them—once she got over her teenage embarrassment that they were too large and gave up researching plastic surgeons who specialized in breast reduction—but something in his sly enjoyment of them brought to mind images of a hefty teenage boy masturbating over *Penthouse* magazine or, worse still, some shadow of his attachment to his overbearing mother. "Jody's beautiful babies," he murmured, more to himself than to her, and then bent down to kiss each nipple, leaving behind wet rings on her jersey.

But what if waiting for this particular weather system to change was like waiting for snow or a sudden frost in Miami: not impossible, but not very likely, either.

"You go upstairs," she said hoarsely. "I'll just tidy up a couple of things here and be right up."

If that cleaning person hadn't come today, she could wash the kitchen floor or scrub the bathtub, any time-consuming chore that opened up the possibility that Thomas would be asleep when she went to bed. She had only herself to blame for being so insistent about hiring a cleaning service.

Once Thomas had left—he was so agreeable; maybe it would have been better if they'd gotten it over with down here, on the living room sofa, even if there was no air-conditioning—she went to the kitchen sink and sprayed her face and the back of her neck with cold, chlorinated water. But as she was drying herself with a hand towel, she realized her intent had been to wash off her loving husband's saliva. She tossed the towel into the sink and, resigned, went up the grand curved staircase that had impressed her so much when the Realtor showed them the house for the first time, all those years ago.

2.

The bedroom was freezing, and when she slid into the bed, the cool of the soft yellow sheets brought up goose pimples.

He was shy, that's what made it all so touching. He liked to leave the lights off and reach for her under the covers, as if they were doing something that had to be kept secret. He buried his face in her chest, mumbling that awful name he had for her, "Jody, Jody," and rubbed against her leg. She could feel his fat, bloated penis bumping her, clumsily. It made her think of a New-foundland puppy, a creature whose gawky, immature, undisciplined behavior was completely inappropriate to its size.

He was at her nipples now, this overgrown adolescent, sucking, but too hard, making her sore and angry. So many men were plagued with premature ejaculation, impotence, and other sexual dysfunctions, but always the wrong men. But as soon as those thoughts passed through her mind, they were drowned out by a roar of remorse. So she lay there, moving her body lightly, trying to set off a spark, something that she, or, less likely, he could fan into a flame. Thomas was in for the long haul at her chest. He was hesitant, always had been, about touching her anywhere below the waist, as if it might be disrespectful to do so.

Dale had been a different sort of lover, a strutting, self-satisfied tease who had absolutely no shame or self-consciousness, who played with every inch of her body until she wanted him so badly she'd find herself pleading with him. With Dale, there had been nothing forbidden or off-limits, no request she couldn't make, no desire of hers he couldn't intuit almost as soon as she felt it. But years ago, she'd trained herself to stop thinking about Dale's un-canny expertise—especially when Thomas was making love to her. It couldn't be a good sign that she was drifting into fantasies of him now.

Thomas was above her, about to make his entry. He had a limited reper-toire of moves, and he always ran through them in the exact same order, like a folk singer who plays the same songs in the same sequence interspersed with the exact same, supposedly spontaneous, patter. Not that she didn't share some of the burden of responsibility, but whenever they made love she was filled with a profound lethargy, as if she'd been drugged. She found it hard to move her legs, tilt her pelvis, give him any assistance or encourage-ment.

"Is this all right?" he asked, more considerate and gentle than her gyne-cologist.

She managed a smile and nodded. "Mmmm," she said. "Yes, it's fine."

She tried to talk herself into feeling cared for, filled with his love and kind-ness, but she felt invaded, as if a salesman had entered the house and was about to start a long tedious demonstration of a vacuum cleaner.

"Is this all right?"

"It's fine," she said, a little more sharply this time.

How had she come to this, a woman of her generation, brought up on the slogans of erotic liberation and revolutionary politics? She'd gone to nude beaches, smoked pot, used a vibrator, watched a pornographic video, and once, on a business trip, when she was much younger, had spent an afternoon in a Seattle hotel room with a total stranger. How had she ended up in an expansive burnt umber air-conditioned bedroom on a wide double-thick mattress, her hands limp on her husband's back, desperately waiting for his assault to be over, as if she were an icy Victorian hysteric? At least those miserable creatures didn't have to pretend to be enjoying it, didn't have to go through the humiliation of clenching and sighing and performing a grand finale as if she were a soprano bringing a big hammy bel canto aria to a predictably shrill close.

When he was finished, he rolled off her, grinning, like a boy pleased with himself after having sex for the very first time. "Thank you," he said, and tenderly wiped his sweat off her neck.

"Thank you," she said. Now that it was over, she did feel grateful, grateful and guilty. If only, somehow, she could find some still place in the relationship or within herself, maybe she could get in sync with him. Maybe that was why she'd started to see Dr. Berman again. She really had to be more open with him about her feelings toward Thomas.

There was a thud from upstairs, as if something had hit the floor in Gerald's room, and then a louder crash and the sound of glass or plastic shattering. She sat up and placed a hand over her chest. It was the explosion she'd been longing for half an hour ago, but not, *never,* from that part of the house. Gerald, she thought, had rolled out of bed and then something, the lamp, had fallen on top of him. Here was her punishment for wanting the distraction of disaster, for worrying about an inconsequential bowl of pudding, for thinking about Dale while Thomas did his best to please her. She leapt out of bed and opened the door to the hall, feeling the warmer air hit her damp, chafed skin. "Gerald?" she called. "Are you all right?"

Thomas ran to her side and the two of them stood there, naked and sweating, their arms around each other's waist, as if they were both afraid to go upstairs and face their fears. "Gerald?" she called again. "Is everything all *right*?"

"Yes, *Jane,*" he called out. "I just dropped my Ace *Hard*ware $5.99 flashlight. I hate to tell you, but it smashed into about ten pieces of cheap *plastic.*"

"You're supposed to be sleeping," Jane said.

"I can't sleep with you shouting at me, *can* I?"

"I don't like that tone, Gerald."

"I told you the more expensive one would last longer."

"You settle down, buckeroo," Thomas said, his smile obvious from the sound of his voice, "and we'll talk about it tomorrow." He pulled Jane to his side tightly and kissed the top of her head, acknowledgment that all was right with their world—their love had been consummated, their house was intact, their son was safe.

Six
As One Door Closes . . .

1.

"What's in the bag, Mr. Sullivan?"

Desmond stopped on the mahogany staircase. The pocket doors to the second-floor parlor were partially open, and Loretta, his landlady, and Henry, the putative superintendent of the building, were seated in reclining loungers, watching television. He'd been in Boston two weeks, and thus far he hadn't walked up or down the staircase more than a half dozen times without hearing Loretta's mellifluous voice asking him "What's in the bag?" or "What have you got there?" even when he was empty-handed. He clutched the crinkly plastic sack closer to his side. "Just some trash," he said, enunciating each word carefully. Surely there was no need to tell her the specifics: an empty wine bottle and two well-read tabloids.

"Just some *what?*" she asked.

"Trash," he said and made a waggling motion with his hand, as if warding off an unpleasant odor.

"Be sure to close the lid on the barrels."

"I will indeed."

"In *what?*"

"In*deed.*"

Henry gave one of his unnerving outbursts of laughter and said, "We can hear you in here. Turn down the volume."

What the housing office at Deerforth College had billed as a grand studio apartment turned out to be a modest room on the top floor of a Back Bay town house. The charming New England kitchen was a sink and a microwave tucked into one dark corner, and the antique furnishings were a small armoire, a rutted library table, and a sagging bed. It was true he had a private bathroom as promised, but no one had mentioned it was down the hall. Still, he couldn't complain about the location or the views; his two round windows looked out to the sailboat traffic in the Charles River Basin in one direction and Charlestown in the other. At night he could see the lights of Cambridge, and the mist on the river and somewhere in the hazy distance, Bunker Hill Monument, an obelisk which, like almost every lamppost in Boston, had enormous historical significance, although no one seemed to know or care exactly what the significance was.

The most unfortunate aspect of the arrangement was the peculiar setup of the house. Loretta Neal lived on the first two floors, and because the place had never been properly divided into apartments, the top-floor boarders had to walk up a magnificently curved mahogany staircase that formed the core of her residence. The doors to her parlor were always partly open. At first, Desmond was charmed by her affability, her Boston accent, even her puckish penchant for having him repeat things he'd already said in a perfectly clear voice. But after answering her what's-in-the-bag inquiry for the tenth time, he began creeping up the staircase, hoping she wouldn't see him.

She called him in out of the hall, as if she were encouraging an old friend to pay a visit. The parlor was a vast oval room with dark paneling, ceiling medallions, and long curved windows looking out to the upper branches of the trees lining the street. The windows didn't open, or at least never were opened, and the room had the musty smell of an underused library. Loretta and Henry's vinyl recliners were plopped in the middle of the floor, distinctly out of place among the antique tables, lamps, and fainting couches pressed against the walls. The television, an immense thing with a whole sci-fi colony of cables worming out of the back, was tuned to an infomercial about a skin care product that eliminated what the spokesperson referred to as "faux wrinkles." As far as he could tell, Loretta and Henry watched nothing but infomercials, and watched them as if they were dramatic programming.

"You're always walking up and down," Loretta said. "This must be the sixth time today, isn't it?"

He attempted a grin. Did she keep a record? "I haven't been counting."

"Me neither. I was guesstimating. Anything you need help with? Henry's just getting ready to leave."

Henry was always getting ready to leave, even late last night when Desmond bumped into him on the staircase dressed in his bathrobe and slippers. He found the attempts to pass Henry off as the building's superintendent insulting. Did they think he would care that he and Loretta were lovers? Desmond guessed Loretta was in her early sixties, a hollowed-out woman with starched too-red hair and the long thin face and spindly legs of a tough, ruined Irish beauty. He'd heard from one of the other boarders that in her youth she'd been the governess for an old Boston banking family and had become the grandfather's mistress. According to the old man's will, Loretta could live in the building until her death, provided she didn't marry. She was given a small income for upkeep of the building, but couldn't make any structural changes. Desmond wasn't convinced there was much truth to the story, but he loved it anyway; it seemed so Bostonian, in a John P. Marquand sort of way.

"Everything's fine," Desmond said.

This comment provoked a disconcerting laugh from Henry. Henry chuckled at almost everything Desmond said, as if he didn't believe a word out of his mouth, including banalities such as "hello." He was a jowly black man, obviously a few years older than Loretta, who always wore a pair of thick black eyeglasses on top of his bald head. Desmond had seen Henry reading the newspaper, watching television, and rewiring an outlet in the hall, never once using the glasses to help him see. Gossip among the boarders claimed: Loretta and Henry had to keep their relationship secret for fear of losing possession of the house due to a race provision in the will; he had been her lawyer twenty years earlier; he had a family stashed away somewhere on the other side of the city.

"Mr. Gutterson isn't bothering you?" Loretta asked.

"Not at all."

Mr. Gutterson was an ill-tempered Yorkshire terrier who lived with a retired schoolteacher at the end of the hall. No one ever mentioned the owner's name, and the one time Desmond had tried to coax it out of the woman herself, she'd said, "I'm Mr. Gutterson's mommy," in such a disturbing tone of voice, he'd dropped the subject.

"My music hasn't been bothering you, has it?" Desmond asked.

"We love music," Loretta said. "As long as it isn't opera."

"We hate opera," Henry said. "Gets you all riled up for nothing."

"It isn't opera." Desmond began backing toward the door. "I should get going. I have to make a phone call." Soon he'd be reporting his bathroom habits and estimated tax payments.

"You can always use ours," Loretta said.

"Thank you," Desmond said. "I need the air." Despite two weeks of frantic calls, the phone company still hadn't installed his line. As a result, all of his calls to Russell had been made from a bank of public phones on a noisy corner two blocks away or from his office at Deerforth with students and colleagues serving as background music.

The night air was heavy with humidity and saturated with light. The smell of the river and the ocean, the rows of stately brick houses, and the reserved, conservatively dressed people who lived in his neighborhood had already become familiar to him. He couldn't decide if it was a good thing or a tragedy that people were so instantly adaptable. There had been moments during the past two weeks when he'd tried to conjure up the New York block he'd lived on for more than a decade and had trouble remembering the exact arrangement of the buildings, as if that whole chunk of his life was fading from his memory. It was a good thing he'd brought along several snapshots of Russell.

There was a row of ten pay phones on the corner of Newbury Street and tonight there were several free, possibly because a good half of the crowd of well-dressed shoppers and diners strolling the street were talking into cell phones. He supposed his life would be easier if he got one of those contraptions, but if he did, he'd have to stop resenting all the people who had one, and that seemed like too high a price to pay for mere convenience.

When Russell picked up the phone after three rings, Desmond's shoulders dropped with relief. Several nights in the past two weeks, Russell hadn't been home when he'd called, and Desmond had stood at the phone booth listening to the traffic crawling past, feeling as if he'd lost control of his life.

"Sweetheart," Desmond said. "It's so good to hear your voice. I was afraid I'd get the machine again."

"I don't understand the phone company," Russell said. "What is the problem?"

"It's ridiculous, really." Desmond supposed that the delay had something to do with Loretta and the setup of the house, and possibly with the fact that he'd forgotten to arrange things before leaving New York; but it was wonderful to hoist up an easy target like the phone company at which Russell could direct some of the hostility and frustration he was obviously feeling toward Desmond. Desmond played up the staggering ineptitude of the people he'd been dealing with and invented a new series of fruitless calls and faxes. "That's the third fax in two days," Desmond said. He gave a detailed description of heading to the English Department office at Deerforth and his conversations with the secretary about similar problems she'd had.

There was a loud silence on the other end of the line, and Desmond realized he'd added too many facts and figures to his scenario; you can usually get away with lying as long as you don't try to make it sound too believable. "Anyway," he said, "I'm pretty sure it's getting hooked up tomorrow. How's business?"

"Too good. I've had to work late almost every night this week. I was there until close to midnight on Monday, sorting through a vanful of furniture we bought, sight unseen, from an estate sale out on the far western end of Staten Island. They were supposed to deliver it at noon and didn't show up until eight o'clock."

Desmond leaned against the phone booth, impatiently listening to Russell's tale of inept movers and broken lamp shades and the struggles of trying to fit three sofas into the basement of the store, wondering if the whole story wasn't another case of too much itemized minutiae. When he finished, Desmond decided to give him a dose of his own doubting silence.

"So . . . anyway," Russell finally said, "how are classes?"

"It's a little soon to tell," Desmond said, even though he'd been longing to discuss his teaching with Russell for days. Somehow, the whole experience didn't feel real to him, and he knew that part of the problem was that he hadn't yet gone over the specifics with Russell. Deerforth had told him he'd be teaching two sections of a course in journalism, but when he arrived, he discovered that one was something called Creative Nonfiction, which, based on the work he'd seen thus far, was basically Noncreative Fiction. The good part was that most of the students in that class were less interested in having their work critiqued than they were in being consoled for their real or imagined afflictions and abuse. He mentioned some of this to Russell and said, "At least it's giving me more free time than I'd expected."

"And you're getting work done on the book?"

A tall blond boy on Roller Blades glided up to the next phone, spilled out a pocketful of change, punched in a phone number using four ringed fingers of one hand, and started up a noisy argument, all without removing a pair of yellow earphones. Desmond turned away and put his hand over one ear. Thus far, he'd unpacked his boxes of notes for the book and lined them up on the library table he was using as a desk. He'd driven out to Waugborn, the suburb where Pauline Anderton had spent her final days, but rather than being inspired by the place, he was depressed by the sight of the ugly decay of the downtown and the clusters of new houses flung into treeless lots. "I am," Desmond lied. "I think I'm getting close to figuring out what's missing. Then at least I'll know what to look for."

"That sounds hopeful. By the way, I forwarded some mail to you today. You got a letter from your editor."

"Oh? How big was it?"

"How big? I don't know. I'd guess it was a note, but I didn't open it. I don't think there was a check enclosed, if that's what you mean."

"No, there wouldn't be." A note could mean anything or nothing at all. Although it didn't make much sense to him that if she'd been too busy to return his calls she'd have time to write bread-and-butter notes. He tried to summon up a picture of her, but it had been over a year since they'd last met and what he remembered most vividly was that she dressed in conservative skirts and jackets and had muscular calves.

"What's all that racket in the background?" Russell asked. "Are you in a bus station?"

Desmond tapped the blond boy on the shoulder. He turned around as if someone had assaulted him, although he didn't pause a beat in his conversation or stop sliding his feet back and forth, obviously in rhythm to whatever music was coming in over the yellow headphones. This was what they called multitasking, something at which this generation was supposed to be gifted. But how much of a gift was it to be adept at doing three things simultaneously when each of them was pointless? He had on a ribbed sleeveless T-shirt stretched over his skinny body and a pair of baggy shorts. And now that Desmond looked, it wasn't blond hair at all, but a bleached-out white mop that had been hacked off unevenly. "Would you mind holding it down?" Desmond asked. "I'm trying to talk on the phone, as you can see."

"Oh, well, gee, I am *sorry*," he said. Instead of turning around, he stared at Desmond. "No," he said into the receiver, "just some guy I was bothering. Yeah, not bad. How am I supposed to know? I can't tell from what he's wearing."

Desmond stared back. He was probably in his early twenties, attractive in an obvious sort of way. Desmond was galled and flattered that he was talking about him so blatantly, and then tried to imagine sneaking him up the mahogany staircase with the Roller Blades on his feet. What have you got there, Mr. Sullivan?

"You still there?" Russell asked.

"I'm sorry, sweetheart, just some kid on skates." He turned his back on temptation. "You know I've been missing Boris the past two weeks. What's he been playing?"

"Now that you mention it, I haven't heard him at all," Russell said. "Maybe he's given up the piano."

Over the past two years, Boris had become such a steady and reliable barometer of Russell's feelings about himself and the relationship, it unnerved Desmond to hear Russell make this announcement so calmly. "That seems unlikely. He's finally making progress. He wouldn't give it up now."

"Maybe he figured he isn't a true pianist and never will be. Maybe he's found a quieter creative outlet. Maybe he's taken up painting."

That was an oddly specific suggestion, one which perhaps contained some clue as to what was going on in Russell's sequestered emotional life. Desmond tried to remember who among their friends and acquaintances was a painter, but no one came to mind. "Listen," he said, "I've been given the class schedule and it looks as if I have a long weekend on Columbus Day. I thought I'd come down then."

"That would be great," Russell said, though not with anything you could optimistically call enthusiasm. "I've been so busy, it seems as if you've just left."

After he and Russell had signed off, Desmond held the receiver to his ear for a moment, looking at the blond boy, and weighing his options. Eventually, he hung up and walked away. Even if Loretta wasn't fazed by a guest, Mr. Gutterson would, in all likelihood, bark up a storm at the sound of a strange voice.

2.

Deerforth College was located fifteen miles into the leafy suburbs, and the next morning, following what had become his new routine, Desmond drove out through a thin drizzle which, given the drought of the past several months, seemed like a nasty tease. The sun came out as he arrived at school, and steam rose up from the damp parking lot.

Deerforth had given Desmond an office on one of the upper floors of the Gothic tower that housed the English Department. He had views from this room, too; the ivy-covered stone buildings, the rolling lawns, the sparkling man-made lake, and the careful crisscross of cobblestone paths, frequently covered with little groups of students, huddled and insignificantly small from his vantage point.

His office, which usually housed someone named Professor Crandersall (currently on sabbatical in Florence) was across the hall from Thomas Miller, the professor Sybil Gale had mentioned at his going-away party. He was a tall, lumbering man who kept telling Desmond he had something important to ask him, but was always pulled away before forming the question. Miller's field was nineteenth-century American literature and, at a depressing lunch with three sullen colleagues, Desmond had been told he'd written a lengthy critique of several of Melville's more obscure works. No one had used the word dull to describe his book, but the implication was clear from the unenthusiastic way they mentioned it: "If you're interested in glancing at it, there's probably a copy floating around the library." Desmond discovered that indeed there was a copy floating around the library, but whether it was dull or not he could only guess. It was one of those dense academic tomes with thousands of footnotes and several dozen appendices, all laid out in breathtakingly small print, the kind of book that Russell's parents took with them for beach reading on their rare vacations to Hawaii or Mexico. Desmond promised himself he'd read it, just as soon as he finished *The Making of Americans*. Maybe he'd send a copy to Russell and have him skim it for him.

Whatever the nature of his scholarly work, Thomas Miller was popular with students. Desmond heard from several that he was a lively, absorbing lecturer and—to cut to the chase—lenient when it came to grades. His height alone must have made them feel they were getting their money's worth. Like politicians, teachers are most effective if they take up a lot of space, and Thomas, who had to be at least four inches over six feet, did.

In addition to Desmond's office and Thomas's, there were two others on the floor. One belonged to a Renaissance scholar on sabbatical and the other was the domain of Celeste Gray. Celeste was a senior faculty member who'd gone to Deerforth as an undergraduate, returned post-doc as a professor, rode out a difficult transition from all-women to coeducational institution, and in general, remained faithful to the school long past the point at which it was considered a virtue to do so. Faithfulness to just about anything other than a pet stays fresh for only eight years before it takes on the rancid smell of indolence or desperation. She was a thin woman in her middle sixties with an acutely wrinkled face, long white hair she wore up in a loose bun, and an air of distracted beatnik brilliance. She taught one course only—Modern Poetry—but seemed to spend most of her time in her office with Helen keeping watch at her feet. Helen was an arthritic malamute, snow white but beginning to go yellow all over.

That morning, the hallway outside his office was uncharacteristically empty and Helen was prostrate in front of Thomas's open door, her blue eyes draped in misery. He went over to pet Helen and Thomas Miller appeared above him, filling up his doorway.

"Poor old thing," he said. "She's stuck with me for the rest of the day."

Because Desmond was gazing up at him, Thomas Miller looked even larger than he did from a distance. His pale polished pate, surrounded by a ring of light brown hair, seemed to be brushing the top of the door jamb. A few days earlier, Desmond had come upon a stash of Professor Crandersall's books and papers, carelessly tossed in a heap in one corner of the office. Stuck between the pages of a book on Verrocchio were handwritten notes Crandersall had made, apparently for a projected essay. They read, in part: "Greatest sculptor in Florentine tradition between Donatello and Michelangelo? . . . look up Ruskin on V's equestrian statue of B. Colleone . . . oh christ, Miller just walked into his office, bet he's got a cock on him like a mortadello . . . bust of Francesco Sassetti . . . Rossellino or Verrocchio? . . . I'd love to chew on his piece, unless it meant talking to the goddamned bore . . . see Pope-Hennessy for details on bust."

When Desmond asked after Professor Gray, Thomas explained that she'd stumbled as she was coming up the stairs that morning and had cracked her shin on the top step. As she was taken away on a stretcher, she'd barked out orders on the care and feeding of Helen. "You don't think they'll keep her overnight, do you? Jane would kill me if I came home with a dog." He laughed nervously at the thought, and then added, "Jane's my wife. Jane Cody. Which reminds me, I have something I've been meaning to ask you. Come into my office for a minute, will you?"

It was a surprisingly narrow room, considerably smaller than Professor Crandersall's and, unlike virtually every other room Desmond had been in on campus, it had no view; the single tiny window looked out to a gabled, slate-covered rooftop. He liked it. Already Desmond had begun to weary of Deerforth's rolling lawns and pampered hedges, all watered hourly despite water bans. The whole campus seemed to be basking in its own loveliness a bit too immodestly, with every manicured tree and artfully designed flower bed lolling and stretching and crying out, "Look at me, look at me!" Books were spilling off his shelves, and the desk was a compost heap of old exams and reams of photocopies. There was a poster of an especially dour and disappointed Melville over his desk. Desmond scanned the room for a photo of Jane, but there didn't appear to be one, just a small photo on the desk of a plump, disgruntled child. A boy, Desmond guessed. Sybil, whom Thomas claimed to remember fondly but clearly didn't remember at all, would want the details of the office, especially the unflattering ones.

Thomas offered him the chair at his desk and carefully lowered himself into a stocky easy chair under the eaves, tugging up the legs of his pants as he descended. "It's a mess, I know," he said, "but in the soul of this man, there lies one insular Tahiti." Desmond nodded and Thomas helped him out by adding, "To paraphrase Melville." Then he quoted a lush, lengthy passage from *Moby-Dick* about appalling oceans and verdant land and inner peace and joy.

Desmond shifted uncomfortably. He hated these academic conversations in which people traded quotations back and forth as if displaying their most valuable baseball cards. Dinner with Russell's parents was a more overtly aggressive version of this —a food fight in which facts and figures, not pies, were flung across the table in the hopes of scoring a direct hit. At this moment the only literary quotation he could think of was from Lewis Westerly's single letter to his eldest son: "Life isn't worth the toilet paper it's written on."

"I've been looking for the right moment to talk with you about your book," Thomas said. "It's a magnificent piece of work. He was a genius, this Westerly, and you, my friend, were a genius for uncovering him."

Embarrassingly undeserved praise, but he'd take it. Certainly no one else at Deerforth had shown any signs of having read the book. "I had a great deal of fun working on it," he said, hoping it came off as modesty.

"Now I'll have to read the novels. As soon as I have a free moment. Is there a logical place to start?"

Desmond gave this serious consideration, seeing the opportunity to introduce a new devotee. "It's a matter of taste, of course."

Thomas slapped his enormous forehead. "*A Matter of Taste.* Of course. I should have realized that from the way you described it. I assume that one's back in print?"

"I'll check for you. So . . . Jane isn't a dog lover?"

Thomas brightened at this offer of more familiar turf. "Oh, don't let her kid you. She loves all animals, even me. Just not in the house. 'This is what you shall do: Love the earth and sun and the animals.' "

Desmond supposed he was quoting something from Whitman, but now he felt less obliged to go out on a limb by risking a guess. Come to think of it, Miller probably hadn't read half of what he spouted but sat at home nights memorizing *Bartlett's*. At least Desmond wouldn't have to go through the charade of praising Miller for his Melville tome. "You said there was something you've been meaning to ask me?"

Thomas started to cross his legs, then reached down to help pull one ankle across his knee. "About Jane, actually. When I told her about your book, she went out and read it and was crazy about it. She's a producer at one of our public TV stations. She's been after me to invite you out to the house for dinner." Thomas leaned toward Desmond as if he were about to offer him an unlisted phone number. "She thinks the two of you might be able to work on a project together."

"Oh? What sort of project?"

Thomas lifted his shoulders to his ears and his chin disappeared into his neck. "I'm not clear. A documentary series of some kind. Biographies. She'll give you the specifics. She's always got something up her sleeve."

Despite everything in his experience that had taught him to view even solid offers of this type warily, Desmond felt lifted by merely having his name mentioned in the same sentence with television. Even public television. What a horribly shallow person I am, he thought; but suddenly the walls of Deerforth College seemed a fraction less confining. He'd have to mention to his class this afternoon that he was working on a TV project even though he didn't know what it was and wasn't yet working on anything.

"I suppose you know a lot of people in Boston," Thomas said.

"Not really. No one, in fact. I'm working on a new book," Desmond said, "so I'm more or less looking forward to the solitude."

" 'Solitude is to genius the stern friend,' " Thomas quoted.

"Mmm. True. Whitman?"

"Emerson. I'll let you know about a date for the dinner."

3.

A few days later, Desmond was sitting at the sidewalk table of a Newbury Street café, eating a cheeseburger. He'd wanted to order a crusty pastry with mocha frosting he'd seen on the dessert tray, but had decided against it at the last moment, imagining how he'd look, sitting there with a cup of tea, daintily slicing through it with the edge of a fork. It was a bright windy day and all the foreign students from Boston University and other nearby schools were out in force, shopping aggressively and turning that particular Boston neighborhood into a perfume ad—threesomes and foursomes of androgynous young people in Armani sunglasses and expensive clothes behaving toward each other in suggestive ways. Deerforth drew an intelligent and relatively sedate student body, but was too far from the downtown nightclubs to give it a competitive edge in the sought-after foreign markets. Most of these kids appeared to have arrived in the U.S. by way of private schools in Switzerland, and judging from their sleek bodies, they all used personal trainers and had access to high-grade drugs. The strong, warm breeze blowing off the river gave them an especially dashing appearance.

The packet of mail Russell had forwarded had arrived earlier in the day. Uncertain what to expect from the note from his editor, Desmond had decided to escape the confines of his room before opening it. Now that the phone company had finally shown up, he found himself waiting more attentively for a call from Russell, and the anticipation made it feel to him as if the walls were closing in. He was still trying to decode the comment about Boris taking up painting. Last night, lying in bed with the window open above him, he'd begun to wonder if it had something to do with the lanky contractor in the building next to Morning in America, who was, after all, a painter of sorts.

Sometimes Desmond worried about his own sexual restlessness. In his pre-Russell days, he'd found himself becoming ravenously promiscuous as soon as he started dating someone. Did it mean he was unable to commit to a relationship, incapable of dealing with intimacy, afflicted with a sexual addiction he'd have to struggle with in some humiliating twelve-step program? What worried him since he and Russell had been together was that he'd felt virtually no sexual restlessness. Did it mean he was getting old, his hormones were getting sluggish? Most worrisome of all was the possibility that it indicated some lack of ambition that perhaps leaked into other areas of his life. Yesterday afternoon, he'd sat down at the table in his room and tried to write a pornographic story about the bleached blond Roller Blader. But halfway into it, he realized the boy had miraculously metamorphosed into Russell, and he couldn't very well construct a lurid fantasy about someone he'd been sleeping with for five years.

The mail Russell had sent was the usual hodgepodge of bills, statements from mutual funds, and pleas for money from hopeless political causes. Sometimes it seemed to him that the utter hopelessness of every political cause he believed in was the most consistent part of his life. There was a postcard from his father, who, according to the picture on the front, was on a cruise in Alaska. "Incredible scenery," he'd written. "Reminds me of the Upper Peninsula, though not as dramatic." Since the death of Desmond's mother, Larry had retired from his law practice and spent most of his time on organized tours of exotic places around the globe, every one of which reminded him of someplace close to home. In theory, travel might be broadening, but most people did it to prove to themselves that, ultimately, they were better off staying on the sofa.

He opened the letter from his editor carefully, using a greasy knife to slit along the seam. Inside was a short note, handwritten on a piece of thin blue paper. "Can't imagine how I forgot to mention sooner, but today's my last day here. Permanent maternity leave. Been crazy the past few months trying to close out a few books. Tried to find editorial match for Anderton bio, but enthusiasm low. Kira Manoly (new girl, British, Tina Brown–esque, gorgeous hair) willing to take a look if finished by January. Otherwise, prospects bleak. Don't despair—they probably won't ask for the advance back and we'll always have Westerly!"

Desmond held the note, letting the wind blow the paper into a backflip.

He was being dismissed. The project he'd been nurturing for years was being passed off to someone with no interest in it or him, someone who had agreed to do his departing editor the favor of *looking* at it, someone whose main qualification was her hairdo. It wasn't just bad news, it was a death sentence. And worst of all, the whole business of his project, his career, was considered so inconsequential, the death sentence was announced in a cheerful little note that had been dashed off so hastily there hadn't been time for complete sentences. A gust of hot wind blew his napkin off the table. He sat watching it float into the pale sky on a strong updraft. He took off his sunglasses and rubbed at his eyes. What am I doing here? he thought. Why didn't I order the pastry? When he put the glasses back on and looked up, he saw Helen strolling down the street with her unmistakable arthritic gait, and her yellowing, windswept fur. What's *she* doing here? he thought. At the other end of her leash was a swarthy Marlboro man in a gray suit, carrying on a lively conversation with a woman. As they got closer to where Desmond was sitting, he realized they were arguing. "You don't take her seriously," the woman snapped. "You're not sympathetic to her problems." "Which problems?" "Primarily? You," she said. "Ah, Janey, you're so indirect." The woman grabbed the leash out of the man's hand, yanked on it and said, "For Christ's sake, *heel!*" Helen complied, the man grinned, and the three of them stopped while Helen sniffed at a parched tree.

She was a tall woman, with long, shapely legs and the kind of robust figure that would have been described as womanly in a more generous decade. Her brown hair was brushed back in a casually unkempt fashion, and loose strands of it were blowing into her mouth in the strong breeze. Underneath the hair was a freckled, weathered face with the untended beauty of a minor European film star who'd started to let herself go around the edges. For one brief moment, Desmond thought she was looking at him, but then realized she was gazing at the half-eaten cheeseburger on his plate. With her free hand, she reached up and adjusted a string of colorful Bakelite beads, and then, as he was about to stand and introduce himself, the three of them moved on. She was wearing an immoderately short skirt that tugged slightly at her hips, and there was something provocative and sensual in her long strides and even in the way she held the leash.

When they were half a block away, she stopped and pulled out a cell phone while the man squatted down to pet Helen. Then the man took her arm and the three of then continued on in the direction of the river.

The breeze came up again and fluttered the letter he still clutched in his fingers. He couldn't have been distracted by Jane Cody—undoubtedly this was she; Celeste Gray was still hospitalized and Thomas had dog-sitting responsibilities—for more than a couple of minutes, but for that brief time, he'd nearly forgotten that his life and livelihood were crumbling around him. He looked down the street again, but Jane and her companions had disappeared.

And then it struck him, the wonderful irony of seeing Jane Cody just as he read this letter. This was fate reminding him that as one door closes, another opens. Jane Cody was his salvation. She, with her long resolute strides and her television connections, was the break he'd been waiting for all these months. This hadn't been a coincidence, seeing her on the street; it had been a sign. What better way to finish the book and revive big-haired editorial enthusiasm than to work with her on a television project? A series of biographies. Surely he could slip Anderton into the mix. A collaboration, a fresh eye to spot whatever it was he'd been missing. The dinner was only a few days away. He tossed back his coffee, bundled his mail, and pushed back from the table. He hadn't received a death notice at all, merely a prod. On his way out of the restaurant, he dumped the pleas for money and bank statements and the editor's letter into a trash barrel. Newbury Street was lined with expensive hair salons and overpriced clothing shops. Maybe it was time he walked into a few of them and saw what they had to offer.

Seven
The Circumstances

1.

Jane often wondered what made people so angry these days. The country was in the middle of a blizzard of economic prosperity and peace, job and real estate markets were booming, virtually everyone you bumped into had gaudy academic credentials, even if they were completely uneducated, and if all that wasn't enough to drive away the demons of fury, you could take pills. Some of the men at her office spent half their time cruising the Internet in search of the best deals on Viagra, Propecia, and Human Growth Hormone.

And yet, after sitting in Dr. Berman's office for fifty minutes, playing cat and mouse with the truth, here she was driving home along the river through a sea of immense, truck-sized pleasure vehicles with drivers hanging out their windows, honking, swerving, swearing, and very possibly getting ready to pull out guns and start shooting. After spending tens of thousands of dollars on something too unwieldy to steer and too big to park, people discovered—surprise!—they had no real need for them and so had to assert the practicality of their purchases by turning the roads into battlefields.

Jane stopped at a red light and almost instantly a frizzy-haired woman in aviator sunglasses stuck her head out the window of the vehicle behind her and started to shout and gesticulate wildly, something about making a right-hand turn on red. Jane gazed at her in the rearview mirror, enjoying the spectacle. The best part of uncontrolled anger was that it made people look fantastically ugly, which was why she preferred to subvert all her own ire into more subtle forms of aggression and, if that didn't do the trick, into good old self-hatred. When the woman in the sunglasses didn't let up, it was obvious her wrath was getting out of line. Jane undid her seat belt and stepped out into the damp heat of late afternoon. As soon as the woman saw her coming toward her armored vehicle, she rolled up her window. There was a wailing baby strapped into a complicated seat in back, and on either side of that, two fuming children with their arms folded across their chests. A golden retriever was panting in the passenger seat. The Whole Catastrophe on wheels, road rage and all.

Jane tapped on the window. "Stop honking at me!" she scolded. "I'm going straight." She pointed. "Straight, see? I'm not turning right at all."

"Then why are you in this lane?" the woman screamed, her face contorted behind the tinted glass.

"Better view!" Jane said.

By the time she got back to her car, the light had changed. And just to prove a point—what point exactly she wasn't sure—she decided to turn right anyway. The woman in the safari vehicle roared past her, and Jane burst out laughing. Jane was heading in the wrong direction and would have to go a good mile out of her way to turn around, but it had been worth it. True, she was running late for her own dinner party, but two days ago, when she had the bright idea of inviting her brother and his wife, she'd called the culinary school in Cambridge and hired some student caterers, so she didn't have to worry about cooking. Her mother-in-law was looking after Gerald (baby-sitting didn't seem, had never seemed, the appropriate term for watching over Gerald), so even if she was half an hour late, no serious damage would be done. Sarah could just add this to the tally of resentments and petty offenses she was doubtlessly keeping on file in the computer Thomas had recently bought her. Thank God it was only another month or so before she moved out and went south to live with Thomas's right-wing sister and her racist (though admittedly sexy) husband. The sister, Beth, was one of those sweet, God-fearing types who attended regular meetings of a prayer group where they discussed "philosophy and miracles," which Jane was sure meant trading statuettes of angels and planning abortion clinic bombings.

"It'll be good for Sarah to have something new to stew about," Jane said aloud. "It keeps her brain cells active."

The comment was addressed to Helen, who was flung out across the back seat like a hunting trophy. Celeste Gray was still in the hospital, and it looked as if she'd be there for a while. After fixing her shin, the doctors had moved on to her kidneys, and Jane suspected they'd run through all the major organs before they let her out. Jane had met Celeste a few times and hadn't liked her. She was one of those older women you're supposed to admire as intelligent and courageous because they're hypercritical and insulting. Despite her initial resistance, Jane had grown attached to the creaky old dog. She had all the virtues of a bloated alcoholic friend, the kind of nonjudgmental lug you could confide in because she had no attention span or memory. ("I just shot my husband and ate his body." "Aw, that's a shame.")

The first week they were watching over her, Jane had been forced to take Helen to work one day and everyone at the station had been so amazed, in that jokey, irritating way, at the spectacle of seeing *her,* of all people, with a *dog,* she realized that most of her co-workers regarded her as a hard-edged, slightly bitter person, the type who had neither the tenderness nor the patience to care about a pet. Chloe Barnes had looked from dog to Jane to dog to Jane with her usual pitying gaze. In truth, Jane was proud of her lack of sentimentality about house pets (a trait Gerald had inherited in an extreme form), but she'd begun dragging Helen into work with her almost every day, just to prove that people didn't know her as well as they all thought. Thomas bled sympathy for the dog—"Poor old Helen, what's going to become of you?"—although he did little to actually care for her. Upon seeing her arrive for one of their talks with Helen in tow, Dale had said, "I never figured you for a dog-lover, Janey." "You seem to forget," she'd said, "that I'm a mother," a comment which she'd meant as proof of her ability to nurture but had sounded like a criticism of Gerald.

Jane adjusted her rearview mirror and said: "I suppose I should have told Dr. Berman that Dale and I exchanged a few kisses last time I saw him."

Helen replied with an unruffled sigh.

"Well, I intended to, but when I told him we'd gone out for coffee four times—which is the truth, if you count the martinis as coffee—he gave me one of those knowing looks of his, as if to say he could see the handwriting on the wall. And believe me, Helen, I'm not paying him all that money so he can cop a superior attitude."

Not to mention that the business of their encounter along the Esplanade last week—mid-afternoon, in a moment of azure beauty when the wind that had been blowing all day just died and the sailboats in the river basin went still, as if someone had flipped the switch on a magnetized electronic game and the surface of the water became a sheet of stretched silk—had been a harmless lapse in judgment, nothing more or less. It was part of Dale's compulsive need to flirt. It would have made more of an event of the whole thing if she'd pushed him away or berated him instead of letting him wrap his arms around her and nuzzle his face against her neck and start nibbling her ear.

"And you have to admit I've been a lot more patient with Thomas since I started having coffee with Dale. True?"

Of course it was true, whether Helen recognized it or not. Over the past couple of weeks, she hadn't felt as overwhelmed by Thomas and the yard and by dragging Gerald to school and shrink and piano lessons and the whole confusing assortment of real and fabricated appointments.

"I should have been discussing this dinner party. Talk about needing to have your head examined." Although she'd planned the whole thing to meet Desmond Sullivan and get him on her side with this documentary project, she'd ended up inviting Rosemary Boyle as well. Rosemary was in the last seconds of her fifteen minutes of fame, and Jane figured Desmond might be impressed that they were friends. Plus she hadn't had time to pull together her proposal as fully as she'd hoped, and Rosemary would be a distraction from specifics. The real insanity had been in inviting her brother and his wife. But if Desmond turned out to be a dud conversation-wise, Rosemary would be entertained just to be in the presence of Brian, with whom, Jane was almost positive, Rosemary had had a furtive encounter of some sort on the beach years ago when Rosemary and Charlie visited on Nantucket and Brian was single and still a student at the Harvard School of Design. And then there was the fact that Brian was supplying some kind of architectural expertise to this restaurant Dale had invested in, so you couldn't tell what interesting observations he might inadvertently make about her ex-husband.

When she pulled into the driveway, she saw the caterers' rattletrap blue van parked near the back door. Maybe she'd call the school next week and suggest they at least repaint the van since everyone she knew seemed to be increasingly concerned with "food safety"—the latest variety of eating disorder to seize the public imagination—and this thing didn't inspire confidence.

She let Helen out of the back seat and called for Gerald. A ghostly, blurred version of Sarah appeared behind the screen door. From this angle, distorted by the loose, dusty screens, Sarah bore an unsettling resemblance to Thomas, or Thomas as he might have looked if you stuck him in a flowered housedress and an unconvincing white wig. As soon as Sarah spotted Jane, she withdrew from the door into the darker recesses of the house.

Helen wandered off to the backyard; that patch of earth was finally getting some use. It was a good thing Helen felt so at home in the unruly grass because it meant she wouldn't have to listen to Gerald complain about having an animal in the house. Gerald had been outraged by Helen's sudden appearance. He claimed, with good reason, that getting a pet should be a family decision and since he was part of the family ("the most important part, as I see it") he should have been consulted. "Your father was doing a favor for a colleague," Jane had told him. "The dog had nowhere else to go. You've heard of charitable acts, haven't you." "Yes," Gerald had replied, and then added, uncannily Scrooge-like: "I've also heard of animal shelters."

As Jane stood in the hallway examining the day's mail, Sarah appeared from the living room and gave a theatrical gasp of surprise. "I didn't see you drive up," she rasped. "You were so late, I started worrying about you."

Started drinking was, obviously, the more accurate way of putting it, given the gravel in her voice and the careful way she was forming her words. Whenever Sarah was looking after Gerald, wine bottles vanished from the shelves of the pantry. Jane would love to know what she did with the empties, probably walked the streets after midnight, dropping them into neighbors' trash cans. "I had a dental appointment," Jane said. "It's right there on the list I left for you."

Sarah grunted. "There's so much on those lists I can barely keep track. I thought it was last week you were at the dentist, no?"

"No," Jane said, making a mental note to drop the dentist excuse in the future. Sarah probably assumed Jane was having an affair, which she'd no doubt be quicker to forgive than something as positive and life-affirming as a shrink appointment. "I had a mammogram last week."

Sarah reached up and adjusted her wig. She had a full head of beautiful white hair, but insisted on wearing a series of synthetic wigs that looked less like hair than your average winter hat and gave her the appearance of a haughty, slightly demented clown. The reason? "They're real time-savers." This from a woman who appeared to spend most of her precious free time peeking through her curtains with a telephone in one hand, reporting to someone on her daughter-in-law's comings and goings. "So many doctors up here," Sarah said. "I suppose I should have Tommy take me for a checkup before I go down to Beth's."

"You're not feeling well?" Jane asked, refusing to look up from the mail.

Sarah snorted with indignation. "Believe me, if I weren't feeling well, the doctor is the *last* place I'd go."

No point in following up on that one. Sarah was one of the sturdiest people Jane had ever met, but she was constantly complaining about her health to prove the strength of her character. She was a farm girl from Upstate New York who'd gone to Albany to work as a secretary and ended up marrying the lawyer she worked for. Thomas's father had died when he was in his late fifties, leaving Sarah with a considerable sum of money and an all-consuming martyr complex. No one knew exactly how much she'd inherited or what she'd done with it, but she frequently found ways of slipping the words "will" and "trusts" into her self-pitying conversations. Thomas was devoted to her, and not for the money. He and Beth had inherited their own substantial sums when their father died. She shuddered to think what kind of terrorist organizations Beth had given her money to. As for Thomas, he'd shown uncharacteristic practicality by investing it in a variety of blue chip stocks and, shortly after they were married—against her wishes—a computer company called Microsoft.

"Where's Gerald?" she asked.

"In the kitchen with the caterers. He took charge of everything the minute they showed up since you weren't home and no one had left instructions for me on how to contact you in case of an emergency."

"Gerald's wonderful with organizing caterers and dinner parties."

"Oh, my, yes." Sarah had her head bowed and was fumbling with a chain holding her beaded cardigan on her shoulders. "It's unusual for a *boy* to be so interested in cooking."

More assaults on the masculinity of a six-year-old. Jane went back to shuffling through the same four pieces of mail she'd been playing with for the past five minutes, faster now than before. "Don't engage" had been Berman's advice. When it came to Sarah, Jane didn't hold a thing back from Berman; if anything, she might have embellished a few details, not to alter the facts, but to emphasize them.

"And Thomas? Is he upstairs?"

"He's out jogging."

Jane looked up at her mother-in-law. "Jogging? I don't think so."

"He started two weeks ago! You didn't know that? You didn't know your husband's been jogging every day?"

"I meant in this humidity," Jane said. It didn't seem very likely that Thomas had suddenly started exercising, but if so, it was something she should have noticed or at least been told about. Jane had another mantra for dealing with Sarah, a complement to "Don't Engage," which she'd thought up herself: "Toss Her A Bone." "Thank you for looking after Gerald," she said. "You're a big help. You should make that doctor's appointment soon since you're only here another four weeks."

"Eight."

"Well. Even so."

"I suppose that's my cue to head back to the barn." "The barn" was what Sarah called the carriage house they'd spent $80,000 rehabbing. With the way Boston rentals were going, they could be getting $3,000 a month easily. But no, because she wasn't living under the same roof as them, Sarah insisted upon pretending she'd been exiled to a "barn" and probably told her friends she was forced to sleep on a pile of straw. As she was heading out the door, she turned to Jane and said, "Oh, for gosh sakes, I almost forgot. Everything's been so confusing here with fancy caterers showing up for a little dinner and you late and all. You had a call a few minutes ago from someone named *Dale*. He said you should call him as soon as you got in."

Jane felt a rush in her chest, similar to the worrisome thump she sometimes felt after drinking too much coffee. There had been no need for either of them to mention it, but she assumed they had an unspoken agreement not to call each other at home.

"Your ex-husband was named *Dale*, wasn't he?" Sarah had her meaty arms folded and resting on the shelf of her bosom.

Don't Engage. "I suspect it *was* my ex-husband. Thomas and I are friends with Dale and his wife."

"Oh, really?"

"Yes. *Really.*"

Sarah said nothing. With her arms still crossed, she made her exit, letting the door slam behind her.

The best thing about having Sarah around was that once she left a room, Jane felt a tide of peace and contentment wash over her. In the silence, she heard Gerald saying, "Leave those dishes on the table. I need the counter space my*self.*" Surely it wasn't possible that his voice was changing already— he wouldn't be seven for four more months—but he did have a strangely deep voice, which, along with his advanced verbal skills and his peculiarly adult interests, could be disorienting.

2.

After being rebuffed by Gerald—"I'm afraid I don't have time for small talk, Jane"—she went upstairs and picked up the phone next to the bed. While she waited for the call to go through, she wrote "dry cleaner" on a pad of paper on the bedside table, a reminder it was time for a general tidying up of the whole second floor. She'd let things go in the past couple of weeks and it was beginning to show. Dale answered with an insulting "Yeah?" which she refused to take personally but still threw her into a defensive stance.

"It's me," she said curtly. "I'm returning your call."

"Janey, I'm in the car. Traffic's a complete nightmare."

"That's what you get for living out in the suburbs." Technically, she supposed she lived in the suburbs, too, but at least they had subway lines in Brookline, not that she used them.

"I'm headed to Providence for a dinner with some developers, and to top it all off, I'm probably going in the wrong direction."

Probably not. Probably not a business dinner either, but she was long past the stage of having to second-guess him. Supposedly, he'd had a long talk with this woman he was infatuated with and had told her they should stop seeing each other. Jane tended to believe him, but with Dale, she always kept a few embers of skepticism glowing. "What's the urgency of the phone call?"

"Now don't get upset, Janey, but Caroline's going to call you tonight. We're going up to her family's estate on the lake over Columbus Day, and she wants you and Thomas to come with us."

"Out of the question," Jane said.

"Well, obviously. I figured I'd warn you so you could have an excuse ready."

The phone cut out. Perhaps he'd entered a tunnel or was passing through some catastrophic electromagnetic field. While she listened to a deafening storm of static, she felt increasingly annoyed that Dale found it so "obvious" that she would turn down Caroline's invitation, as if her friendship with Just Caroline meant nothing and these coffee meetings the two of them had been having were immensely significant. When the phone cut back in, Dale was still babbling on, oblivious of the fact she hadn't heard a word. ". . . I mean it wouldn't work, under the circumstances, and with—"

"What circumstances are you talking about?" Jane interrupted. "We've had a few discussions about your marriage, which in my book is barely enough to qualify as a friendship, let alone a 'circumstance.' "

She heard him sigh and then say, "Janey," in that slightly annoyed, slightly amused way of his that made her body shudder with sour memories of hurt and anger and infatuation. Without too much effort, she could still feel his arms around her and his rough cheek rubbing against her neck and the swampy smell of the river on that windy afternoon. "Whatever you think is best," he said with weary resignation.

"It's not a matter of what I think is best, Dale, it's a matter of figuring out a way to refuse without hurting Caroline's feelings." The signal cut out again, an electronic shriek sliced into her eardrum, and then a teenage boy's voice came on talking about beer commercials. A perfect replacement for Dale.

She hung up the phone and paced around the bedroom picking up socks and underwear and a stack of student papers Thomas had been reading before he went for his "jog." She certainly didn't welcome one more distraction or complication for this evening, especially if it involved a conversation with Caroline. Caroline was so proud of the mythic family estate in New Hampshire, it would be impossible to get her off the phone once she started bragging about it. Jane had told Rosemary to arrive at 6:30 so they'd have a chance to talk, and if she was even remotely on time (unlikely) she'd be showing up soon.

She picked up a blouse she'd flung across the back of a chair and was about to hang it up when she remembered that this was what she'd been wearing the afternoon she and Dale had walked along the Esplanade with Helen and she'd let him wrap his arms around her and kiss her and press himself against her when the wind died and the sailboats went still. She put the blouse up to her nose and inhaled, but there was no trace of the spicy smell of Dale's body, just a faint whiff of verbena from the French moisturizing lotion she'd bought a couple of weeks ago. She hung it in the closet and slammed the door shut with resolve. She wasn't going to let herself travel down this road or slippery slope or whatever it was. The whole business of having these secret meetings with Dale had been a mistake. The only good thing to come out of them was the inspiration for the documentary series. In between discussing Caroline and his own plans for the tacky restaurant he'd invested in, Dale had listened to her refine her concept, although she had presented most of it as something she'd been planning for months. She'd close that deal, advancing her own career and proving to Dale she wasn't as unmotivated as he assumed, and then leave him to settle his marriage in whatever way he chose.

Jane heard a car pull up in front and looked out the window in time to see Rosemary Boyle emerge from the back seat of a taxi. She was wearing a loose black sheath of a dress with narrow shoulder straps, and when she stood up, it fell into place with remarkable precision. Jane hadn't much thought about what she was going to wear, certainly not this rumpled pullover she'd worn to Dr. Berman. (The last thing she wanted was to give Berman the idea she paid special attention to what she wore to see him, which meant she usually spent a good half hour trying to pick out something appropriately nondescript.) She went to the closet, rifled through the uninspiring collection of dresses, shirts, and jackets, and emerged holding the blouse she'd just hung up. It would have to do. Good color, went with everything, and, even if she hated to admit it to herself, there was something exciting about wearing an article of clothing that knew so many secrets.

When she turned around, Thomas was standing in the bedroom, T-shirt in his hand, sweat dripping off his pale body. His face was the most peculiar shade of purple-gray she'd ever seen, like a piece of chicken that had been boiled in grape juice, and for one moment, she was so touched by the sight of him, she nearly ruined her outfit by rushing over and embracing him.

"Look at you," she said. "Where have you been?"

"Two blocks up Beacon, two blocks around, and back. Which is twice as much as I was doing last week."

"But in this weather, Thomas?" She heard something in her voice she hated, a condescending mothering tone which, ironically, she wouldn't dare use with Gerald. "What possessed you?"

He looked down at himself and slapped at his stomach, sending out a spray of sweat. "I'm afraid I might be getting a little out of shape."

He said it with such hushed sincerity, she laughed, and, trying to reassure him, said, "You look the same as always, Thomas. This *is* your shape." She went to him and kissed his sweaty shoulder. "If you keep this up, I might have to join you." He wouldn't keep it up, she was certain of that, but for a moment, the idea of the two of them jogging together through the neighborhood made her feel calm and reassured. The doorbell rang. "It's Rosemary," she said. "I'd better go down before she rings again and breaks Gerald's concentration."

Eight
Dinner Conversation

1.

After driving through heavy traffic for ten minutes, Desmond's back was plastered to the seat with sweat. Anticipating the heat, he'd worn a sleeveless T-shirt and hung his brand-new dress shirt (sale price $112) on a hook in the back seat. It was important to make a good first impression on Jane, his last best hope for professional redemption, and impossible to do so with a sweat-dampened shirt clinging to your nipples.

Jane and Thomas lived in a shady enclave in Brookline. The streets were quiet, cool, overhung with towering maple trees and sycamores; he felt as if he'd entered a gated community even though the main shopping street was a mere two blocks away. The houses were enormous, ranging in architectural style from Tudor to Bauhaus, all filtered through a Marie Antoinette fever dream of gracious living. But that wasn't fair either; there was some overlay of New England discretion—or was it Puritanical shame?—in the neighborhood. All the immense houses were practically blushing with modesty, peeking up over a carefully sculpted privacy hedge, or revealing just enough of themselves through a screen of pine trees to let you know the essence of what you were missing. The Miller-Cody manse was at the loop end of a cul-de-sac. By the standards of this neighborhood, their house looked almost shabby—a generous Queen Anne Victorian with a turret, a wraparound porch, and a lot of lacy ornamentation skirting the eaves, all of it in need of a fresh coat of paint. Unlike its neighbors, it was fully exposed to the street with only a hint of unkempt lawn separating it from the sidewalk.

He parked just beyond the driveway, took off his T-shirt, and wiped down his back with it. He slipped on the dress shirt standing on the street and gazing up at the house.

Jane answered the door, talking into a cordless phone she had cradled against her neck. It was the same woman he'd seen the week before, dressed in the same creamy blouse and colorful Bakelite necklace. She motioned him into the house and made a gesture of annoyance toward the phone. Her voice had the tone of husky, almost bullying self-confidence which he'd heard her use on the street and which he found inexplicably reassuring. Desmond didn't want to appear to be listening, but there wasn't much to look at in the front hallway: a chair, a brass coat rack, and a little table with letters on it.

"I know what you mean," Jane said, "but I haven't had a chance to talk it over with Thomas. He might have plans. No, no nothing like that, it's just that Thomas has allergies. And Gerald is so . . . urban." She looked at Desmond and shrugged, apologizing for something, although he didn't know what. "Well, I'll get back to you after we've had a chance to talk it over. You'll never guess who just walked in. Desmond Sullivan. Yes, that one. I'm trying to get him on board this project I told you about. I will."

She switched off the phone and tossed it onto the chair by the door. "My ex-husband's current wife," she told Desmond. "She wants me to tell you she loved your book." She reached back to lift her hair off her neck and then stopped with her elbow pointed out, as if a thought had just occurred to her. "If you were me," she said, "would you go away for a weekend with your ex-husband and his new wife?"

It struck Desmond as a peculiarly personal question, especially since they hadn't even exchanged names. He supposed she was being ironic, but there was something sincere in her wistful expression and the way she was standing with her hand clutching at her hair. "Not just the two of them and you?" he asked.

"No!" She dropped her hair. "I didn't give that impression, did I?"

"No, no. Just making sure." He tried to imagine how Russell would respond; Russell generally had more success in social situations that required irreverent spontaneity, while he fared better in situations in which silence could be interpreted as discretion. He opted for the simple truth. "I suppose I'd have to go," he said. "Just to prove to myself and to him that he didn't matter to me one way or the other anymore."

She seemed to consider this point. Desmond handed her a bottle of wine. She glanced at the label and tossed it onto the chair with the phone.

"There's a good chance this dinner is going to be a fiasco, so don't judge me by it. I invited too many people. I'm not doing the cooking so at least the food should be edible. My recommendation is to ride with it and have a good time. I'd love to meet with you next week and discuss my ideas for a series of biographies I'm putting together. I've set up a meeting with an executive producer to try to get some seed money. He and I have worked together so long now, it might be useful to bring you into it, to give some weight and freshness to the proposal. Assuming you're interested in getting involved?"

"I could be."

"That's great." She took a small appointment book from a drawer in the table in the hall and scanned through the empty pages. "Is next Thursday all right? Around 3:30?"

"That sounds . . . fine," Desmond said. He'd been anticipating the standard business of introductions and facile compliments about the house, but these were clearly beside the point, as if, unbeknownst to him, he and Jane had been friends and business partners for years. And something in her blunt, amiable manner did make him feel he could dispense with all of his usual wariness and get right to the risky business of being friends with her. The phone rang again. Jane looked at it for a moment. "It's probably just my brother calling with an idiotic excuse for being late. He's supposedly coming to dinner, but his wife is twelve months pregnant, so you never know."

She was several inches shorter than Desmond, but she had a way of holding her chin up and at a slight angle so that she appeared to be looking down at him, not with condescension, he decided, but as if she were lining up her defenses in case there was an attack at some later point in the evening. Several buttons of her blouse were undone, exposing a surprising amount of cleavage, making it obvious that she genuinely liked her ample body. Forty, Desmond guessed, and determined to be happy about it.

She nodded toward the back of the house, inviting him to follow her.

"Don't mind the mess," she said. "Gerald is six. Although hopelessly tidy, come to think of it." She had on a pair of white, low-heeled sandals that clacked against her soles as she walked. They didn't exactly go with the rest of her outfit but drew attention to her slim, shapely legs. Beautiful ankles, Desmond thought, although that wasn't the kind of thing he was used to noticing on anyone.

"So, briefly," Desmond said, "what is your idea about the series?"

"I've been trying to put together a series of biographies for years now, but I never found a theme to make it all cohere. When I was reading the Westerly biography, it struck me that it was a mistake to focus on the greats in history when the mediocrities on the edges tell us so much more about the culture. I'm thinking in that direction. Westerly might be a good place to start, unless you're working on someone even more marginal at the moment." They were passing through a front parlor, a thin room filled, in a desultory way, with new sofas and chairs in light shades of brown. Neither pretty nor ugly, the furniture was so aggressively bland and self-effacing it was almost invisible. Desmond had the distinct impression no one ever used the room. "You are working on another biography, aren't you?"

"I'm very close to finished," Desmond said. "A singer named Pauline Anderton."

"Oh good, another one I've never heard of. I hope she had a shameful secret tucked away in some closet."

"I was hoping that, too, but I've finished most of the research and I think she told all of her shameful secrets to anyone who'd listen."

"Well, maybe we can tweak things a bit," Jane said.

They'd come to a narrow, wainscoted hallway off the kitchen. Two young men wearing blue jeans and chef's aprons were standing at the kitchen counter chopping vegetables and talking in low voices. When they spotted Jane, they looked up and smiled, slightly embarrassed and intimidated. They had on baseball caps with the brims turned backward. A plump, oddly large child was standing on a chair, using a canvas pastry bag to decorate the top of a cake. "The little one is mine," Jane said. "Gerald, care to say hello to our dinner guest?"

The boy looked up from his work, red-faced and angry, and said, "I nearly spoiled the whole thing, *Jane.* Is that what you want?"

Desmond recoiled at the voice, a bizarrely adult growl, dripping with resentment and a surprisingly well-developed sense of irony. The kid had

Thomas's coloring and a bloated version of his shape. His hair was close-cropped, almost as if his head had been shaved, making his face look perfectly round.

Jane was not the least bit put off; if anything, she seemed eager to encourage him and engage in a test of wills. "As I remember it," she said, "I merely asked if you wanted to say hello. Correct me if I'm wrong."

"He*llo*," he mocked and went back to his work.

"Difficult age," Jane said. "He usually has hair, but lice or fleas or something were going around his school. I'd be worried about getting them, but he isn't one of those touchy-feely kids."

Helen was splayed out on the kitchen floor, her eyes trained on the caterers.

"He must be happy to have Helen around."

"He's not a dog person, either."

She had her hand on a screen door leading out to a porch, and as she was about to push it open, Desmond said: "I saw you walking Helen along Newbury Street last week."

Without turning around, she said: "Really? You recognized the dog?"

"Yes."

"Was I alone?"

"No," Desmond said. "You weren't."

Jane held the door open, blocking his way with her arm, and smiled at him. "I hope you won't take this the wrong way," she said, "but I was afraid you were going to be one of those dashing men with slicked-back hair. Light up the dinner party and then head off for an assignation before dessert. I'm so glad you're not."

He knew he should have been insulted on at least three different levels even though—or perhaps because—her appraisal of what he wasn't was so accurate, but he found himself pleased that she approved of him, even if it was for all the wrong reasons. "I tend to make the worst of what I've got," he said.

"That's a very becoming trait in a man," she said, "as long as you're not married to him."

2.

She led Desmond out to a wide, unpainted deck that still smelled of fresh cedar. The land behind the house dropped off precipitously, creating the illusion that the deck was floating off the back of the house. There was a stand of trees somewhere at the edge of the lawn, and rising above it was the skyline of Boston, glittering through the haze of the sticky twilight. A long table was set for dinner, and beside it, in a black wrought iron chair, a woman was gazing at the city and sipping from a wineglass. Although she must have heard them approach—Jane's sandals slapped against the new boards—she sat turned away, as if she were deep in thought or hard of hearing. Or more likely, Desmond thought as he took in her appearance, striving to make a dramatic entrance, even though they were the ones entering. Her dark hair was gathered in a tight little knob that sat on the crown of her head and added length to what was already an exceptionally long and graceful neck.

"It's a great view," Desmond said. In fact, he was tired of views by now and longed for a filthy air shaft every once in a while, but it was the kind of view that demanded comment.

"If only it were a great city," the woman in the chair said.

Jane introduced her as Rosemary Boyle, "the writer." He had a dim memory of having heard the name and said, "Ah," in a tone he hoped suggested impressed recognition.

"Rosemary and I have been friends since college," Jane said.

"More or less," Rosemary added cryptically.

"Rosemary's here to teach at BU and hating every minute of it."

"Not every." Rosemary seemed to be leaving open the possibility that this could be one of the exceptions, providing you kept her properly entertained.

Jane strolled back into the house. Desmond looked down at the lawn, the carriage house, and back at the skyline, grabbing at easy observations that might lead somewhere. Everything he said was answered with an enigmatic comment that was clipped enough to sound unkind without being specific enough to be insulting. She was the physical opposite of Jane, a meticulously slim woman with two pencil slashes for eyebrows and a dark purple bow of a mouth. Everything about her was so tight and smooth, she looked as if she'd been zipped into her pale skin. She was holding her wineglass in a limp-wristed grasp that suggested debilitating ennui. As the evening wore on, it became obvious to Desmond that she'd decided that appearing to be completely uninterested in almost everything somehow made her more interesting, probably a manifestation of low self-esteem, but an irritating one. She ran her eyes up and down Desmond, then turned away, leaving him feeling as if he'd been given an exam and had flunked with flying colors.

"Jane tells me you're teaching out at Deerforth with Thomas. I suppose it's hideous."

Desmond felt a pang of sympathy for his colleague, not to mention himself. "As a matter of fact, the campus is gorgeous," he said.

"Yes. That's what I meant."

Professional jealousy, Desmond assumed. The Boston University campus appeared to be made up of subway stops and traffic lights with a few Burger Kings thrown in for atmosphere.

"It's been great having Thomas out there to help me settle in. He's extremely kind."

Rosemary shrugged. "It's easy to be kind when you're as depressed as he is."

He was tempted to follow her down this path until they were taking open swipes at each other, but in addition to the fact that he was getting a little long in the tooth for this kind of boxing match, he couldn't be entirely sure she wouldn't report back to Jane on her opinion of him, and he didn't want to sour what looked like a promising relationship. It was always hard to judge female friendships, which, in most cases, turned out to involve a good deal more intimacy and exchange of information than most marriages. It was usually safest to assume you were talking to a small discussion group, even when you were one on one. "So," he said, "how many books is it you have in print . . . now." The "now" was tossed in at the last minute as a way of suggesting that no matter how hard he tried, he couldn't keep up with her output. Hopefully she wasn't unpublished.

"The three collections of poetry, the book of stories, and of course, *Dead Husband.*"

Of course. He had heard of her, had heard her interviewed more than once on National Public Radio, although he never would have connected this cool, austere woman with the widow he'd heard on air, heartbroken and elegiac, her voice practically melting with melancholy and regret.

"Congratulations on all your success."

She toasted herself with her wineglass. "If I'd known the memoir was going to do so well, I would have written one years ago."

Desmond nodded. Surely she had to wait for her husband to die, although maybe there were other deaths she could have exploited: *Dead Mother, Dead Sister, Dead Dog*. Come to think of it, it probably wasn't too late for her to turn the whole thing into a lucrative cottage industry.

"Is *your* book still in print?"

He nodded, feeling a gesture was less of a lie than saying yes would have been. "I'm sure Jane's mentioned her ideas about her and me working together."

Rosemary drank down the rest of her wine and dismissed the possibility. "Jane and her ideas," she said.

A few minutes later, Thomas walked around the side of the house and down the sloping lawn holding on to Gerald's hand. The heavy humidity—everything was sweating, from the glasses to the furniture to the vegetable chips—seemed to have drained the color out of the sky and the trees, and the two figures looked like blurry cutouts on the overgrown grass. The row of low lanterns lining the pathway down to the carriage house below blinked on, and Thomas turned and waved up to Desmond and Rosemary with the kind of overdone enthusiasm that Desmond always found slightly embarrassing.

"I'll be right up," he called. "Gerald's going to help his grandmother sign on to the Internet. Aren't you?" He swung Gerald's arm, but the boy didn't turn around or speak. "Do you two need anything up there?"

"Common interests would help," Rosemary said.

Thomas laughed at this and walked on. The lanterns were making eerie, poignant shadows on the lawn and magnifying the difference in height between father and child. Thomas was stooped slightly, obviously talking in a low, gentle voice to his son as they made their gradual descent. The sight of the two of them plodding along in the dim light stirred in Desmond a faint, jumbled longing—for a child, he assumed, although it wasn't quite that clear. Russell occasionally mentioned the possibility of trying to adopt but Desmond had never taken the talk all that seriously, assuming it was Russell's metaphoric way to express his disappointment that dogs weren't allowed in their building. Still, he felt a lugubrious nostalgia for something he knew he'd never have, and wanting to include himself in this blurry twilit vignette, he called out, "Have fun, Gerald," in a voice that was itself a little blurry.

The child stopped abruptly, turned, and said, "I *intend* to," with the same disconcerting sarcasm he'd used in the kitchen.

"I'll bet Thomas is a wonderful father," Desmond said, a bit shaken. "You can tell he loves his son."

"Can you think of a better excuse for staying with Jane?" Rosemary said.

3.

Jane's brother and sister-in-law arrived moments after the plates had been brought out to the table. Jane got up to answer the doorbell, and a few minutes later an immensely pregnant woman in a summer sundress printed with colorful Adirondack chairs tottered out to the back deck. She was short and small-boned, and she appeared to be balancing her stomach in front of her as if it were a tray of drinks she was about to serve to the guests. She had a Peter Pan haircut and a smile so broad it seemed to swallow up all her other features. There was something in her smile and her otherwise hesitant demeanor that struck Desmond as almost morbidly apologetic, begging forgiveness—not for being late, but for showing up at all. Thomas kissed her rather tenderly on the forehead and turned her around by the shoulders to show her off to the rest of the table. "Doesn't Joyce look radiant? 'If the radiance of a thousand suns were to burst forth at once in the sky, that would be' . . . well, not nearly as radiant as you."

"As long as no one bursts forth at the table," Rosemary said.

Thomas fussed over Joyce's chair, the bald top of his head shining in the candlelight when he bent over. Shortly before the caterers brought out the plates of food, Jane had carried out a mismatched assortment of candles, everything from absurdly thin tapers in glass holders to fat scented tubes that reminded Desmond of cafeteria-sized cans of beans. She'd set them down on the table and the porch railing, and the light was restful and somehow cool, despite the increasingly thick humidity. Desmond hadn't been able to shake Rosemary's comment about Thomas being depressed, but his kindness toward Joyce struck him as simple generosity.

"Any day now?" Desmond asked her.

Joyce was awkwardly trying to inch her chair closer to the table. "Two more months," she apologized, turning down her mouth.

Rosemary made a muffled grunt and went back to her wine.

As Jane and her brother crossed the deck, Desmond could hear them bickering—with practiced annoyance, not real anger—about Aunt Somebody, whom he apparently didn't phone often enough.

"I call her when I can," the brother said. He attempted to sit in Jane's seat but she pointed him toward the chair opposite Desmond.

"Well, you'd better start calling her when you can't." She looked around her plate and chair for her napkin, but came up with nothing. "She doesn't even know when the baby is due."

"November," Rosemary announced. She obviously had no intention to eat, and passed her napkin across the table to Jane. "Although I'm fully prepared to assist with the delivery if someone miscalculated."

Brian was several years younger than Jane, and Desmond found himself distracted by his handsome, silent presence on the opposite side of the table. He was recognizably Jane's brother, but it looked as if the family features had been tested on her before being perfected for him. He was pale and gaunt, not in an unhealthy way, but as if he was troubled by profound doubt—a man of the cloth who'd devoted his life to God and then, when it was too late to switch professions, discovered he was an agnostic. His dark hair was cut in flawlessly clean lines above his ears and up around his temples. Vain, Desmond thought, taking in the gray silk shirt and the perfectly knotted green tie. Here was a man who knew how to wear clothes; Desmond's expensive efforts at dressing up for Jane's sake had apparently failed miserably. Brian was an architect, which perhaps explained the affected haircut and some element of fastidiousness in his erect posture.

Joyce was a children's book editor at one of the few remaining publishing houses in Boston. A perfect profession for her, Desmond thought, listening to her talk about an illustrated book for five-year-olds she'd just bought that day. As with a lot of people who work with or for children, there was something childlike about Joyce: her colorful, little-girl dress, her short, little-boy haircut. Rosemary was staring at Joyce as if she were trying to remember who she was. When Joyce finished describing her book purchase and apologizing for going into such detail about it ("I guess it's not really all that interesting"), Rosemary said, "Did your publishing house bid on *Dead Husband?*"

Joyce looked momentarily distressed and glanced toward Brian for help. He, however, had barely looked in her direction since they'd sat down. She confessed she had no idea: the children's editors didn't have much connection with the adult division. "They probably couldn't have afforded it," she apologized.

"Too bad," Rosemary said, making it clear the loss was not hers.

The food was what food was these days: a meeting of the UN in the middle of a large dinner plate with a dusting of something green around the edges. Jane complained that this was the last time she'd use the catering school since everything they'd ever served ended up looking and tasting the same, with variations only in the inedible parts of the meal: the elaborate garnish or the plate itself. None of which, Desmond noted, prevented her from eating with immoderate enthusiasm. She leaned forward slightly as she ate, her colorful beads swinging out from her chest.

"I think it's delicious," Thomas said. "Are you enjoying it, Joyce?"

"Very much. Too much. I've gained forty pounds. Fortunately, it's all baby."

"Not all," Brian said, making eye contact with no one.

Jane had apparently been waiting for just this opening. "I suppose we get to critique *your* body next?"

"Oh let's," Rosemary said. She'd pushed her chair back from the table as the food was brought out, and, for the last ten minutes or so, had been gazing at Brian with flirtatious boredom. So far, she hadn't even bothered to pick up her fork, concentrating all of her energy on the wine. But rather than loosening her up as it did most people, it seemed to be making everything on her body tighter. It looked to Desmond as if someone were slowly twisting her bun of hair, reeling in her skin, narrowing her eyes, and sharpening her gaze.

"I'm fascinated by how threatened men become when women actually eat enough to sustain themselves or, God forbid, gain a pound," Jane said. "It tells you something about their true feelings toward women. I don't include Thomas. I gained eighty pounds when I was pregnant with Gerald, and he loved it."

"She looked like a butterscotch pudding," Thomas said.

"I hope that's not what we're having for dessert," Rosemary said.

"We're having cake," Jane said, and then added quietly, "courtesy of Gerald."

Grudgingly, it seemed to Desmond, Jane brought up a restaurant Brian was helping to design. She mentioned it in a general way without asking him about it directly, as if she were giving him an opportunity to contribute to the conversation, should he desire to do so. "Is that the one Dale owns?" Rosemary asked, drawing out the name in a demeaning way.

"Jane's ex," Thomas translated for Desmond.

"Not owner," Brian said. "He's one of a dozen investors. They're treated like anonymous blood donors; drain a few pints of plasma out of them, hand them a cookie, and send them on their way." He dusted off the front of his shirt. "Surprisingly enough, he's not the worst of them."

"I never liked Dale," Rosemary said. "I tried to warn you against him, Jane. I told you it would end badly."

Jane filled her glass from a sweating pitcher of water with lemon slices floating on top. "You did, but I thought it was because you wanted him for yourself."

"No one has Dale for herself, that's the whole point."

Desmond had the strong impression that Dale was the man he'd seen on Newbury Street the other day. Jane was sitting back in her chair nursing the cold water and fingering the neckline of her blouse. He looked toward Thomas to see how he was reacting to all this, but he was sitting with his elbow on his knee and his head propped up in his hand, listening to something Joyce was telling him about book sales in a quiet voice. This was probably the look of glazed sympathy he had when listening to students discuss their final papers. But on second glance, he wasn't glazed at all. There was something about the way he was hunching his broad shoulders and covering up his chin and mouth with his long fingers that made Desmond think he was trying to shrink himself down to Joyce's size, the way you might if you were talking to a small child you didn't want to frighten. My God, Desmond thought with a shock of recognition and more than a little amusement, he's completely infatuated.

By the time the cake was brought out, the air had grown uncomfortably still and heavy. The Boston skyline was now barely visible through the haze; the lights rose up from the streets and buildings surrounding the whole baking city in a sick orange halo. The cake was not the aesthetic masterpiece Desmond had been expecting; the creamy flowers around its rim were sloppily done and unevenly spaced, facts that Desmond found comforting somehow, given Gerald's age. While she was cutting through a row of pink flowers with an absurdly long knife, Jane told the assembled crowd that she and Desmond had a meeting with an executive producer at WGTB next week to discuss their project, a series of biographical documentaries. "Tell us about your new book," she said. "It's going to be part of the series, although we're not sure where it will fit."

The whole evening had been leading up to this moment, but now that it had arrived, Desmond wasn't sure he was up to the challenge. The shirt he'd cared for so meticulously was damp with sweat and his face felt flushed. He'd had perhaps one glass of wine too many, and on top of all that, he found himself oddly uncomfortable with handsome, wry Brian sitting across the table from him. He stalled for a few minutes by exclaiming over the cake and drinking a tall glass of water, then started off slowly, explaining that he was working on a biography. "Of Pauline Anderton," he said.

There was a long moment of silence which Rosemary broke by saying, "I give up."

"I'll bet Thomas knows," Jane said. She wiped the knife on a damp napkin and cut off another slice. "Thomas has an encyclopedic mind." It wasn't the first complimentary thing she'd said about her husband this evening—she'd complimented him quite often—but this, like all the others, sounded emotionally neutral, as if she were describing the reliability of a favorite automobile not the attributes of a man she was married to.

Thomas mulled this over, his lips pursed, ready, it seemed, to blow out a candle. "I believe she was a singer," he said. "And I'm going to go out on a limb here, and say she was known for falling off the stage, most notoriously at Carnegie Hall toward the end of her career."

"Oh goody," Rosemary said, "a tragic drunk."

Over the years, Desmond had grown used to the fact that most people had either never heard of Pauline Anderton or mis-remembered her in an outrageously unflattering way. Falling off stages, driving a Cadillac through a plate glass window, even, in one case, murdering a backup singer. Whatever defensiveness he'd once felt on her behalf had faded long ago. He patiently explained that while she had collapsed on stage several times late in her career, Anderton had never sung at Carnegie Hall.

"Too bad," Jane said. "There probably would have been great footage."

As Desmond was describing her early triumphs in Florida, her discovery by Walter Winchell, he felt something or someone pressing against his leg. He cleared his throat and sat up a little, but there it was again, a steady, gentle pressure that was definitely not accidental. He looked to the far end of the deck; Helen was prostrate near the railing, gazing at the skyline mournfully. So much for that possibility. The dinner table was narrow, not really suitable for six people, and earlier in the evening, he'd felt his knees brush briefly against someone's leg several times without thinking anything of it. He glanced over at Brian, but he was staring off into the middle distance as he had been doing for the bulk of the meal.

"I think my mother might have listened to her," Thomas said. "She could even have some of her records stashed away somewhere, here or in Beth's house or that friend's cottage she goes to in June."

"The elderly have become one of the few remaining nomadic tribes on the planet," Rosemary said. "It's an interesting phenomenon. Someone should do a book on it."

Jane pointed a finger. "Give it a whack, Rose. You could call it *The Living Dead.*"

It didn't seem likely that Brian would be playing footsie with him under the table, his pregnant wife on one side and disapproving sister on the other, but even the possibility, however remote, made Desmond feel lightly, carelessly aroused. What was it Jane had said, Ride with it and try to have a good time? What was the point in drinking too much and risking blowing your career if you weren't going to indulge in a bit of inebriated recklessness? He pushed back against the leg with a gentle rocking motion.

"She asked you if she's still living," Thomas said.

Desmond looked down to the other end of the table where Joyce was leaning toward him, apparently fascinated by Anderton's life story. He pulled his leg back, felt himself blush, and said, "No. No, she died almost ten years ago. Just outside Boston."

"I can certainly understand coming here to die," Rosemary said. "It's coming here to live that I don't understand."

4.

After coffee had been served, Desmond asked for directions to the bathroom. The kitchen was clean and dark and smelled of a citrusy detergent, and the dishwasher was churning. The caterers might not have been the best cooks in the world, but they'd left the place spotless. Earlier in the day, Desmond had gone into a shop on Newbury Street that sold alternative remedies for an amazing variety of problems. He'd walked past the place dozens of times, vowing never to enter despite a fascination with the shelves of pill bottles and the scrubbed, lab-coated clerks. When he finally broke down and went in this afternoon, he'd been delighted to see that in addition to selling treatments for everything from broken bones to cancer, Healthy Living sold tablets and capsules and tinctures for Uneasiness, Insecurity, and Confusion, exactly the sorts of ills he was trying to cure. When he asked the clerk if she had anything to heighten mental clarity, she'd shown him a bottle of tiny white pills which, she assured him, had been used for centuries in Turkey. (Everything in the store seemed to have been tested in places like Romania, Albania, or a remote mountainous country known for its appalling health care.) He felt quite certain she would have been equally unruffled by a request for something to help finish your biography of Pauline Anderton. It was time for his evening dose. He opened a cabinet over the stove, but instead of glasses he saw an elaborate display of cake decorating utensils, pastry bags and assorted nipples, food coloring, and tiny spatulas. Gerald's, no doubt. He decided to forgo the water and started chewing up a handful of pills. You can't OD on them, the clerk had assured him, an admission of ineffectiveness if ever he'd heard one.

He'd been directed to a lavatory off the kitchen, a small room at the end of a long hallway that had obviously been a closet in the not so distant past. There was no window, but when he turned on the light, an exhaust fan in the corner of one wall came on with a whir. He pissed into the toilet loudly, chuckling over the possibility that Brian had been rubbing his leg. Clearly Brian was one of those narcissistic heterosexual men who liked to shove himself on you just so he could go home and reassure himself that someone had made a pass at him. If Desmond had tried to push it any further, Brian would undoubtedly hide behind Joyce with indignant contempt. And yet, Desmond felt his cock thickening in his hand as he mulled over the whole incident, and he gave it a few bemused tugs as he finished up. There had been a loud rumble of thunder earlier, so the dinner party would probably break up within the next ten minutes. He looked at himself in the mirror as he washed his hands. Not the light-up-the-dinner-party type, but, if Brian's taste was any indication, not hopeless, either.

When he opened the door, Brian was standing in the narrow wainscoted passageway a few feet from the door. He was leaning against a counter with his arms folded across his chest and his fingers wrapped around his biceps.

He was smirking attractively, and Desmond felt embarrassed, as if seeing someone about whom he'd had a powerfully erotic dream.

"Sorry I kept you waiting," Desmond said.

Brian shrugged. "It takes as long as it takes."

"Right." He had his legs thrust out into the passageway so Desmond couldn't get by him without elaborate contortions. "Cozy little bathroom," he said. "Did you design it?"

Brian laughed at this. "No one de*signed* it. Jane stuck a toilet and a sink in a closet. She has as much aesthetic sense as a field mouse."

"I gather you two aren't very close."

"Not in age, looks, politics, religion, or hair color. Otherwise, we're like twins."

There was something so unbecoming in his languid tone and the attempt to boost himself up by running down Jane, Desmond felt the erotic charge of the moment dissipate into annoyance. He motioned toward the hallway with his chin, indicating he wanted to get by.

Brian pulled in his legs but reached out and fingered the collar of Desmond's shirt. "Nice material," he said.

"Cotton."

"Oh." He dropped the collar and brushed it back into place, pushed himself away from the counter with his hands, and went into the bathroom. Before he closed the door, he said, "My office is in Cambridge. Give me a call sometime, Desmond. I'll give you a tour of the stately homes of New England."

Christ, Desmond thought, what a lot of nervy bullshit that was, with his wife sitting out on the deck, seconds away from going into labor. He hated this type of cad on principle, marrying for security and acceptance while running around with men on the side. He adjusted himself in his pants and started walking toward the kitchen. When he looked up, he saw Gerald standing at the end of the passageway glaring at him. He had a large tub of ice cream tucked under one arm and a dripping spoon in his hand. When their eyes met, Gerald stepped back into the shadows. Desmond stopped for a second and felt the blood rush from his face. Then he reassured himself the child was only six, probably hadn't seen anything, and wouldn't understand what had been going on even if he had.

In the kitchen, Gerald was standing near the sink wearing a hard little pout.

"Good ice cream?" Desmond asked, keeping his tone as cheerful as possible. When the child said nothing, Desmond tried again. "What flavor is it?"

"I'm not supposed to eat ice cream before bed," Gerald announced. Something in his deep voice and the tone made it sound like a proclamation of his moral superiority.

Desmond winked at Gerald and said: "I won't tell anyone. It'll be our secret."

"I'm not supposed to keep secrets with strangers," Gerald stated, as if Desmond had proposed something unwholesome.

"No, of course not. Good idea. Well, you sleep tight."

Before Desmond had a chance to make it out of the kitchen, Gerald said, "I saw you talking to Uncle Brian."

Desmond stopped and turned. "I'm sure you did," he said. "He's a nice man, your Uncle Brian."

"He doesn't like me," Gerald said. "He called me fatty and told Jane she should put me on a diet."

"Oh. Well that wasn't very nice." In the dim kitchen light, Gerald looked a good deal smaller and more pathetic than he had a few minutes earlier. A sad kid more than anything, clumsy, shorn, and wearing a striped jersey that was stained with melted ice cream. Desmond went over to him and squatted down until he was Gerald's height. "I think you're the nice one, not your uncle. Do you want me to help you put away the ice cream?"

"What makes you think I'm finished?" Gerald said.

So much for that attempt at bonding. Difficult age, Jane had said. And would continue to be a difficult age for the next forty years, Desmond guessed. He could feel Gerald glaring at his back as he walked out to the porch and a loud clap of thunder rattled the windows.

Nine
True Enough

1.

"It's cramped," Desmond said, "but there's something appealing about living out of an armoire and a boxy little refrigerator. I guess it makes me feel young again. Like a student."

Jane was still trying to catch her breath after attempting to impress Desmond by climbing the three winding flights of stairs without stopping— as if he would notice or, in the unlikely event he did, care. "Why do you suppose it is," she said, holding her breath so she wouldn't gasp, "that the idea of being young *again* is so appealing when being young the first time around was such hell?" She glanced in his direction; in this room, he looked even more awkwardly tall and thin than he had at dinner the other night. She could see, through the disguise of graying hair, wrinkling skin, and the vague credentials of "biographer," the gawky adolescent fending off insults and vainly attempting to fit in. It was obvious from his slightly hunched posture that he still wasn't comfortable in his skin, which probably explained why he spent his time writing about other people's lives. "It *was* hell the first time around, wasn't it?"

"Hell might be a little strong, but close enough."

"You're lucky. Everyone I know who had a loud, happy youth has spent the last twenty years battling disappointment and depression." Not that she hadn't spent some of the past twenty years battling disappointment and depression, too, but at least she could go to Dr. Berman and complain. If she went and told him her problem was a happy childhood, he'd think she was insane, and she'd find herself slapped with one of those thirty-year analysis sentences with no chance of parole.

Desmond offered to make her a cup of tea and she surprised herself by accepting. "I can't believe Deerforth set you up in a place like this," she said. "Barking dog and all. And where's the bathroom?"

"Down the hall."

"Oh, God. People in bathrobes lined up for the shower?"

"I don't have to share it."

"Something to be thankful for." Jane walked over to one of the round windows and rested her elbows on the sill. Warm, humid air was blowing in from the east, smelling of traffic and dust and the ocean. From here she could see the sailboats in the river basin. She'd never realized how many sailboats there were on the Charles, but since that afternoon with Dale, she saw them every time she looked in the direction of water, dancing across the surface of the river, unfettered, sails fluttering, like especially tall ice skaters. Best to file that observation and images of that whole long afternoon—river, boats, and abrasive kiss—into a locked chamber somewhere, perhaps of her heart. The room was probably stirring up memories. Awful as it was, there was something about it that filled her with intense longing—for what, she wasn't sure. Maybe Desmond was right and it was the simple, obvious thing: youth. Which in her case, she quickly realized, was just a synonym for bachelorhood.

"They could at least supply an air conditioner," she said.

"Who'd have guessed it would stay this hot this late in the season? It's strange weather, isn't it?"

Jane nodded noncommittally. A day didn't go by when she didn't worry about the rapid rise in global temperatures, the scrambled features of the seasons, about the peculiar new intensity of the sun that scorched skin, even in winter, about the extreme storms brewing in the clear waters of distant oceans, but there was something so dreary about the people who spent their time obsessing over matters they couldn't control, she'd rather not be counted among their ranks. Standing with her back to the window and the sultry summery breeze blowing against her hair, she started to feel a little faint. Perhaps it was from the heat, or the exhausting climb, or something in the atmosphere of the pale green room. There was paint peeling from the wall in one corner, a patch of water stains and plaster dust and a hint of yellow floral wallpaper from some earlier era. She sat on the soft mattress of the bed, crossed her legs, and tried to regain her composure. "I know what it is about this place," she said. "It's your archetypal Parisian atelier."

"I've thought that, too. It must be the view and the round windows. Although I can't say I've ever been in a Parisian atelier."

"Neither have I," Jane said. "I don't suppose anyone has. Unless they have them at DisneyWorld."

Although she *had* been to Paris. Twice. Dale had taken her there for a week after she'd discovered he'd been having an affair, and she had decided to give him a second chance. It had been an attempt at a second honeymoon. April in Paris. Aside from racing through a couple of churches which didn't interest either of them all that much and a museum that had secretly bored her—as a group, the Impressionists had lost their appeal for Jane when their paintings started showing up on neckties—virtually all they'd done was wander through the city in lazy circles with no idea what they were looking at, then go back to their hotel and fight, fuck, and eat, usually in that order. Then, three months before Gerald was born, she and Thomas went to Paris for ten days on his semester break. Thomas had designed a rigorous itinerary that hit every major cultural and artistic highlight of the past several centuries and had delivered a beautifully researched lecture to elucidate the significance of each block of granite they stepped on. Oddly enough, she ended up feeling as if she'd seen more of the city the first time around. What Desmond's room really brought to mind wasn't being young or single, but rather the hotel room she and Dale had stayed in on that trip. The hotel was called the Claude something, and theirs had been a dark, incommodious room, and she hadn't thought about it in years, and she wished the memory of it hadn't stabbed at her so violently and unexpectedly. "It has Bohemian charm," she said quietly. "But at this stage of my life, I doubt I could live like this."

"No," Desmond said. He had his back to her and was preparing the tea with a plastic electric kettle, the kind of cracked and stained appliance you'd expect in this kind of room. "It definitely wouldn't do for a family of three."

She could feel a headache coming on. She hadn't been thinking about a family of three at all; she'd been thinking about herself. Maybe Desmond saw her as part of an undifferentiated mass, Janethomasgerald. But sitting on the bed and bouncing her legs, she didn't know whether to feel insulted over this loss of individuality or concerned that she herself hadn't included her husband and child in her configuration of "this stage of my life."

Desmond brought her a steaming cup and she cradled it in her hands, wondering what she was supposed to do with the tea bag and why she'd accepted his offer when she'd never much cared for the subtle, watery pleasures of tea. In an hour and a half, they were meeting with David at the station to pitch their idea and try to wring some money out of him. She'd read the first several chapters of the manuscript of the Pauline Anderton biography, and after discussing it with Desmond a few days earlier, had decided that this was the best place to start. Anderton would make a perfect subject for a twenty-minute pilot they could use to sell the rest of the series. There was TV footage of Anderton, a local connection, and enough falls from grace (or whatever was the appropriate term for Anderton's career highs) to make it salable.

Desmond hunched over the library table he had set up as a desk and fidgeted with a tape player. It was impossible to be in a room this size, sitting on a stranger's bed, breathing in the smell of his soap and shaving cream, without feeling a little awkward; the whole setup was just one notch too intimate, even though there was no sexual tension between them. Not that Desmond was unattractive. He had on a pair of slim green pants that were either a thrift shop find or an expensive designer knockoff of the same style, a lime green polyester shirt, and an inch-wide tie. He was a little old for this nerd rock star look, but he pulled it off convincingly enough so that even if it wasn't flattering, it wasn't ridiculous. It was quite obvious he was gay—something in his polite, slightly ironic manner gave him away; not effeminate exactly, but self-conscious enough to put it outside the bounds of traditional masculinity—but she wished he'd do her the favor of slipping the information into the conversation so she wouldn't have to tiptoe around the subject.

"Should I assume you're single?" she tried.

"Well." He turned from the tape player with a look of distress. "This usually works fine, but I'm having a little trouble with it right now. The buttons are jamming. I really want you to hear her voice before the meeting. I shouldn't have opted for the cheapest model."

Cheap diversionary tactic, too, she thought. Maybe he was still in the closet, a depressing, boring possibility. She hardly knew any gay people who were still in the closet. Then again, if they were, how would she know? She'd often wondered if Rosemary didn't have some lesbian tendencies—it might go a long way toward explaining why she'd married Charlie—but she hoped not; if she found out ten years hence that she'd been a dyke after all and had never once made a pass at her, Jane would be crushed. Desmond appeared to be nervous, too, with a slight sheen of sweat on his forehead. Not the best way to make a good first impression on David, who valued cool, capable characters like Chloe and mistrusted apprehensive types like himself.

"So you *are* single?" she tried again.

"No," he said. "Not really. I have a lover."

Lover was infuriatingly vague, although no heterosexual would use it in this context. "Oh?" Jane said. "Is it a long-term relationship?"

"We've been together for five years." Then he looked up from his busy-work at the useless machine and said, "He and I."

Thank God that was out in the open. She put her teacup on the floor, took off her suit jacket and hung it from the bedpost. She sprawled out on the mattress with her head propped up in her hand and kicked off her shoes. "Five years is infancy," she said. "Although your average gay man acts as if it were three quarters of a lifetime. I have a theory gay relationships age in dog years. What do you think?"

"I can't say I know much about 'your average gay man.' "

Open mouth, insert foot. "I didn't mean it like that," she said. "But understand, Desmond, I don't have a homophobic cell in my body, so I just blurt out whatever comes to mind."

"It's fine, really."

Clearly it wasn't. She'd said something insulting and then promptly made an even bigger fool of herself, all while spread out like Cleopatra on his bed. She wasn't sure why, but she wanted him to like her and approve of her. It went beyond the potential of a working relationship. She found he was easy to talk to, which was more than she could say of most people these days, Helen aside. It didn't hurt that they knew no one in common with the exception of Thomas, and she couldn't imagine that Desmond would find himself in a heart-to-heart with him. "I'll give you an example of how blasé I am on the topic of homosexuality," she said. "I have a strong suspicion Gerald is going to be gay when he grows up. Or is gay now, if that's how it works." It was the first time she'd given voice to this particular concern, and she was shocked to hear herself say it. It was such a monumental confession, to herself as much as Desmond, and such a profound betrayal of her son, she scanned the little room, half expecting to find that everything looked different. But the center was holding and all was quiet. Desmond was merely nodding in a calm, disinterested way, as if her words didn't surprise him at all. Maybe he'd drawn the same conclusion when he met Gerald at the house. She picked up her teacup, sipped from it, and found the warm, gingery water comforting. Now that this worry about Gerald had been released from her archive of shameful thoughts and was dispersing in the humid air of the room, it didn't seem like such a terribly big deal. "I'm not even upset about it," she went on, encouraged. "When I decided to put him into therapy, it wasn't with any thoughts of changing him. I just want to make sure he's happy with himself, however he turns out."

Desmond had his head under the table and was checking the cord for the tape machine. Generally speaking, she found people who had trouble managing the most simple mechanical tasks—turning on a tape player, operating a dishwasher, using an electric can opener—infuriating. Their ineptitude was usually nothing more than an obvious plea to be taken care of. In Desmond's case, it appeared to be genuine ignorance, which was much more forgivable. He crawled out from under the table and said, "That's good. But in your heart, I suspect you'd prefer that your son . . ." He stopped there.

This sounded to her more like an admission of dissatisfaction with himself than anything else, confirmation of her suspicions that at least some of the balloons and chanting associated with Gay Pride were a matter of trying too hard. "I love him for who he is. And of course Thomas adores him. And I'll tell you something else, Desmond; if Gerald does end up going to a shrink twenty years from now, I'd like the shrink to know that whatever else he says about his parents, he had a mother enlightened enough to send him to a psychologist at age six."

"Get the shrink on your side, you mean."

"I hadn't thought of it in those terms, but now that you mention it, why not?" One of the most troubling aspects of dropping Gerald off at Dr. Garitty week after week was not knowing what he was saying about her and, even more worrisome, about her relationship with Thomas. Garitty refused to divulge much of interest about her conversations with Gerald, which surely couldn't be ethical practice when the patient was a six-year-old.

"It sounds like a workable but complicated plan."

"I'm a complicated woman. Which doesn't prevent me from being a complete idiot some of the time. Half the time."

Desmond said, "I doubt you're ever an idiot."

"No, not a complete one, anyway."

He gave her an exceptionally magnanimous smile, one that put her at ease about her series of confessions and blunders. Although his real motivation might have been finding an excuse to display teeth that appeared to have been professionally whitened. She'd been pondering having hers whitened for a couple of months now, but worried it might be a first step down a very treacherous path that ended ten years later with a $25,000 facelift. She'd started to hear women not much older than her, perfectly reasonable, intelligent women, too, talking about what they intended to have "done," as if they were discussing altering a jacket. Jane considered plastic surgery an overpriced form of self-mutilation; a pointless one, too, since everyone agreed that the people who'd had the best things "done" were the ones who looked exactly as they had before surgery. In July, she'd had lunch with Sonia Clark, a former co-worker at the station. Sonia was fifty-three and married to a successful financial type, and after Jane had complimented her once too often on how rested she looked, she revealed that her recent "vacation" had been three hours on an operating table, followed by six weeks of at-home recovery. Jane had been appalled by Sonia's giddiness over it and so repulsed by the idea that she'd subjected herself to such a bloody renovation, she'd had trouble finishing her lunch. Although to be fair, she had written down the surgeon's name on a list somewhere.

"Are *you* in therapy?" she asked.

"Not at the moment." A cloud of some kind passed over his face. "I went once when I was practicing law in Chicago. She helped me make some changes in my life, but once we started going deeper, I left. I suppose it wouldn't hurt to go back at some point."

"Well, whatever you do, don't go when you're depressed or in a crisis. You're vulnerable and completely at the shrink's mercy. The only reason I started going to my old doctor again last summer was because I wanted to rub his face in how healthy I've been since I left treatment." Even she didn't believe that, but she liked the sound of it. "What's your lover's name?"

"Russell." Desmond pushed a button on the machine and something loud and unpleasant, a shout that was equivocally musical, came blasting out of the tiny speakers. "Russell Abrams." Desmond lowered the volume and the whole thing promptly went dead. The dog on the other side of the wall started to yap. Desmond took the tape from the machine and studied it for a moment. "This looks fine, so it must be the machine."

"We can listen to it in the car on the way to my office. If you don't mind me saying so, I'd guess from the look on your face you don't like discussing Russell."

He seemed to cringe slightly, probably an indication that he either missed him desperately or was having an affair. "To be honest, I'm finding it a little harder to be separated than I expected. I hope he is, too."

Despite what she'd said—and was fairly certain was true—about her lack of biases against homosexuals, there was some essential way in which she didn't think of gay relationships as the equal of heterosexual ones. It wasn't the lack of children or even the rampant sexual infidelity. It had more to do with the fact that most male couples she met seemed too fundamentally compatible to be bothered with the kind of jockeying for position that she saw as an integral part of love. It was possible Desmond was having trouble being apart from his lover, but if they were a heterosexual couple, the phone would have rung by now and the refrigerator would be plastered with photos and a spouse would be climbing the stairs at this very minute, hoping to catch someone red-handed.

"I'll be seeing him over Columbus Day. When you're visiting your ex-husband, assuming you decided to go."

"I decided not to go," she said, "but Dale's wife has been talking to Thomas. He seems to think it would be good for Gerald."

Desmond picked up a black canvas briefcase and started tossing tapes and papers into it. He went to the small walnut armoire near the bed and opened the door. The top shelf of the thing was lined with little bottles of vitamins and other health-foody-looking items. He studied them for a minute, then turned to her. "Do you think I should take something to increase mental clarity, reduce ambivalence, relax me, or energize me?"

Jane pushed herself off the bed and stood beside him, studying the rows of bottles. "Midlife crisis?" she asked.

He nodded. "Long-term. Care to join me?"

"Why not? Do you have anything for Everything In General?"

2.

She longed for one of those glittering New England autumn days, with blue skies and bright sun and brisk wind, but when they stepped outside, the humidity was so heavy, it could well have been midsummer rather than early October. A few of the trees in front of the stately brick houses along Marlborough Street had started to change color, but given the weather, they looked unsettlingly incongruous. She and Brian had grown up in Chevy Chase and so, technically speaking, were Southerners, although that particular identity was one she'd never been eager to claim; it didn't fit her image of herself. As soon as she got to Smith, she began telling people she was from Washington, D.C., a geographically more neutral territory. The ruse worked so well, she started moving her childhood north in increments. By the time she entered graduate school, she'd almost convinced herself she'd been born in Connecticut. These days, it seemed as if the weather from her childhood had decided to throw her a curve by migrating north with her.

Desmond squinted up at the sun and put on a pair of bottle-green dark glasses that struck her as unnecessarily stylish. She put her arm through his as they walked along Marlborough Street. "You're not nervous about this meeting, are you?"

"Not nervous," he said. "Anxious maybe."

"Don't be either. It's going to be casual."

"What are we asking for?"

"Tons," she said. "Major sponsorship of the entire series, the full backing of the station. Two or three million, minimum."

"That much!"

"If we're lucky, we'll get ten grand, which doesn't sound like much, but as seed money, it's crucial. Once the station shows its support, I should have no trouble scraping together another fifteen grand for the pilot."

"Where does that come from?"

"You start at the top, combing through the roster of big corporations with public relations problems: ugly law suits, cans of tainted food, a diet pill that made eight people lose their hearing. Oil spills are obviously the best—all those birds—but I don't think there's been anything too grim in that department in the last couple of years. Then you start working your way down through thousands of little foundations with a couple of dollars they want to get rid of. It all adds up, that's the important thing to remember."

"You've done your homework."

She had done her homework, at least in a manner of speaking. She'd given Chloe a memo requesting some information; thirty-six hours later Chloe had come into her office and dumped a bulging file of grant applications on her desk, explaining that she'd have given them to her sooner but she'd had to fix some major computer glitch, which she tried in vain to describe to Jane. If delegating responsibility was Jane's forte, well, there were worse things than that. This whole project had made her feel professionally renewed in ways she hadn't anticipated. Working on it was so much more gratifying than moping around cocktail lounges and coffee bars with Dale Barsamian, and besides, it gave her something to talk about with Dale Barsamian when she did mope around with him.

Once they were speeding along Storrow Drive, the river basin on one side, the glinting windows of Back Bay town houses on the other, Desmond pulled the tape out of his pocket and slid it into her tape player. "This could take a little getting used to," he said. "Don't expect perfection. It's from one of her live recordings late in her career. The second half of the recording doesn't have much to recommend it, but the first half is quite strong. It has a few signature numbers and some great raw emotion. Judging from the tape, she didn't really start hitting the bottle until intermission."

There was a smattering of applause and then a gruff, sandpapery voice thanked the crowd. "This next number is one I learned from Dorothy herself, Miss Judy Garland. I love ya, Judy. Give the kids a kiss g'night from me."

It began promisingly: a string section played the melodic line from "Over the Rainbow" in rich, torchy tones. A flute came in with a few decorous trills, obviously meant to suggest a happy bluebird flapping its way across a pastoral scene. Not that she was prey to obvious sentimentality, but something about this particular song always got to Jane, and she felt a little catch in her throat. The orchestra pulled back and in a soft voice cracking with emotion, Anderton sang her first word, a gentle, sibilant "some." This was followed by an odd second of silence during which you could hear Anderton gathering her breath. And then came a shattering "WHERE," like a clap of thunder directly overhead. Another moment of disorienting silence was followed by a rushed, breathless "ovah the rainbow" as if she were speaking the line.

It wasn't simply that the voice was aggressively loud—like Jane's old gym teacher screaming at her for doing clumsy jumping jacks—but it also had a gravelly quality that made you want to clear your own throat as you listened. And this was before she started belting down cocktails! Then there was the bizarre lack of consistency in her pronunciation, from the crass, Bostony "ovah" in the first line to the absurdly pretentious "eau-verre" a few verses later.

Jane tapped the tape player. "Do you mind if I lower it a bit?"

"No, not at all."

That helped. This was one singer who'd never be accused of subtlety, but once Jane let herself relax into the song a bit more, she found that there were some audible gradations of the overpowering belt. She sang in character, if not always on key. Anderton ended with a remarkably understated and touching "why oh why can't I?" as if she genuinely wanted to know. The music faded out and Desmond ejected the tape.

After a moment of reverential silence, he said: "Well?"

When Jane was alone in her car, she tended to listen to pop music of the blandest sort. If she was in the right mood, she could tear up listening to one of those fashion models with a microphone singing a cornball rendition of the latest mush from an animated Disney film. Dale, who claimed to know something about jazz, had taken her to hear singers he considered great; mostly she'd found them irritating show-offs who put perfectly beautiful melodies through a meat grinder. In general, she hesitated to venture much of an opinion about music since some snob was always coming along and telling you why your taste was contemptible. If it was a choice between listening to more of this tape and tuning in to a religious fanatic call-in show, she'd probably opt for the latter. And yet, against all odds, she found herself shaken by it, and perhaps a little haunted.

"I don't know if it's good," she told Desmond, "but it's . . . real."

"That's it exactly," Desmond said. "It's the one thing pop singers never are anymore. They can be strong or accomplished or loud, but they're almost always packaged and overrehearsed, carefully modulated for a particular audience. You listen to them and you have no idea who they are or where their voice is coming from. No honesty."

Jane had lost the thread of her initial idea, but it was gratifying to know she'd at last said something right. "How close were she and Judy Garland?" she asked.

Desmond tipped his hand from side to side. "Hard to say. She often mentioned her in concerts, the kind of thing you just heard, or: 'I'm sending out a special hello to my pal Judy,' but I haven't been able to find any evidence the two actually met."

"No letters, anything of that sort?"

"I found one memo Garland sent to her lawyers asking them if they could get 'that broad in the housedress' to stop mentioning her in concert. That's really about it. Anderton was famous for performing in simple outfits."

When she asked Desmond when he'd be finished with his book, he looked out the window at the river flashing past and the low collegiate buildings of Cambridge on the other side of the water. Something was holding him back, he explained, some missing piece of information. He had all the facts, the dates, the times, the places. "But," he said, "I still don't have the essential *truth* of her life, the *core* of who she was. Until I find that, I don't have a coherent narrative of a life so much as a collection of incidents. 'The clothes and buttons' of a person, to use Mark Twain's phrase, but not the person herself."

The subject seemed to fill him with a degree of melancholy that struck her as just a touch overdone. "I hate to interrupt," she said, "and I don't mean to be indelicate here, but can't you just make something up, some essential truth, then fit the other pieces around it?"

Judging from the grim, disbelieving look he gave her, it was a bad idea, maybe even an appalling one. Probably an indication that he thought she had subnormal intelligence or, worse still, no integrity. She was confident of her intellectual abilities, but she sometimes worried about the integrity issue. It had taken her a good two years of working on *Dinner Conversation* to get over the impulse to call in friends at the last minute and hand them a character and a script. What had finally decided her against it was not "honesty" and the even more amorphous "principles," but the realization that people being themselves always made for a better show than people acting a role. Right choice, wrong reason. But rather than try to back out of this blunder, if that's what it was, she stumbled on, digging the hole deeper: "I know you wouldn't end up with the essential truth in the way you mean it, but you'd probably end up with something that's true enough."

You could say the same thing for the narrative she was writing in Dr. Berman's office. It wasn't the whole truth and nothing but the truth, but it was true enough to get the important points across. After all, most people, shrinks included, were more comfortable with an edited version of reality and only the most profoundly masochistic individuals look at themselves without a shade over the bulb. Look at that libelous "memoir" of Rosemary's.

Desmond was either so horrified he couldn't speak or, she'd rather think, genuinely stumped at how to respond. "It doesn't work like that for me," he finally said. "It's a matter of sifting through the pieces and listening to everything, over and over if need be, until the truth emerges. If I were to leap at some convenient assumption or . . . well, lie, which is what you seem to be suggesting, I'd never know who the person really was. Which would end up being an enormous disservice to the subject, even if he tried to stay locked up in a closet, like Westerly."

"I'll leave you to your standards," Jane said. "Which end up being a lot harder to live up to when you're working with television deadlines. Just do me a favor, when we go in to talk with David, don't contradict me. It's best to present a united front. We can work out all the rest afterward."

3.

She led him through the reception area of the studio as if she owned the place and greeted everyone with the studied geniality of a company president who'd made a point of being on a first-name basis with the underlings. "I'll show you around the soundstages," she said. "Most of them are down here on the first floor. We've still got half an hour to kill." But as they neared the elevators, she started chatting with a tall man with a gaunt, Abraham Lincoln face; when he made a move toward the elevator door, she discreetly indicated to Desmond that he should get on. "We're going up to five," she told the man. Once the doors had closed, she started slathering on praise for a proposal of his she'd read two weeks ago and then introduced him to Desmond as Keith Sommerstone, esteemed creator of, among other films, *Insects,* one of public television's most successful documentary series. He got out at the third floor and Jane immediately pushed the button for the lobby. "He's got a vacuum cleaner on the funds around here," she said as they descended. "He could propose an eight-part series on whittling and get a green light."

Desmond was convinced he had something to learn from Jane's self-confidence, even though he didn't entirely believe the self-confidence itself—any more, it was obvious, than she did. He suspected she was the kind of person who left everything undone until the last second, and then faked and fibbed her way out of the corner into which she'd painted herself. But the important point was, she did get out. And with her help, he'd get out of his corner as well. She had ambition and wasn't afraid of it; that was the difference between them. He'd always thought of ambition as a first cousin of greed and envy and, although not closely related, at least on the same family tree as murder. Getting where you wanted necessarily seemed to involve machinations whose sole purpose was to get your rivals to drop their guards so you could charge ahead of them and then slam the gate shut. And if the rivals didn't get out of the way, you just resorted to plan B and mowed them down. But Jane's ambition was tempered by a benign lack of clarity: it was apparent she wanted this series to go over, even if she herself wasn't certain of her motives. The idea of making up an essential "truth" as the center of someone's life was appalling, but she'd delivered the suggestion with such sweet sincerity, he felt grateful to her for trying to help him out. Since arriving at the station, he'd noticed a definite increase in his pulse rate, an indication of just how desperately he wanted this series to fly.

In addition to the show Jane produced, several news, cooking, and gardening programs were filmed at the studios of WGTB. Desmond knew you always had to expect that movie and media personalities would be smaller and less impressive (although generally better looking) in person than they were on screen, but it hadn't occurred to him that the studios themselves might be so morbidly ordinary. As Jane gave him a tour of the building, he found himself marveling at the ticky-tacky, taped-together, temporary appearance of things: everything out of sight of the camera could have been part of a high school production of *Our Town*—metal folding chairs behind a news anchor's desk, backdrops on which the painted scenery ended in mid brush stroke, a wastebasket filled with oily paper behind a chef's kitchen counter.

"If you look at anything too closely," Jane said, catching his glance, "it starts to look seedy. I'm talking about the studio, not life."

Maybe so, but he'd often thought that it was true of life as well. The young couple who lived above him in New York were so loving on the street, but so volatile and vicious in private. Then there was Peter, who appeared to have been living a double life for a good portion of the time Desmond had known him. Or, to take a more frightening example, his own carefully hidden ambivalence about Russell, which perhaps, given recent events, hadn't been hidden carefully enough.

Jane slipped her arm through his as she had on the street. He was flattered by her attention, but he couldn't tell if she genuinely liked him or was trying to convince herself she did. Maybe—according to her theories—they were essentially the same thing. "I won't even show you the set of my show. Imagine a windowless conference room in a real estate office and you've got the general idea. We stick a vase of fresh flowers in the middle of the table and it looks like the Four Seasons. That's the genius of it. Anyone can make a lovely set look lovelier, but to transform a wreck into something beautiful is a talent."

They were passing through a room set up with rows of long tables equipped with telephones and pitchers of water. "Fund-raising," Jane said. "Every time a right-winger gets up and makes a speech against us, we have to take on more volunteers to handle the pledges. I've even flirted with the idea of voting Republican myself as some contorted way of keeping the station alive."

The offices of *Dinner Conversation* were on the second floor of the building. In the outer room, two men and a woman—all looked young enough to be Deerforth students—were clustered around a computer. The young woman was a dark beauty with a Lady Godiva mane of curly hair, dressed up in a bell-bottomed pants suit. She looked up at Jane and bit her lip anxiously, as if she'd spotted blood rushing from Jane's forehead.

"Chloe, Carl, Otto—Desmond. Any disasters I should know about?"

"Everything's on track," Chloe said "Dershowitz called earlier to cancel for next week, but I talked him into coming on."

"You should have asked me," Jane snapped. "What makes you think I wouldn't have welcomed his cancellation?"

"You're the one who invited him."

"That isn't the point, Chloe, and you know it."

The point, it was obvious, was some kind of rivalry, but rather than pout over what was clearly an unfair accusation, Chloe apologized. One of the boys moved away from the computer screen, and Desmond could see a garish color photo of a naked woman. "We were just trying to figure out if this is really Courteney Cox's body," he said to Jane. "What do you think?"

"I think it's not her body even if it is. If anyone comes in, tell them I'm still out. Desmond and I have a meeting with David in fifteen minutes, so I don't want any interruptions."

Chloe tilted her head to one side and all that lush hair—or whatever it was—slithered over her shoulder. "Good *luck*, you guys," she said in a voice so drenched with sympathy they might as well have been headed straight to the ER for heart surgery.

4.

David was a short man who was letting himself go physically. When he stood up to shake hands, Desmond couldn't help but notice that his stomach was pressing against the bottom buttons of his pink shirt and his thighs straining against his chino pants. He had a round, meaty face and a small goatee that was being used to compensate for an absence of chin. Something in his look of exhaustion suggested a man who'd lost his appetite but was resigned to eating everything on his plate. There was a certain weary dignity to men like this, the ones who were determined to pay their dues and make good on their promises, especially if they didn't lose it completely and end up with blood on their hands and a body or two stashed in the basement somewhere.

"You got the copy of Desmond's book I sent up?" Jane asked.

David pointed them toward a couple of chairs in front of his desk and took a cursory glance around the office. "Ummm . . ."

"Maybe Chloe forgot to send it up. I'll have her get on it this afternoon."

Desmond didn't believe a word of it, and there was something in the annoyed way David was pursing his small mouth and stroking his goatee that suggested he didn't buy it either.

"The book is practically a classic," Jane said. "One of the most important biographies of the last decade. Wouldn't you say, Desmond?"

She'd warned him not to contradict her, but surely she didn't expect him to back her up on this one. "That might be overstating it just a bit."

David had his hands in front of his mouth now and he was impatiently tapping his fingertips together. He glanced at his watch, signaling that the introductory chitchat was over, and said, "So what are we discussing today?"

Jane took a folder out of her briefcase and opened it on her lap. She leafed through the pages. From his seat beside her, Desmond could see the pages were mostly half-finished lists and old news clippings. Either she'd taken the wrong folder with her or hadn't prepared for this meeting. But if she was thrown off, she didn't let it stop her. "Let's say I told you I wanted to propose a series of six fifty-minute biographical documentaries of American artists from assorted fields—literature, music, dance, and so on," she said. "What would your first question be?"

"Who," David stated flatly.

"Right. And if I told you: Hemingway, Sinatra, Isadora Duncan, your reaction would be?"

He picked up a paper clip and started to unwind it. "Been there."

"I completely agree. How about Fitzgerald, Billie Holiday, Fred Astaire?"

"Been *there*." The paper clip was now a straight piece of metal he was twirling impatiently between his stubby fingers.

"Steinbeck, Tony Bennett, Gene Kelly."

David frowned but said nothing. The office turned quiet and through the window Desmond could hear a great sigh as a truck passed on Soldiers Field Road. Desmond wanted to leap out of his chair and scream "Get on with it." He made what he hoped was a discreet swipe at the sweat trickling down his forehead. Jane lifted a sheet of paper from the folder. At the top she'd written: "Goals For June" and underneath that, a half-finished sentence in illegible script. As if reading from the sheet, she said, "What if I said, Lewis Westerly? What if I said Pauline Anderton? What if I said Terry Benson?"

Terry Benson?

"I'd have no idea who you were talking about." David's voice had the same bored tone it had had earlier, but he'd stopped twirling the paper clip. "I'd *assume* you were talking about some forgotten American geniuses. Is that where we're going here?"

"Not quite." Jane inched forward on her chair. "I see it this way, David: people are tired of hearing about the extraordinary. They don't watch television for edification, they watch it to feel better about themselves. How else do you explain talk shows and court TV and the cop things with the pathetic bare-chested junkies handcuffed and shoved into cruisers?"

Desmond could hear Jane turning the crank on her peculiar mediocrity argument. He disagreed with the small portion of this argument he understood and saw it as a highly unlikely selling point. And right now, sitting across from David, watching the paper clip in his hand and feeling sweat trickling down his back, he felt very much like a salesman. "We're talking about geniuses of a different sort," Desmond said. "We're talking about artists whose genius is found in the honesty of their art. People are turning to real-life talk and court shows, as Jane said, because it's honest, even if it is ugly. So much mass-produced, commercially viable art is synthetic and dishonest, you can't be sure of a point of view or a true emotion. Pauline Anderton, the singer Jane just mentioned, wasn't a perfect performer, but when you listen to her, you hear something true."

"Even if it is ugly," Jane added.

"And these are the people we'll be profiling," Desmond added. "The artists of truth."

David was fiddling with the paper clip, and Desmond could sense this meeting would be over in another ten minutes, at best. Desmond gave a quick summary of Pauline Anderton's career, making note of a few of the highlights he found more interesting and then, when he sensed that David wasn't quite convinced, dragging out the old standbys of alcoholism, her husband's cancer, and a mild gambling addiction.

"And this would tie in with Desmond's upcoming book," Jane said, "which we could easily use for fund-raising purposes."

David tossed down the paper clip, a sure sign that he'd heard enough. "I see what you're getting at here," David said, "but here's the problem: we can't do a bio series on people whose life stories are told every other week on Lifetime, but we also can't do a series on some drunken housewife with a ten-minute career. Even if her story is interesting, who's going to turn on the show to bother to find out?"

"You're not seeing the potential in this," Jane said. "You do promos, you get Desmond on some radio shows to talk about her, make a teaser showing her doing a header off the stage. People will be riveted."

"Still, they never heard of her."

David pushed back his chair and an alarm went off in Desmond's head and he saw himself falling down a long dark staircase. "Anderton," he said, "may not be a household name, but look who she palled around with: Judy Garland, Mel Tormé, Frank Sinatra."

David's chair rolled back toward his desk. "Sinatra?"

"I've been in touch with Liza Minnelli, who's more than willing to consider doing the narration."

"Really? You think you could get her to appear on film?"

"I don't see why not," Jane said. "You said she's been helpful all along, didn't you, Desmond?"

What amazed Desmond was that it had happened so effortlessly, this lapse into complete fabrication. Although he had to say, there was some grain of truth in it: Anderton did talk about Garland and had recorded some of Mel Tormé's songs. Not true, but to quote Jane, true enough. At least for the moment.

Ten
The Spin Cycle

1.

Gerald was sitting at the table in the kitchen, grudgingly drinking his breakfast glass of milk. Jane had read that many children dislike milk, and Gerald's pediatrician had told her it was nothing to worry about. Go to the supermarket, he'd advised her, and look at all the products designed to disguise the buttery flavor of milk and its white viscosity. Sure enough, there were shelves of the stuff—powders and syrups and granules. So why did she take Gerald's feeling of revulsion toward milk so personally, as if it were a subconscious rejection of her? She insisted he drink a glass of milk each morning for his bones and his teeth, but the real reasons she made sure he choked down every drop were undoubtedly more complicated.

Thomas was driving Gerald to school in half an hour, and he still hadn't returned from his morning jog. It worried her that he was being so consistent about jogging. As far as she could tell, he'd missed only two days in the past two weeks, and there hadn't been much improvement in the weather. She had managed to talk him into going out in the mornings when it was cool, although he still ended his runs pink and sweating.

"Did you finish your milk, sweetie?"

"Lyuuuck!" He shuddered, and handed her his empty glass.

She set a plate of toast in front of him and sat down at the table with her coffee. Gerald's hair was beginning to grow in, which made him look less like a convict, but it was at that awkward middle stage of growth: spiky bristles sticking out all over. "What are you doing in school today?" she asked.

"Something *stupid* and babyish probably."

Oh, Gerald, she wanted to tell him, I hope you don't talk like that in front of your classmates. He had only one friend in school that she knew of, an eight-year-old girl named after the city in which her parents had met: Plattsburgh. He sometimes went to her house to give her cooking lessons. Last week, her mother had called Jane to complain that Gerald was condescending to Plattsburgh and creating "self-esteem issues." As if her name wasn't a guarantee of that. If only she knew how to talk about any of this without hurting his feelings. He took a bite of his toast, chewed for a few seconds, and then let his mouth drop open. A lump of masticated bread plopped onto his plate.

"Gerald! What was *that?*"

He held up his toast. "What's *this?*"

He was making it sound as if she'd just tried to poison him, an effective tone to take since her conscience wasn't clear. "It's your toast, my dear, what do you think?"

"What's *on* it?"

"Listen, mister, we ran out of butter and I haven't had a chance to go shopping, so I used margarine. Which happens to be good for you." That was unlikely, seeing as everything, including breathing, was unhealthy.

"I hate it! You know I hate it!"

"Gerald, sweetie, I will go shopping today and I will get you some butter. Sweet, unsalted, not in quarters but in a one-pound block, just the way you like it. All right?"

"That doesn't do me much good this morning."

Where had he learned to talk like this? What gremlin crawled up the stairs to his third-floor "apartment" each night and gave tutorials in sarcasm and bullying? If only she had the option of blaming it all on TV, life would be easier. But Gerald had almost no interest in television, aside from the occasional cooking show. And what was the right thing to do now? Punish him? Run down to the store on the corner and buy some butter? Get to work at the churn? She picked up his plate and put it into the sink, ran water over it and turned on the disposal. "I can offer you the following: cereal, banana, or peanut butter sandwich."

"Lyuck, lyuck, lyuuuuck."

Thomas walked in the back door, mopping his face with his T-shirt. "Morning, boys and girls. What's the racket in here?"

Jane watched as Gerald looked from one parent to the other, made a mental calculation of some kind, and said, "Nothing. I wasn't hungry, that's all."

It was a clear-cut case of divide and conquer, but she wasn't going to enter into the fray by further explanation. It was better to allow herself the luxury of believing it just didn't matter.

"Is that so?" Thomas asked, "Well, maybe if we have time, and you decide you *are* hungry, we can stop on the way to school and pick you up a bagel. How does that sound?"

Gerald shrugged. "I'd prefer a muffin."

Thomas chugged down a big glass of water. "We'll see about that," he said, mild but in control. His skin looked firmer, and that girdle of fat that clung to his waist was definitely shrinking. Perhaps he'd changed his diet as well, in subtle ways she wouldn't necessarily notice—smaller portions, skipping lunches. People like Thomas, thinkers who ordinarily didn't register on exercise as a part of daily life, didn't take up jogging all of a sudden unless something was troubling them, unless they felt they needed to spruce themselves up.

"How come you're so wet?" Gerald asked.

"I've been running in the heat. And when you get hot, your body perspires, and the water on your skin evaporates and cools you down."

"Do you *like* running?"

Thomas cocked his head. "Do I like it? You know, I hadn't thought of it in that way. I was viewing it more as a daily trip to the dentist. Although now that you mention it, I am beginning to enjoy it. It gives me more patience. It's helped me put some things in perspective."

"What kinds of things?"

"Little things," he said. "I hope they're little. Now you better get ready or we'll have to skip the muffin."

Little things. He could be talking about students, the ever-grating English Department, a paper he was trying to finish on *The Confidence-Man.* And yet the weary tone of his voice suggested it was something more personal. She owed it to him to tell him that she was seeing Dr. Berman again. It was a simple, matter-of-fact way to start opening up to her husband. She could even report on what she was discussing with Berman, since she hadn't opened up to the good doctor very much.

Gerald turned as he was leaving the kitchen. "Why do we have to go to New *Hamp*shire? I hate New *Hamp*shire."

Thomas knelt on the floor in front of him and said, "We've been asked by some very nice people, and it would be rude to say no, and there's a beautiful lake, and even though you don't realize it yet, you're going to have a good time."

"I hate water."

Thomas chuckled and gave him a gentle nudge toward the hallway. When they could hear him stomping up the stairs, he grabbed a banana and said, "I have to run. I have to take Sarah for her checkup later this morning. What do you have on today?"

"Too much to remember." He came and kissed her on the forehead, and as he was leaving, she said, "Thomas, I wish you hadn't told Caroline we'd go to the lake."

"Oh? Why is that?"

His back was to her, but there was something unsettling in the way he'd asked, almost as if he was testing her, or possibly trying to trip her up. From the moment they'd met, she'd been careful never to mention Dale in ways that would make Thomas think she had any good feelings for him lingering on the edges of her subconscious. It wasn't exactly a struggle, since she wasn't aware of any lingering good feelings.

"I don't know," she said. "It might be awkward."

"There'll be lots of family and friends floating around. I think it will be fine. It will be good for Gerald."

"He hates New *Hamp*shire."

"He's never been, Jody. By the way, I was on the deck and overheard some of the toast discussion. Don't take it all so seriously. He's only six."

2.

When she got out of her appointment with Dr. Berman, she felt worse than she'd felt in weeks. What she'd wanted to discuss with him was her inability to tell Thomas she was back in therapy, but the more she thought about it and the harder she tried to find a way to bring it up, the more impossible it seemed. It was the kind of thing she should have mentioned immediately, in the first or second session; telling it now, after months of twice-weekly meetings, would probably make Berman think she was acting out or resisting treatment. She gave up the idea and rambled on in a monotone about how abandoned she'd felt when her parents had died. That was always good to kill time, and it was the kind of topic that seemed to please Berman. It was probably useful, in a therapeutic sense, even though she was almost certain she'd worked through all that material years ago. And yet, driving back to her office, she felt so frustrated, she called Desmond from her cell phone and asked him if he'd like to meet her later in the day for coffee. He'd love to, he told her. He said it in such a heartfelt, relieved voice, it was obvious he was lonely, sitting around that grim room reading student papers and listening to Pauline Anderton. She felt such a flush of sympathy for him, she decided to go all out and suggested they meet at the Ritz.

It was late afternoon when she walked into the golden lounge on the second floor of the hotel. She scanned the room and realized that she was probably underdressed, but that wasn't necessarily a bad thing. She'd been to tea at the Ritz one other time and had left wondering if all the ladies in pearls and boiled wool jackets weren't paid actors, hired to sit politely nibbling on their sandwiches and straining their tea. Desmond was sitting at a table in the corner, smoothing down the pink tablecloth with his hand. He stood and grinned when he spotted her, but as she was making her way toward him, she saw an expectant look on his face, his eyes a little more wide open than usual, something hopeful in the grin. She'd made a mistake in suggesting this place. Why invite someone to the Ritz unless you had some good news to announce, something to celebrate? Why not meet at any boring coffeehouse unless you were going to report that the station had okayed your proposal and was coming up with the money?

"You're looking pretty lovely," he said. He held out a chair for her.

"Too bad. I was hoping I was underdressed."

"Sorry to disappoint you. You look perfect."

You could always count on a gay man to flatter you. And when one did, she usually ended up feeling only halfway complimented. The myth about their superior taste made no sense to her, but experience had taught her it was frequently true. You couldn't discount the praise, but given a moment to think it over, she invariably felt a sputter of disappointment. It was like drinking nonalcoholic beer—tastes like the real thing, but where's the buzz? He was wearing a tie and a sports jacket, which probably meant he'd called ahead to find out if there was a dress code. He looked handsome in a slightly disheveled way, and she was so grateful for his flattery—or half compliment or whatever—she practically delivered a panegyric on his outfit.

"I don't believe you," he said, "but I appreciate it."

The room was filled with proper Boston ladies, the same cast or identical stand-ins she'd seen here last time, and a few young couples, one nestled together on a love seat feeding each other cookies. Desmond nodded toward a corner where a woman dressed in pale purple was playing a harp. "We should either be much older or in love with each other."

"Let's just be voyeurs," she said. "It always sounds to me as if harpists are playing Debussy. Which is odd because I have no idea what Debussy sounds like."

"Not like this. Unless I'm mistaken, she's doing a medley of Rodgers and Hart."

She wasn't about to admit she couldn't name a single song she was absolutely certain had been written by that particular team. Basically, she lumped the whole of the American songbook under the "show tunes" umbrella. "Thomas would know the composer immediately, along with the date it was written and who first recorded it. He's full of information." She thought this over for a moment. "And wisdom, too."

"I had an interesting conversation with him this morning," Desmond said. "I was telling him I thought I needed a bit more time to solve my problems with the biography and he quoted something from Emily Dickinson. 'Time is a test of trouble, not a remedy.' I'm not sure I agree, but it made me realize I've been counting on time to fill in the gaps on the book. I have to be more aggressive in sorting it out."

There was something grandiose about the way Thomas pulled quotations out of thin air, like a magician yanking a quarter from behind someone's ear, knowing very well that it's not the quarter or the quotation you're supposed to applaud, but the magician's ability to produce it. And yet, you could sometimes get the inside track on what was going through his mind if you listened to what he was reciting. "Time is a test of trouble." What trouble had he been thinking about, other than Desmond's? This morning he'd made that vague comment about jogging giving him more patience. Perhaps he was waiting out her season of discontent, hoping it wasn't strong enough to survive more than a few months. Exactly what she was hoping.

The waiter came around bearing triple-tiered trays with delicate sandwiches and scones dotted with currants and little cakes coated in dense frosting. She wasn't hungry, and she had no intention of eating, so she chose the three cakes that looked the most caloric. Leaving something that fattening on the plate would make her feel especially virtuous.

"You and Thomas are an interesting couple," Desmond said. He was selecting sandwiches from the tray, thin, crustless items that cried out to be eaten in an affected way, pinkie in the air. She wondered how he'd manage with those.

"Interesting how?" she asked.

"Well, for one thing, Thomas is a bit academic. He's very studied and careful." Dull seemed to be the word he was trying to avoid. "And you're much more spontaneous."

"Not always," she said. Even so, she appreciated hearing it. She wanted to think of herself as spontaneous and free-spirited, despite the fact that she spent vast amounts of time attempting to be organized and disciplined.

"And yet you seem to work together very well as a couple."

She strained her tea into her cup and dropped in a couple of cubes of sugar. (She'd been hoping for coffee, but they probably would have sneered at her if she'd dared to ask for it.) She liked the picture Desmond had of their marriage—two distinctly different people with different tastes and personalities who still functioned well as a couple. That was the way she hoped people saw her marriage to Thomas. It was the way she'd seen it for the first couple of years they were together, before she felt swamped by petty annoyances, before Gerald became quite so verbal. "Thank you for saying that," she said. "Sometimes I think about the marriage going through regular, predictable cycles, like the weather. Or like a washing machine. Some are smooth and quiet, some noisy, but in the end, they all work together and eventually get the clothes clean."

"What cycle are you in now?"

The cakes were staring up at her, daring her to take a bite. She sliced off such a thin sliver of the chocolate cake, it crumpled into a heap on the plate, and she scooped it up with a spoon. "Probably the WASH cycle. Warm Affection mixed with Subtle Hostility. It's a low-key mode. What about you and Russell?"

He pondered this for a moment. "The SPIN cycle: Separation Producing Increased Neediness. A lot of chugging and rattling. I was hoping it would be closer to RINSE—Recaptured Independence . . . Negating Symbiotic . . ."

"Entanglement?"

"Exactly." He picked up one of the cucumber sandwiches and, making what looked like a noble attempt at being not too dainty, popped the whole thing into his mouth. "I miscalculated, it seems. But I guess I'm talking about my own feelings, not the cycle of the relationship."

"What about Russell's feelings?"

"I don't know. I'll find out this weekend."

"It's trouble if you're not both on the same cycle. The unbalanced light goes on and everything grinds to a halt. My brother and Joyce come to mind."

He seemed to perk up at the mention of Brian, which probably meant he'd been charmed by his looks—good looks, if she could believe everyone's opinion except her own. "Another interesting marriage," he said.

"That's one way of describing it. He's been stuck in the raging narcissist cycle for years. I was married to one of those once."

"Dale?"

She nodded. She looked down at her plate, astonished to realize she'd finished every last crumb of the chocolate cake. She'd been so intent on not eating it, she hadn't even tasted it. "Are you worried that Russell isn't missing you enough?"

"Probably. It's what I deserve, so . . ."

"But people never get what they deserve, so you've got nothing to worry about. Anyway, all you have to do is wait for the happy-days-are-here-again cycle."

She liked herself as he seemed to see her—strong, capable, independent. Not part of the undifferentiated mass of Janethomasgerald as she'd feared, but part of a loving, healthy family. Which wasn't so far from the truth. She liked his belief in her, his faith that she could help see him through whatever block he was having with this book. She wanted to live up to his image of her.

Later, as they were making their way down the staircase to the lobby, he

said to her, hesitantly, "So, Jane, was there a reason you wanted to get together? Something you wanted to tell me?"

She'd wanted forty-five minutes of companionship, wanted to be around
someone with whom she had a relationship uncomplicated by fabrications
and omissions. Someone who approved of her, even if, in truth, he didn't
know her all that well. She stopped on the staircase and let him get a few
steps ahead of her. "Can you believe I almost forgot?" she said. "We're going
to get the money! I haven't had the official word, but I've had the unofficial
official word we're getting a green light. And not only that, it seems nearly
certain we'll be getting more than the ten grand I thought we'd end up getting."

He bounded up the stairs and put his arms around her. "You're brilliant,
Jane."

This was what she'd come for, and standing on the stairs with the harpist
above plucking out something silvery and melancholy—Debussy? The Bea-
tles?—she believed him for almost a full minute.

Eleven
Home Alone

1.

Desmond was gazing out the window of his office at the still surface of the lake in the middle of Deerforth's campus. It was the period of Pauline Anderton's life after her husband died that he found so puzzling. All indications were that her husband had tolerated her singing career while belittling her talent with backhanded compliments. ("For people with talent," he once wrote to her, "singing's no big deal. For someone like you, it takes courage. To hell with the critics.") Desmond didn't understand why she'd abandoned her singing after his death. If she hadn't turned down every offer to perform or record, she might have become a more confident and polished artist.

"Ahmthina turrin mamuth inna crag ed."

Desmond turned away from the window. He'd almost forgotten the student was still in his office. Roger, Roger . . . Lovell, was that it? He was a desperately thin boy who seemed—was it possible, at age nineteen?—to be losing his hair. He wore baggy, sweaty T-shirts, and enormous eyeglasses that made him look a little like a bug or some prehistoric creature. Colleges ought to offer makeovers as part of the whole package, along with job placement and health care. Based on his prose, Roger was exceptionally bright and capable, but he spoke so rapidly, everything came out in a garbled wad, and it was almost impossible to tell what he was saying.

"I see," Desmond said.

"Gugugugugugood. Gla yagree."

Had he said he was thinking of turning his mother into a crack head? Maybe so. He was enrolled in the Creative Nonfiction class and the consensus among the other students was that his memoir lacked tension and dramatic coherence. Maybe, one girl had suggested, he'd have a stronger story to tell if his father had cancer or his mother had a drinking problem.

"I'm not sure I *do* agree with you," Desmond said. "You might want to continue writing as truthfully as possible about your childhood and see what story emerges from that naturally."

Roger started to roll his hands over each other so quickly they became a blur. "Yabba gadda gedda sumthin inna . . ."

He should tape Roger and play it back at a lower speed to find out what he'd said. In the meantime, it was probably best to check out. Desmond turned back to the window. Based on the letters and postcards Anderton had sent, she and her husband had hardly had a loving marriage. It wasn't likely she'd gone into such deep mourning after he died she couldn't perform, so what was it that had caused her to drop the ball professionally? He was certain the answer to this would cast a long shadow over the rest of her life and fill in the missing pieces.

"Yathinga heron addis beda?"

Desmond looked at Roger again. The kid was leaning forward in his chair, eyes immense behind the glasses. "A hearing aid?" Desmond asked.

"Nanananana. Heron addis."

He felt like suggesting he just do away with mom altogether. Dad, too, while he was at it, claim he grew up in an orphanage. There was dramatic tension for you. Everyone in the class had signed up for it because they wanted to write nonfiction, but they made so few distinctions between what had happened in their lives and what had happened in the scores of memoirs they'd read, it might as well be a course in science fiction. "A heroin addict? Claim that she's a junkie?"

"Yayayayaya. Mayme ayes."

"Maniac?"

"Nono. Mayme AIDS. GivarAIDS."

Give his mother AIDS. One more suggestion along those lines and he'd feel duty bound to report Roger to the dean. "Let's think about that, all right? In the meantime, maybe you should write something more detailed about your brother. I found some of the pages about him to be the most interesting you've got so far. Just follow the little details of your relationship with him. That business about him falling out of the tree was genuinely touching."

Desmond stood and ushered Roger out before he had a chance to tell him he didn't have a brother at all. He shut the door behind him and packed up the last of the papers and lecture notes he was taking with him on his New York trip.

Discounting the last ten minutes, it had been an exceptionally good week. If he were prone to Jane Cody–style hyperbole, he'd call it a triumph. On Monday, Jane had told him about the near certainty of getting the money. "It was you," she'd said as they were standing on the staircase at the Ritz. "Your whole concept of what the series should be was brilliant. But what really clinched it was that inspired business about Liza Minnelli."

This wasn't the first time she'd praised him for that particular lie; despite her compliments about his ideas for the series, it was this fabrication that seemed to please her most. And, curiously enough, it was that moment of ruthless prevarication that he kept replaying in his own mind. Not his clarification of Jane's ideas, not his succinct analysis of Anderton's life and talent. "I've been in touch with Liza Minnelli." It was exhilarating to discover something new about himself, to find that he had a hidden talent for on-the-spot mendacity. It made him think he was more creative and spontaneous than he'd guessed.

On Tuesday, he'd started making phone calls to arrange interviews with some key figures in Pauline Anderton's life. First there was an older couple in Waugborn, the Boston suburb where Anderton had spent her final days. This pair of garrulous boozers had been friends of Anderton's sister and drinking buddies of Pauline's right up to the end. They loved to tell amusing anecdotes about the fun they'd had with her, anecdotes that usually started with a fond "Remember the time we went to . . ." and ended with a drunken mishap and some variation on the comment, "Yeah, she almost died that night," delivered as if it were the surprising and hilarious punch line to a joke. With careful editing, their stories could provide dramatic, colorful testimony to Anderton's decline.

He'd received a cooler reception from Anderton's daughter, Lorna, a forty-something (going on sixty, he was sure) woman who had a collection of Anderton memorabilia on display in the sunporch of her house in Gulf City,

Florida. Desmond had spent a few days with Lorna in the early stages of his research and had found her to be a suspicious person who acted as if he were trying to siphon money out of her bank account but who eventually had come around. She didn't seem the least bit surprised or disappointed to hear that the book was still unfinished, and was wary of the new project. "A TV show?" she'd asked. "Well, we'll have to get back to you on that one."

It was only a little after noon, but already the Deerforth campus was emptying out and beginning to feel like a lush, shadowy park. College campuses, along with youth, are wasted on the young. From his office window high above the rolling lawns and colorful trees, Desmond could see students packing cars and lined up for the shuttle bus to Boston with their knapsacks and suitcases heaped up around their feet. The start of a long weekend. There was something about the whole indulgent concept of a "long weekend," not to mention the very words themselves, that suggested romantic possibilities. He'd told Russell he was going to arrive on Saturday, but he'd woken up this morning so caught up in this autumnal urge for going and the predatory desire to make this long weekend as long as possible, that he'd decided to bring his schoolwork with him and leave today.

As he was about to call Russell's store and tell him about the change in his plans, the phone rang.

"Is this Desmond?"

A recognizable voice, although one he didn't recognize. "Yes?"

"You're never in your office, Desmond. I'm surprised I caught you. It's Brian Cody."

Desmond glanced toward the door to make sure it was closed, and then to make sure it stayed closed, stretched out the phone cord and turned the deadbolt. "Brian, hello." He lay down on Professor Crandersall's puffy, bedspread-covered sofa and put his feet up on the armrest.

"You sound as if you're in a rush."

"No, not exactly."

"Not too busy taking care of your students?" There was a faint suggestion of something lewd under this, as if he assumed Desmond spent the bulk of his time prowling the streets or luring students into his office so he could "take care of" them. Desmond had found that most of the closeted men he knew assumed that all openly gay men spent at least ten of their sixteen waking hours pursuing or engaging in sex. It was an insulting assumption that took profligate promiscuity for granted and discounted the possibility of professional pursuits and emotional fidelity; the actual number of hours was probably much closer to six.

Since the dinner at Jane's, Desmond had thought about Brian from time to time, usually with bemused annoyance. In one brief fantasy, he and Brian had spent some quality time together, assuming sexually humiliating Brian in his own office could be considered quality time. Fantasy was one thing, but Desmond had never entertained any notions of actually calling him up. When he looked up Brian's office address in the phone book, it hadn't been with the intention of dropping by for coffee. One balmy Wednesday a couple of weeks after the dinner at Jane's, Desmond had driven home from Deer-forth via Cambridge and walked past Brian's office. If you were going to cook up a harmless fantasy—and he'd read somewhere that all fantasies are harmless—it helped to have a few authentic details to use for set design. The building was on a noisy street and the front window was artfully covered with opaque shades, so there'd been no risk of being spotted by or spotting Brian.

"I've been fairly busy with your sister," Desmond said. "We've started working on a project together."

This didn't impress him. "Mmm. So I've heard." There was a rustling of paper, as if he was unrolling blueprints while cradling the phone against his neck. "Look, I'm just calling to tell you that offer of a tour of the city is still on. You haven't forgotten, have you, Desmond?"

Desmond hated the condescending tone in his voice when he said his name, and making an attempt at stabbing back, he said, "No, *Brian,* I haven't forgotten." But this, he realized, was seduction through sarcasm, probably the very thing Brian had been hoping to provoke.

"Then give me a call. I'll give you my number. I've got some free time next week, so maybe we can work something out. Have you got a piece of paper there, Desmond?"

"I think so, *Brian.*"

Later, driving along the Merritt Parkway with a Pauline Anderton tape playing in the background and the Connecticut landscape passing by the windows, he realized he'd forgotten to call Russell and tell him about his change of plans. But stopping in Connecticut and finding his calling card and talking over the roar of passing traffic seemed too taxing. Unlike Desmond, Russell liked surprises.

2.

As soon as he walked into the apartment, he was overwhelmed by the reassuring exhaustion that always overtook him when he returned home from a long trip. The sounds of the New York traffic, so distinctly different in volume and tone from the traffic sounds in Boston; the dusty odor of the dirtier New York air; the familiar smells of carpets and houseplants and gas from the pilot light on the stove that always blew out on breezy afternoons. As he lowered his bag to the floor beside the red velvet sofa in the living room, he realized how cold and emotionally empty his life in Boston was, and, taking in all the clutter Russell had been collecting for five years, how colorless his life in this apartment had been before Russell had tricked Desmond into letting him move in here. What a fool he'd been for thinking he had to leave this behind, even temporarily, to get a hold on his life. This *was* his life. This was where he belonged, here in this apartment flooded with the burnished light of late afternoon, and the primitive portraits and embroidered pillows. He let his knapsack slide off his shoulders, and went to the kitchen to get something to eat.

He and Russell were erratic housekeepers. Once or twice a month they'd go on extravagant cleaning binges that could last for a couple of days. They'd spend hours doing laundry, and swinging around vacuum cleaners and harsh chemical sprays. Then, gradually, they'd slide back into genteel squalor. But there was nothing genteel about the squalid kitchen this afternoon. The sink was stacked high with dishes, the wastebasket was overflowing with trash, and the little table by the window was covered with junk mail and stacks of unread newspapers. Russell read history voraciously, but seemed to view current events as inconsequential. The tragedies and victories of the past at least had a beginning, a middle, and an end; until you could see the whole picture, he wasn't interested. All the nondescript 1980s junk he sold at Morning in America suddenly took on a thin veneer of Cultural Significance when you factored in the Black Monday stock market crash, the ravages of AIDS, and the all-too-plausible announcement of Reagan's Alzheimer's disease.

Well, maybe this kitchen mess was a good sign, evidence that Russell needed Desmond around to hold his life together. The freezer was crammed with TV dinners, frost-covered loaves of bread, and boxes of mini-pizzas. What a poignant image this stockpile conjured up: Russell slumped over a plastic tray of pseudo-food. He might as well be eating protein pills. The bottom half of the fridge was virtually empty. Nothing to eat. So much for that idea.

Desmond checked his watch. In all likelihood he had another hour, hour and a half before Russell showed up, assuming he came straight from the store. There was time for Desmond to settle in and assert some dominance over the place, take back some of the space. Assert his right to be here. After all, he was the one who had bought this apartment. He took a swing through the bedroom—another dumping ground, laundry heaped up on a chair—then went out to the living room and circled into the kitchen. He made a stab at attacking the dishes, but as he was attempting to find the sponge under all those food-encrusted dishes, his back stiffened with resentment and he abandoned the project. Back to the fridge, but there was *still* nothing to eat in there. In the living room, he turned on the radio. Russell had it tuned to a Top 40s funk station—since when did he like this music?—and Desmond found the thumping bass a hammer on his skull. He looked in vain for the remote control and finally gave up and shut the thing off. He collapsed on the living room sofa and picked up a magazine called *Hello,* apparently a British version of *People* or maybe the *National Enquirer.* Desmond leafed through the pages, bored by the pictures of the Royal Family and the only slightly more attractive, unrecognizable British TV stars proudly showing off their grim London town houses. It was a mystery what Russell could possibly find interesting in this.

He looked at his watch. Seven minutes had passed since the last time he'd checked. He went to the kitchen, but nothing edible had materialized, so he decided to go out to get something to eat. As he was opening the door, he heard the young marrieds, Tina and Gary, arguing in the hallway. The last thing he needed was to attempt polite chitchat with those two. Now he was a prisoner in his own apartment. Except it suddenly didn't feel like his own apartment; it felt like Russell's. And Russell felt like a stranger.

A beer and a soak. He'd have to clean the bathtub first, no doubt about that, but that at least would eat up ten more minutes.

Desmond drew a bath and lowered himself into the warm water. Better already. He rested his beer bottle on the floor beside the tub and pulled a magazine from the rack near the toilet. A men's "fitness" magazine. Now here was real pornography. Clinical text describing exercise and diet and skeletal structure accompanying lurid photos of big-breasted, dewy, depilated men bending over benches or hanging from chin-up bars with their legs in the air. He skimmed through the pages, searching for a model who looked anything at all like Russell, but no one could match the lean economy of his musculature. He flipped to the back of the magazine and found himself staring at a photo of a carefully groomed man in a phone sex ad who bore a striking resemblance to Brian Cody. He stuffed the magazine back in the rack and finished his beer.

By the time he'd dried himself off, he'd killed almost an hour. He went into the bathroom wearing the damp towel and squeezed himself around the foot of the bed. It was obvious from the way the blankets were pulled back on the unmade bed and the way the pillows were dented that Russell had been dividing his time between his side of the bed and Desmond's, probably an indication of how much he missed him. Desmond sat on his side of the mattress. The afternoon was fading quickly, but the room was still bright with sunlight and uncomfortably warm. There was a fat yellow book on his night table, the cover a sampler of different type faces and sizes, a loud, ragged jumble of letters announcing the title: *Becoming the You You Deserve to Be.* They should call this genre of book shelf-help, since, as far as he could tell, no one read past the first few pages before hiding them away in a bookcase. They all seemed to boil down to the same simple message: it's all right to be selfish and self-centered. And what if it turns out you deserve to be a homeless, penniless wreck? How awful to think that Russell, in his anger at Desmond for leaving town, in his loneliness, had descended from Trollope and Tocqueville to "Dr. Ashley."

The book was bulging with something stuck between the pages. It fell open when Desmond picked it up, and inside was a pair of large, brown eyeglasses. Not a pair that Desmond had seen Russell wear. He slowly opened the bows and slid them onto his face. The room went blurry. Whoever they belonged to had worse vision than Russell. He looked down at the book. Bifocals. He'd never understood how people navigated their way through this bifurcated world. And with all this laser surgery going on, one day soon all glasses would be nostalgia items, right up there with typewriters.

He put them back in the book and set the book on the night table, careful to leave it exactly where it had been. He wasn't going to leap to conclusions. Maybe Russell had had his prescription changed. Unlikely, and besides, these weren't new glasses. He swept back the sheets. No bodies there. There was no reason to assume anything. He looked back at the idiotic, infuriating "book." If Russell was cheating on him with a man who read *Becoming the You You Deserve to Be,* he was getting what he deserved. On the other hand, if Russell was cheating on him, maybe he, Desmond, was getting what *he* deserved. As he looked out the window beside the bed to the courtyard in the middle of their building, Boris started to play the piano. So he hadn't quit after all, hadn't moved, hadn't taken up *painting.* He started playing a slow, halting rendition of "Night and Day." Like the beat beat beat of the tom-toms indeed. For the first time in the years Boris had been playing, Desmond wished he were able to flip a switch and turn off the practice session. He sat on the edge of the bed, his head in his hands, looking down at the floor. There, poking out from under the mattress was a black sock. He reached down and grabbed it. Inconclusive. Everyone wore socks and they were all more or less the same size. He stared at it for a moment, listening to the piano, feeling a fluttering in his chest that was either grief or rage or maybe both at the same time. The simplest thing to do would be to get dressed and leave, wait an hour and call from around the corner, telling Russell he was arriving ahead of schedule. Give him time to bury the evidence, if that's what it was. He slipped on his underpants, T-shirt, and socks. But as he was trying to find his shirt, he heard the door to the apartment open, footsteps in the hallway, creaking floorboards. Now he was trapped. Caught. Caught double if Russell wasn't alone.

"Desmond?"

He was standing in the bedroom, slim and bespectacled, alone, a wry smile in his eyes. "You're early," he said.

"I am," Desmond said, wondering if maybe it wasn't more a matter of being late.

Twelve
A Relaxing Weekend

1.

"Her bread is terrible," Caroline whispered, "but I have to buy a few loaves to support her efforts. I can stop at the food pantry tomorrow and donate them."

It was Saturday afternoon, they'd been at the farmer's market for twenty minutes, and thus far Caroline had done nothing but give money to animal causes and make a series of mercy buys. She was on a first-name basis with most of the farmers, bakers, and craftspeople who had tables set up under the yellow and white striped canopy. As she led Jane through the tables, she greeted each one, chatted briefly, and then pulled out her wallet and made a purchase. The pies and cookies and limp lettuce and brown cauliflower and the little jar of herbal salve were all stowed in the woven straw backpack with the leather straps Caroline lugged from vendor to vendor. The backpack, like everything else at the Wade family estate, had been purchased by Nana someone or other and used by generations of Wades for the same purpose. Virtually every dish towel on the estate, every coat hanger, every threadbare chenille bedspread had been fetishized.

As they were driving from the estate to this market—the tent was set up in a field near the center of a surprisingly bucolic New Hampshire town—Caroline had stressed the importance of supporting the farmers and craftspeople, keeping the local economy strong and healthy, helping to combat the invasion of Wal-Mart and similar chains. Jane agreed with the whole concept on a political level and was ready to shop herself into bankruptcy, but once they arrived and she got a good look at the bruised, insect-infested vegetables, the pale uninspired lumps of bread, and the hideous pencil holders made from soup cans—to select only one example of the crafts, and not the worst one—she'd begun to wonder if it might not make sense to let survival of the fittest take its course; let the talented gardeners and whatever else thrive while the others got into more suitable fields and allowed their fantasies to die dignified natural deaths. It was probably unspeakably churlish to suggest that not everyone should be encouraged to live their dreams. The generous thing to do was to judge people on their ambitions rather than their achievements. Which was all very nice, but when it got down to having to eat someone else's ambitions, Jane would rather bow out.

Jane watched as Caroline chatted with a round, doughy baker who bore an uncanny resemblance to his undercooked loaves. Surely Caroline's attitude toward all of this meant that she was a better person than Jane was or ever would be. As if Jane needed one more example of Caroline's moral superiority. She could hear Caroline complimenting the young man on a batch of brownies she'd bought from him the weekend before—and had probably tossed into a Goodwill bin on the drive home.

Jane looked over at a nearby table laden with an appalling assortment of crocheted potholders and lap blankets and other yarny items that were less easy to identify. The woman selling the stuff was seated behind the table in a green and white webbed lawn chair clicking long knitting needles. She looked as needy and earnest as everyone else here and had on a long crocheted vest with panels from—was it beer cans?—worked into the design. Two points for the efforts at recycling, but not a fashion statement that was likely to catch on. Still, she was undoubtedly another worthwhile cause, not to mention that she was geriatric, which meant you could excuse the shoddy workmanship.

"Beautiful day, isn't it?" Jane said, picking up an orange and brown . . . something from the table. She beamed at her with her kindest smile. "The sun is so welcome this time of year."

The woman looked at Jane through milky blue eyes. It was a warm day and

Jane had worn a chartreuse tank top and a pair of purple shorts and white sandals. The knitter took in her outfit and seemed to form an opinion. "It's not so welcome if you've got *skin* cancer."

Oops. "No. Well, I imagine not." Don't Engage. Toss Her A Bone. "You do lovely work," Jane said. "I wish I could knit."

"Everybody wishes they could *knit,* but no one wants to take the time to do it. You have to work at it." She held up her gnarled, arthritic hand. "You wish you looked like *this?*" She frowned with disgust. "I didn't think so."

Don't Engage. "What is this?" Jane asked, indicating the orange and brown socklike thing she'd picked up.

"Hold it up!" the woman ordered. "Goes over the ketchup bottle to make it look prettier at the table."

"Ah ha." If you were out to make a mercy purchase, it probably helped to buy something truly useless and support a wretched, ill-tempered hag like this. "How much is it?"

"Twenty-five dollars."

Jane somehow managed to prevent herself from screaming "You must be joking!" but astonishment evidently showed on her face.

"It's an original pattern," the woman defended. "And it takes me *ten hours* to make one of them." This was an outright lie. In ten hours, Jane could make a sock for every bottle in the house and the last time she'd picked up a pair of needles had been in high school home ec class. "You want bargain basement, go down to Wal-Mart."

Upon hearing mention of the enemy, the woman selling pressed leaves at the next table looked over.

"It's just that we don't eat much ketchup at home, that's all," Jane said. Do Not Engage. "I'm allergic to tomatoes."

The woman shook her head with undisguised revulsion. "Everybody's got an *excuse.* All right, go ahead, take it for five."

But I don't want it for any price, Jane thought as she reached into her bag. "Here, why don't we compromise? Here's twelve." There had to be someone she could give it to.

The beer can vest rattled as the woman leaned forward in her webbed chair and snatched the bills out of Jane's hand. "Took me two *days* to make that. Twelve dollars! Pffft."

Jane's mouth dropped open. Had the woman actually spit at her? If not, it was near enough. And she was supposed to stand here and take it! "Well if twelve dollars is such an insult," she said, "and it's so un*bear*able to part with the thing, why sell it at all? Why not just have it framed and donate it to a museum?"

People at the other booths were starting to stare at her, all the farmers and bakers in their simple jeans and work shirts, staring at her in her summer clothes and city sandals, making her feel like the world's oldest adolescent. Caroline was finalizing her purchase and making frantic hand signals to her which Jane couldn't read. She should simply leave the hideous item here on the table, but that would probably cause a riot. She stuffed the bottle cover into her bag—what a practical design, and undoubtedly extra pretty when covered with ketchup—and walked away, leaving the old woman clicking her needles, and, for all she knew, laughing and spitting at her. This should count as two good deeds done today. Or six.

Caroline rushed over. She took Jane by the arm and led her down the aisle of tables and out from under the canopy into the unseasonably hot sun. It had been years since Jane had spent any significant time with Caroline, and in the interval, she seemed to have grown more beautiful. Or not beautiful exactly, but lovely. Everything about her was fresh and fair and lovely—the long lean lines of her body, her soft corn silk hair, her smooth pink skin. She had on a lemon yellow dress that floated around her slim body. She even smelled lemony, despite her cigarettes.

"I took you at your word about supporting these people," Jane said, "but it nearly cost me my life."

They walked across the bumpy, browning field, toward the lot where they'd left the car. Caroline looked over her shoulder, apparently to make sure no one was tailing them, listening in on their conversation. "I try to avoid that woman," she said. "She and her husband are big NRA supporters and they've been connected to the local militia. There was even talk they were involved in a bomb threat at the State House in Concord last year."

"Oh, shit."

Caroline hitched the pack off her shoulder and carefully set it in the back seat of her ancient Citroën. The car smelled of worn, sun-roasted leather and cigarettes. Caroline put on her sunglasses and lit up a Chesterfield. Amazingly, given the studied, careful way she did most things, she never used a seat belt, while Jane, a slob by comparison, had an absolute mania for them. Especially when she was driving with someone as reckless behind the wheel as Caroline. Once Jane had strapped herself in with the quaint lap belt, she pulled the bottle cover out of her bag. If Caroline weren't here, she'd rush back and toss it at the woman.

"Don't give it a second thought," Caroline said, looking over. "Two dollars?"

"Twelve. I talked her down from twenty-five."

Caroline shook her head. "The farmer's market committee is trying to think of a way to keep her out next year." The engine turned over and sputtered to life and there was that odd Citroën lift and they were off. Caroline went through a stop sign, not obliviously, Jane noted, but aggressively. It was nice to know that even Caroline wasn't immune to road rage.

"I don't know how much more evidence of consumer fraud you'd need than this," Jane said. "Keep it, and I won't feel as if I wasted my money." Jane stuffed the sock into the glove compartment, noting that it was already full of parking tickets.

Once they were on a deserted, winding road, Jane settled back into her seat. She'd been dreading the whole awkward weekend, and especially had been dreading this kind of excursion, when she and Caroline would be together alone. But so far, it all had been strangely pleasant, as if she and Thomas and Dale and Caroline were just old although not especially close friends; as if this ill-advised weekend would end up neutering her flirtation with Dale. Thomas had been wise to insist they come. Even Gerald seemed to be enjoying himself. "Thanks for inviting us up here," Jane said. "I had some doubts when you first asked us, but I'm glad we came."

"I'm the one who should be thanking you," Caroline said. "I'm surprised you didn't hang up on me that day I called you. Frantic."

"Let's not talk about it," Jane said. "It seems like a very long time ago."

"It wasn't that long ago, Jane. Whatever it was you said to him seems to have helped."

This caught her interest, like something speeding past in her peripheral vision. She knew she ought to ignore it, but she couldn't help spinning back for a double take. "Oh?"

"I don't know what had been going on, but whatever it was, I think it's over. I know I asked you to tell me everything, and yet, for some reason, I don't want to know anything." She gripped the wheel with both hands and shrugged. "I'm just grateful to you, that's all."

Jane looked out the window beside her. They were passing by a sunburnt open field with a weathered white farmhouse off in the distance. There were children playing under an old maple tree that looked half dead, and she could smell cows; shit, in other words. She didn't like the country and never had. She often felt frightened when she was surrounded by trees and undeveloped land, and the inky dark and thick silence of the nights unsettled her. Undoubtedly, it had something to do with being uncomfortable with herself, but then again, what didn't? And yet, there were benefits to living among animals, close to insects and the soil; at the moment, she felt peaceful in the warm car, breathing in manure and dust and secondhand smoke from Caroline's cigarettes. Maybe she really had done Caroline a good turn after all. Maybe it didn't matter that she and Dale had passed a few flirty moments as long as he was more responsive to his wife. She'd talk to Dale this afternoon and clear it all up. "Speaking of gratitude," Jane said, "thank you for being so kind to Gerald."

"Gerald, " Caroline said, laughing out a lungful of smoke. "What a little charmer."

Did she mean it? Of course she did. Caroline was fluent in four languages but didn't know the meaning of the word irony. As for Gerald, he seemed to have fallen in love with her as soon as he laid eyes on her willowy blond loveliness. He followed her around like a smitten paramour. And Caroline was amused and smitten in turn. Would he like to go fishing, canoeing, learn to play tennis, go out sailing with her? No? Well, how about they go up to the attic together and go through her grandmother's trunk? You never knew what fun old clothes you were going to find there.

"You find him charming?" Jane asked, realizing that she was pleading for a more detailed compliment, not caring how desperate she sounded.

"Oh yes," she said, mildly enough to be believable. "I have a feeling he's going to be a very talented designer or artist when he grows up. He has an eye for color and line."

Code for homosexual. But Caroline was being genuinely complimentary, no edge in her voice, and Jane realized, as they drove through the flickering golden light, that she was a little smitten, too. The warm breeze was blowing in the window, scattering Caroline's fine golden hair. She swept it off her face with her right hand, the sun glinting off a hammered silver bracelet she had clamped around her wrist. Jane pulled down the sun visor and looked at herself in the narrow mirror. If Caroline was a perfectly ripe peach, she was a head of broccoli. Freckles, wrinkles, and dark circles. She wasn't living her life properly, that was her problem. Study Sufism and you end up looking like Caroline, run around in circles for ten years and you end up looking like Jane.

They turned onto the long sloping drive that led from the road through the Wade estate and down to the lake. The pines on either side of the drive had to be a hundred feet tall, and the dirt road itself was covered with a blanket of fallen needles and bright leaves. The leaves parted for the Citroën as Caroline shifted and they sped downhill. And then they rounded a curve and the Georgian brick manor house appeared in a clearing, surrounded by acres of yellowing grass. The house itself seemed to be gazing off at the limp green lake and the low rolling mountains. How Dale's pulse must have raced when he saw this estate for the first time. No need to pretend that this view didn't have something to do with his decision to marry Caroline six months after they met. Dale could make all the money he wanted with his real estate deals and his restaurants and his developments; he could make more powerful friends than he could keep track of; he could accumulate dozens of academic degrees and become fluent in ten different accents; but here was the ultimate prize, the one thing he couldn't buy outright and had to marry into: class.

Perhaps breeding explained Caroline's tolerance for all the people at the farmer's market, for Gerald, for Jane herself. Perhaps it explained her emotional generosity, the mild but seemingly genuine interest she had in Thomas's conversation. This world of proud lineage and family tradition, of inherited wealth and social standing, of gracious hosting and polite conversation, of solid brick houses and hundred-acre estates was so different from the disjointed incoherence of Jane's alcoholic background, she and Caroline might as well be different species. She felt simultaneously like a visitor at the zoo and one of the caged animals on display. The only thing that made her feel slightly more at ease was knowing that Dale didn't belong here either. They rattled up to the side of the house and Caroline turned off the engine. The car made a few shuddering protests and sank. Caroline opened her door and stepped one foot out, then seemed to think better of it and turned toward Jane. She put her hand on her knee. "You're a good friend," she said. And leaned over and carefully placed a lemon-scented kiss on Jane's cheek.

Jane practically swooned. She wanted to grab Caroline's hand. Leave Dale, she wanted to say. Let me live here instead. Let me try to be more like you.

Dale was sitting at the kitchen table, talking building codes on the wall phone with the cord stretched across the room. There was a tall glass in front of him filled with ice and—probably—liquor, and he was swirling the ice with two fingers in lazy, distracted circles. His feet, encased in black sandals with Velcro straps, were propped up on the chair beside him. His body language was completely out of sync with his barking tone of voice, so you couldn't tell whether he was having a pleasant, relaxing afternoon in the country or a hellish business crisis. Of course, he probably didn't know himself. Caroline went to the rounded aqua refrigerator—all the appliances in the house were masterpieces of 1940s and 1950s design—to put away a package of goat cheese.

"Where are Thomas and Gerald?" Jane asked quietly.

Dale moved the mouthpiece under his chin. "Down by the lake with the dog. Father-son outing."

Dale had on shorts and a polo jersey; only Thomas and Gerald, both of whom had put on long pants and a sweater that morning, had dressed for the season rather than the weather. She suspected there was some hidden meaning to the comment about "father-son outing," but she didn't care enough about his opinion of either Thomas or Gerald to try to figure it out.

Caroline was loading the freezer with loaves of bread. "Jane had an encounter with Wilma Wyndam at the farmer's market," she said.

"The Nazi?" Dale asked. "Fuck this call," he said, pushed himself out of his chair and slammed down the phone.

"I made the mistake of buying something from her."

Dale laid a brotherly hand on her shoulder and looked into her eyes. "Thanks for supporting our local militia."

Caroline grinned at him and walked out to the cold storage room with a bag of apples. Once Jane was sure she was out of earshot, she said, "I'd like to talk with you."

"I'll look you up when I've averted the current disaster."

2.

Desmond had given her his unfinished draft of the Pauline Anderton manuscript so she could search for a hook they could use for the documentary. She was lying on a faded chintz-covered chaise longue tucked under a dormer window in the third-floor bedroom where she and Thomas had spent the night, reading the manuscript. Helen was curled up on the floor beside the chaise, and she was stroking her fur with one hand. From here, she could see Thomas sitting in a dark green Adirondack chair on the lawn and Gerald reclining under a tree reading a 1920s *Harper's Bazaar* he and Caroline had found in the attic this morning. Caroline was three stories below on the loggia, curled up on a wicker chaise—another family heirloom—a cigarette in one hand, a leather-bound copy of *The Decameron* open on her lap. She'd tied a bandanna around her head to keep her hair from blowing in her eyes, and from here she looked like a frail beauty reclining on the deck of an ocean liner. Other family members were showing up later in the day, but they were staying in the many guest houses scattered around the estate.

"Some people are just born with it," she told Helen. "Not you and not me, doggie, but definitely Miss Just Caroline Wade."

Jane had finished a chapter of the Anderton biography in which Anderton, before being discovered by Walter Winchell, had backed out of a potentially career-making spot on a national radio broadcast because her husband had a head cold and insisted she stay and care for him. With characteristic bluntness, she'd tossed off the unfortunate clash of events as if none of it mattered. There was a quote from a postcard she'd sent to her sister: "Don't bother tuning your radio Saturday night. Deal blew up due to Michael's cold. Who cares? I hate g.d. New York anyway. I'd rather stay in Hell City, FLA, and spill hot soup on the slob. They wanted me to do one of those Cole Porter numbers. Hate them all."

In the book, Desmond interpreted this incident and Anderton's reaction to it as an example of the ways in which Anderton had been a victim of the narrow roles available to a woman in the 1950s. Jane saw it differently. She viewed the whole radio disaster as a willing sacrifice Anderton had made for love. She'd given up a part of her career for the sake of a man she loved deeply, no matter how often she referred to him as a slob or a bastard in her letters. It was probably best not to point it out to Desmond and confuse him further.

A breeze blew in the window, stirring the warm, slightly musty air. The climate was now so unpredictable—hot one day, cold the next—it was like living with an unmedicated manic-depressive who, at any moment, could fly into a frenzied rage and start ripping down the wallpaper. Two days ago there had been massive tornadoes in Texas that killed eighteen people and turned an entire small city into a heap of rubble; a hurricane "of biblical proportions" was threatening St. Kitts. No wonder people everywhere were so uneasy, so fearful. This bedroom, now so warm Jane was beginning to feel drowsy, had been cold last night. The room had twin beds, but when she complained about the chill, Thomas had crawled under the covers with her and cuddled against her back, enfolded her in his big arms and rubbed his feet against hers. They'd listened to the night sounds of the old house and the old-money estate, the creaking of trees against the roof, the shudder of antique windows, the faint smack of the lake against docks and shoreline. When she felt him rocking against her, lightly, shyly sliding his penis along the back of her thigh, she was overcome with loneliness. He started to make love to her, and she found herself drifting away from her own body until she was perched on one of the creaking tree branches, quietly watching him nuzzling and sucking and prodding. When he finished, he slipped back into his own bed and she stayed somewhere outside herself and watched as she buried her face in her pillow and silently wept.

The smell of Caroline's cigarettes wafted in on the breeze and she gazed out the window again. There was Thomas, there was Gerald, the pieces of her life spread out on the rolling yellow leaf-covered lawn below her. How nice it all looked in this late afternoon autumn light. How nice it all looked from a distance.

"You look comfortable."

She turned and Dale was leaning into the room, his hands gripping the door frame, dressed in khaki tennis shorts that made his olive skin look even darker. How did he maintain this disconcerting tan? Probably made furtive visits to a downtown tanning salon run by a homely high school dropout who was in love with him.

"I am comfortable," she said. "It's wonderful here, like taking the cure at a sanatorium. It's so peaceful." And yet watching him walk into the room with his slow, rolling walk, she felt a tremor of anxiety unbalance the melancholy peace she'd felt only a moment ago. The muscles in her body tightened, and she heard a faint ringing in her ears, something high-pitched and very far away. "Did you resolve whatever problem you were having down there?"

"Nearly. They're having some major conflicts between the restaurant design and code requirements. Americans with Disabilities Act, of course. A huge pain in the ass and a killer expense."

"It's awful," Jane said. "Imagine having to cut into your profits just so a few disabled people can have the same quality of life as the rest of us."

He held up his hands. "I just said it was a pain. That's all. Your sarcasm flares up like an allergic reaction around me, Janey."

She shrugged. She hadn't meant to say what she'd said, but he was right, it just happened when she was around him.

Dale looked so silly in this room with its faded wallpaper—pink roses against a soft green background. The incongruity of his burly body and the pastel femininity of the room were almost laughable. It even smelled a little like old face powder up here. Thomas was so much taller than Dale, his head nearly brushed the low ceiling of the room; and yet Dale had the larger, more commanding presence (a word she hated, but like other words she hated—cute, sermonize, marvelous—it had its uses), so much so that she could feel him filling up whatever room he entered. He went to the bureau across the room from her and lifted one of the antique silver hairbrushes.

"I wonder how many decades it's been since someone actually used this thing."

"It's a museum piece," she said. "Usefulness is beside the point."

"Apparently. Have you noticed there are no Touch-Tone phones in the house?"

"Don't knock it, Dale, just because neither one of us has a family history we want to preserve."

When Jane and Brian's parents died, Brian was about to start college. Of course there were no retirement funds set up or insurance policies. A group of concerned relatives had cleared out the house and sold everything off to help raise money. She had no silver hairbrushes or chenille bedspreads, just a jumble of vague memories that grew vaguer every year.

"I wasn't knocking it, Janey. As you probably figured out, I like all the pomp and most of the circumstance."

Jane watched him carefully, taking in his body as he languidly set down the hairbrush and straightened out the bureau scarf. She'd never completely trusted Dale, not for one minute of their marriage, and she didn't trust him now. She felt cornered in the chaise longue, but she didn't know where she'd stand or what she'd do with her hands if she got up.

"You didn't tell me Gerald was in therapy," Dale said.

"No," she said, thrown off guard, "I didn't. Who did?"

"I asked him about his gymnastics classes and he told me they were really therapy sessions."

She should have made it clearer to Gerald that Dr. Rose Garitty was a gymnastics instructor to everyone, not just Sarah, but she hadn't wanted to make him think there was anything wrong with going to therapy. She'd have to figure out a new way to frame it.

"He's okay, isn't he?"

"Of course he's okay. He's just a little . . ." She waved her hand at the subject, hoping to get rid of it.

"He's just a little boy," Dale said. He slipped his hands into the pockets of his shorts, gave them a tug so they rode up his thighs. "What is it you wanted to talk about?" he asked, raising his eyebrows.

Watching him walk toward her, she felt her whole body stiffen. She'd never had a panic attack, but maybe this was how they started. She gripped Helen's fur more tightly, but the dog flopped over on her side, sighed and went deeper into sleep, no help at all. Dale sat down on the end of the chaise, an inquisitive, mocking expression around his lips. She pulled her feet in close to her butt so her knees were up under her chin and some of the manuscript slid off her lap and onto the floor. Dale looked at the fallen pages with his head tilted, but Jane said nothing. Her whole body was trembling now. She wrapped her arms around her shins and squeezed so he wouldn't notice. She could smell his body, warm and oily, like a toasted pecan.

"Hmmm?" he said. "What did you want to talk about?" He put his hand on her ankle and massaged up and down with his thumb.

"Don't do that," she said. Her voice was so hoarse and thick with desire, even she recognized it for what it was.

"Don't do what?" he asked and slid his hand up to her knee and then down the back of her thigh.

"Caroline is right below us."

"Yes, I know. And Thomas and Gerald are out on the lawn. And we can see all of them from this window and if they were to look up they'd see sunlight reflecting off glass."

"That's supposed to make me feel better?"

"I like Thomas," Dale said. He rested his chin on her knee. "He told me more about the history of this area in five minutes than I learned from coming here for five years."

"He's like that," Jane choked out. "He knows everything. Everything, Dale."

"Oh?"

A terrible wave of heat was spreading over her whole body; all of her exposed skin, she worried, must be flushed and hot. She let her head fall back on the chaise and turned her face toward the window while he kissed her knees and slowly slid his hand down her leg until the tips of his fingers were somewhere inside the legs of her shorts. Everything outside looked so peaceful, the falling leaves and Gerald turning the pages of the magazine and Thomas with a book open on the arm of the Adirondack chair. If she could just step outside her body now, she'd be able to find the strength to stop Dale, she'd be able to walk out of this room and down the stairs and outside, she'd be with them, out on the lawn in afternoon sun where she belonged. But that wasn't likely. She couldn't even gather enough strength to stop herself from trembling.

"Don't," she whispered.

One minute, it seemed, you were living your life and shopping for dinner and making plans for your career, you were full of resolve and good intentions, full of love and sacrifice and generosity, and then, without warning or transition, you were sliding off the edge of your world, unable even to reach out a hand to prevent yourself from falling into oblivion. Sweet, hot, sheltering oblivion.

"Stop," she whispered. He pushed down her knees and crawled up onto the chaise until his chest was between her legs and his face was nestling against her stomach. "Please. Please stop."

Something in her tone—what was it?—woke Helen. She got up, crossed the room, looked at Jane with disappointment, and hobbled out to the hallway.

"Janey," he whispered, and ran his hands up the sides of her body and cupped her face.

"Please," she said. "Stop. Please, please, please, please, please."

Thirteen
Childish Behavior

1.

The bedroom was hot, even with the windows open and the ceiling fan spinning slowly overhead. The honking and braying of the traffic on West End Avenue was filling what little space in the room wasn't taken up by the oversized furniture, making the air seem even heavier and denser. With the shades drawn against the afternoon sun, it felt and looked like midsummer. Russell had taken the air conditioner out of the window too early, probably on one of the few cool days they'd had this fall. How kind of him, except it was the sort of chore he always left to Desmond, and the fact that he hadn't waited until Desmond returned to let him do it was just one more piece of suspicious information to slip into the file of evidence Desmond was carefully compiling in his head: self-help book, eyeglasses, air conditioner, possible weight loss, sideburns. (Suspicious or not, this new flaring facial hair had one thing going for it: very unbecoming.)

Russell was in the shower. His parents had called that morning to announce that they were attending a conference of the American Psychological Association at a vast hotel in Midtown Manhattan and would love to have dinner with them. "Notice," Russell had said, as soon as he'd clicked off the phone, "that they waited until the last minute to call. They've probably known about this conference for months, and ordinarily, I would have had something planned for a Saturday night."

Like what? Desmond managed not to ask.

Russell's incessant grumbling about Gloria and Leon was an indication of his devotion to them; he'd arranged his life and career in ways that were guaranteed to displease them mostly because he was afraid that he'd fail at any attempt to earn their approval. Better by far to take himself out of the running than to risk losing the race. Russell's parents usually showed up in New York two or three times a year, most often unannounced, and the four of them would grimace through a tense dinner. Afterward, Russell would retreat into a thousand-page book for several days.

Listening to the hiss of the shower, Desmond felt defeated by all that he understood about Russell's defenses. What was the point in knowing someone this well when it helped bring their betrayals of you into the light?

The most unsettling part of the past twenty-four hours hadn't been Desmond's gnawing suspicions and jealousy, hadn't been the way Russell acted so blasé and accommodating; it had been the way anger routinely rained down on Desmond and then, unaccountably, rearranged itself, molecule by molecule, into lust. Russell would turn his head a certain way or rub at his eyes, or make some other unsurprising, inconsequential gesture, and Desmond would find his whole body dripping with rage. Next thing he knew, he'd be lurching across the room, wrestling Russell to the floor or down onto the bed or pushing him up against a wall, unbuckling and unbuttoning.

At some point last night, Desmond had come to the realization that it was all a matter of reclaiming his territory. Maybe that's what lust boiled down to in the end, a battle over property lines; his had been rekindled by the discovery that a sleazy developer was possibly digging a foundation on his land. It would have been easier, and probably a lot less exhausting, if they'd had one terrible fight and someone, preferably Russell, had ended up getting clobbered.

Desmond maneuvered his way around the furniture to the bureau and opened the top drawer. Inside was a jumble of ties and undershirts and socks, his and his, undifferentiated, tangled up together the way their lives and their identities were now tangled together. How foolish he'd been for agreeing to Russell's suggestion they store their clothes in the same bureau; he should have known that as soon as you give someone what he wants, he loses interest in it.

Underneath a pile of white socks was a pair of black lycra shorts, part of a posing outfit Russell had bought for a sweaty, exhibitionist yoga class he'd attended twice. He tugged at the stretchy material, feeling a strong urge to take hold of each leg and yank them apart at the seams. Instead, he buried his nose in them and inhaled deeply, hoping to catch a whiff of Russell's body. But no, there was no hint of anything more personal than the recycled plastic they were made of and Tide.

He tossed the pants back and began groping toward the corners of the drawer. Early this morning, as he and Russell were lying side by side on their too-big bed, Desmond had reached over and picked up the idiotic self-help book. He'd read the title aloud and asked, "Yours, sweetheart?" trying to sound disapproving in a lightly bemused way.

"Melanie left it here the other night," he said calmly. "She insisted I read it, said it changed her life."

The book, Desmond noted, was closed flat with only a scrap of a *New Yorker* cover someone had been using as a bookmark between the pages. Assuming Desmond hadn't dreamed the things up, that meant Russell had taken the glasses out and hidden them away somewhere. What else would you do with a smoking gun?

"How has her life changed?" he'd asked.

Russell put down the book he was reading, a volume of short novels by Thomas Mann. "Well, for one thing," he said, "her latest crush is on an honest to God, unconflicted, uncloseted lesbian."

"Ah. Progress."

"Yes, it is." He mulled this over for a moment and added, "Although it's true this woman has been in a relationship with a very wealthy woman for the past fifteen years and they have two kids together and are partners in a small advertising agency . . ."

It usually turned out that the people who claim they're looking to change their lives are really looking for a way to justify making the same mistakes over and over. No wonder these self-help books were so popular.

As he poked through the array of generally unused clothing, Desmond knew that if he found the glasses in the dresser drawers, then at least he'd know Russell had stashed them away. By the time he'd rummaged his way to the bottom of the bottom drawer, the bedroom floor was littered with under-pants and jerseys and T-shirts, and he was sweating.

"Looking for something?"

Russell's hair was wet from the shower, and there were traces of shaving cream around the edges of his silly muttonchops.

Their eyes met and it was apparent to Desmond they'd seen each other's cards. Even so, he found himself saying, "I'm looking for a sock."

"Top drawer. Same as always."

"Right."

He crammed the clothes back into the drawers. Russell stood at the closet door, naked, pondering which combination of clothes would displease his parents most. His back looked lean and muscular, a perfect combination of skin, bones, and sinew. What a great, gorgeous front the human body is, a splendid storehouse for secrets and deceptions.

He went to Russell, thinking he'd like to strangle him and found instead that he was running his hands down his back. "Better not," Russell said. "We'll be even later showing up at the restaurant than my parents and lose our edge."

2.

"You just know the food's going to be vulgar in this kind of amusement park," Gloria Abrams said. She took off her glasses and let them fall against her chest on their leather cord, folded up the menu, and tossed it into the middle of the table. "Not that I expected anything else. Morganthal said the dinner they had here last night was 'pretty good,' so I should have known it would be a disaster. I couldn't believe the paper she delivered this afternoon. Complete drivel from start to finish. I was so enraged by the end of it, I could barely stay seated."

Desmond felt Russell grab his thigh under the table and squeeze tightly, his usual signal that he was trying to control the anger he felt toward his mother's scathing disapproval of everything, each shred of which he took personally. Yet, given the current state of things, it felt like a vestige of their former intimacy rather than intimacy itself. Desmond reached down and put his hand over Russell's. "We could have gone somewhere else," Russell said.

"Unfortunately," Gloria said, "we're staying in this hideous hotel, so it was too convenient to resist the temptation to crawl down here and get a table." She gazed at Russell as if she were looking at him for the first time. "Interesting sideburns, darling. I hadn't noticed that look as a new trend."

"I'm trying to start one. My goal is to get photographed for the Style pages of the *Times:* 'Son of infamous child psychologist wearing childish facial hair.' "

"Well, *bonne chance.* You always were ambitious."

Gloria had her long white hair pulled off her face and woven into a complicated braid that she wore draped across her shoulder as if it were a pet snake. She was an attractive woman who frequented hairdressers and manicurists and dance classes but seemed to be preserving the beauty of her face and figure mainly through sheer force of will. She was in her late sixties, and the sunken appearance of her cheeks and hazy pallor of her green eyes gave her an intimidating elegance. If only, Desmond had often thought, Gloria weren't Russell's mother, the two would have been great pals. She was exactly the kind of confident, intelligent, belligerent woman Russell found irresistibly glamorous.

"Oh, no!" she whispered. "There's that Simmons woman. She isn't coming this way, is she? Check for me, will you, Leon?"

Without lowering his menu, Leon said, "She walked past."

"You see how they all avoid me? They're terrified of me, as if I'm strolling around with a bomb in my briefcase. Which, by the way, I am, and plan to deliver at eleven tomorrow morning."

Gloria had based her career as a child psychologist on the theory that treating children like mere children was an insult to their intelligence and integrity, and that most would grow into happier and healthier adults if they weren't forced to waste the first twelve years of their lives playing games and reading silly, witless books. Recently, she'd done a reversal of sorts by publishing a series of papers which attempted to prove that personality and adult behavior were largely the result of the genetic equivalent of Russian roulette and had almost nothing to do with parental influences on either nature or nurture. "Absolving herself," Russell liked to point out, "of any responsibility for the way her children turned out." That might have been the case, but

Desmond had always felt that she was motivated most strongly by a terrible fear of receiving the endorsement of her peers; they, after all, had dismissed her early work and to prove to herself and everyone else that those initial attacks had been personal, she had to make sure they dismissed everything that followed. It wasn't all that different from the stand Russell took with Gloria and Leon.

As Desmond sat politely listening to her describe the paper she was going to deliver tomorrow morning, it occurred to him that Gerald Cody-Miller was, in many ways, Gloria's ideal child: a shrewd, sarcastic, self-possessed adult in an undeveloped body, a six-year-old who showed no discernible interest in childish things and was insulted by any suggestion that his opinions were less valuable than anyone else's. Jane would undoubtedly take enormous comfort in Gloria's harsh theories. He'd have to buy her a copy of Gloria's first book as soon as he got back to Boston.

"I met a child I think you'd find interesting," Desmond told her. "His mother claims he's scoffed at every toy that was ever put in front of him, practically since birth."

"Wonderful. And have they forced them on him?"

"No, I don't think so. They buy him computers and pastry bags and food processors."

Gloria clapped her hands together. "Just delightful. I'd love to meet him. Children are such extraordinary creatures."

"As long as they're not childish, right, mother?"

"As long as they don't have childishness forced on them." She reached across the table and patted Russell's arm. "For some, it comes naturally."

"Yeouch," Russell said, as if her touch had burned him.

The restaurant was located somewhere in the confusing maze of lobbies and gift shops and coffee shops and theaters and big blank ballrooms in one of the many Midtown shopping malls that were trying to pass themselves off as luxury hotels. It had taken them fifteen minutes of walking up and down hallways and stepping into and out of elevators before they found the right eatery. It was so immense, loud, and impersonal, with such a mob of waiters and diners rushing in and out, it could easily have been an airline terminal. At least an airline terminal held the promise that in a matter of minutes you'd be up in the sky somewhere and away from it all. You had to eat your way out of this glass and steel box, no easy task judging from the immense platefuls of food being whisked past the table.

Leon finally put down his menu and yawned. "We should have let Desmond make the reservations. That last place you chose was wonderful."

Leon and Gloria tended to heap praise on Desmond for small, insignificant triumphs like picking out a decent restaurant, while completely ignoring his career, as if it were an embarrassing disfigurement they'd trained themselves not to notice.

"Desmond's been in Boston," Russell said. He tried to remove his hand from Desmond's thigh, but Desmond held it tightly in place. "I would have been happy to make reservations for you. Especially if you'd given me more time. Hint hint."

"We called at 11:30 and it's now 7:30," Leon said, "which by my calculations is eight hours."

"I have 7:50," Gloria said. "I hope your watch isn't going bad, Leon."

Leon frowned and knocked back the dregs in his wineglass. While Gloria had the posture and sleek tidiness of a retired ballerina, Leon Abrams tended to look like a sofa that needed reupholstering. He was two years younger than Gloria but appeared to be aging at a much faster clip. It often happened that one person in a couple siphoned all the health and energy from the other. In Pauline Anderton's case, she'd enjoyed an unprecedented string of vitality beginning virtually on the day her husband had been diagnosed with cancer. On more than one occasion, Desmond had tried to engage Leon in a conversation about his work and academic career, but Leon had merely smiled wanly and assured him that it wouldn't interest him, which, Desmond had to admit, was probably the truth. He didn't really know what an economist did, in a practical sense, and his interest in money went only as far as making sure he had enough to meet his monthly expenses.

A robust young woman dressed in stiff black and white approached the table, flung her hair around and took their orders, uttering vaguely obscene, carefully rehearsed murmurs of approval at each of their choices ("Mmmm, that's my favorite." "Oooo, you're going to *love* that." "I haven't tried that one yet, but I've heard it's *sinful!*"), so that by the time she'd left the table, they all were a little uncomfortable.

"Deerforth College," Gloria said, stroking her braid. "Didn't we know someone there, Leon? It wasn't George Forstein, was it?"

"I'm afraid so."

"That friend of yours who killed himself?" Russell asked. "The biochemist?"

"I don't think either of us ever considered him a friend, did we, Leon? He married that woman who made jewelry and went around selling it out of the trunk of her car. She insisted on having all those babies." Gloria held out her palm, as if she'd just offered them the explanation for the suicide.

"Did this happen at Deerforth?" Desmond asked hopefully, thinking it finally might give him something to discuss with senior faculty.

"No," Leon said. "His behavior became so erratic, even Deerforth wouldn't keep him. In retrospect, he probably had a brain tumor."

"He had a horrible marriage," Gloria corrected. "He was bored senseless by that wife, and on top of that, he was lazy. How are things at the store, darling?"

"Interesting segue, mother. Things are fine. If you come down tomorrow I'll give you the employee discount on any purchase over fifty dollars."

"Ah, well, if you throw in shipping, I'll consider it."

Before Russell had a chance to lob back the next sarcastic rejoinder, the long-haired waitress and a coterie of helpers lugged overflowing plates to their table, set them down in front of them, and then stood back admiring their handiwork. Every gesture, every comment from the staff seemed to have been scripted by an army of market analysts in the home office of whatever multinational corporation owned this hotel. Even the arrangement of the food on the plate appeared overly rehearsed.

"They must use shovels back in the kitchen," Gloria said, giving the pile of food on her plate a nudge with the back of her fork.

Desmond looked in dismay at the greasy mound of pasta in front of him, one more obstacle to overcome today. The only thing more appetite-suppressing than slow service was having the food delivered this quickly. The evening was not going well. No worse than these evenings usually went perhaps, but Desmond was beginning to feel like a corgi, desperate to run circles around the table and herd everyone together, to reassure Russell, if only for a moment, that his was a convincing facsimile of a happy family.

A few years ago, he realized that Russell read as voraciously and ambitiously as he did to please his parents; but given the push-me pull-you nature of their relationship, Russell usually told them he was reading a mindless potboiler or scandal-mongering memoir to shock and dismay them. There was some potential for actual conversation in Thomas Mann, since he wrote the only novels in world literature Leon didn't consider "gossip with commas."

"Leon," he said. Leon looked up from his plate of food hopefully, as if he'd been waiting for something to interest him. "When I came home last night, Russell was reading a collection of Thomas Mann's short novels. Is there one that's a particular favorite of yours?"

"I do have a favorite." He went back to his food, swallowed a mouthful of pasta, and said, "But I don't think it's one Russell would care for."

"Why not tell us the title?" Desmond said. "We can take bets on whether or not it's one Russell cares for." Russell nudged him under the table. "We can play a little parlor game after dinner," Desmond went on, "and see who can quote the most lines from it."

Leon sighed. As he was about to mention a title, Russell cut him off. "I don't know what Desmond's talking about. I'm reading a self-help book. It's all about reaching your full potential."

Desmond felt his face grow hot. He didn't want to hear any more about that book, not now or ever. Russell wasn't reading it and never would read it. Bringing it up was a slap in his face, recrimination for trying to referee Russell's boxing match with his parents.

"The problem with helping people reach their full potential," Gloria said, "is that it's basically the same thing as eliminating hope. People are happiest believing the fiction that they're only using twenty percent of their talent and intelligence. Help them become all that they can ever be and they'll really have something to be depressed about."

There was a muscle twitching in Russell's face, just under his cheekbone. Maybe she was suggesting that Russell had reached his full potential in running the secondhand shop, reading self-help books, and co-habiting with Desmond. When the waitress came back and delivered her canned questions to make sure everyone was happy, Russell asked for directions to the men's room and got up from the table. After a moment of awkward silence, Gloria said, "You're good to put up with our little family squabbles, Desmond."

"Why wouldn't I?" Desmond said. "I'm part of the family."

She looked slightly stunned by the comment as well she might have been; Desmond couldn't remember ever being so blunt with her before. He was a little stunned himself. He'd always felt most comfortable standing on the periphery of these mudslinging contests, safely ensconced as a spectator in the stands. He wasn't sure what had compelled him to step into the middle of it.

"You are indeed," Gloria said. "I didn't mean to imply you weren't. Sometimes I'm just not sure what Russell *wants* from us." She was looking directly into Desmond's eyes, stroking her braid, challenging him.

"You'd have to ask him, but I'd guess it's what we all want—childish things: finger paints and facile compliments."

"Oh, dear. Not my specialty."

"No. That's why seeing you make the effort would be so meaningful."

Gloria said nothing, but she stopped stroking her hair.

"Rough weekend?" Leon asked.

"Possibly."

There was nothing left to say, at least nothing anyone wanted to say, so they sat in silence trying to chip away at the mountains of food in front of them. When Russell returned to the table, Gloria sat back in her seat and gazed at him. "You know," she said finally, "those chops, or whatever you call them, the sideburns, are really quite becoming. They balance out your face."

"Wouldn't you know it," Russell said. "I was just looking at them in the mirror and decided to shave them off."

3.

As soon as Russell had left for work the next morning, Desmond called Peter at the apartment he'd moved into shortly after Velan had kicked him out. "Please come down," Peter begged. "I want to show off the place. It's a fresh look for me. Clear, clean, no more of that designer crap. And I really want you to meet Sandy. You're going to love him."

"To be honest," Desmond said, "I was hoping I might get a chance to talk to you alone. After I've met Sandy, naturally." Naturally, he'd have to put up with a show-and-tell of apartment and boyfriend, a tour of the rooms and discussion of the furniture. He'd have to sit patiently while Peter and Sandy groped each other in front of him. People always have to display new real estate and relationships before the paint starts to crack on both.

"Come at noon," Peter said. "You'll get the whole picture."

Peter's current digs were in a new development near the West Side Highway. The building was a sleek glass column surrounded by other sleek glass columns in various stages of completion. The whole neighborhood seemed to have been invented in the past five years and had the feeling of an extraordinarily well-heeled frontier town. What a perfect place to start a new life, a faceless building at the edge of the known world with the grinding and crashing of construction playing in the background twenty-four hours a day. But the noise, along with the bright sunlight and the unseasonable heat and the dusty yellow air, seemed to disappear as soon as Desmond entered the building's calm lobby. Here was the future, a carefully controlled environment that allowed you to see the outside world while shielding you from its every danger and inconvenience. Never mind about global deforestation and dwindling species of plants; there were trees here and exotic red flowers, the air smelled sweet and was filled with soft, seductive sounds that could have been music or bird calls. The cool, golden elevator lifted Desmond to the twenty-third floor with smooth efficiency, and he stepped off, pleasantly disoriented, as if he'd been transported to another world.

Sandy opened the door for him. He gripped his hand as if he were trying to crack a walnut. "It's just *great* to finally meet you, Desmond," he said, emphasizing his words with the overdone enthusiasm of someone trying to lure you into a pyramid sales scheme. "Not that I don't feel as if we're friends already."

Desmond had been expecting youth and vitality, but Sandy couldn't have been more than thirty. He had light hair cut in a geometric flattop and the solid body and perfect posture of a hefty dancer. Everything he was wearing—gray polo shirt, knee-length khaki shorts—appeared to have been ironed within the past hour, and his skin was so clean and glowing, it looked as if it had been polished with a rag. Good with children and dogs, Desmond thought, everyone's favorite uncle, probably planning to impregnate a lesbian friend or adopt a baby. He led Desmond into the apartment, his shoulders thrown back with proprietary confidence, silently proclaiming that no matter how long Peter and Velan had been a couple and despite the fact that he Sandy didn't live here, he Sandy was in control.

The clean, clear decor Peter had touted over the phone turned out to be a long living room with views of the Hudson furnished with two matching bone-colored love seats and a glass coffee table. There were a few framed travel posters leaning against the walls and a stack of books on the floor that looked as if they'd been placed there by an interior decorator. The sun was blazing right outside the window, but thanks to some technological miracle, the pane was cool to the touch.

"Nice, isn't it?" Sandy asked. "I told Peter no clutter. I go through with a trash bag every time I come over. He'll be out in a minute. Take a seat." He tugged up the legs of his shorts, lowered himself onto the love seat opposite

Desmond, and spread his arms out across the back. You'd have to say he was an attractive man, yet there was something corpselike about the antiseptic spotlessness of his skin; and the forced baritone of his voice and muscularity of his calves seemed to be obvious instances of protesting too much. "Peter tells me you're up in Boston," he said.

"I have a teaching position for one semester." Desmond started to describe Deerforth College.

Sandy nodded in the eager, polite way of someone feigning interest, then took advantage of a pause and said, "I grew up outside Boston. A small New England town called Stoneham." It would have sounded charming enough, if only Desmond hadn't had the misfortune of once getting lost in the bland sprawl of this particular suburb. When Sandy asked him if he'd heard of it, Desmond felt the kind thing to do was say he hadn't. "I'll have to show you around some time," Sandy said.

"That would be wonderful."

"And your lover runs a secondhand shop. I think I might have been in there once," he said, as if congratulations were therefore in order. "What do you think of Boston?"

"It's growing on me."

"It's funny you should use those words." Sandy leaned forward with genuine amazement, a smile lighting up his face. "Just this morning I was telling Peter I think I've *out*grown Boston."

"Well—"

"And you're working on a book of some kind?"

"Yes, I'm—"

"I love to read. A couple of us at Merrill Lynch formed a reading group. We get together once a month and discuss a book. Are you in a reading group?"

It didn't matter how Desmond answered any of these questions, since it was obvious Sandy was asking them so he could toss in his own opinions. After offering an annotated list of the books his group had read over the past sixteen months, Sandy sprang up from the love seat and clapped his hands. "I'm being rude," he said. "What can I get you to drink?"

"Oh, maybe a—"

"I'm going to have a Pepsi. But Peter probably has a bottle of wine hidden away somewhere if you like."

"Soda would be fine."

When Peter finally emerged from the bedroom, he dashed over to

Desmond and embraced him tightly. He swept his hand around the room and then nodded toward the kitchen where Sandy was rattling ice. "Can you believe how far I've come since the last time we were together? Can you believe it? God, it's good to see you."

What he obviously meant was that it was good to have Desmond see him in his present state of bliss. He'd lost weight, cut his hair into a variation on Sandy's crew cut, had his bushy eyebrows trimmed, and—a wild guess, but Desmond would have put money on it—had something done to his face with a laser. His skin was taut and raw. There was no denying he looked younger and more rested, but Desmond found himself disconcerted by the way this old acquaintance had started to resemble his new boyfriend. The two were wearing almost identical outfits and similar pairs of leather sandals. Good for him, Desmond tried to convince himself, although suddenly, unaccountably, he found himself flooded with fond memories of Velan's disarming drunken wit.

Sandy passed out glasses and sat beside Peter on the love seat. Peter put his arm around Sandy's shoulder, the two kissed, and Desmond sat facing them, feeling as if he were watching an unimaginative puppet show. "Tell me the truth, Desmond," Peter said, nodding his head toward Sandy. "Am I the luckiest guy in the world, or what?"

Talk about your rhetorical questions. "I'd say you're pretty lucky." If there was anything more excruciating than being dragged into the middle of someone's marital discord it was being seated in the front row for a performance of their honeymoon. Especially if you'd recently heard the bell tolling on your own relationship.

"And he told you he's from Boston? Small world, isn't it? Let me tell you . . ."

The window was behind them, and Desmond could see harsh sunlight flashing off a crane, sending a message in Morse code—unreadable, but still more interesting than Peter's paean to Sandy's extraordinary skills at preparing delectable low-fat dinners. Strange, Desmond thought, how staying in a difficult relationship with a difficult person had lent Peter a certain amount of dignity and gravitas. Sitting beside perfectly pleasant and pleasing Sandy, Peter looked like a two-dimensional copy of his former self.

When Sandy got up and left for choir practice at a church he belonged to, Peter raised his eyebrows and lifted his hands, as if struck dumb by his extraordinary good fortune. "He's even religious," he finally said.

Desmond nodded, wondering why this was supposed to be considered a virtue. He didn't understand the attraction to and reverence for organized religions, many of which struck him as fairy-tale justifications for self-righteousness, bake sales, and murder.

"I didn't know it could be like this, Desmond. I didn't know I could be so happy." With this confession, Peter seemed to be overcome with emotion and buried his face in his hands. Now, obviously, was not the best time to bring up Desmond's concerns about Russell. Peter pulled himself together, wiped at his eyes and said, "I don't suppose you've seen Velan since you've been back."

"No," Desmond said. "I haven't. I've been a little preoccupied."

Peter shook his head with dismay and ran his hand across the plateau of stubble on top of his head. "Bitter. He's turned bitter."

"Oh?"

"And have you heard the latest? He's going to AA meetings. Unbelievable. He hasn't had a drink for *weeks*." He held up his hand and started counting off the list of Velan's offenses on his fingers. "Hasn't had a drink in almost a month, hasn't smoked a cigarette in two months, goes to a therapy group of some kind, and just got a promotion. Oh, and some kind of exercise routine where they strap you to a board and stretch you out like a piece of taffy. Can you imagine it?"

"Frankly, no."

"And, and he started taking antidepressants. He was never depressed a day in his life. I'll tell you what his problem is. His problem is that he thinks we broke up because I started seeing Sandy." He shook his head in disgust.

"That wasn't the reason?"

"That was a symptom. The problem is that Velan's impossible. I'm lucky I got out of that relationship alive. Everything has to be his way or no way. I couldn't breathe without running it past him first."

Not, Desmond wasn't about to point out, that Sandy wasn't doing the same thing, simply with a different aesthetic.

"And here's the kicker. Are you ready for this? Velan's started 'seeing someone,' to use his delicate euphemism. Knowing Velan, it's highly unlikely he's 'seeing' much of anyone since most of his dating time is probably spent flat on his stomach with his face buried in the pillow."

"Yeah. Well." Desmond tilted his glass up to his mouth, dismayed to realize he'd already drained it dry and chewed up all the ice. "It sounds to me," he said, "as if you and Velan are still in close contact."

"We talk every once in a while," he said quietly. He picked a book from the top of the pile near the love seat and examined its cover and spine as if he'd never seen it before. He put back the book and looked at Desmond apologetically, all the anger in his voice and face exorcised.

Thank God Desmond had kept his mouth shut, hadn't been duped into letting out his true feelings about Velan. He'd give this little separation four months, six maximum, before Peter and Velan were once again a model couple, visiting a counselor twice a week and planning a trip to Tuscany. Desmond's promiscuous sympathies trotted over to Sandy, devout young man, off singing God's praises while his boyfriend subconsciously mooned over a lost love. "You miss Velan," Desmond ventured.

Peter rubbed at his face with his hands as if he were washing it with soap. "I've been with him—I was with him—so long, it's like he's a part of me, and now that part, gangrenous or not, has been amputated. A confession, all right? I feel amazingly revitalized with Sandy. Like I'm walking around with this stronger, stiffer hard-on. Metaphorically speaking."

"Right."

"But somewhere in the back of my mind, I'm waiting to go back home and show it off to Velan."

"I suppose you're going to have to tell him that."

"Yes, I suppose I am. When I'm ready."

Having unburdened himself of this confession, he relaxed back onto the love seat, looking much more like the man Desmond had known for many years now. "So tell me everything," he said. "I want to hear all about your adventures. Don't hold anything back. What do you think of these love seats? Too austere? Sandy picked them out. He's great, isn't he?"

4.

That was a predictable waste of time, Desmond thought as he was ejected from the cool lobby to the steaming sidewalk. He hadn't really believed Peter was going to solve anything for him, but he hadn't planned on spending quite so much time discussing the virtues of ABC Carpet and Home.

By the end of dinner the night before, Russell and his parents had settled back into their ready-aim-fire conversational style, and Desmond had felt exiled for having the audacity to try and pull them together and include himself. Even so, when they parted at the hotel's elevators, Gloria had embraced Russell and told him she planned to visit the store when the conference broke up on Sunday afternoon. Maybe something good had come out of it.

Not, apparently, that Russell saw it that way. When they stepped out of the hotel, Russell went on the attack: "I don't know what you said when I left the table, but whatever it was, I wish you hadn't."

"I didn't say much of anything."

"That pathetic attempt by my mother to compliment me, after thirty-five years of criticism. She likes my sideburns. Please. And then she looks toward you as if to say, 'See, I did as you suggested and he completely rejected me.' "

"You do an amazingly good imitation of her, you know."

"I've been very careful never to ask them for anything, especially praise. I make one quick trip to the bathroom and you undo all those years of work. I assume she'll never make it to the store, but even the suggestion makes me uncomfortable. And bringing up my reading habits, to try and impress Leon. I've never been interested in impressing them."

"My intentions were good, sweetheart."

"But ultimately, Desmond, it isn't your business."

Two months earlier, he would have welcomed these words as an indication of a healthy distance between them. But now they stung. "Since when aren't you my business?"

"You give up a certain number of rights when you make a unilateral decision to move away for a handful of months, and, as you're walking out the door, as much as tell a friend you're embarrassed by our commitment to each other. And then you come back for a visit, still not ready to talk, just hump away for twenty-four hours, like you've hired me and want to get your money's worth."

"You didn't seem to mind about the humping part. Not, I gather, that you're in desperate need."

There was a conversation stopper, at least for a few minutes. The problem with silence, so welcome at some moments, was that it could mean anything: "How dare you suggest such a thing" or "How did you find out?"

Finally, Russell said, "What's that supposed to mean?"

"You tell me, Russell. Why should I have to do all the *work* in this relationship?"

true enough

Thinking back on it as he walked away from Peter's newly minted neighborhood, Desmond saw that the conversation had, at that point, hit a patch of black ice, one of those invisible hazards of driving in unpredictable climates, and gone into a swerve. The only way to wrest control of the vehicle, he'd been taught, is to steer into the swerve—face it head-on—which unfortunately happens to be completely counterintuitive. Rather than discussing the book and the eyeglasses and his own suspicions and calmly pumping the brakes, he followed his heart and swung the wheel back and forth wildly, as if he were driving a bumper car. In the volley of indirect insults and evasions that followed, they'd narrowly missed hitting a tree, but had ended up stuck in a snowbank on the side of the road, Russell acting as if Desmond had offended him, Desmond refusing to beg for more information.

When he looked up again, he realized he'd sauntered downtown and was walking along the edges of Times Square. He glanced around, looking for a familiar landmark. In the years before he met Russell, he'd often wandered down here when he was feeling lonely, stuck in his work, or swamped with unspecified anxiety. He would stroll through the movie theaters, the bookstores and arcades, the strip joints, until he was anesthetized by the sweet stink of flesh and the heat of anonymous intimacy. Nothing looked familiar today. The community of furtive men—bound together by rampaging loneliness and lust—had been replaced by groups of shopping and sun-dazed tourists. Families in loud, insignia-emblazoned T-shirts and sneakers swarmed the streets, clutching shopping bags, carrying children, stupefied by spending. It was all supposed to be so much more upright, now that the porn and prostitutes had been driven out; yet there was something far more obscene about this vulgar hunger for stunningly pointless stuff. And at least the cock and pussy hounds of old had the decency to display a little guilt and self-hatred.

He should leap on the subway, go to Russell's store, tell all and make amends. But like Peter, he'd have to do it when he was ready, and he wasn't ready yet.

When he looked up again, he was standing in front of the Disney store. The doors were open, and they seemed to be sucking their victims in, right off the street. It made the peepshows and plastic penises, the inept photography of the porn magazines and grimy amateurism of the banished theaters seem quaint, cozy, and downright wholesome. In the five years he'd been with Russell, the world had changed completely. If he'd ended up here with the unconscious intention of avenging Russell's betrayal of him, he'd come to

191

the wrong place. But there was cool air blowing out from the store, and inside he could hear the siren call of lush, cheap music. If you couldn't fight your own fate, how could you possibly hope to fight Disney? Maybe there was some childish thing in there he could buy as a present for irascible Gerald.

Fourteen
Specific Plans

1.

If Dr. Berman had been merely overweight, it was very likely Jane wouldn't have noticed. She herself made no claims of physical perfection, and she rarely scrutinized bodies, male or female, looking for flaws. These days, people talked about an extra ten or twenty pounds as if they were a sign of emotional or moral decay, which just went to show how prudish and puritanical the country had become. But Berman was obese in an exaggerated way she found distracting. As soon as she walked into his office last summer, after a two-year vacation from treatment, she could tell that he'd added another thirty or forty pounds to his frame.

She sat opposite him in his office—a tidy sterile room he'd painted yellow, probably in the hopes that patients would find it cheerful—trying not to notice the way he filled up his chair to overflowing. Almost as disconcerting as his size itself was the fact that it seemed to matter to her. Not that it was anything she could discuss with the good doctor. He frequently coaxed her to talk about *their* relationship, a topic she found entirely beside the point and nonetheless embarrassing.

Instead of talking about *them,* she should be telling him exactly what had happened in New Hampshire, the entire disastrous course of events, which, she'd promised herself as she drove out here, was what she was going to do, no matter how humiliating, demeaning, and painful. Berman had his stubby fingers laced together and resting on his belly and was gazing at her with his patented look of calm, benevolent inquiry, his head tilted toward his right shoulder at a nearly imperceptible angle. She loathed these awkward moments of silent staring, but she knew that if she didn't allow them every once in a while, didn't force herself to sit, speechless and utterly still, he'd think she was chattering to fill time and avoid an important issue. She wanted to be sure—and hated herself for wanting it—that he didn't think of her as one of those neurotic time bombs she saw in his waiting room, pinched, nervous men and women sitting there, ready to implode.

The hideous vertical blinds over the window were directing sunlight in her eyes. Best not to start complaining about that, she reminded herself, or Berman would see the whole thing as another diversionary tactic. The session was almost half over and so far she'd managed to talk exclusively about Sarah, another useful time filler.

As the silence began to stretch thin, Berman's eyes opened wider—his speechless "Well?"—and she saw that he was rapidly approaching boredom.

"I think I mentioned that I went to Dale's wife's family's estate over the weekend." She kept the tone casual, as if it were of little consequence.

"Yes, you did mention it."

Of course he wasn't about to ask her if she'd had a good time, something as direct and simple and conversationally *normal* as that, something as helpful as that. Better to hand her some rope and see if she used it to hang herself.

"It's a lovely place—trees, water, mountains. Or maybe they're officially hills. It's New Hampshire, so they're probably mountains. I wasn't taking in much of the scenery. Among other things, it was unseasonably hot. Not that there are reliable seasons anymore. It's one of those old family estates Grammy or Gammy or Bammy bought back in the good old days, when you could have indentured servants and didn't have to pay taxes. I'm sure the acreage is haunted by the ghosts of people who died keeping the Wade family in firewood and ice." Maybe she was beginning to sound unappreciative and resentful of Caroline, who had, after all, been lovely in every possible way. Considering what had happened, she couldn't even utter Caroline's name. "Still," she said, "an impressive place in its self-reverential way." She brushed some lint off her skirt and adjusted her wristwatch. "We came back a day early."

The head tilted just a fraction more to the right. "Oh?"

"Dale was involved in some business crisis back in Boston. He was completely preoccupied, and we felt we were in the way."

"Both you and Thomas felt you were in the way."

It was one of those annoying statements that was really a question, a prod in a particular direction, not asking for information directly, but restating what she'd said in the hopes that she'd stumble along and reveal more than she'd intended to reveal. After all these years, she knew every one of Berman's tricks, the inflections and wordings he used to prompt her. Somehow, she still fell for them; before she could stop herself, she was saying, "Yes, we had a family discussion and we agreed we were in the way, with all the phone calls and his bad mood and whatever was going on behind the scenes."

"You and Thomas discussed it and were in agreement." He was nodding, not necessarily an indication that he believed her.

"Yes. And then we left."

That should be blunt and unambiguous enough to satisfy him, nothing to echo back to her as a verbal trap. It was the truth, too. They had left. So why did she feel so hollow and defeated right now, so magnificently frustrated? She could see her plan for telling *all* slipping out of her grasp. Not that she intended to go into detail. Some people claimed to give their shrinks the whole hard-core, X-rated version of their lives, fantasies included, but that was mostly bragging and flaunting of conquests. It would take some doing to make the episode on the chaise longue pornographic; she'd been fully clothed throughout, a detail that mattered very much to her at the time and mattered more, as a point of pride, now. But clothed or not, she'd been so undone, physically and emotionally, by the way Dale had touched her—kept touching her, refusing to stop—and by the smell of his body and the hot sting of his breath, she'd been unable to move for half an hour after he straightened himself out and left the room. And when she finally did get up, she felt bruised and raw, still tender from the release of all that pent-up passion, still wet. Two hours later, she had to sit at the dinner table having polite conversation with Caroline and Thomas, with Gerald sitting there scowling at her as if he'd witnessed everything. When Dale stood behind Caroline and put his arms around her and kissed the back of her neck, she'd felt a wave of jealousy and relief that was so confusing, she went out to the porch and smoked one of Caroline's cigarettes.

Thinking about what had happened that afternoon, she felt a miserable trickle of arousal. With the sun shining in her eyes, she felt needled and panicked. Berman wasn't going to help her sort all this out, she could see it clearly now, and she wanted out of this room. Either that or to collapse against Berman's big, soft stomach and make a full confession. She was so desperate, the thought of his plump hands smoothing down her hair struck her as appealing. And yet, she could see the distance between what she wanted and what she knew she was going to get opening up in front of her. "The sun," she said, way too loudly, "is right in my eyes!"

"Would you like me to close the blinds?" Berman asked.

"No," she said. "I'd like you to dim the sun. Of course I'd like you to close the blinds."

Berman heaved himself up out of his chair and fiddled with a beaded cord, letting in a wider flash of white light, and then, finally, shutting it out altogether. The room was suddenly dark, as if a lamp had been turned off, quieter somehow, the atmosphere more unexpectedly intimate. He returned to his seat and looked at her with his bland, forgiving expression, refusing to be insulted by her tone.

"Now I should apologize for my sarcasm," she said.

"Do you want to apologize?"

"Oh, please, Dr. Berman, please. I've been coming to you for a total of three years, off and on; I've poured thousands of dollars into your bank account, I've talked my throat dry, and you're still tossing rhetorical softballs at me as if I hadn't progressed out of the batting practice stage. As if I'm just another one of your patients."

She looked up at him. Nothing. He appeared to have absorbed this comment as unflinchingly as he absorbed everything else she said. Their eyes met for a few seconds and then he reached over and turned on the light beside his chair. "Oh shit," she said. "Now I have to apologize for *that* slip and explain that I really *do* know I *am* just another one of your patients and that I'm *not* some special case, but that—shoot me—I'd like to think I'm a little bit more sane and sensible and self-aware than that sunburnt skeleton I see in your waiting room every Tuesday or some of the other wrecks—whose lives, I know, believe me, I know, are undoubtedly more organized and orderly and focused than mine—and would like to hear *some*thing from you other than the usual, predictable, textbook therapeutic, Psych 101 jargon."

Jane clutched the arms of her chair, trying to prop herself up, trying to look in control, even though she felt a peculiar weakness in her thighs. She was melting. Maybe she was having a nervous breakdown. That at least would be something concrete, something you could slap a label on. Berman was his placid self, but in the soft shadows, his face looked handsome and disconcertingly sensual. She'd probably have to lift her shirt and unhook her bra to get a reaction out of him. Fortunately she hadn't said *that* out loud. He raised one eyebrow and crossed his feet at the ankles, like a polite schoolgirl. Expensive brown socks with flecks of gray, she noted, undoubtedly presents from his wife.

"All I mean," Jane said, "is that I'd like you to say something unpredictable. Does that make me a horrible person? And please don't bounce that question back in my face; it's obvious I think it *does* make me a horrible person or I wouldn't bother to ask."

Berman shrugged, a gesture she hadn't seen him use before, and the newness, the unpredictability of it alarmed her. In an unfamiliarly stern tone of voice, he said, "Maybe you'd like to say something unpredictable yourself."

"Me?"

"Yes, Jane, you."

"Such as what?"

"It's up to you. But if you're looking for a suggestion, you might start by telling me what happened in New Hampshire."

Had he ever, in all the years she'd been coming to see him, called her by her first name before? She thought not. In phone messages, he called her Ms. Cody and in person, he avoided her name altogether. "I thought I just told you what happened."

There was something hard and determined in Berman's eyes. Apparently she'd insulted him with her earlier rant and now he was getting back at her. "I know you think you did," he said.

His head came over again and his dark, small eyes narrowed and he unclasped his fingers and put his hands somewhere in the direction of his hips and she saw the whole situation very clearly: he knew exactly what had happened in New Hampshire. He'd probably known what had been going through her mind from the moment she mentioned having coffee with Dale, had probably known it had been drinks that first time, not coffee at all. So in addition to the humiliation of him knowing that she'd been carrying on a heavy flirtation with her ex-husband and had had a—what would you call it? A fully clothed orgasmic encounter?—he knew she'd been avoiding full disclosure. He was now in a position to sit in judgment on two counts. And, on top of it all, she was paying him for this.

They were back to their staring contest. She commanded herself not to blink. "I did tell you what happened."

"Good," he said.

She experienced a moment of triumph and then, somewhere deep inside her, heard a door slam shut. She glanced over at the digital clock beside Berman, the clock with the vast, bright numerals, just so no one could mistake the time and squeeze another sixty seconds out of his day. She had another six minutes to fill. It was like being trapped in a vault with a time-release lock. She hated most sessions with Berman these days, but these early morning sessions were the worst. What a way to begin the day. She should try yoga or meditation, something where you didn't have to pay for the privilege of providing all the entertainment yourself. "So as soon as we got back from New Hampshire," she said, "Sarah came over to the house to tell us that her heat wasn't working. As if we didn't know it had been in the eighties all weekend."

But now Berman was merely staring at her, not nodding, not encouraging her with his usual, subtle head movements. A numeral clicked over on the digital clock. Five more minutes.

2.

The morning air, damp and with a trace of Canadian cool in it, woke her up as soon as she stepped outside. The entire session had been like one of those brief, intense naps that leave you drooling and disoriented. It was over, that was the best you could say about it. She could cancel her next appointment, just to show him . . . something. She turned right and walked along the sidewalk, buoyed up by the sudden appearance of autumn and the cancellation plan, then realized she hadn't left her car in this direction. She turned around and walked back, past Berman's building. But after walking another half block, she couldn't be sure she'd left it in this direction either. A light changed on the corner and traffic roared up Commonwealth Avenue. The trolley through the center of the street screeched along the tracks. She looked across the trolley tracks, hoping she'd left the car there. She was edging toward panic. She'd find the car eventually, but it troubled her that there was such a wide, dark hole in her memory.

She looked down the street, vaguely in the direction of Back Bay. Somewhere in that tangle of buildings was Desmond's small, quiet room with its circular windows and pretty, obstructed views. What a joy it would be to live in that kind of stripped-down, uncomplicated arrangement, one in which there wasn't room to hide anything. So what if you had to walk down the hall to reach the toilet. Her throat tightened, and her breathing became more strained.

If Berman looked out one of his windows, he'd be able to see her, spinning in circles, muddled, pacing back and forth like a lunatic. He wouldn't look out one of his windows; he lined up his patients with barely a minute between appointments. A truly crazy person who didn't have control over herself would grab one of the passersby and beg for help. She wrapped her jacket around her more tightly and it came to her at once: she'd left her car on a side street just steps away.

But as she headed in that direction, she thought about Desmond again, about his simple room, his simple, absentee relationship. Maybe he was unhappy from time to time, unsatisfied, lonely, but surely he wasn't misplacing his car and walking zigzags at ten in the morning. That was what she wanted, that simplicity. There was only one thing to do, one way to turn the day around, make up for not having told Berman about Dale: prove Berman's suspicions wrong. Call Dale and call the whole thing off. By the time she went back for her next session, the whole business would be in the past and it wouldn't matter that she hadn't brought it up. Her life would have the simple clarity of Desmond's and she'd use all of this energy to move their joint project forward. Progress. Going to Berman had done her some good, after all. It wasn't time and money down the drain.

She'd call from the goddamned cell phone as soon as she got to the car. It was Wednesday. Dale seemed to have free time on Wednesday afternoons. They'd meet and talk about what had happened and she'd explain why their little flirtation was over. Then she'd go visit Desmond and make specific plans for the next couple of weeks.

Fifteen
Insert Coin, Pull Lever

1.

"You know, of course, that this entire area of the city was once part of the harbor, a swampy tidal basin they started dredging in the late nineteenth century. Imported a lot of Dutch engineers who were used to this kind of project—dikes and so on. Most people don't realize it, but the ground here is still spongy. It's sinking. Residents are trying to save on water bills by drilling wells on their tiny plots, undermining their own foundations. Shortsighted, to say the least. They'll see how much they've saved when the supporting structures of their buildings start to collapse."

Desmond nodded. He and Brian Cody were standing on the corner of Commonwealth Avenue and Dartmouth Street, surveying the wide, tree-lined boulevard as a dusty breeze blew around them. They'd been together for over an hour, and so far, the tour of Boston had gone very much like this: Brian pointed out some of the historical and architectural features of a particular neighborhood and then gave a quick excoriating summary that emphasized an architect or developer's poor judgment, lack of taste or professional expertise: the hideous concrete mistake of City Hall Plaza; the technical oversight that resulted in windows falling out of the Hancock Building; the ill-conceived, inelegant renovations owners had done on town houses in the South End. The message in every case was that if he'd been hired or consulted for the job, it would have been done with more taste, expertise, and professionalism. The tour had been a show of narcissistic self-confidence, but underneath that, Desmond sensed a foundation as spongy and suspect as the ground they were now standing on. Which was—not that anyone was mentioning it yet—a few short blocks from Desmond's room.

"Still," Desmond said, "it is a beautiful street."

"It has its moments. This Beaux Arts birthday cake here is one, discounting the new windows, of course."

"Where do you and Joyce live?"

"A Cambridge apartment. I started renting it when I was in design school, gutted it completely and redesigned the entire floor plan. It's perfect for my needs."

"And big enough for the three of you, once the baby's born?"

He tipped his head doubtfully from side to side. "I may have to give up a corner of my study for a nursery, as long as I can soundproof it. Alternately, I'll try to do something interesting with the walk-in closet in the entryway. It would be nice to have more rooms, but I'm not moving out to the suburbs to get them."

Although Desmond agreed with most of Brian's aesthetic opinions, he wanted to challenge him and counter the snobbery and self-aggrandizement in much of what he said. Giving up a corner of his study was an act of spectacular generosity? And what kind of person sticks his baby in a closet, walk-in or not? "I can't imagine you fitting into suburban life," Desmond said, hoping there was an insult buried in the comment somewhere.

"That building over there," Brian said, "was once a finishing school for proper Bostonian girls. Now it's a finishing school of a different sort: a plastic surgery center. They completely destroyed the interior—ironic when you think about it, making something ugly for the sake of beauty."

The warm wind and bright sun stung Desmond's face. He was beginning to feel sandblasted. Brian still looked dashingly pale, unaffected by the elements the way many architects, Desmond had noted, tended to be. He had on a snug green suit, and was wearing a pair of tiny, dark green sunglasses that made him look like an actor going incognito so he'd be recognized.

"Wouldn't it make more financial sense for you and Joyce to own?" Desmond asked.

"Some people are renters and some are buyers. It's in my nature to be a renter."

Thus far, Brian hadn't mentioned Joyce's name once. If Desmond hadn't met his wife, he'd find it hard to believe Brian wasn't a bachelor. When they were touring the Italian neighborhood in the North End of the city, Brian had spoken at length about the trip "he" had taken to Italy and the hotel "he" had stayed in in Rome and the way "his" time in Bologna had influenced his own work. It wasn't until Desmond pressed him for details, asking specifically if he'd gone alone, that it became apparent the trip under discussion was his and Joyce's honeymoon.

When Desmond returned from New York, he'd called Brian's office and left a message, thinking it would be good for his ego to arrange a distraction, especially one that involved ambivalent flirtation. Brian had returned the call promptly and here they were, four days later. But throughout this boring tour business—on the whole, Desmond probably would have preferred one of those gossipy, inaccurate spins around the city in a retired amphibious military vehicle—Brian had been cold and evasive, so much so that Desmond had begun to wonder if he'd been mistaken about his intentions all along. It didn't matter that much to him; merely placing the call had made Desmond feel marginally better about whatever it was Russell was or wasn't doing.

They circled a few more blocks and eventually wound their way back to the commotion on Boylston Street. From the corner where they were standing, Desmond could see the front of the Boylston Hotel; Jane had pointed it out to him one day and said it was a good place to get drunk, should the urge hit him. What a miserable betrayal of Jane, to be spending the afternoon with her brother under these circumstances. What a deeper betrayal of Joyce, but after all, he didn't know her, not really, even though he was firmly convinced that he would be a better, happier, and more interesting person if his allegiance were to her and not her narcissistic, pansexual husband. At least Desmond was doing his best to wedge her name into the conversation every once in a while. That must count for something. Brian, too, seemed to be gazing at the Boylston Hotel. Perhaps he'd had a nefarious encounter there, or maybe he was about to launch into another one of his disparaging rants. Just to discourage him, Desmond said, in a tone of voice he hoped wasn't overly friendly, "Do you give this Welcome Wagon tour to every new arrival?"

"No," Brian said. "Not unless the new arrival interests me."

Since Brian had shown absolutely no interest in Desmond's writing, teaching, life in New York, opinions of what they were looking at, or general impressions of the city, there was only one way to interpret the comment. But even that was a stretch considering that Brian had rarely looked in his direction throughout this long, opinionated excursion. Sooner or later Desmond was going to have to make a move, if for no other reason than because he was tired of looking at buildings, and wanted to get off the street. "You know," Desmond said, "I live only a few blocks from here."

"Yes," Brian said. He brushed dust off the sleeves of his jacket, finally acknowledging the existence of the outer world. "I do know."

"You asked Jane?"

He seemed offended by the suggestion. "I don't ask anything of Jane. If I did, she'd come back with a mile-long list of favors."

"There's a great view of the river from my window. You can see Bunker Hill Monument, too, if you get just the right angle. Shall we head back there?"

"That's fine with me. I could use a cup of coffee."

Desmond had run out of coffee a few days ago, but hopefully it wouldn't come to that anyway.

As they were crossing Newbury Street, he heard someone call out Brian's name in a weary singsong, and looked up to see Rosemary Boyle coming toward them. Her hair was pulled back in its tight bun and her eyes were carefully hidden behind a pair of round sunglasses. She looked from Brian to Desmond and back again, seemed to make the obvious assumption, and said, "Out for a stroll?"

"Brian's taking me on a tour of the city," Desmond said. "The low points of all the architectural highlights."

She turned her mouth down slightly. "Thank you for not inviting me," she said. "If I was forced to read one more plaque about the historical significance of a bronze duck, I'd lose my mind."

"You'd better watch out," Desmond said. "You're next on the list; he gives the tour to all newcomers."

"In that case, I'm off the hook. Brian and I are yesterday's news." A gust of wind cut down the street and ruffled her gray cashmere sweater. "Right, Brian?"

"I know better than to disagree with you, Rosemary."

"Yes, you do. That's because I trained you when you were young." Brian was still young, Desmond decided, possibly seven or more years younger than his sister. Rosemary lifted a black leather briefcase she had in her right hand. Unlike everything else about her, this was untidy; there was a clump of frayed newspapers and Xerox sheets sticking out of the top and the plastic handle of a portable umbrella. "Student papers," she said. "A ream of scintillating analyses of poetry in America. Compare and contrast Wallace Stevens and . . . I forget who else. I was supposed to 'correct' them weeks ago. I'm headed over to one of Boston's many romantic little boîtes where I'll plant myself at a corner table until I've read every page."

"Do you have to grade them?" Desmond asked.

"They're interested in psychoanalysis, not grades. I figure out exactly what everyone wants to hear about themselves, then I tell them the opposite. They love it."

"I'll have to try it with my students."

"It wouldn't work for you. You've crafted a nice-guy persona for yourself, so you have to give them what they want. Otherwise, they'd storm the dean's office and demand your resignation. I'm considered a cold, spiteful bitch, so they want to be scolded and dominated by me. They'd be happiest if I came to class in spike heels and black leather pants."

"I'm surprised you don't," Brian said.

"The pants are at the cleaner. Well, I'd invite you to join me for a drink, but it looks to me as if you two have a few more sites to see."

They said their goodbyes, but as they were turning to leave, Rosemary put her hand on Desmond's arm and told him that she'd read his Lewis Westerly biography and had found it fascinating. Desmond was stunned, both by the fact that she'd read the book and by the tone of sincerity in her voice, a complete shift from her usual ironic sniping. "Thank you," he said. "Thank you for reading it."

"Much to my surprise, it was a pleasure. Of course, it's always a pleasure to read about the torment of someone's hidden sex life. You feel as if you've caught them red-handed."

2.

Miraculously, Loretta and Henry, installed in their recliners, merely nodded when Desmond and Brian climbed the staircase. ("A potential fall hazard," Brian said, hand shaking the banister, "but at least they haven't destroyed the place with a shoddy renovation.") In Desmond's room, Brian went to the round window and stared out at the windswept river, evidently contemplating something, possibly the sight of Cambridge just across the water. Desmond wondered if he was suddenly plagued by guilt, although that seemed doubtful. Surely you had to acknowledge the existence of other people in order to experience guilt, and a man who referred to his honeymoon as "my trip to Italy" wasn't a likely candidate for that.

When he finally turned from the window, he glanced around the room slowly, taking in every detail with a blank expression that did little to hide his disapproval. He looked down at himself and then met Desmond's gaze; it was the first time he'd looked at him directly since they'd been together, and his pale eyes were softer than he expected. Desmond was shocked to realize that he'd missed an essential fact about Brian: he was shy. "What do you think Rosemary meant," he asked, "when she talked about . . . catching someone red-handed?"

There was a rueful tone in his voice that Desmond found almost touching. It didn't make sense to try to demonize Brian. A lot of gay men he knew complained about the scruples of married men they'd had affairs with, as if cheating with someone of the same gender as your spouse put you in a morally superior position.

"Rosemary was talking about the subject of a biography I wrote. He had a private life that was very different from his public persona."

Brian sat on the edge of the bed and unbuttoned his jacket. "How so?"

"Most strikingly, he had a reputation as a compulsive womanizer, but in his journals, he wrote almost exclusively about 'playing gin,' code, I discovered, for picking up young men on the street. There were at least two gin games recounted every week for the last couple decades of his life: 'Disappointing game,' 'Big win,' 'Dealt a marvelous hand this afternoon,' and so on. I asked one of his ex-wives about his card playing and she scoffed at the idea, said he hated to play and usually cheated when he did. These secret pickups were the center of his life."

"Maybe his marriages were the center of his life and these were simply outlets."

"That's what he tried to tell himself, but looking at it objectively, you wouldn't draw that conclusion."

Brian crossed his legs. "It sounds as if he was confused."

"I don't think he was. He knew what he wanted, he just didn't want to take responsibility for his desires." As Desmond looked across the room to where Brian was sitting, he saw clearly that the afternoon was at a crossroads. Brian looked vulnerable and a little lost, sitting on the edge of the bed tucked under the eave, his shirt tightly buttoned and his pants carefully zipped. If Desmond didn't take decisive action immediately, he'd be presiding over a therapy session that would last until dusk, listening to Brian's marital problems and wayward desires and possibly, a more horrifying thought, confessing some of his own. "Tell me, Brian," he said. "Do *you* play gin?"

This question seemed to catch Brian off guard. He cleared his throat and said, "I've been known to, from time to time. Depending on who I'm with."

"Let's say you're with me."

Brian looked off in the direction of the window, apparently contemplating an honest answer. The last thing Desmond needed at this point was another rejection. He crossed the room and sat on the bed beside Brian. He gripped the back of his neck, pulled him toward him, and gave him a blunt, hard kiss on the lips, partly hoping it would make him uncomfortable. It didn't. Brian wrapped his arms around Desmond's shoulders so tightly, their lips were mashed together. Desmond hadn't done this with anyone other than Russell in five years, and he was struck, as if this were the first time he'd kissed someone, by the shocking intimacy of the act: the shared saliva, the exchange of breath, the brush of skin against skin. Brian's body had a strong soapy smell with a trace of nervous sweat under it and his mouth tasted like stale mint. Strange smells, reminding Desmond that he was doing this with a stranger, which wouldn't be bad if he didn't know the stranger's name, along with the names of his sister, wife, and assorted relatives. He worked his hands against Brian's chest, pried himself away from him, and stood up. Brian misunderstood the gesture. He slipped off his jacket and was unbuttoning his shirt as if it were about to burst into flames.

Shit, Desmond thought as he grudgingly took off his own shirt, I should have opted for the therapy session. Brian kicked off his shoes and stepped out of his pants. He had a smooth, pale body, tight and surprisingly muscular. He hesitated for a moment about the underpants, then seemed to decide to leave them on. Well, why not? If you were going to go to the trouble of buying aquamarine bikini briefs, you might as well show them off. He wondered who was going to end up laundering these things. Hopefully not Joyce. Brian sat back down on the bed with his legs spread. Desmond realized, looking down at this attractive and absurdly available body, that there was nothing he wanted to do with it. He felt panicked by the inevitability of what was about to happen, as if he was willingly boarding an airplane he knew was destined to crash.

"Nice abs," Brian said in a husky voice.

It was a ridiculous attempt at a compliment. Not only that, there was something about the exercise-video nature of the word "abs" that put the last nail in the coffin of Desmond's desire or whatever it was that had propelled him this far. It was too late to walk away from this, so he walked closer to the bed. Brian drew Desmond toward him and stuck his tongue into his belly button. From where he was standing, Desmond could see a scrap of view out the round window and an unfortunately larger scrap of his own reflection in the mirror over his bureau. If you eliminate all desire and passion from sex, the whole thing begins to look unfortunately similar to playing a slot machine: insert coin, pull lever, numbly hope for the jackpot to spew out. Goddamn Russell. He'd talked Desmond into all those years of monogamy, gotten him used to sex connected to emotion—to love, if you wanted to get specific—and then went out and broke the very vows he'd insisted upon.

Brian was moaning as he buried his face deeper into Desmond's stomach. Obviously some kind of belly button obsession, which, given Joyce's delicate condition, Desmond was not going to think about too seriously. Instead, he thought about Russell, about the infuriating possibility that he was engaged in something along these lines at this very minute. Except in his case, he was probably enjoying it. Conjuring up Russell's name and the image of his face and body helped. Desmond looked at himself in the mirror again. Oh well, he thought, insert coin, pull lever, take your chances. It's only a quarter.

Sixteen
The Walsh Kids

1.

Jane gazed out the window of the rented van as Desmond drove through downtown Waugborn, an architecturally neutered area in which every building—most brick, many nearly a hundred years old—had been partly sheathed in beige vinyl or white aluminum, stripped of their individuality and integrity. Once, this probably had been a collection of family businesses selling the necessities of life; now it looked like a row of portable storage units housing makeshift martial arts schools, video rental outlets, and grimy magazine stores with advertisements for a multitude of lottery games plastered on their windows. A handwritten sign on one proudly proclaimed: "We Had Two $50 Winners This Year Alone." That told you everything you needed to know about what constituted winning in a place like this.

Waugborn was about fifteen miles from downtown Boston, but Jane had never driven through it. She occasionally read about it in the paper, usually a lurid story of a prom at which there'd been a drug overdose or a shooting, or a report of a tractor trailer overturning and spilling hazardous material onto a watershed area. This was one of those towns people had moved to in order to escape the dangers and congestion of urban living. Now it was as densely packed as the inner city but lacked the city's conveniences and cultural benefits. Unless you consider a store that sells "balloons for every occasion" a cultural benefit. It was mid-afternoon, balmy and aggressively bright. Jane had on her darkest sunglasses, both to cut down on the glare and to hide her own exhausted eyes. The dusty downtown streets were populated by hunched teenaged boys cradling cigarettes and young mothers wearing windbreakers, pushing strollers, and in general, looking as weary as she felt.

Suburban blight. She'd suggest it as a topic for *Dinner Conversation,* haul in a few sociologists and urban planners, try to book the mayor of Waugborn or a similar disaster area, a few parents worried about their kids getting gunned down in the junior high. In terms of the pilot, this shot through the window of the van would be a perfect visual metaphor for Anderton's life, or at least the end of it: the loss of identity, the death of a career. Come to think of it, it was a perfect visual metaphor for Jane's own blighted heart, full of contorted emotions. It didn't make sense to her that you could feel so energized and renewed one minute and thoroughly depleted the next; so filled with excitement and erotic anticipation at ten in the morning and so flattened by guilt and self-loathing by noon.

"Anderton's brother-in-law grew up in Waugborn," Desmond said, "and her sister, Margo, spent the majority of her life here. After Anderton's husband died, she moved up here to be with Margo and her husband. She came to love the place."

"Was she schizophrenic?" Chloe asked. She and Tim Gough, an undergraduate from Emerson College doing an internship at WGTB, were seated in the back of the van surrounded by lights, tripods, and an assortment of video equipment they'd borrowed from the station. "A lot of people who have neurological chemical imbalances are misdiagnosed as alcoholics, drug abusers, and anorexics."

Wouldn't it be a tremendous relief, Jane thought, to have something as neat and decisive, something as blameless and clinically sanctioned as a neurological chemical imbalance? That way, you could explain away your own rotten behavior, your own choices. You wouldn't have to slip so deeply into the murky regions of right and wrong, wouldn't have to be consumed by regret. Maybe a pill or a transplant or a treatment would numb all your imbalanced longing and lust and the rest of the unwieldy baggage she'd been carting around recently. Including—possibly, who knew?—love. Come to think of it, she did feel as if most of the chemical compounds in her brain had taken it upon themselves to have a blow-out party.

"There's no indication of schizophrenia," Desmond said. "No family history of it or any other mental illness."

"Oh." Chloe sounded crushed. It would be a tough job to turn Pauline Anderton into a victim, but if anyone was up to the task, it was Chloe. She was clearly horrified by the degraded downtown, and probably horrified by the ordinariness of it, too.

"You're sure you're comfortable using this equipment?" Jane asked.

"Pretty much. The camera I used for my senior project was a little more sophisticated than this stuff, but one of the guys at the station spent about five hours going over everything with me. And Tim's majoring in media studies."

Silent, long-haired Tim was so in awe of Chloe, he'd barely shown signs of life since they left the station. Today Chloe had come to work wearing a dark business suit. With her fashion-model frame and cascading curls of raven hair, even this conservative outfit look inexplicably fetching. Everything Chloe wore would make Jane look like a drab, harried lawyer or an over-the-hill hooker. There was no point in trying to do something about her fashion sense now; in five years, when she hit her mid-forties, she'd turn invisible, assuming she wasn't already. But for the past few weeks, despite all the chemical imbalances in her brain, she'd felt wondrously *visible* for the first time in years. It didn't matter that she wasn't turning heads on the street, that people like Chloe had sorted her into the remainder bin; someone was actually seeing her when he looked at her, and approved of what he was seeing. Too bad—too inconvenient—that the someone was Dale, but you can't have everything.

Jane could tell Desmond was disappointed that Chloe and an unpaid assistant were doing the taping. Maybe he suspected something. She wasn't going to press the issue; reassuring him would only make him more doubtful and might raise too many questions. This was just a preliminary taping and Chloe would do a good job with this as she did with everything else. Jane had seen her senior thesis film, a thirty-minute documentary about her mother and her mother's family, all gorgeous camera angles of her gorgeous mother sitting in pools of gorgeous fading sunlight. Of course, given the fact that it had been made by Chloe, it was a story about one woman's triumph over adversity, even though, as far as Jane could tell, the most adversity mom had to overcome these days was traffic on the Long Island Expressway as the family shuttled back and forth between their Park Avenue duplex and the house in East Hampton. Despite herself, Jane had watched the end of the film fighting back tears, mostly because it was such a bald, blunt love letter from a child to her adored mother. Jane never had felt that way about her own Scotch-soaked mother, and if Gerald ever made a film about Jane, it would probably fall into the horror movie genre.

They'd left behind the morbid downtown and had entered a sprawl of houses pressed too close together with a few browning hedges between them and an occasional lonely tree, like something preserved for its historical significance. Desmond pulled up in front of a low mint green house with faded green and white metal awnings over the windows. "This was Margo and her husband's house," he said. "That window above the garage was Pauline's room. There were only a few houses around when they lived here, but they've developed every available inch of open land."

Not exactly Graceland, but there was something interesting in the way the paint was peeling around the trim and in the rust stains dripping from the awnings. "Who lives there now?" Jane asked.

"I'm not sure. It was sold years ago. After Pauline died, Margo got sick and she and her husband moved to Florida."

"What's the architectural style?" Chloe asked.

"I think it's called a raised ranch," Desmond said. "Although it could be a split-level. I can't remember exactly what I call it in the book. We should have brought along an architectural consultant."

This was an obvious reference to Brian, a reference Jane was not going to pursue. Two days ago, Rosemary had called and mentioned that she'd bumped into Brian and Desmond in Boston. There was nothing wrong with that, but the fact that Desmond hadn't said anything about it had given her pause. "I guess they were headed for Desmond's apartment," Rosemary had said. Having been at Desmond's apartment, that didn't seem likely. And yet . . .

"I'll call it a raised ranch," Chloe said. "Sounds exotic." She made a note in a black leather notebook while Tim hooked his stringy yellow hair behind his ears and watched her with slack-jawed admiration.

Jane wanted to think she'd once been like Chloe, young and ambitious and exacting, but she knew it was more simple and complicated than that. Yes, she'd been ambitious, but usually impatient to *be* somewhere and annoyed with the process of *getting* there. Desmond pulled the van away from the house and continued down the block. Maybe this impatience had infected all of her life. Maybe she'd been so eager to be in love with Thomas, with a man who loved and respected her, had been so eager to be a reliable wife and mother, after having failed once at being a wife, she hadn't paid enough attention to the tiny details involved with getting there.

They stopped in front of an even more unpromising house, a brown, vinyl-covered raised ranch or bungalow or Gothic cathedral for all she knew. Planted in the front lawn was a cut-out piece of plywood depicting a woman bending over at the waist and showing her bloomers. In the big picture window, two egg-shaped people in sweatshirts were waving cheerfully.

"Wow," Chloe said, awestruck. "This is right out of Diane Arbus."

Maybe so, but they looked content in their house, happy to welcome their guests, thoroughly pleased to be themselves.

2.

"I would say you don't look a day older than you did a couple of years ago," Mr. Walsh told Desmond, "but I guess you'd know I was lying. Wouldn't he, Jean?"

"Oh, sure," Mrs. Walsh said. "Dennis knows how old he looks."

The last time Desmond had interviewed these two, a couple of years ago now, they'd called him every male name that began with a D—Dennis, Donald, Douglas, Drew, Derrick, David, Daniel. You'd think they might have landed on Desmond once, purely by chance, but it had never happened. He'd stopped trying to correct them, figuring it couldn't matter all that much, even though he found the whole business infuriating. Best not to alienate them. They were important to him, the only link he'd found to this part of Anderton's life. They'd given him eyewitness information about her final years, her death, her burial. And their batty behavior, gaudy house, and cheerful, inappropriate laughter could be major assets on screen. They were all sitting in oversized furniture in a small room at the back of the house paneled in something that was supposed to be wood. The windows looked out to what had been a field two years ago and was now a tidy circle of new houses

212

which, like the furniture, were much too big for the setting. Desmond was willing to bet they all had four or five bathrooms, each with a slew of water-thirsty tubs and toilets and shower stalls.

"They finally got rid of that barren wasteland we had out there," Mr. Walsh said, following Desmond's gaze. "Came in and put up those houses in a few days."

"It feels so much more private now," Mrs. Walsh added. "Before, anybody could be out in that field looking in the windows."

"I see what you mean," Desmond said.

The disappointingly amateur team of Chloe and Tim was setting up the lights and video equipment while he and Jane tried to make conversation. It was probably a good thing Jane was being cautious with the fifteen grand they'd been granted, but he wasn't convinced that the camera crew was the best place to get economical. Mr. and Mrs. Walsh were sitting on a red plaid sofa shoved against one wall, both in navy blue sweatshirts, looking like a pair of plumped pillows. They had similarly round bodies and sagging jowls and matching receding hairlines. Tim, who, in tight blue jeans and a baggy yellow T-shirt, looked almost prepubescent, held a light meter up to their faces, took a reading, and reported back to Chloe.

"Should I introduce you to the new kids while we wait?" Mrs. Walsh asked. She took a sip from her glass of apple juice, a Scotch-and-water if ever Desmond had seen one.

Jane looked at Desmond warily. "They won't be here for the taping will they?"

"Oh, sure, they'll be here through the whole thing. But they're quiet. Aren't they, Denny?"

Not the kids, Desmond thought. "Yes, they're very quiet."

Mr. Walsh clapped his hands and the lights went on in a tall glass cabinet against one wall. Inside was Mrs. Walsh's collection of ceramic figurines, many of whom Desmond had met the last time he was here. The collection had multiplied significantly in two years, so much so that the shelves looked as crowded as Brighton Beach on a steamy July afternoon. Mrs. Walsh un-locked the cabinet and took out the figure of an androgynous boy. He ap-peared to be wearing too much rouge and his pants were hanging low in back, revealing the crack of his lush behind as he bent down to French kiss a puppy. "This is Carey," she said, "our youngest. He's a collector's item. And this one here's his sister, Cookie." Cookie was a nymphet in hot pants whose toes were being licked by a kitten, to her obvious delight. You had to wonder how people got away with selling these things on the open market. Jane looked at Carey suspiciously before handing him back to Mrs. Walsh.

"Do you buy these on the Internet?" she asked.

"Oh, no," she said. "They just arrive here when they need a good home."

Desmond had played along with this the last time he visited, but in the presence of Jane, the little game struck him as humiliating. Mr. Walsh had gotten up to refill the juice glasses, and Desmond suddenly wished he hadn't turned down their offer of a drink so quickly.

"Oh and here's the one you were so smitten with last time," Mrs. Walsh cooed, pulling out a bare-chested boy with a fishing pole sticking up between his legs. "He was excited to hear you were coming today."

"He looks it," Jane said. "Did Pauline like your collection?"

Mr. Walsh emerged from the kitchen with two full glasses and handed one to his wife. "She kept threatening to smash up the whole case," he laughed. "She was a great one for joking around."

"I think we're set over here," Chloe said. "Whenever you're ready."

Mr. and Mrs. Walsh went back to their plaid sofa. Mr. gripped his wife's knee, while Mrs. grinned into the camera. They were old pros at this, loved to talk about Pauline Anderton or, Desmond suspected, just about anything else, but it might help to reassure them. "I know we've covered most everything you have to say in the earlier talks I had with you, but we want to get some of it down on videotape for our film on Pauline. So I'd like you to relax and enjoy yourselves, and don't worry about repeating things. This is very informal. As much as possible, pretend you're talking to me for the first time."

"We don't remember what we told you last time, so that should be no problem," Mr. Walsh said. He was stroking his wife's knee in such a casual, distracted way, it was almost as if he were scratching himself. Maybe that's love, Desmond thought, and then stopped himself from pursuing it further. He'd given up looking for a definition of love. Any definition was bound to be as unreliable and fleeting as the thing itself. "Is there anything you'd like to add here, Jane?"

She pulled a strand of hair back from her face and he saw, for the first time that day, the dark circles of exhaustion around her eyes. "Tell us everything you know," she said. "Don't worry about trying to say nice things about Anderton. Our goal is to present her whole life, so if some of it is a little unflattering, it isn't going to matter. The best way to honor a person is to tell the truth about her, without judging any of it."

"In that case," Mr. Walsh said, "I wish we had some filthy gossip, but basically, we were just good pals."

They didn't need much prompting once they got going, remembering the first time they'd met Paulie, the first time they'd had her over for dinner, the way she liked to regale them with stories about the people she'd met when she was at the peak of her fame. "Not that we believed all of it," Mr. Walsh said, staring straight into the camera.

"Not that we believed most of it," Mrs. Walsh said.

Desmond had heard the bulk of this before, although the Walshes seemed to be adding new details as they went along, perhaps inspired to embellish by the presence of the camera.

"Margo had a fit when she heard Paulie was coming to move in with her," Mrs. Walsh said. "And Carter, the husband, he came stomping over here and told us he'd move out if that big so-and-so moved in with them." She used her fingers to pick at her thin, curly hair. "I guess they were worried she'd come in town with that giant personality of hers and suck up all the oxygen."

"Either that or start singing," Mr. Walsh chuckled.

"Still," Desmond said, "you told me they all got along quite well."

"Oh, I don't mean they didn't get along once she arrived." Mrs. Walsh brought her face down to her glass and sipped off the top inch of liquid. "It's just that they had a fit when they *heard* she was coming. Wasn't that it?"

"They were afraid she'd be bored living out here surrounded by trees. Not that they needed to worry about that with the police showing up a couple times a month."

There was a bowl of hard candy on the table between Desmond's and Jane's chairs and Jane was poking through it as if she was looking for a particular flavor. Her hand stopped moving and she glanced up. "Police?" she asked.

"Oh, if Paulie had tossed back a few drinks and was in a good mood," Mr. Walsh said, "she'd get belligerent and start throwing around the furniture. The sister was always afraid the TV was going to go through the window and spoil their reputation in the neighborhood."

"Not that anyone would have cared," Mrs. Walsh added. "We were always open-minded and didn't get in each other's business. As long as she didn't bust up *our* furniture."

"What would she do if she was in a bad mood?" Jane asked.

Mrs. Walsh chuckled and took another sip of her apple juice. "Well, if she was in a bad mood, you didn't want to be around. I think that's why Margo spent so much time in the hospital, just to get away from her sister."

Desmond was thumbing through an indexed file of transcripts of his previous interviews with the Walshes. The room was getting increasingly hot, probably from the lights, and he wished he could take off his sweater. "I believe you told me Margo had some early signs of Alzheimer's and that was why she was in and out of the hospital."

Mr. Walsh shrugged dramatically and smoothed his sweatshirt down over his stomach. "It could well have been that," he said. "Either way, we don't believe in snooping. If Margo and Carter needed help, they knew we were here."

Chloe passed a note to Jane. She opened the folded slip of paper and showed it to Desmond. *"Elder Abuse?? Common w/ Alz."*

"Are you suggesting Pauline was beating up her sister?" Jane asked.

The Walshes looked at each other. "I'm not sure you'd call it beating her up," Mr. Walsh said. "Would you call it that, hon?"

"No, I'd say more like roughhousing. The usual sibling rivalry stuff. I doubt there was ever any bloodshed. Underneath it all, they loved each other. Deeply."

Desmond didn't know what to say. The last time he'd been with this hapless couple, they'd told him touching stories about Pauline Anderton and her final days. Admittedly, they'd mentioned a few scenes in restaurants, a drunken fight with a neighbor who was now dead, but nothing quite so tawdry as this. He was tempted to tell Chloe to turn off the camera, but it didn't seem right to stop them just because they were contradicting themselves. He put down his file, popped one of the hard candies into his mouth and tried to crack it in half with his teeth. It was this portion of Anderton's life, and the years leading up to it, that still didn't make sense to him. If her behavior was bordering on violent, it had to mean she was unhappy—with herself, her life. Perhaps with her decision to scrap her whole career and move to this undistinguished part of the country. That was one way to make sense of it in light of what he already knew. He made a note: she wished she'd gone back to singing after her husband died.

Mrs. Walsh sighed and sipped. "We always thought Margo would be the first one to go, what with the Alzheimer's and the cancer and the heart problems and that kidney thing."

"Didn't she have diabetes?" Mr. Walsh asked.

"Probably. And Paulie was strong as an ox. You never know how your life is going to change and rot. The kids are the only things that remain unchanged, innocent for eternity. That's why I love them so. I think Pauline was jealous of them, them staying so young and her getting fatter and meaner every day.

She blew up like a balloon at the end there." Mrs. Walsh puffed out her cheeks and thrust her chest forward and seemed to expand on the sofa. "It got so she could hardly fit through doors."

"Now wait a minute," Desmond said. "I've seen pictures of her from her last years, and there's no indication she was that fat."

"Oh, she knew how to hide it," Mrs. Walsh said. "I'll give her that. She'd wear cute little sweaters so you couldn't tell."

Mr. Walsh nodded in agreement. "We didn't hold any grudges against her, even after she ruined that Christmas party of ours. By the time we got back from Arizona that winter, she was dead and Margo and Carter had moved on to Florida, which was where Margo always said she wanted to live. I guess it was a good thing they took in Paulie after all because she ended up leaving them some money."

Desmond was crunching the sour ball between his teeth, leafing through his notes. It would have been equally annoying but not nearly as humiliating if Jane hadn't been here to listen to all these contradictions. He found the page he was looking for and scanned it quickly. "You *told* me," he said, "that you were here when she died, that you went to the burial. 'We had a good long cry at the grave site.' That's a direct quote."

"Well sure, we went to the grave site. We went that summer. I can't guarantee about the tears."

"I definitely cried," Mrs. Walsh said. "I cry about everything. Are you sure you don't want a little drink to wash down that candy, Davie?"

"Now that you mention it, a drink might be nice. Jane?"

"I could use a splash of something."

3.

When Chloe complained that the sun had started to shine into the lens of the video camera and that they'd have to rearrange the lights, Jane and Desmond went out to the backyard to get some air. It felt more humid than it had earlier in the day, as if yet another spell of summer weather was blowing in, even though it was the third week in October. Jane hated it. There were about seven days in the year when the temperature was tolerable now. There had been at least four weather disasters described as "the storm of the century" in the past six months alone. Jane took a pack of cigarettes out of the pocket of her skirt.

"I didn't know you smoke," Desmond said.

"No, neither did I. Anyway, I don't. Not really. I hate the smell of cigarettes and the taste of them and what they do to you, but I love the matches." It was true. She pulled out a small, green box of Rosebud wooden matches, slid it open and struck one. She loved the bright flare of light and heat. She shook out the match and put its ashy remains back in the box. She'd sneaked a cigarette from Caroline's pack in New Hampshire, smoked it outside in the cool night air, and now she was up to three or four a day. Just what she deserved, punishment for her bad behavior, although a complicated kind of punishment, since she enjoyed the compact drama of lighting up and inhaling until the little cylinder of tobacco was used up and gone.

She turned back to Desmond, but he was staring mournfully across the Walshes' wooden fence to the neighboring yard where a hodgepodge of plastic toys was spread out across the yellowing grass. She found those big, smooth, garish jungle gyms and tricycles and kiddie pools among the ugliest things on the planet and had felt partly relieved that Gerald had never shown a flicker of interest in any of them and was, from time to time, openly disdainful of children who did. Another part of her was worried that it might mean he was doomed to miss out on some important piece of childhood and that it was her fault: perhaps he was trying to please her by dismissing toys as "ugly" and "stupid." This morning, Desmond had given her a book by his lover's mother which he said she'd probably find interesting. He hadn't elaborated on why she'd find it interesting, but it seemed to indicate he thought either she or Gerald needed help on the question of child rearing.

"It sounds as if Pauline Anderton was quite a hellion," Jane said.

He shook his head. "What troubles me is that it contradicts so much of what they said before."

"Don't you often find there are several versions of the truth?"

"Yes, but usually not from the same source. And then all that nonsense about Anderton getting obese. I've seen pictures of her shortly before she died. I hate to think the Walshes are that unreliable."

"Sometimes people like to perform for the camera," Jane said. "I've seen it before."

"They did take to it, didn't they?"

In this awful glare of sunlight, Desmond looked older than she'd seen him look before. More gray in his hair, and more crepey wrinkles around the eyes. Jane put out her cigarette carefully and slipped the butt into the pack. It was so easy to offend people with cigarettes these days, it was almost refreshing. She'd have to carry a pack around as a weapon, even after she'd given up this latest bout of indulgence. "Is that all that's troubling you?" Jane asked.

"The Walshes? Well, no." He put on a pair of sunglasses and squinted across the yard. "In addition to everything else, Russell and I can't seem to get our footing in dealing with each other. The last couple of times we've talked, I've had the feeling the air is leaking out of our relationship."

"Should I press for details?"

"Please don't. It would probably embarrass both of us."

That was vague enough to mean anything, but if he was referring to some situation with her brother, he was right, she really didn't care to know.

"Have you interviewed Anderton's sister? Margo?"

Desmond shook his head. "She's in an old-age home in Florida, with advanced Alzheimer's. I talked with her on the phone once, but she was fairly incoherent. The last time I talked with Anderton's daughter, she said her aunt only has a few more months."

"Maybe she's covering up. Maybe she's afraid Margo will tell you something truly unflattering about Pauline."

"No, I believed her. The daughter's pretty straightforward. Lorna's like her mother in that."

"Where do we go from here?"

"You're the executive producer. If we've got the money, I think we should go down to Florida and interview Lorna relatively soon. She might be able to clear some of this up. It would be good to get some shots of her collection of Anderton memorabilia."

Their money. She shouldn't have told Desmond the station was coming through with the seed money until they actually did, but at the time, she was so certain they would, it hadn't seemed to matter. Given how long it was taking David Trask to come back with an answer, she'd started to wonder. Dale had already made it clear he'd be happy to invest, so she'd take him up on his offer. He was rolling in dough these days. His income and net worth had probably quadrupled since Massachusetts had chucked out rent control and handed a blank check to landlords and real estate developers. He might as well throw some of it at the arts. If she really tried, she could probably get him to set up a foundation of some kind. A very small one. She'd ask him for ten thousand, which ought to be more than enough to get the two of them plus their camera crew down to Florida.

"When would we go?" she asked.

"That would depend on Lorna's schedule, but hopefully before Thanksgiving. I'll talk to her. We can set a date and make the reservations."

Jane rattled the box of matches. "Good," she said. "I could use a vacation."

Seventeen
The Piano Lesson

1.

"Have you decided what you're going to do about the baby's bedroom?" Desmond asked.

There was a long silence from the other end of the line, and then Brian said, "I'm still mulling it over."

"It's getting a little late, isn't it? I thought the baby was due—"

"Any day now. That's true. I can put something together quickly. I did most of the work on my apartment myself, all in the course of a couple of weeks, so it won't be a problem."

He was still mulling over where to put the baby's bedroom in *his* apartment. One thing was certain, they weren't going to put the crib in *his* bedroom because *he* wasn't planning to take time off and couldn't afford to have *his* sleep interrupted. It was amazing, really, the way Brian managed to avoid ever mentioning Joyce or any decisions that *they* were making as a couple or plans the two of *them* had ever made together. Given what had happened in Desmond's room a couple of weeks ago, you wouldn't expect him to go into a lengthy description of their happy marriage, but you'd think he might mess up once or twice and let the name slip out. Desmond found it hard to listen to the two-mouthed behemoths Melanie had mentioned in Morning in America before he left town, the ones who spoke exclusively in the first person plural, but there was something about Brian's refusal to acknowledge his wife's existence that was eerie. It must have been exhausting dodging "us" and "we" as if they were poisoned darts. The whole thing was surprisingly unbecoming.

"What does Joyce think about the baby's room?"

"You know, Desmond, I really didn't call to talk about the baby's room, okay? I called because I have a little free time this afternoon around four, and I was wondering if you'd like to get together. I could drop over."

"I have a couple of appointments here at school," Desmond said. "And then there's a department meeting of some kind at four." Specifically, the kind of department meeting to which he hadn't been invited. "So I'm afraid I won't be home until much later in the evening."

It sounded as if Brian's receptionist had come into his office. There was a discussion about a client on another line, and then he said, "Well, tell them I'll call back, I'm busy." When the door had clicked shut, he said, "Not that I'm counting, Desmond, but this is the third time I've suggested we get together and the third time you haven't been available. So frankly, as I see it, three strikes and you're out."

Desmond preferred to think that Brian was the one who'd struck out, but that was nitpicking. "It's too awkward," Desmond said. "Joyce is about to deliver, I'm working with Jane . . ."

"That might be so, but I wish you'd thought of that before you invited me back to your place that day and came on so strongly."

"I apologize, but I think this is for the best. It's not as if I'm single either, you know." It was reassuring to bring Russell into the conversation in some form, especially since they hadn't spoken in five days and their last conversation had ended on a sour note. There was a knock on Desmond's office door. "Who is it?" he called out.

"Ee rolovel."

"Come in, Roger," he said, happy for a legitimate distraction. "I'll be right with you. Take a seat."

"Yayaya. Dolemmeinerup."

"I have a student here," Desmond said, "so I should be hanging up."

"I guess you should. I didn't mean to snap at you before, it's just that there's a lot going on in my life right now, and it's all starting to get a little overwhelming. But don't worry, I won't call again."

"Maybe when the baby comes, you'll fall in love with it, and everything will fit back into place." Desmond didn't believe it for a minute, but it was the generous and encouraging thing to say. Desmond thought he'd handled the whole call pretty well. Everything had been done with clean efficiency and without ambiguity. Maybe those sugar pills he was taking for Ambivalence had finally kicked in. It was discouraging to think he'd lost his ability to have meaningless sexual affairs, but nice to see he still knew how to end them. "Job well done," he said aloud.

"Yayayaya. Thanyaverymuss."

Roger Lovell. He'd forgotten about him. He was nervously fidgeting in the chair across from Desmond, grinning, adjusting his big, insect-eye glasses. Now that the weather had turned a bit cooler, he'd layered a few baggy, long-sleeved T-shirts under his usual outer layer, making him look more like a restless scarecrow than ever. Even if he hadn't been trying to get Brian off the phone, Desmond would have been happy to see Roger. Roger had taken Desmond's suggestion for writing more about his brother, and last week, he'd turned in a ten-page story about helping his younger sibling regain the confidence to climb trees after having fallen out of one and broken his arm. It was the most charming and sensitively written piece of Creative Nonfiction the class had yet produced.

"Yes, well, job well done, Roger. I'm proud of you, I really am." Desmond reached out and shook the boy's hand, a surprisingly cold thing considering how much time he spent clasping it and rolling it around. "It's simple, clear, full of emotion, no histrionics." He nodded toward Roger's beat-up vinyl briefcase. "How were the written comments from the other students?"

"Kina fusing."

"Confusing?"

"Kinda, yayayaya."

"In what way?"

Roger snapped open the briefcase and pulled out a wad of papers, most of them smudged with food and coffee stains, many covered in comments written in absurdly large script. Desmond tried to get a glimpse into Roger's briefcase to see what else he was carrying around. He remembered Roger telling him he was a math major, although it could have been biology. It always happened that his interest in a student's personal life spiked if she or he turned in a coherent piece of work. Up to that point, they tended to form a pleasant blur in his mind. He saw what looked like a row of pill bottles before Roger snapped the briefcase shut.

It was hard to make out all of the long, garbled speech that followed, but it sounded as if most of the students had found the story unfocused, boring, and pointless. (What else could "poless" mean in this context?) Most shockingly of all, almost everyone had commented that they "dinna baleeit." How was it possible that they didn't believe this straightforward vignette when no one had balked at perky Esther Feldman's claims that she'd been brought up in a dark closet for the first six years of her life, or at Bill Moretti's story about his grandmother being sold into white slavery? No one had doubted the veracity of the two students who wrote supposedly autobiographical stories about helping their parents commit suicide, one with a shotgun. Helping your brother climb a tree was the one thing they found lacking in credibility?

"You have to decide for yourself if any of this criticism rings true for you, Roger, but my advice would be to ignore it and keep writing."

"I'mga reryeit. Maygima quawralegic."

Desmond looked at his watch. He wasn't going to change his mind about meeting up with Brian, but this conversation was enough to make him wish he had so little pride and so few scruples that he could. "A quadriplegic?"

"Yayayaya. Moramatic."

Had he said romantic or dramatic? At this point, it didn't seem to matter much. Desmond was clearly swimming against such a strong current of opinion, he was destined to drown anyway, so why not relax and enjoy the scenery as he was pulled out to sea. Roger's generation had fact and fiction so thoroughly confused, there was no point in trying to make a distinction. Old television shows were accepted as historical documents and carefully staged and scripted media events were considered "real life" dramas. When faced with a scrap of genuine emotion, it was easier to fall back on cynicism.

"That's an interesting idea, Roger. Unexpected. Romantic, dramatic. Excellent."

"Yathinso?"

"Yes, I do think so. And why not do something really *believable* while you're at it and make him the world's youngest quadriplegic IV drug user with HIV, hepatitis C, and ADD."

At the mention of the last illness, Roger's eyes lit up. How did Desmond know, he mumbled, that he and his brother both had ADD?

Later in the afternoon, Thomas stuck his head into Desmond's office. He was about to call Jane. Did Desmond have any messages for her?

"Tell her to hurry up with those Florida tickets," Desmond said. "I'm dying for a suntan."

2.

It was a gray afternoon with a low, heavy sky and down on the street, twenty stories below, people were bundled up in sweaters and long coats. From the floor-to-ceiling window where Jane stood, the Public Garden was a distant blur of red and brown. It was windy and the trees were slowly being stripped of their pretty, dying leaves. At long last, a welcome spell of autumnal weather, even if it hadn't arrived until November. She couldn't wait for winter, assuming it came this year. She'd like a long spell of Arctic air to settle in and freeze the ground, the ponds, the river, and—what a comforting thought—her own heart. Dale was in the bathroom, shaving and talking on his cell phone. He was a man who needed to be in constant touch with his minions; electricians and plumbers and painters and builders. This dance of codependence was what made the world go round. They had the skills, he had the money. Most important of all, he had the forceful, ruthless male energy needed to hold it all together. When they were married, she'd often watched him at work and thought to herself that she could do what he did and do it with more grace and decency. But listening to him these past few weeks—"Then tell him to go fuck himself," he was saying over the sound of running water. "We'll get Tom to do it for half the price."—she realized how foolish she'd been. There was something about his brash bullheadedness that inspired people; it had inspired her to start this documentary project. And now it was his money that was funding it.

He came out of the bathroom, his dark, damp skin set off by the thick towel he had wrapped around his waist. The Boylston Hotel specialized in thick towels and expensive soaps and cotton sheets, meaningless little luxuries that seemed to mean so much. Dale knew one of the hotel's developers and so had access to one of the apartments—executive suites, in the silly, ego-stroking language of this world—on the upper floors. She'd rather not know how often he'd used this place and with whom, so she never pressed for details.

"New problems?" she asked.

"Business as usual. But I should get over to the site right away, stave off a meltdown." He ran the back of his hand down her face and gently across the tops of her breasts. She'd put on her skirt, but was wearing only a bra, a new one, above it. She was completely unselfconscious around him, as if they were an old married couple, and still, she felt the warmth and texture of his hand every time he touched her, as if they were young lovers. The best illusions of both worlds: intimacy and ardor. In the waning days of their marriage, she'd been suspicious of everything he did and said, wary of his motives every time he kissed her. Now that she was in no position to judge or question him, she accepted everything gratefully: their time together in these rooms, his fingers against her skin, his advice, his money. Dale was, by nature, a lover not a husband, the way some men are built for basketball, others for racing horses. Maybe she wasn't built to be a wife, an unsettling thought. She watched him cross the room as he took off his towel and dried his face with it.

"If you're going to leave with me," he said, pulling on his pants, "you'd better get ready. I'm sorry to rush off, but I have to be across town in twenty minutes."

"I ordered a sandwich from room service while you were in the shower." She'd ordered one for him, too, but there was no point in mentioning it now. She picked her blouse up from the chair by the window and slipped it on. "I think I'll wait for it. I can't remember if I had lunch or not and I'm starving."

"I'll bet you are, Janey. You've earned it." He buttoned himself into a white shirt, knotted his tie, and shrugged himself into his jacket and overcoat. Every trace of the hour and a half they'd spent together was erased from his body and face. He kissed her on her raw, bruised lips, searched through his pockets for his watch, then headed to the door.

"How does the rest of your week look?" she asked, buttoning up her blouse.

"I'm not sure. I'll call you at the office when I have a better idea."

That was typically noncommittal. "You have my cell phone number, don't you?" she asked. "I turn it off when I get home, but otherwise—"

"I'll get it from you next time we talk." He gave her a crisp, ironic salute and left.

The silent, ivory anonymity of the room overwhelmed her as soon as he shut the door behind him. Everything here was so pleasant, the bland furniture, the deep carpet, the thick drapes that sealed off the room from the outside world so effectively, but it all lost its charm once he'd departed. Soon, a chambermaid would come in and strip the bed and tidy up the bathroom and make it seem as if nothing had ever happened here. That was supposed to be the appeal of hotel rooms when you were having an affair, so she didn't understand why it didn't appeal to her at all.

She was putting on her shoes when room service buzzed, and she hobbled over to open the door, one shoe on, one off. A slender man with cropped graying hair was holding a tray at his shoulder. "Room service?" he asked. He was smiling and handsome, but Jane couldn't help thinking he was too old and intelligent to be doing this. What personal or professional disappointment had led him to this kind of employment? Obviously, it was going to be one of those awful afternoons when everything was coated with poignancy.

"Just put it on the table by the window," she said.

He took the covers off the plates and started to arrange two settings on the round maple table; towering roast beef sandwiches, a half bottle of red wine, a bud vase with a yellow rose, the entire romantic late afternoon lunch she'd been imagining when she'd called in the order.

"Don't bother with all that," she said, digging through her bag. "Just leave it."

"Shall I open the wine?" He had a deep, cultured voice. An actor, poor man, which would explain everything.

"No, it's fine, really. I'll do it myself."

He fussed a bit more, then presented her with the check and a pen. "If you'll sign here . . ."

"I'll pay for it," she said. She didn't know what the arrangement was with the room, but the last thing she wanted was to start racking up charges against Dale's account. She handed him a stack of bills and told him to keep the change. Kindness, she hoped, was made up of small generous gestures like this that added up bit by bit, no matter what you did to those nearest to you. Although at this moment she felt more like a spoiled, extravagant Lady Bountiful. As she let him out, a woman passed in the hallway holding the hand of a child, an unsteady little boy of about three, overdressed in a gray flannel suit with short pants and a cap.

"Hello, young man," the waiter said. He knelt down and shook the boy's hand.

"Can you say hello?" the mother cooed, grinning proudly.

"Hello, mister," the boy said.

Something about the boy, so tidy and polite, captivated Jane. "He's adorable," she said. The mother looked up at her and a shadow of confusion crossed her face.

Jane closed the door and went to the mirror. Her blouse was buttoned incorrectly and her hair was puffy on one side, as if she'd just crawled out of bed. She was still wearing only one shoe. She fixed herself up, brushed down her hair, put on the other shoe. Awful woman with her perfect string of "pearls" against her cream-colored sweater and her perfect little child. She hated women who paraded their children around and had them perform for strangers as if they were trained monkeys. Gerald could never accuse her of having done that. She took a few more swipes at her hair and then felt a hollow thump in her chest. Gerald. She looked at her watch. Ten to four. She ran into the bedroom, found her briefcase on the bureau and fumbled with the clasps. Her appointment book was on top. She leafed through it, looking for today's page; a storm of notes fluttered to the floor. She squinted, afraid to open her eyes and face it head-on. But there it was, just as she'd feared, a note that Thomas had written for her over a week ago stating that he had a department meeting today and therefore wouldn't be able to pick Gerald up at his piano lesson in Cambridge as he usually did. The lesson ended at four. She'd need half an hour—at least—to get out of this room, down to the garage, across the bridge, and all the way to the other side of Harvard Square. She yanked her sweater over her head, scurried around the room looking for anything she might have dropped. Calling the school now would only take up more time. She'd call from the car. She found her jacket and her bag, cursing herself for her forgetfulness.

She took one last swing through the rooms; for the past three weeks she'd lived in fear of leaving something important behind in this bland landscape where any personal item would be as damning as a drop of blood on a white bedsheet. Nothing here but all that perfectly good food going to waste. Sixty dollars down the drain, but worse still was the sight of it, sitting there peacefully waiting for someone to come along and eat it. Poignant. She grabbed the bottle of wine, stuck it in her bag, and ran out.

There was a young man in the elevator, dressed in a dark overcoat, staring straight ahead, carefully avoiding eye contact. If Dale were here, he'd make some joke with the man and they'd have a good laugh and wind up shaking on a deal to build the World Trade Towers North before landing in the lobby. There was something unnerving about the man's studious avoidance of her, as if he knew that half an hour ago her head had been flung over the side of a king-sized mattress while her ex-husband stroked her throat and fucked her, and her poor, difficult son was hammering out scales, confident that his mother would be there to pick him up when it was over. But no, he couldn't know anything. To him, she was just another forty-year-old nonentity who was starting to sweat. The elevator stopped two floors down, letting in a couple in their sixties, nicely dressed, she smelling of some faint and expensive perfume. They were wearing big smiles, professionally polite, but she was grateful. The elevator made it down only one more floor before stopping again. As three men in suits were getting in, her cell phone rang. She pulled it out of her bag and tried to hold it to her ear discreetly. Undoubtedly everyone else in the elevator had cell phones, but they all looked at her as if she'd just farted.

It was Thomas, asking her if she wanted him to pick anything up on the way home. "I thought you had a department meeting," she said.

"I do, but I should be home by six. By the way, I have some good news for you, Jody. It looks as if Celeste is going to be released early next week. Helen is going home!"

The elevator bell rang. They stopped at the ninth floor, let off the three men, let on a young man in a jogging outfit. Helen was leaving. Jane felt something catch at the back of her throat. "That'll make things easier," she said, although she could barely get the words out.

"What's that gong? You remembered about the change in schedule, didn't you?"

"Of course I did. I'm on my way to pick him up now. His lesson ends at four."

The woman with the expensive perfume checked her watch and looked at her again.

"Oh, good. Are you near Harvard Square?"

"I'm in Central Square. I'll be there in five minutes."

When she clicked off and looked up, the friendly couple were glaring at her with open disdain.

Yes, she thought, as she ran across the cold concrete of the parking garage, you let yourself get farther and farther off the trail until you're completely lost in the dark forest and your life is a ruin of confusion and you find yourself running through an underground garage with your briefcase dangling off your shoulder and your helpless son stranded.

As she was bending to unlock the car door, her bag slid off her shoulder, the wine bottle fell out and cracked against the concrete floor. She felt warm wine on her ankle. If she'd left the bottle in the room, the sad waiter could have enjoyed it. No time now for regret. She climbed into the car and backed out of her space.

She fished through the change cup on her dash, but couldn't find the garage ticket. The scrawny man in the booth with the patch of pink skin along his neck had seen it all before and wasn't impressed. "Thirty dollars," he droned.

"Thirty dollars? I was here for less than two hours!"

He pointed to a sign beneath his window that said something about lost tickets and full prices, some infuriating bit of rules and regulations.

"I asked you when I arrived," she said, "if there were any spaces on this floor. And you told me you'd just come on duty so you didn't know."

There, that ought to satisfy him, prove to him that she'd come in when she said she had. He pointed to the sign again, and she saw that she could present sworn affidavits, photos, and DNA samples and it wouldn't matter at all. He had his job to do and he was doing it and had been doing it while she languished away an afternoon in a hotel room. Choose Your Battles, she told herself and handed over a fifty dollar bill. "Keep the change," she told him. More kindness, unless it was self-flagellation.

She drove through the tangle of crowded Back Bay streets until she was out on Massachusetts Avenue. Three more stoplights and she'd be on the bridge to Cambridge. She checked her watch again. Two past four. Not nearly as bad as she'd feared. Gerald would be coming down the winding staircase of the music school clutching his books. She'd call the school in one minute. She was scarcely late at all.

Halfway across the long, flat bridge over the river, traffic came to a complete stop.

She looked to either side of her, but all she saw was the cold expanse of gray water. No sailboats today, just the low sky and a froth of whitecaps whipping across the river. She pulled out the cell phone and called the school. The receptionist with the affected accent had no idea what she was talking about and grudgingly transferred her to the security guard who sat at a desk in the lobby. She'd picked this school, despite its inconvenience, because it had a solid reputation and was housed in a magnificent red-stone mansion on a lovely side street near Harvard Square. What she hadn't taken into account was that the teachers, used to prodigies, apparently, had little patience for Gerald, who tended to play in a thundering style and blame his weaknesses on his teachers. He'd gone through two in the past eight months.

"He's probably standing in the lobby waiting for me," Jane explained. "If you could just put him on."

"There are about a dozen kids here," he said. "What's he look like?"

"He's six," Jane said. "Tall for his age. He has light hair and he's wearing a light blue jacket with a hood. Although I doubt he's wearing the hood."

"Let me look." But no, no one by that description was in the lobby.

"He's a bit plump," Jane said, realizing that the delicate euphemism for his size made him sound like a turkey.

"Sorry. If I see him, I'll tell him you're running late. What's his name again?"

After she'd hung up, Jane reminded herself of Gerald's awkward maturity and, at times, unsettling fearlessness. Most likely, he'd sit down in the most comfortable chair in the school and bury his head in a magazine, silently berating her for being late. One thing about a child with Gerald's personality, you never had to worry about him talking to strangers. So why was she so panicked? Guilt, that was the only explanation. She had the heater on in the car, and the whole interior was starting to smell like fermented grapes. She checked her watch again. Eight past four. Not too bad, but there was no sign of the traffic breaking up. Maybe there was an accident ahead, or, more likely, some rich, spoiled students were stopping traffic to protest some imagined assault on their privileges. She leaned on her horn, a useless exercise, and one that only made her feel more nervous.

And then, thinking about how much she'd always hated Cambridge—or the smug superiority of Harvard anyway—she realized she had one more option. Brian's office was two long blocks from the music school.

"He's in a meeting," she was told, which was what every receptionist and secretary in the world is paid to tell everyone.

"This is his sister," Jane said. "Please ring him and tell him I need to talk to him immediately."

"I'm sorry, but as I just—"

"You don't understand," Jane said quietly. "It's an emergency. *It's an emergency!*"

While she waited for him to come on the line, she bent down and tried to rub the wine off her stocking with a rumpled piece of tissue paper while vowing not to lose her cool like that again.

"I have clients coming by in the next hour," Brian said. "I have three projects in trouble. I can't drop everything to help you out with day care, Jane."

She could hardly wait for his baby to be born, assuming it ever was. All the real work would be handed over to Joyce, who would probably accept it gratefully, but a certain amount of mess would almost certainly splatter onto Brian's brow. "We're talking about your nephew," she said. "I've never asked you for anything and this would take all of half an hour out of your day, probably more like twenty minutes." She spit on the tissue and rubbed hard.

"What are you doing?" he asked.

"Nothing. Please, Brian, this is important."

"I'm sorry, Jane, but I don't have a free minute this afternoon. Don't you have a baby-sitter or your mother-in-law or someone?"

She didn't believe him. It was more of his selfishness, one more round in the pitched battle they'd been engaged in since they were children. She was probably as bad as he, except that she, in her very worst moments, wouldn't take it out on a child. "If I had someone else, I wouldn't be asking you."

"The answer is no."

Fearing he was about to hang up on her, she said, "You don't have time for Gerald, but apparently you have time to squire Desmond Sullivan around town."

That silenced him. She hadn't been planning on saying it, hadn't been planning on mentioning it ever because it was none of her business and made her uncomfortable, but he'd backed her against a wall and it had slipped out. It seemed as if minutes passed with neither of them saying anything, and for once in her life, Jane actually felt close to her brother as she listened to his harsh breathing.

When he finally spoke, his voice was weary. "Why is it that I never call you with these kinds of crises?"

Thank God he was giving in. "Wait until you have a child," she said. But the relief passed as suddenly as it had come over her and was replaced by the realization that giving in was an admission that something had, in fact, happened between him and Desmond. "You'll see," she stammered. "You'll see that . . . things come up you can't elicit."

"Elicit?"

"Predict. Things you can't predict."

"I can predict right now that this will never come up with me. I will never call you in the middle of the afternoon, completely out of the blue . . ."

She could see the traffic ahead starting to move, a little break in the line of cars. "I'm more grateful than I can say. Please . . . if you could leave right this minute . . ."

3.

When she arrived at the school, Gerald was sitting on the steps leading to the street with his arms folded over his music books, and the corners of his mouth turned down. Daylight Saving Time had ended last weekend and it was nearly dark. The rooms of the school were lit in warm, golden light, and even through the closed windows of her car she could hear pianos and the rasp of cellos. Gerald was wearing a baggy, orange sweatshirt, not the blue jacket she'd described to the security guard. Why hadn't she noticed it this morning? The whole afternoon might have gone differently if she'd given the guard the right description. Brian was pacing on the sidewalk, wrapped up in his dapper tweed sports coat and a long, dark scarf. She'd always thought there was something suspiciously vain about him, although she'd been too absorbed in their rivalry to pinpoint exactly what his vanity made her suspect. How had she missed what now struck her as so obvious it was almost embarrassing? It was a little before five, and now that she was here and Gerald was fine and within thirty minutes they'd be at home and Gerald would be standing at the kitchen counter cooking, the panic of the past hour dissolved. All things considered, she'd handled it rather well.

Gerald opened the door, tossed himself into the passenger seat and slipped on his seat belt, all without looking at her.

"Hi, honey," she said, and gave him a kiss. She wasn't going to make a big deal of this and alarm him retrospectively. "How did the lesson go?"

Silence, and then he said, "Have you been *drink*ing?"

"Excuse me?"

"It smells like *wine* in here."

Brian rapped lightly on her window, his fingers tightly encased in brown leather. He motioned for her to roll down her window. "Mission accomplished?" he asked.

She nodded toward Gerald and lowered her voice. "I don't want to make a big production of this, but I hope you know how much I appreciate it."

"As I was walking over here, I realized it's the kind of thing you'd do for me. Not that I'd ask."

The gloves were definitely a bit too much for this time of year. Thomas usually didn't get around to wearing gloves until midwinter. She turned back to Gerald. "Did you thank your uncle for coming to meet you?"

Gerald said nothing.

"Gerald? I asked you a question: Did you thank your uncle Brian?"

"Thank you," Gerald said to his chest. "Now could we *please* get going?"

"All I can do is thank you again," Jane said. The scarf, too, seemed an affectation. The temperature was probably in the fifties.

"You could also give me a ride back to my office."

She moved some papers around on the back seat and he climbed in. "Take a right at the end of the street and then another right," he said. "What's that smell in here?"

"It's wine," Gerald said.

4.

Gerald was banging his legs against the seat, obviously trying to get a rise out of her. Maybe it was best to simply let him blow off some steam in this harmless way. He hadn't said a word since they dropped off Brian, not that he'd been talkative when Brian was in the car, and now they were almost home. She decided to make one last stab at civility. "Was your teacher happy with all the practicing you've been doing, sweetie?"

Bang bang bang, and then he slid a little lower in his seat and actually kicked the dashboard.

"I asked you a question, Gerald." Carefully enunciating each word, she said, "Did the teacher notice how much practicing you've been doing?"

Bang bang bang, kick kick *kick*.

"Gerald! Enough!"

He fluttered his legs rapidly, like a swimmer racing to the finish line, and then exploded: *"Where were you, Jane?"*

She wished then that she hadn't been so quick to allow him to use her first name. It had sounded cute when he was two, a tiny boy calling his mother Jane, so incongruously grown-up in that incongruously grown-up voice of his. But now it seemed to put them on an equal footing, as if they were peers, as if she had no authority over him. Saddest of all, there was no turning back; it was unlikely now that he would ever call her something as tender as mom. "I told you, sweetheart, I was stuck in traffic. There was a terrible accident and I was stuck on the bridge. There was nothing I could do."

"Doubtful."

"You're being very rude, young man." Bang bang bang. "And please stop that annoying thing you're doing with your legs."

He gave the dashboard one last kick. "Grandma said you'd probably forgotten me."

"Grandma? You called Sarah?"

"I called her when you didn't show up. What was I supposed to do, sit around and wait to be kidnapped?"

"The security guard was looking for you. You didn't hear him?"

"He was looking for someone named Jerry and since that isn't my name, I paid no attention."

"Exactly what did your grandmother say to you?"

"She said she hadn't heard from you and didn't know what you did with yourself half the time. Then she asked me if you and Dale had spent a lot of time together when we were up in New Hampshire, and then I saw Uncle *Brian* come in and realized he was looking for me."

She pulled into their driveway. It was bad enough that Sarah was continually trying to drive a wedge between her and Thomas, but trying to turn her own son against her was purely sadistic. Sarah had answered that one call from Dale, months ago now, and desperate to have something to use against Jane, had come to all kinds of conclusions. At least she could have the decency to keep them to herself.

As she got out of the car, Helen, poor, fading beast, came up from the backyard, making a noble effort at wagging her tail. She'd lost weight in the time she'd been with them, despite Jane's attempts at fattening her up, bringing home special packages of hamburger and ground chicken. Helen went over to Gerald, but he ignored her completely and made straight for the front steps. From this angle, he looked tall, erect, and adult, and she didn't want to let him go.

"I want you to come back here right this minute," she said. "I want you to come back here and pet Helen, right on the head." He spun around and made a great show of marching back and running his hand across Helen's head as if he were wiping crumbs off a counter. "No, I don't mean like that, I mean with a little bit of genuine feeling. She's going to be gone very soon, and I want you to look back at the time that she was with us and remember that you did something nice and kind and decent for her. Do you understand?"

He touched her head, a little more gently this time, and immediately withdrew his hand. "She smells funny," he said.

"She smells like a *dog*, which shouldn't surprise anyone because that's what she is."

"May I go now, Jane?"

"Yes, you may." But when his key was in the lock, she said, "And from now on, I'd like you to call me mom or, if you can't manage that, mother would be acceptable."

She strode across the damp, leafy lawn, nearly tripped on a stone in the middle of the dark path, and knocked on the door of the barn. No, not the barn, the carriage house, the very nicely, expensively appointed carriage house. She looked down with dismay at her wine-stained stockings, but she had to take care of this now, before the whole situation got out of hand. Eventually, she heard Sarah shuffling across the floor, and when she'd finished rattling the locks, she opened the door wrapped in a blue and red and yellow blanket. Undoubtedly, it had taken her this long to answer the door because she was searching for this attention-getting prop, a not-so-subtle reminder to Jane that she was freezing to death in the overheated "barn."

"May I come in?" Jane asked.

Sarah opened the door wider. "It's your house."

"Thomas and I own it, if that's what you mean, but I've never once come in unless I was invited."

"No. In fact, I can't remember the last time you *were* in here, *Jane.*"

So the gloves were off!

The washing machine was running in the room off the kitchen and the whole house smelled of bleach. Jane couldn't remember the last time she was here either, but she remembered the smell; Sarah seemed to have a bleach fetish. She washed everything in bleach, she cleaned every surface with it, for all Jane knew, she bathed in it. As soon as Jane left, she'd probably disinfect the air with it. Jane sat on the sofa and Sarah, very carefully and slowly, lowered herself onto a Bentwood rocker piled high with worn cushions and pillows. It was one of the few pieces of furniture Sarah had supplied herself and, judging from the looks of it, the only piece of furniture Sarah used. She wrapped the blanket around her shoulders and forced an unconvincing shiver to run through her body. It was so unattractive, a robust woman like Sarah playing the infirm old lady. Jane wasn't going to play nice-nice, not today. They'd gone past that.

"If you're cold, you can turn up the heat," Jane said. "We installed the most efficient and reliable heating system we could find, so there's no need to sit here shivering, wrapped in blankets."

"Oh, don't worry about me, Jane." Sarah reached up and touched her big white wig. What was the point, Jane wondered, of going to the trouble, expense, and discomfort of wearing a wig if it only served to make you look worse than you did without it? "I won't be here much longer, so I'm not going to be running up your heating bills."

"You know where the thermostats are and you know how to use them and I know for a fact no one has ever mentioned heating bills. The rest is up to you." Jane adjusted a pillow behind her back to make herself more comfortable for what was coming, and found it was pushing her off the cushion. She reached behind her and tossed it to the far end of the sofa. Sarah watched, stone-faced. "Listen, Sarah," she said. "I think you know why I'm here."

"Not really. Unless I forgot to pay the rent this month."

All $100 of it, always paid in fives and tens to make it look like they were gouging her. Don't Engage. "I just brought Gerald home, safe and sound. There was a traffic jam getting into Cambridge. When I realized how bad it was and how late I was going to be, I called my brother and had him rush down to the school from his office and wait with Gerald. He wasn't alone for more than a few minutes. Ten at the most."

Sarah stared at Jane for a very long time, then said, "I'm glad to hear it." She put her feet up on a crocheted stool, another piece of furniture that belonged to her. Perhaps she spent her days trying to figure out how best to avoid touching anything that Jane had come in contact with. She folded her hands on her lap, and in a flash of panic, Jane saw a busty version of her husband and her shrink sitting opposite her. "All I know," Sarah went on, "is that when he called here, he was so terrified, I thought something terrible had happened to him. I thought he was hurt or lost. I tried to calm him down, but I didn't know what to tell the poor thing."

"You may not have *known* what to tell him, but apparently what you *did* tell him was that I'd forgotten about him. You tried to 'calm him down' by telling him that I'd abandoned him like some abusive mother who leaves her kids stranded in a shopping mall."

Sarah said nothing to this, merely stared at Jane with self-righteous contempt. She pursed her mouth and made a soft, sucking sound.

"There was a change in our usual schedule," Jane said, "and, I admit, I forgot where I was supposed to be and when. And then, on my way to pick him up, I was stuck in a traffic jam. *That* is what happened."

"Oh, yes, Jane, I'm sure it is. I am sure that's exactly what happened."

Jane leapt to her feet. "Well it doesn't matter if you're sure or not, Sarah, does it? What matters is that I *fucked up* and when I realized I'd *fucked up*, I dealt with it as quickly as I could, and Gerald is safely at home and everyone is fine and I'd like to put the entire unfortunate incident behind me."

Sarah's mouth was actually twitching, and when she spoke, her lips were drawn so tightly, they were white. "Don't you *dare* use that filthy language around me! Who do you think you're talking to, Miss *Cody*? Why don't you go take a look at yourself, all dirty and disheveled! You dis*gust* me!"

Everything that Sarah had said to her over the past seven years had slid off the surface of Jane's defenses. She'd chalked all of it up to a sick rivalry for Thomas's affection. But these words knocked the wind out of her. She felt unsteady on her feet and was afraid she was going to cry. "You've never liked me," she said softly, a reminder to herself, as much as to Sarah, that this wasn't about whatever she imagined had happened this afternoon. It wasn't about Dale because she couldn't know anything about that, whatever she suspected.

"I'm the mother-in-law in the barn. I'm not allowed to have an opinion. But I told my daughter the first time I met you, I called her right up on the phone and I said, 'That woman is never going to make my Thomas happy.' "

Jane could feel tears rolling down her face, but she wasn't about to reach up and brush them away. Now Sarah looked like Gerald, like Gerald and Thomas. Sarah and Gerald and Thomas, a trinity. And she was the outsider. She'd always been the outsider and maybe that was why she'd started up this ridiculous affair with Dale, because she wanted to feel like she belonged somewhere. "Thomas has been happy," she said. Her voice was weak, as if she were the old woman. "He's been happy with me, and he's been happy with Gerald, and he loves this house. That might be hard for you to accept, but it's true."

It was true. It was undeniably true. She had made Thomas happy. She'd made him forget the woman who'd left him, and she'd given him a son whom he adored. She had made a home for him. She'd even taken in Sarah, made room for her nemesis in her own household. What more did she want, blood?

"You're a fine one to go talking about what's true," Sarah said. "You with all your lies and your lists. You want to hear truth, I'll tell you some truth. I got the results back from those tests of mine the doctor took last month, and I'm about six months from dead."

"What are you talking about?"

"My whole body's full of cancer. Every damn inch of it."

Jane sat back down on the sofa and wiped her eyes, not sure what to make of this. "Thomas said the doctor gave you a clean bill of health."

"I didn't tell him. I didn't tell anyone. You're the first person I mentioned it to. And I don't plan to tell anyone else, so please don't go spreading it around."

Jane found that she was taking in short, shallow breaths. Sarah had made the announcement of the cancer as a big "Gotcha! Score one for me!" Still, Jane was struck dumb by the news. And moved, in some unexpected way, by the fact that she'd chosen to tell her at all. She wanted to cross the room and take Sarah's hand. "I'm so sorry," she said. "I'm so sorry. What did they say . . ."

Sarah waved one of her big hands. "I'm not going into detail. And don't be sorry for me. Just know one thing, Jane, I plan to make sure everything's *right* before I crawl into the grave. For Thomas and for Gerald, and even for you. So let's not dance around each other anymore."

5.

Back in her own bedroom, Jane sat on her bed and stared at the phone. Now she saw clearly that the whole desperate day had been headed toward this. Be like Chloe, she told herself, learn from your mistakes. It would be a relief, a huge sigh of relief once she'd done it. She called his private voice mail. No personal message from him, so at least she didn't have to hear the sound of his voice.

"It's me," she said. "I can't do this anymore. Let's pretend it never happened. No hard feelings, all right? And please, don't call me back. Let's just leave it at this."

Like all heels and rakes and cads, Dale was a man of honor; he'd respect her wishes and she wouldn't hear from him. In six months or more, they'd bump into each somewhere and act as if nothing had happened. She took off her clothes and stuffed them all into the bag for the dry cleaner. But no, she didn't want any reminders of her last afternoon with him, so she stuffed them into a plastic bag, tied it closed, and tossed it into the wastebasket.

Eighteen
The Other Widows

1.

Eight months later, I returned to the cabin where he died. It was mid-June and the sun was warm. Yellow irises were blooming on the shore at the far end of the pond. I sat for hours on the dock until the light began to fade and I knew it was time to move on.

Desmond closed the book. Luckily, he'd decided to read the final pages of *Dead Husband* here, in the privacy of his shrinking room, instead of at his office at school, or worse still, in a coffee shop or some other public place where someone might have witnessed him shedding real tears—twice in the past hour.

This was hardly the reaction he'd anticipated when he went out last night and bought a copy of Rosemary's slim, successful memoir. There was that absurdly bad title, for one thing, and for another, there was chilly, churlish Rosemary herself. He'd been expecting one of those self-serving, pity-me tomes, full of trumped-up anguish and insulting jabs aimed at everyone who had the misfortune of crossing the author's path. What he found instead was a love story and one of the more moving love stories he'd read in years. Although billed as a memoir of widowhood, it was really a portrait of a complicated and loving marriage. More pages were devoted to the living Charlie than to the corpse of the title, and Rosemary herself came off as a fiercely independent woman who also managed to be an unapologetically devoted wife. More to the point, she came off as a person with something of importance to say on the subject of love.

He kept waiting for Jane to make an appearance in the book, but the closest to a mention he was able to find was reference to a friend named "Karla" (quote marks Rosemary's) who lived in Detroit and had made a second marriage to a loutish man for money and security after divorcing a handsome skirt chaser. This was in a chapter called "The Other Widows," a list of friends and relatives who'd lost their husbands, not to death, but to lovers, divorce, or, in one case, disappearance. "The world rallies around them, touched as they are by the glamour of abandonment and betrayal, rather than the stench of death." That was one way of looking at it.

He checked his watch. It was almost nine o'clock. He had no idea what Rosemary's social life was like, but it was a Saturday night and therefore unlikely she'd be asleep, assuming she hadn't drunk herself into a stupor. And even if she had, he didn't object to the thought of rousing her. Earlier in the evening, he and Russell had had one of their most distressing conversations yet, and surprisingly, he found himself longing to talk about it with Rosemary.

In the middle of a desultory exchange of news items—Roger Lovell this, Melanie that—Russell had mentioned that the person who'd been subletting his studio apartment in the Lower East Side for the past five years had called him to say she was moving out of the city. A job in Houston, poor thing. "You shouldn't have any trouble finding someone," Desmond had said. "No," Russell said, "assuming I decide to look for someone." Ah. And did that mean he was thinking of finally giving the place up? "Those are two of the three available options," Russell had said.

Desmond hadn't thought about this enigmatic statement until after they'd hung up. Replaying the conversation in his head, the only third option he could think of was that Russell would keep the place and not sublet it or, to narrow it down even further, move back in himself. If it was supposed to be a threat, it wasn't a very credible one. For one thing, the place was so tiny, it wouldn't accommodate Russell's collection of cocktail shakers, let alone the rest of his life. But why raise it as a possibility, even obliquely, unless the thought had crossed his mind? Twice in the past five years, there had a been a change in tenant in the apartment, and twice Russell had made noises about giving the place up. The sublet racket he was running, like most housing situations in the city, was technically illegal, and the only way he could justify keeping his name on the lease was by keeping the rent a mere $50 above what he paid. Desmond had always encouraged him to hang on to the place. You never knew when it might come in handy for some friend who suddenly found himself homeless or some elderly relative who was sick of the suburbs and thought Avenue C might be a nice change of pace. Desmond often found an image of the tiny, dark apartment floating into his mind when he and Russell were having an especially vituperative argument or when he was feeling closed in by Russell's stuff, both the physical and the emotional kind. He'd frequently imagined suggesting to Russell that he think about moving back into the studio, but he'd never imagined Russell coming up with the idea on his own. He'd redialed the New York number to ask Russell for clarification, but there was no answer, so instead he lay on his bed and wept his way through the final pages of *Dead Husband.*

Too bad if Rosemary was asleep or passed out; part of the price of fame was taking calls from troubled fans. She answered her phone with an unpromising rasp. "Friend or foe?" she demanded.

"Neither, I'm afraid," Desmond said. "Friend of a friend is the best I can do."

"Ah, Mr. Sullivan. Friend of many friends it seems." She coughed and cleared her throat.

"I didn't wake you up, did I?"

"Not yet. What can I help you with?"

"I was wondering if you'd like to meet me somewhere for a drink."

She sighed deeply and with what sounded like genuine dismay. "I doubt it's as simple as all that. What's your ulterior motive?"

"I'm not sure I'd call it an ulterior motive. I wanted to talk to you about *Dead Husband.*"

"Oh, Christ. I was hoping for something a little more challenging. I'll tell you what: if you bring a bottle of inexpensive red wine, I'll let you in. That way we get to have our drinks and I don't have to change out of my jammies."

As he was creeping down the staircase, Loretta called, "Where you headed, Mr. Sullivan?"

"Out," he said. He was officially done with filling in Loretta and Henry on every detail of his life. The final straw had come when they'd grilled him about Brian Cody, about his dark good looks, his exceptionally fashionable wardrobe, all in a way that Desmond found insulting, as if they were amazed that someone who looked like Brian would be visiting someone who looked like him.

It was a mild night, remarkable (or frightening, he wasn't sure which) for early November in Boston, and as he walked along Marlborough Street, he could hear the music and laughter of dinner parties spilling from open windows. Someone in a house somewhere behind him was playing Chopin on a piano, not well, but with halting tenderness. It was an etude, one of those melancholy Chopin etudes full of rivers and flickering light and longing. Boris had studied this piece last year, and Desmond and Russell had lain in bed together listening to him struggle through it night after night for more than a month until finally he could play it from beginning to end without stopping, gliding over his own mistakes as deftly as a skier absorbing bumps on an uneven slope. Desmond hadn't been able to figure out why he had found Boris's gawky performance so touching, but now, listening to this other, slightly more accomplished pianist, he heard the elusive ghost of the piece as it was intended to be played and heard the performer reaching for it, fingers outstretched, inching close but not quite taking hold. You could hear the longing in the performer as clearly as you could hear it in the music itself. He and Russell had been reaching toward something, too, but it seemed as if they'd missed it and he had no idea how to get back on track. Perhaps Rosemary, unlikely expert that she appeared to be, could tell him how to do it.

2.

She lived in a narrow brownstone one block from the river. The immense buildings of BU loomed above her street, making it feel both protected and closed in by the institution, the way much of Boston felt protected and closed in by its many universities. She buzzed him in, and he climbed the staircase to the second floor, the polished wood of the banister and walls gleaming from the reflected light of a brass chandelier. He knocked, and from somewhere inside, he heard her call out, "It's unlocked."

He entered into a long, dark hallway, and followed the light into the living room. There, seated on a cluttered red sofa, was a hugely fat yellow cat. It looked at Desmond as disdainfully as Rosemary had the first time he'd met her, slowly roused itself, and, with a sullen backward glance, disappeared through an arched doorway. "Take a seat," Rosemary shouted.

Easier said than done, Desmond thought. Most of the furniture in the round, candlelit room was covered with newspapers and books spread open. Not quite what he'd expected, given Rosemary's meticulous appearance, but he brushed some cat hair from the overstuffed sofa and sat. There was a bay of curved windows opposite him, and through them he could see a towering wall of scattered lights in what appeared to be a building of classrooms. It was as if an ocean liner were parked outside. An open copy of his Lewis Westerly biography was sticking out from under the sofa, and embarrassed by the sight of it—it was open to page 107—he tapped it out of sight with his foot.

Rosemary emerged from the kitchen with a wineglass in one hand, waving lightly at the air around her head with the other. "Fucking toaster oven burns every fucking thing I put in it. I was trying to play the hostess and defrost some cheese things the previous tenant left in the freezer and look what happens." Desmond stood, but she motioned him back into his seat. She had on a man's red silk bathrobe and a pair of red velvet slippers. Her hair was loosed from its usual tight bun and fell around her shoulders, dark and sleek. "I'm sorry about the mess," she said. "I haven't had many visitors here so I've let the place go completely to hell. It's been quite thrilling to watch the deterioration. Next I suppose I'll leave out containers of rotting food and dirty undies. It came furnished, so I had to mark my territory somehow."

Desmond handed her a bottle of wine. "I didn't give you much notice."

"I hate people who do; they tell you they're coming next Tuesday meaning you damn well better have the place presentable and something edible in the fridge. I prefer these last-minute arrangements. Someone calls you up with despair in his voice and demands to be seen right away. You light a few candles in the hopes they'll hide a multitude of sins."

"Did I have despair in my voice?"

"That's how I interpreted it. Why else would I have invited you over?"

She took a sip from her wineglass, handed it to him, and headed back to the kitchen with his bottle. He wasn't sure if this was his drink or if he'd been assigned the task of holding it for her, but when she reappeared a few minutes later, she was drinking from a glass so full she had to sip carefully. She sat at the opposite end of the sofa, one leg tucked under her. "Your wine is much better than mine," she said. "You don't mind finishing up that stuff, do you?"

He was insulted by the request but flattered by her honesty. "I guess not," he said.

Rosemary frowned, as if she was disappointed by his answer, proof that she wasn't dealing with a worthy opponent. She threw an arm across the back of the sofa, and the red silk robe slid open. Desmond could see the curve of one pale breast and the dark edge of her nipple. She was watching him over the rim of her wineglass, and flustered, he turned to the window. The lit-up building offered some dull conversational inspiration. "How are your classes going?" he asked.

"Oh, please. You don't really think I'm the kind of person who sits around my apartment wondering how my classes are going, do you? I put in my time, they send me my paychecks; as for the children . . ." She shrugged.

"And yet," he said, "I suspect you're a good teacher."

"Of course I am, albeit in a monstrous Miss Jean Brodie sort of way. I get personal with them immediately, talk endlessly about myself, and ask all kinds of inappropriate questions about their sex lives. I don't know what they learn, but at least everyone stays awake, which is more than someone like Thomas Miller can claim."

Or Sybil Gale or any number of the professors Desmond had taught with, each of whom claimed to care more about his students than Rosemary. What if she turned out to be the truly devoted teacher and they turned out to be self-absorbed academics who couldn't read the pulse of the students sitting and snoozing in front of them? Still, every harsh word out of her mouth made the sad, thoughtful narrator of *Dead Husband* seem more like a fictional creation. He looked at her warily and said, "How much of what you say should I believe?"

"I'd suggest taking the all-or-nothing approach. It's so much more relaxing than having to engage your mind and judge every word out of my mouth. Plus, as you can tell, I'm ever so slightly drunk." She gazed out the window, and then turned back to him with a mournful droop in her eyes. She wasn't wearing any makeup, and her pale, naked face, eyebrows carefully plucked into thin lines, looked like an unfinished portrait. With her hair loosed from its bun, the skin on her face was less taut, more carelessly draped around the bones of her cheeks.

Desmond found his eyes wandering back to her exposed breast and thought that if he could do so without there being any consequences, he'd like to reach in and cup it, feel the softness and weight of it in his hand. She seemed to be trying, with a mixture of derision and depression, to seduce him into making this kind of overture, although from his point of view, it wouldn't be an overture but the whole symphony. She caught him staring again and said, "Are you looking at my tits with desire or envy?"

"Just looking."

"I should blush, but I don't know how." She stretched back on the sofa, basking in his discomfort, and said, "Just so we can get this out of the way, what is it you wanted to say about that book?"

"I wanted to tell you how much I liked it. I hated coming to the end, and, to be honest, I was deeply moved by the way you talked about love. And more specifically, about your marriage."

"Did you weep?"

"Yes. More than once."

She frowned and lifted her wineglass to her mouth. "People are always telling me they wept reading it. It makes me think there's something wrong with me for not shedding a single tear while writing it. Since we're both in the scribbling game, I'll let you in on a secret: I think one of the great tragedies of our time is the way people insist upon being ironic about everything. Look at me; I'm practically drowning in the stuff. I have to undercut everything I say with irony, and in addition to being time-consuming, it's emotionally exhausting. And worse than that, the huddled masses in this country have equated irony with its lesser cousin, sarcasm, mostly thanks to good old television. So when I sat down to write the book, I decided to hell with irony, let's try something new here; let's get really sophisticated and go for heartfelt sincerity and big-time earnest.

"There were several hundred thousand ways I could have written about that relationship, since my feelings about it and about Charlie himself shifted by the minute through all those endless years of our marriage. And believe me, they were endless, each and every one of the fifteen. So I thought, okay, let's just pick an attitude and stick with it. And then it hit me: true love. Why not? Give the people what they want. Out with irony, in with love. And boy oh boy, did it ever work. If you don't believe me, call my accountant."

She got up from the sofa, and he followed her into the kitchen, a small, spotless room that looked as if she rarely entered it. There was still a thin layer of smoke from the toaster oven hovering in the air near the ceiling.

Desmond opened the window a crack to let in a warm breeze, and watched as the smoke dispersed. Rosemary poured herself more wine, but when Desmond held out his own glass, she dumped in a mere splash.

"Can't you do a little better than that?" he asked.

She pouted, but filled up the glass, and for the first time, Desmond felt a flicker of approval from her. He was still reeling from her description of her book, a confession of complete cynicism as far as he could tell, but delivered in a confusingly earnest tone. When they returned to the living room, he went and stood at the windows, gazing out at the wall of lights, while she repositioned herself on the sofa. The big yellow cat stalked back into the room and gave Desmond another disgruntled look, as if to say, "Still here?"

"I didn't figure you for a cat person," Desmond said.

The cat sprang up to her lap and she began running her hand down its back in long, languid strokes. "I love my pussy," she said. "Fuddy and I have been together a long time."

Desmond watched the performance for a few more minutes. When she dropped her guard, stopped insulting you and lapping at her wine, she looked remarkably vulnerable, especially tonight, dressed in that red robe, her hair falling around her shoulders. He decided to take a chance at provoking more insults and said, "You know, Rosemary, I don't believe what you just told me about your book. I don't believe you calculated the whole thing, cooked up a scheme with your accountant. I think you wrote it from your gut."

Rosemary pushed the cat off her lap and brushed clumps of fur from her robe. "A romantic. That's charming. Not to me, but to a lot of people. The book is full of truths, Desmond, truths of the human heart. If it weren't, you wouldn't have responded to it as you did. And the desk in my bedroom wouldn't be stacked to the ceiling with mail from readers wounded by love and death and the rancid bore of daily living. Is the book completely *honest* about my relationship with Charlie? Only he and I know, and neither one of us is talking."

She raised her thin, carefully plucked eyebrows, as if to say, Any more questions? He ought to invite her into his Creative Nonfiction class, have her give a lecture on this very point. Really, she should be the one teaching it. His students seemed to have grasped half of what she was saying—the withering dismissal of honesty as a concept with any relevance—and then done her one better by tossing truth into the trash heap as well.

"I had a very interesting call from Jane about an hour ago," she said, "just after you called me."

The tone in her voice suggested she had some tragic piece of news she couldn't wait to report. Desmond moved away from the window and cleared off a chair opposite her. "Everything all right?"

"In the long run, yes. In the short term, a big stir. Joyce . . ."—she flicked her hand—"whatever her name is . . . Cody, I suppose, finally decided to go into labor, and guess where Brian was?"

"I have no idea," Desmond said, probably too eagerly. At least not at my place, he thought.

"No one does, that's just it. In any case, not at home. Thomas Miller ended up rushing her off to the hospital and poor Jane was calling all the likely suspects, trying to locate her brother. I have a feeling you might have a message from her on your machine, although I assured her you were headed in this direction for a visit."

"What bad timing. I wonder where Brian could be, on a Saturday night?"

"Frankly, Desmond, I thought you might be able to answer that question."

No, he was happy to be able to tell her, he had no special insight into Brian's whereabouts. And that was the honest truth.

"My apologies for misreading our little encounter on the street. I had the most wonderful time imagining what was going on with you two while I sat at that café, attempting to read my students' papers. I hate when someone all of a sudden develops a conscience and shoots your plans to hell. He couldn't stand the thought of cheating on his wife?"

"I couldn't stand the thought of cheating on mine. After I did, that is. Which is too bad because I don't think Russell, the wife in question, is having the same crisis of conscience."

"You're one of the other widows." There was a candle burning on the coffee table in front of the sofa, the flickering light sending shadows up to the high ceiling. Rosemary leaned down and put it out with her fingers, a surprisingly indirect signal, given her blunt personality, that it was getting close to closing time. "I have a certain amount of envy toward you, touched as you are by the glamour of abandonment and betrayal. Also because you, unlike me, have the possibility of making your dead husband feel sorry for what he did to you."

As he was walking home through the dark quiet streets of Back Bay—no piano music now—it seemed to him that perhaps Rosemary had offered him some advice, even if unwittingly. He should follow her example and send

Russell a letter full of truths of the human heart, of his human heart, possibly adding a few details that might provoke the faint stirrings of regret. Knowing that it didn't necessarily have to be honest made the whole project seem easier and a lot less threatening. They were leaving for Florida in a week. He could send off the letter before he left and wait to see where the chips fell.

3.

As soon as Desmond left, Rosemary snuffed out the rest of the candles, turned out the lights, and headed for her bedroom. The goddamned cat was curled up on her pillow. The Realtor had told her this was the best apartment she had to offer, but cat sitting was part of the arrangement. Fortunately it was an independent creature that required little attention beyond the occasional bowl of nasty food. There was no threat she was going to form an emotional attachment to the thing the way Jane had with that ancient dog she'd been taking care of. Poor Jane attached herself to so many unlikely people and things—both husbands, that obnoxious child, the dog, the highly unlikely project with Desmond. She wasn't a good judge of character, which was just another way of saying she didn't have a clue about who she was or what she wanted. Or maybe she knew but refused to admit it, which was pretty much the same thing.

Rosemary poured the rest of the wine into a juice glass, shooed the cat off the pillows, and climbed into bed. She loved to lie in bed in this darkened room that belonged to someone else and look out at the great wall of lights on the other side of the street. Funny how such a big, imposing, impersonal thing as that could make her feel less alone, while a warm, furry cat cozied up against her stomach threw her into an existential crisis.

She took a few more sips of wine and gazed at the big, enfolding building until the lights became a blur. She wrapped Charlie's robe around her more tightly, pulled her knees up toward her chest, and, as she had done on so many nights over the years since the goddamned son of a bitch had gone and died on her, wept until she was exhausted and was finally carried off to sleep.

4.

It was after three A.M. when Thomas got home from the hospital. Jane was sitting in a chair in the living room, the radio tuned to the all-night jazz station, and a single lamp lit behind her. She was sleeping when he came in, or half asleep. Either way, she gave a start when she saw him. The whole of the long, confusing evening came back to her, and she groaned. He was wearing a blue windbreaker and was holding a can of beer. He'd earned it, there was no question of that, but it was so unlike him, drinking at this hour, that she started to laugh softly. He turned down the volume on the radio, and with a weary rasp in his voice, asked her what she found so funny.

"With that jacket, that beer, you looked like a soccer coach, that's all."

As he walked past her chair, he touched the top of her head, and then sprawled out lengthwise on the beige sofa. It was strange, she thought, that they'd moved in here almost four years ago, and she couldn't remember ever before sitting here with him like this, in the quiet middle of the night.

"Do you know, I used to *be* a soccer coach?" he asked. "It was maybe twelve years ago, before I met you, when I lived out in Watertown. A little neighborhood league that didn't last very long."

The news shocked her, partly because she couldn't imagine him standing on a field and coaching, partly because it made her realize she didn't think much about what his life was like before they met. "How was your team?"

"Everyone had fun, but I can't remember if we won very often or not."

That was probably the only part of it she would have remembered. If only more of whatever it was he had had rubbed off on her in the past six years. "How are Joyce and the baby?" she asked.

"Both fine. Considering all the tension at the start, it was a pretty easy delivery."

Shortly after midnight, Thomas had called her to say that Brian had finally showed up, claiming he'd gone to a movie and had rushed to the hospital as soon as he heard Jane's many messages to him. It was an insultingly unlikely story—who went to a movie without telling their ultra-pregnant wife where they were going?—but it was easier for everyone to pretend they believed it.

"So you stayed in the waiting room?" Jane asked him.

He hoisted the beer can to his mouth and shrugged. "I wasn't going to go into the delivery room. I just wanted to be sure everything went smoothly."

She was ashamed of Brian—abandoning his wife, leaving Thomas there to pick up the pieces. On top of that, she was ashamed to be his sister and, here was the hardest point to accept, to be so much like him in so many ways. Narcissistic, self-centered, unfaithful, unreliable. "Poor Joyce," she said. "What's going to happen to her? She deserves so much better."

"Joyce isn't as fragile as you think, Jane." There was something steely in his voice, as if he took this very personally, as if he were defending himself as much as he was defending Joyce.

He's in love with her, Jane thought. It became so obvious to her now—all the attention he lavished on her, the compliments he paid her, the interest he took in her work, the way he diligently read the children's books that she'd edited—she couldn't imagine how she'd missed it before. Then again, how typically self-centered of her to have missed it. How surprising that she finally recognized it. They were in love with each other, or infatuated with each other. When you thought about it, they were made for each other: two kind, honest, intelligent people. What a decent, happy, healthy couple they'd make. "She'd be happier married to someone like you," Jane said.

"She's married to your brother."

"*You'd* be happier, Thomas, if *she* were your wife."

"Oh, Jane," he said. He closed his eyes and rested the beer can on his chest. His breathing was heavier, with a slight whistle in it, a sign that he was about to fall off to sleep. "I'd be happier if *you* were my wife."

Nineteen
The Last Dinner

1.

Chloe knocked lightly on Jane's office door, pushed it open a crack, and peered inside in that halting, apologetic way of hers, as if she were afraid she'd find Jane in there torturing a small animal or rolling around on the carpet naked. Or maybe she was afraid she'd find Jane doing exactly what she was doing: staring out the window at the gathering clouds, watching the wind torment the trees, and banging a pen against her desk with nervous distraction.

"Is there a problem?" Jane asked.

Chloe looked over her shoulder. She was catching on; she knew enough to know that there was always going to be someone standing behind you, peering over your shoulder, ready to knock you off your pedestal. "I don't think so," she said. "Did one of the guests cancel?"

"Not that I've heard." Jane wouldn't have minded especially if one of the guests had canceled. They were doing a conversation on the recent turn of events in another of those kindergarten sex scandals that should have dropped out of the news decades ago. If Jane had booked the guests herself, she would have loaded the table with experts who'd debunk and discredit the recovered memory industry, but Chloe had done most of the booking for this particular discussion, so the guests would be a group of therapists who made their livelihoods convincing people they were miserable, and state prosecutors who'd made careers out of putting innocent people behind bars. This was the fourth show Chloe had booked, and even if Jane didn't agree with her point of view, she had to admit—grudgingly—that Chloe did a masterful job of making sure the guests all arrived on time, were prepared to speak, and knew the importance of staying on subject. It was the thrill of the new for her. At her age, everything had the thrill of the new, and it was infectious. She swept back her curls and tapped her long fingers on the door jamb. "I was just upstairs. David asked me to see if you were free. To have a talk with him."

She was nervous and it showed, and it was so uncharacteristic of her to display any professional discomfort or doubt, Jane started to worry. "What does he want now?" she asked.

Chloe pulled her head back so her chin was tucked into her neck, a gesture she apparently intended to come across as astonishment. "I wouldn't know!" she said. It was the first time Jane had seen Chloe look unattractive in all the months she'd been at the station. Jane had been hoping to see her look frazzled or homely or frantic since the day she arrived, but now she felt let down, the way you might feel let down by seeing weakness in an overbearing parent you longed to see diminished but needed to be strong. (The way Jane had felt betrayed by her own parents when they had up and died, father following mother into the grave at an early age, as if neither had taken into consideration the consequences for her and for Brian. Not to mention the consequences for Joyce and Thomas.) And besides that, Chloe's gesture was thoroughly unconvincing. A bad actress doing Lady Macbeth.

Jane pushed herself back from her desk and stood up, and Chloe came to life, as if seeing Jane trying to rouse herself from her stupor was cheering. She smiled brightly and announced that their tickets for Florida had arrived this morning. "Everything's set," she said. "Tim got the time off from work, and I got an incredible deal on the van. And you're going to love the price of the hotel."

"You're exceptional in every way," Jane said. "I mean that."

They were leaving for Florida in less than a week, and although she hated to fly, didn't like the stifling humidity of the South, and had discovered that the area of Florida they were visiting had so little to recommend it, it was generally passed over by guidebooks, she couldn't wait to get out of town. She went into the bathroom and splashed cold water on her face. Then she looked into the mirror, hoping she'd see conviction and competence, something that might please David Trask, even if she wasn't quite up to intimidating him these days. No such luck. Her hair was too long and stringy, had lost some of its luster, and her face was gaunt. She still couldn't get Thomas's words out of her mind, what he'd said the night he came back from the hospital. If only she didn't have a guilty conscience, she would have asked him what he meant. But as it was, she had to assume the worst. And worst of all, she longed to talk it over with Dale. He was the only one who knew what was going on. Or had been going on. It had been two weeks since she'd left the message on his machine telling him she couldn't see him anymore, and just as she'd predicted, he was doing the wretchedly honorable thing by not calling her back.

2.

David was pacing in front of his wide window, the sky a dark field behind it. "The threat of rain," they'd said on the weather this morning. But how could it be considered a threat when it had scarcely rained all fall and everything seemed to be drying up? They should do a *Dinner Conversation* on the glib giddiness of weather reporting. She'd make a note of it when she got back to her office.

David looked unhappy, as he often did these days. A little over a year ago, he'd made the colossal mistake of marrying a beautiful, younger woman— for love. It was generally assumed that David had family money—who in public television, aside from Jane, didn't?—and he wasn't unattractive, but he'd married out of his league. It was obvious to anyone who knew anything about women like Mara Kray that David was a stepping-stone on Mara's path to somewhere else. She needed a bigger and more glamorous audience than she was likely to find in Boston, and Jane supposed it was only a matter of a year or two before Mara hooked up with a better connected and more powerful man. In the meantime, she tended to flirt with good-looking nonentities, her male counterparts, and publicly humiliate David in a gentle, conde-scending way. In the gray morning light, his skin looked sallow.

As she took a seat in front of David's desk, she noticed, with a quick stab of dread, that there were coffee cups and a few plates of half-eaten pastries stacked up on a table in the corner. This had to mean there had been a meet-ing here this morning, one to which she had not been invited. David was still pacing, had made no moves toward sitting down, and aside from mumbling a few words of greeting, was being unusually silent.

"Meeting?" she asked, desperate to break the ice.

He stopped pacing and stared at her for a moment, apparently trying to decide how to respond, stroking his wispy goatee with his index finger. "Chloe told you?"

That cleared up that suspicion: Chloe was now officially inside a loop she'd been booted out of. She indicated the table with her chin. "I was guessing."

"Ah." He seemed to be relieved by this and sat at his desk. "Good guess."

"I assume it wasn't anything that concerns me, because I assume that if it were something that concerned me, I naturally would have been included. Especially since you were serving breakfast."

He put an arm across his chest, rested his chin in his hand, and scrutinized her. In a matter of seconds, she saw the look of restive discomfort and apol-ogy melt off his face, replaced by a look of barely controlled contempt, and she understood her tactical error. She was living up to her reputation for being hard-edged and sarcastic. Difficult. And in doing so, she was making his job infinitely easier than it would have been if she'd played against type and sat there like a wounded bird.

He let his hands drop to his desk and rose up taller in his chair, puffed up on self-righteousness. "The meeting concerned a lot of people, Jane." He nodded at her and arched one eyebrow, as if to put her in her place.

She'd been told, by more than one person, that she never knew her place. "Including me, correct?"

"Yes, including you."

"And I wasn't told about it."

All those years with Dr. Berman had at least produced some shred of self-awareness. She knew very well what she was doing here: Trying to divert at-tention away from the significant issue—the content of the meeting to which she pointedly had not been invited—and onto the irrelevant insult of not having been included. Trying to give herself a moment of reprise before he told her what he was going to tell her, which was, obviously, that *Dinner Conversation* was about to grind to an official stop.

"I called you up here *now* to tell you about the meeting, Jane. Do you want to hear about it?"

She felt a terrible wave of pride swell up inside her, and she leaned her elbows on his desk with as much casual arrogance as she could muster. "Let me guess," she said. "The announcement we've been waiting to hear for the past twelve months: *Dinner Conversation* is on the way out. Correct?"

He glared at her, not even grateful that she'd done him the huge favor of making this unhappy announcement. "Correct. I'm truly sorry."

She tossed it off. "The only surprise is it didn't come sooner." Her legs were beginning to feel peculiarly heavy in the chair, and the strange gray light was making her slightly dizzy. "When?"

"We figure we'll do the last show sometime in early January."

That was a blow. In the last few seconds, she'd done some calculating and had concluded the show would probably run for another six months. "That obviously means you have a replacement lined up." She nodded, trying to look impressed by his skills and foresight. "What is it?"

"We're working on a few ideas, nothing final. I'm sorry, Jane, I know how much this show has meant to you over time."

"Granted, it has a certain nostalgic appeal, but I'm not about to shed tears over it. I'm going to need more time to devote to the series, so it all works out pretty well. How's Mara?" Toss her into the conversation just to remind him that he had problems, too. Just to balance things out here. Just to change the subject.

"I'm afraid I have another bad piece of news for you." This time he got up and went to the window where unpromising slashes of rain were beginning to strike the glass. "I heard last night that the funding we'd been counting on from the station has been turned down."

"Oh, really? Well, I'm not . . . shocked. I've got proposals out to about thirty-five other foundations, so this was really just a small bit of seed money." The small but essential seed money, the money she'd been counting on to pay back her loan from Dale.

David leaned against the window and folded his arms across his chest, telling her, without actually saying it, that the meeting was over and she should get up and leave now. There was some kind of new and awful self-confidence in this gesture. All the years they'd been working at the station, he'd been her boss, but somehow, she'd always felt she had him in her pocket. She thought for a moment that perhaps she should just sit there and make him all the more uncomfortable, but he didn't look uncomfortable at all. She'd be reassigned to another show, but unless it was her own, unless it was the series, she'd be starting at the bottom again.

She stood up, dismayed to discover that her foot had fallen asleep. Somehow, she made it to the door. As she was about to walk out, David said, "Mara, by the way, is fine."

"Wonderful." She lifted her dead foot a few inches off the floor and tried to shake it discreetly. "Give her my best."

3.

She wanted pills. She wanted to wait in line at Walgreen's with all the other prescription junkies and hand in her slip and be given a cheap, amber vial of small, expensive pills that would, within a matter of hours, *minutes,* make her feel better about everything. She didn't want a solution, she didn't want to sort through her feelings, she wanted to simply not care. She'd been so infuriatingly shortsighted when she went into her I-hate-drugs monologue with Dr. Berman all those months ago.

Everything she hadn't told Dr. Berman or had told him in some abbreviated or altered form was piling up on top of her, and the weight of it was starting to crush her. As she sat in Berman's office, looking at him as he looked at her, each waiting for the other to speak, she thought about how, in the last month, their relationship had changed. His signals weren't as easy to read, his silences were more ominous, his eyes were more stern. He'd lost respect for her, she could tell. It shouldn't matter, since her own respect for him was a little soft, but somehow it did. She knew she ought to either break down and tell him everything, or drop out of treatment altogether, maybe find another shrink with whom she could make a fresh start.

I'd be happier if you *were my wife.* Tell him that. Start there.

"Something I forgot to tell you," she said.

He raised his chin, nothing more encouraging than that.

"The dog left a few days ago. Remember I told you about Helen, my husband's colleague's dog?"

Yes, he remembered. He remembered everything. For all she knew, he remembered things she hadn't even told him.

"I got up at six A.M. and I took her out for a long walk, all around the neighborhood. It was still dark, dark and colder than I'd expected. She was walking more slowly than usual, as if she knew she was leaving that day and was taking it all in for the last time. I took her down to a park near the house, and I let her off her leash and she just stood there, looking at me, with a let's-get-it-over look on her face. Do you say 'face' for dogs? Anyway, we went home and she watched as I packed up her leftover cans of dog food, the bag of treats. She watched me the whole time, didn't even go to the dish of food I'd put down for her or get her usual drink of water. And then, when Thomas left for work, she followed him out to the car and got in the back seat, all without prompting. She just went along with him, didn't fuss. But as she was getting into the car, she turned and looked at the house, almost as if she knew I was up in the window. She seemed to be saying, 'How can you do this to me?' I could barely watch."

"You told me the dog missed her owner."

"Yes. That's right."

"Her owner was released from the hospital and she was going back to her."

"Yes."

"Don't you think it's possible you're the one feeling the loss? Aren't you talking about your sadness, Jane, not hers?"

Her sadness, her loss. Her sadness about Helen, which wasn't even about Helen but about everything else she'd lost in the past several months, a list that seemed to be growing by the hour. Her face began to feel uncomfortably hot and, before she knew what was happening and had a chance to apply the brakes, she began to weep.

"I'm sorry," she said. "I'm sorry. I didn't mean to do this." She pulled a handful of tissues out of the box sitting on the table by her chair and mopped at her face. In addition to whatever else she was feeling, she was panicked that Berman might get out of his chair and try to comfort her. What would she do if he came over and put his hand on her shoulder? All the time she'd been seeing him, off and on all these years, she'd maintained a perfectly poised demeanor, had never once shed a tear, and now she knew why. It was this awful fear that he'd console her. Except she'd been sobbing for a good few minutes and he didn't seem to be doing anything.

"I'm going to Florida in four days," she said through her tears. "I'm afraid to fly. I hate all the little noises and the way the coffee smells and the way all the seats and the bins feel so cheap and everything rattles when you take off. I want you to write me a prescription for something to make it easier."

Without blinking, Berman reached one of his hands into a pocket of his chair and pulled out a prescription pad. "I'm qualified to do that," he said, and began to write.

She needed help and he was going to give it to her, and all she had to do was ask for it. She was so relieved and grateful, and so embarrassed by her own ignorance of this simple arrangement, she wept even harder.

Twenty
Welcome to Florida

1.

The gray smoke of clouds floated past the window at a leisurely pace. There was nothing quite as soothing as flying, nothing that provided such a sharp, comforting contrast between illusion and reality. On the inside, the calm hum of air filtration systems and the predictable routine of flight attendants and the bland monotone of the pilots; on the outside, the violence of metal and jet fuel ripping the sky apart, cutting up the delicate chemicals of the atmosphere in an effort to hurry people to places they usually didn't want to go. Desmond loved being lifted out of his life, plucked up into the chilly ether where everything was clean and carefully controlled and simultaneously safe and dangerous, where you could travel at extraordinary speeds through subzero temperatures without effort or discomfort, without even having to press your foot on a pedal. And if ever there was a moment when he longed to be rescued from the foundering boat of his life and strapped into a comfortable chair, it was now. How many mistakes could he make thirty thousand feet above his whole world?

Two female flight attendants were standing in the aisle one row in front of them, loudly discussing the injustice of the airline's scheduling policies. It was true that all the glamour had been drained from air travel, but that only made it as dull, in a reassuring way, as a trip to the Grand Union.

"I'm sick of it," one of them said. "I'm sick of being pushed around."

"No kidding," the scrawnier of the two drawled. "And yesterday they drug-tested me again. That's twice this month."

"Oh shit." The untested woman reached a pale, braceleted arm into the overhead bin and tossed a pillow, doll-sized and stiff, to the passenger seated below.

"The whole thing was so humiliating I went out and had a complete blowout last night."

Jane shoved a magazine into the seat back in front of her. "Aren't they sup-posed to be discussing something important right now?"

"Your lunch?"

"I was thinking about emergency landing procedures and flotation de-vices, but lunch would be nice. What have you got to read over there?"

He handed her a copy of the same airline magazine she'd just been look-ing at, and she flipped through the pages as if she'd never seen them before. She was nervous. At the airport, she'd stepped out of the taxi and dropped her purse onto the sidewalk and dropped her keys as she was stooping to pick up the purse and dropped her purse again as she was stooping to pick up the keys. If he had to put money on it, he'd guess that she, like the emaciated flight attendant, wouldn't pass any drug tests with flying colors today. "Take care of Jane," Thomas had told him yesterday morning. "She likes to boss people around, but underneath, she needs someone to watch out for her." And then, with great tenderness, as if he were revealing to Desmond one of his wife's most lovable traits, he said, "She wouldn't admit it, but she hates to fly."

A smile had lingered on Thomas's face for a moment, and Desmond had felt as if a curtain had been pulled aside and he was being offered a glimpse into a hidden corner of their marriage. He'd assumed that Thomas was the one who needed to be coddled and babied—Thomas with his shiny, baby head and his overbearing wife and his mother in the carriage house and his monstrous child whom he adored—but now he saw that was Jane's percep-tion of things. In reality, it was Thomas, solid and steadfast and dull, who ended up protecting Jane from her own worst impulses. In preparation for this trip, she'd had her hair cut shorter and permed, and it made her look de-fenseless, the way people always look when their efforts at dressing up produce unflattering results and their desire for beauty is revealed while the beauty itself remains elusive. The way he looked, no doubt, in the overpriced gray Armani jersey he'd bought yesterday in a moment of shopping self-indulgence that instantly soured into self-loathing. The back of Jane's neck was exposed and the perm was so recent, her hair appeared to fit her head badly, like a hat she'd bought for the color, despite the fact that it was the wrong size. She kept pulling at the curls in back, perhaps trying to loosen them up. She had on a gray flannel suit, just right for November in Boston, even this warm November, but a big mistake for Gulf City, Florida.

The plane bumped, as if its bottom had just scraped over a boulder, then rose up. The cabin was shot through with milky sunlight, and when Desmond looked out again, there was a field of dark blue beneath them. They were over the ocean now, making their way south along the coast. Within minutes, they'd be flying over Manhattan. For one reckless moment, he imagined that if he gazed out the window, he'd spot Russell down there, walking along Broadway, maybe reading the letter Desmond had written after visiting Rosemary and had finally put into the mailbox.

He'd gone through eight drafts of the thing. He started out with a raw, emotional plea he'd typed in a wine-fueled frenzy of sentimentality. "I don't care what you've done or with whom, I don't want you to move out, if that's what you're contemplating. I'll be back in a little more than a month. We'll work it out then. Let me finish this semester and finish this book. I feel certain I'm very close to finding what I'm missing, and all I'm asking for is the quiet space to do it." The next morning he'd woken up, reread the page-and-a-half letter and found it a bit too conciliatory. It wasn't strictly true that he didn't care what Russell had been up to. "I don't know what you've been doing, or with whom . . ." he revised. That afternoon, as he was reading over the second draft in his office at Deerforth, he'd been struck by the pleading tone in the part about finishing his book. He scratched out the "quiet space" and penciled in "I need a little fresh air, too." At midnight, sitting at his desk, he'd retyped the fourth draft. "I *know* what you've been up to." And the next morning: "If you want to move out so badly that you'd consider returning to that cell on C . . ." Over lunch, red pencil in hand: "I haven't exactly been crying into my pillow every night, you know." The many drafts were so jumbled in his mind, he wasn't entirely sure what was in the version he'd mailed, but he was fairly certain there was some veiled reference to a handsome, bi-sexual architect, and to the wonderful emotional freedom he was experiencing now that he could lay claim to a larger portion of his own identity.

Jane grabbed the armrests of her seat. "Where did Tim end up?" she asked.

"Somewhere in the back," Desmond said. "I can't figure him out. I don't know if he's a dolt or a genius, although I have the feeling it's either one or the other, no middle ground."

"He's twenty," Jane said, "meaning he was raised in a completely different culture from the one we know, so you and I have no basis for judging his intelligence. He might as well be a different species. Within ten years, he'll be ruling the world with his computer and media talents and we'll be extinct. We think in terms of pages, he thinks in terms of screens—computer, TV, movie. And therein lies the future."

Desmond supposed there was some truth to this, and yet what fascinated him about Tim, and about so many of the students in their late teens and early twenties he'd taught over the years, was that for all their computer savvy and sophistication, for all the cultural advantages and freedoms they'd been handed growing up in a time of peace and prosperity and sexual liberation, they seemed, in most emotional ways, to be right back in the 1950s, obsessing about a Saturday night date or an unreturned phone call, a crush or a crisis of insignificant proportions. If anything could save the human race for another couple of generations—unlikely, but not impossible—it wouldn't be advances in technology and scientific intelligence, but this lack of emotional development that pulled people back to their simplest needs and desires and left them stumbling over their deepest insecurities. In the end, there was nothing more compellingly human than that.

"I'll bet Chloe is up front eating lobster," Jane said. She sighed and handed the magazine back to Desmond. "I've never liked lobster. And lately, I can't even look at the poor things, trapped in their holding tanks at the supermarket."

In the airport lounge, Chloe had started chatting with a gray-haired businessman from Atlanta who, ten minutes later, had her ticket upgraded to first class so they could continue what must have been a riveting conversation. Chloe had seemed genuinely surprised by the attention: "Wasn't that nice of him?" she'd asked as she was gathering up her things for early boarding.

"Just for the record," Jane said, "no rich older man ever found me so interesting or attractive he offered me a first-class ticket. You have to be exactly the right blend of pushy, pretty, and emotionally needy, and I've never been good at keeping the pieces of my personality well balanced."

"Just for the record," Desmond said, "you seem very well balanced to me."

In the end, being a good friend usually came down to talking people out of their perceptions of themselves, especially the accurate ones.

"You wouldn't think I was a hopeless alcoholic if I ordered a Bloody Mary, would you?" Jane asked.

She was beginning to sound maudlin. People often get maudlin when they board airplanes and leave everything of importance behind them and can't decide whether they're afraid of crashing or hoping for it. When the drink finally came, Jane mixed together the tomato juice and the miniature bottle of vodka with the precision of a chemist, took a sip, and began rummaging through her enormous leather purse. "You know," she said, "I truly cannot remember the last time I had a whole day in which I wasn't responsible for doing a single thing." She took out a small vial of prescription pills and popped one into her mouth. "Vitamins," she explained. As she was about to put the bag under the seat, she reached into it and hauled out an appointment book, overstuffed with sheets of stationery, newspaper clippings, ragged slips of paper. She opened it up randomly and a few unevenly folded pieces of paper fell onto her lap. "This is what my week usually looks like," she said. "Gerald's doctor appointments, my shrink appointments, my shameful secrets. Not that I have any." She handed the book to Desmond. "It's perfect airplane reading."

It wasn't possible that the drink and the pill had taken effect already, but Jane seemed to be sinking more deeply into her seat. As long as he didn't end up having to carry her off the plane, he didn't mind. Once, many years earlier, he'd been involved with a pothead boyfriend who'd been so easily amused by lighting up a joint, he required blissfully little in the way of gifts, expensive entertainment, or conversation. If Jane had offered, he wouldn't have turned down one of her little yellow pills. She fumbled with the seat until she was partly reclining, then let her head drop back and her eyes close. The book was a hodgepodge of notes, most of them typed or scribbled on loose paper; the pages of the memo book itself were practically untouched. There were reminders about bills and facials and dinner guests, notes about *Dinner Conversation*, shopping lists, and menus. It wasn't possible that something this disorganized could help clarify anything for anyone; it wasn't an appointment book but an admission of defeat; handing it to him was a cry for help.

"You have an awful lot going on," he said.

"I do, don't I? And that's one book of many." She turned her head toward

Desmond, her face resting in a nest of her too-curly hair. "The lure of the fresh, naked page gets to me at least once a month, the hope that starting a new appointment book will be the same thing as starting a new life."

One thin strip of paper was entitled "Things For Gerald." A list of toys and books she intended to buy for Christmas or birthday presents, he assumed; on closer inspection, it proved to be something else. "Spontaneity, joie de vivre, physical confidence." Good luck finding any of those things in the aisles of Toys "R" Us. That was about as likely as him finding the character traits he'd been searching for in bottles of organic sugar pills and herbal extracts suspended in alcohol. The list covered half the page. At the bottom she'd written, in tiny print, the word "smiles." This was exactly the kind of scrap he would have celebrated finding if he'd been writing a biography of Jane, but with her sitting next to him, about to fall into a drug-induced sleep, it was embarrassingly intimate.

He reached over to put the book on her tray table, but she touched his hand lightly. "Keep it for me?" The tone of her voice, soft and girlish, made it sound like a plea. "It would be such a vacation for me to not have to think about any of that for the next few days."

"It's only fair to warn you," he said, "that when I'm alone in my room, I'll probably pore over every word, snooping into your life. It's part of my job."

"It doesn't matter. It's all written in code, and lately I've been having trouble keeping the code straight. You're welcome to all of it, Desmond. I trust you." A few minutes later, she added, in a voice heavy with sleep, "If you discover anything interesting in there, be sure to let me know, especially if it turns out I'm a halfway decent person."

The plane flew into a patch of turbulence and then got caught in an updraft that lifted it to a higher altitude. Two men in T-shirts and shorts who'd looked drunk as they'd stumbled into their seats, whooped with delight as if they were on one more ride at an amusement park. Jane had fallen asleep, and as they bumped higher into the sky, her head rolled gently from side to side, barely making a dent in her new curls.

2.

As recently as three years ago, the last time Desmond had visited Anderton's daughter, Lorna, and her collection of memorabilia, this stretch of the Florida panhandle had been a piney wonderland of shabby motels and tourist cottages scattered along the beaches and roadsides as if they'd been dumped there from a fast-moving truck. There were dark bars and unwholesome, oddball restaurants with gaudy signs. "Home of the Topless Oyster," "All You Can Eat Shrimp," "Ho-Made Po-Boys." He'd been fascinated with the run-down glamour of the place, imagining that if he were a completely different person—a married truck driver from southern Georgia, let's say—he'd come here to spend vacations with the family. Now even that shaky fantasy couldn't support its own unlikely weight. The area around the airport was being brutally developed with big concrete hotels thrown up by multinational chains and strip malls with the usual cast of retail characters and restaurants. It was as if some fungus had arrived in the hold of a plane, transforming the landscape close to the airport first, and starting to spread.

Jane was comatose in the passenger seat of the van, and Chloe and Tim were in back, playing an electronic game that made strange bleeps and elicited groans.

He supposed people found the growing uniformity of the world comforting. You didn't have to react to this landscape or these shops or restaurants because they were all identical to ones you'd seen thousands of times before in hundreds of other places. The food you bought at the big chain restaurants was so familiar, you didn't have to worry yourself with actually tasting it. The world was bursting at the seams with information and "content," information's brand-new sibling, and in order to assimilate all of that, you had to neutralize as much sensory input as you could.

Fortunately, as they got closer to Gulf City, the development thinned, leaving more of the seedy disrepair he remembered fondly from his last visit—roadside bars and motels, a few weed-choked vacant lots. A naval base that had been in Gulf City for decades had closed at the end of the 1980s, and the town was still reeling from the abandonment, refusing to pick up the pieces and start anew, like a bitter husband who couldn't accept that his wife had left him. Russell had accompanied him on that other visit and had declared Gulf City, "a real place, even if it is a really awful one." And yet all of it, the drinking dives and dying malls, the hot-sheets motels and the little restaurants named after the owner, were circumscribed by the incongruous beauty of the wide, green expanse of the Gulf waters and the white sand that seemed to stretch for miles.

Chloe had booked them into the Gulf City Hotel, which turned out to be a flat-roofed two-story motel painted in uneven shades of brown that reminded Desmond of pecan shells. The V-shaped building was broken into two long wings that angled out from either side of a glassed-in coffee shop and office, and it seemed to be embracing the parking lot, and, by inference, your most sacred possession: your car. Except today, there were only three cars in the lot; not much to protect.

As soon as she spotted the place, Chloe put down the electronic game and started making bleeps of her own. "This isn't a hotel," she cried. "It's barely a *mo*tel. Talk about false advertising!"

"If you ran a place that looked like this," Desmond said, "would you advertise honestly?"

"I guess I should have known something was up when they told me the price."

"It's fine," Jane said, although, as far as Desmond could tell, she'd barely opened her eyes. "We're only here for a few nights. As your executive producer, I approve."

Chloe stepped out to the pavement of the parking lot and waved her clipboard in front of her face, indicating either the intensity of the heat or a bad odor. She was wearing black Capri pants and a skimpy white T-shirt and a pair of thick-soled, open-toed sandals that made her look especially tall and narrow. Her face was flushed a dark, pretty shade of copper, and her hair hung halfway down her back in long tendrils. In Boston, she'd stand out for being exceptionally attractive and perhaps only slightly underdressed, but walking across the parking lot of this unpromising motel in a remote finger of Florida that had been dubbed the "redneck Riviera," she looked almost cartoonishly young and thin. And her confident stride in those thick sandals made her look more vulnerable than poised. She pulled open the glass door of the office and the white sunlight flashed in Desmond's eyes. If he was seeing through Chloe's well-made defenses to the weaknesses underneath, they were all in trouble. He looked up to the white sky and had a strong premonition that things were not going to go well here.

3.

The air-conditioning unit was clattering like an antique fan, and his room was so cold you could store meat in it. The walls were paneled with dark wood. In the dim light cast by an eggplant-shaped lamp on the bureau, the walls looked slick, as if they were coated with many years' worth of nicotine or were dripping with humidity. The place smelled of mildew and cigarettes. So much for the charm of undercapitalized businesses. Where was the Holiday Inn with its sanitized toilets and its spotless mediocrity when you needed it? Desmond sat on one of the double beds and started to take off his shoes, but looking at the shaggy orange carpeting, he thought better of it. Three nights. For three nights he could put up with anything. He pulled open the orange drapes, and the room was flooded with a burst of sunlight so bright it seemed to gobble up the room's flaws. There was ocean, the soft, shifting green of the Gulf, rippling in the wind like a field of grass. When you had this outside your door, how could it matter what color the carpet was or how dirty the walls? The white sand, fine quartz blown down from the Appalachians, started at the foamy edge of the water and sprawled—through spiky grass and scrub pines—right up to the back wall of the motel. He pulled the drapes shut. The funny thing about dazzling sun and pretty views was that they made you want to share them with someone else. Better by far to have a dank room that made you want to run away.

He turned the TV on and off, checked out the bathroom, unpacked a suitcase, and made a call to Lorna, confirming their meeting with her tomorrow morning. He pulled down the orange bedspread and jammed four thin pillows under his head and, for the next hour, read through Jane's lists. The business of biography had taught him that people were always the best sources of information about their own lives, providing you didn't believe much of what they said about themselves. You had to look for the longing between the lines, look for the person they were trying hard to be, learn how to read the essential lies they told to themselves. If you took Jane's lists at face value, you'd have to conclude that she was the hardest working wife and mother on the planet. But if you really wanted to know what occupied her mind, you'd have to decode the little check marks that showed up in the corner of certain pages of the appointment book. Poor Thomas, he thought, leafing through the numerous mentions of him scattered across the pages; he was the man Jane so eagerly wanted to love, which wasn't necessarily the same thing as being the man she did love.

He took a short nap, and when he woke up, decided to try the beach. On the same shopping spree that had produced the gray Armani shirt, he'd bought a $58 bathing suit, a satiny, bile-colored thing chosen solely for the technologically advanced way it emphasized his crotch. He pulled it on, looked at himself in the tarnished mirror over the hotel bureau, and fell back onto the bed laughing. It was about as appropriate for this beach and his body as a pair of space boots. It made him look like a skinny, jaundiced middle-aged man with a saggy pouch in the crotch that was as erotic as a knobby knee. Age is a sneak, hiding little clues to its presence all over your body, wrinkles and bags and dark circles and creaky joints you're unaware of until you trip over them just as you're trying to make a good impression.

It was between seasons, too late for the summer crowds that drifted down from Georgia for the Gulf breezes and the fishing, too early for the German tourists who flocked here in the winter. The beach stretched for miles in either direction, empty except for a few children running along the edge of the green water, screeching and splashing. The water was cooler than he expected and he dove in quickly and swam straight out from shore until he was warm and panting. When he stopped and looked back, the shore seemed impossibly far away. Hotels were lined up along the beach like barricades protecting the rest of the town from the waves. He rolled over onto his back, letting the salty broth of the Gulf buoy him up, and gazed at the blank sky arching over him. Love was a little like swimming, he thought. You float along in effortless comfort, not really taking into consideration that at any moment you could be dragged down under the surface and drown.

Tomorrow when they went to visit Lorna, Jane and Chloe and Tim could photograph the house, take shots of the collected career clutter. He had his questions for Pauline Anderton's daughter written down in a carefully composed list that narrowed in on those final years after her father had died and Pauline had gone into retreat. Why had she given it all up when she needed the money, finally had freedom, had club owners (albeit owners of minor clubs) hounding her to perform, and one legitimate record company ready to welcome her into their studio? Look how well he'd done, he thought as he paddled back to shore, in the privacy of his hollow room. If his relationship with Russell was the price he ended up having to pay for finishing this project, it just might be worth it after all.

As he was walking up the beach wrapped in a towel, he saw Jane sitting on the cramped cinder block patio behind the motel. She had on a blue, beachy bathrobe with big yellow flowers splashed on it, and her face was partly hidden by her sunglasses. She was holding a book in her hands, although she didn't seem to be reading it. As he got closer, he saw that it was the copy of *Playing with Childhood,* Gloria's harsh critique of parenting that he'd given her weeks earlier. He pulled a chair beside her and she peered at him over the top of her sunglasses. "Do you like my outfit?" she asked.

"Better than I like mine."

"Opposite ends of the same impulse—trying to hide your flaws by showing them off or covering them up. Thomas gave me this," she said, and fingered the lapels of the robe. "What's your excuse?"

"Low self-esteem." He tapped the cover of Gloria's book. "What do you make of this?"

"It says everything I've ever thought about children and childhood." She slid her sunglasses back up to her face and scratched at the back of her neck. It was late afternoon, and she couldn't have been out here for more than twenty minutes, but already her skin, newly exposed by the hairdo, looked scorched. "But reading it in someone else's words made it sound heartless. Poor Russell. If this book is any indication, he must have been raised in a laboratory."

"Gloria likes to get on her soapbox and be outrageous enough to make people listen. I think Russell probably had a fairly normal upbringing."

The corners of Jane's mouth turned down, and for a moment, Desmond had a horrible feeling she might get weepy. Having met Gerald, he should have known better than to fling around the word "normal" so casually. Trying to recoup, he said, "What matters is that, eccentric or not, Gloria was a loving, devoted mother."

"I'm sure she was. I'm not so sure I have been."

"According to your lists," he said, "you spend half your day doting on Gerald, driving him from one appointment to the next, taking him to museums, classes, lessons."

She waved off the significance of this with both hands. "A hired hand could do that. I'm talking about inside. I never felt that *hunger* to be a mother, that gnawing hunger so many women talk about. I always assumed

I'd have a child at some point, but it wasn't with any urgency. If anything, it was with resignation, the way you assume you'll probably have your wisdom teeth extracted at some point." She looked off toward the water where two little girls were digging in the sand at the edge of the waves. The sun was beginning to set and the sky along the horizon had started to turn pale green and pink, like an unripe tomato with a faint blush of color. The wind had picked up some since he'd come out of the water, and Desmond could feel the fine white sand blowing against his ankles. He didn't know how to respond to any of this; talk about parenthood had a vague, intangible quality to him, like listening to people talk about their vacations in places he had no particular interest in visiting.

"It's not something you can talk about with anyone," she went on. "I suspect Rosemary feels the same way about children, but I'd never talk about it with her. Nothing's considered more hateful in a woman than not wanting to bear children. Even women who abandon or abuse their kids are regarded with less suspicion, since they at least had them in the first place and there's always the chance they can be reformed."

"You had Gerald," he reminded her.

She shook her head slowly, back and forth, her tight new curls unmoving. "Almost from the day he was born, he was a completely independent person. I'd look down at him in his crib and he'd be staring at me with this indignant look in his eyes, as if he was saying: 'What do *you* want?' It must have been a response to something I was doing without even knowing it."

"Everyone probably feels that way at some point."

"They *don't,* that's the odd part. I used to meet with a group of new mothers to talk about feeding and sleeping and trying to fit motherhood into our lives. After a month, I had to drop out. I couldn't understand half of what they were saying, and it made me feel as if I wasn't a real mother. Worst of all, that I wasn't a real *woman.*" She paused. "I'm sure none of this makes sense to you."

He had his own problems with feeling like an impostor. There were moments when he was dining or drinking or having a conversation with a heterosexual friend or colleague, even an abundantly tolerant person, and saw a look of benevolent curiosity cross his or her face, and felt, suddenly, as if he'd been cast off to some vast plain of ambiguity and otherness, where his features were shifting and his gender was indistinct. Then he'd be overcome by his own curiosity—perhaps a bit less benevolent—about himself and where he belonged among women and men in the big picture of life. More than once, he'd felt that way with Jane herself. But never, he realized as he gazed down the beach, never with Russell. He'd always felt solidly in place with Russell, unambiguously male, even when engaged in the least manly of activities.

"But when you're with your husband," he said. "Then you know who you are—a real mother, a real woman. No?"

"Oh, well," she said, and set Gloria's book down on the white plastic table beside her. "Dale could make anyone feel like a real woman."

He was silent for a moment, hoping that the Gulf breeze would blow this little slip out to sea, but it must have blown it right back into her ears, for she turned her head away and took off her glasses. "Shit," she said and reached into the pocket of her bathrobe for a pack of cigarettes.

The colors of the sky had darkened and spread along the horizon like a stain. A gust of warm wind blew and an empty soda can rattled across the edge of the patio. One of the little girls on the beach screamed and ran up to the road where her mother was sitting on a low seawall.

"That appointment book I gave you," Jane said. "I'd love you to do me a favor and throw it out. I can't decipher the code anymore and even if I could, half of it is lies, stuff I made up to impress someone else or kid myself."

He reached out and took her hand. "Jane," he said. "Why are you telling me all this?"

The wind shifted and the soda can rattled back across the patio. "I honestly don't know," she said.

Twenty-one
Pancake Breakfast

Jane woke up hungry. She couldn't remember what she'd eaten yesterday. Very possibly nothing. Desmond had asked her to have dinner with him last night, but she was too exhausted—from the flight, the pills, the drive, the exertion of all the confessing she'd done on the beach. She wasn't sure what had brought that on, but lying in bed in the dank motel room with a frame of morning sunlight around the curtained window, she didn't regret it. She felt lighter than she'd felt in a long time, possibly the result of letting go of so many pent-up worries. Although it could be that she was coming down with a head cold from sleeping in this refrigerated cell.

She wanted to stand and look at herself in the mirror across from the bed, but it was midwinter in here. As for walking across the cracked tile floor of the bathroom, that was out of the question. Something was wrong with the air-conditioning system. Maybe even these artificial climates were going wacky. She grabbed a pack of cigarettes from the shelf attached to the wall beside the bed. The cigarette thing had gotten out of hand. At the airport on the way home, she'd toss out however many she had left and that would be that. Berman would probably tell her that taking up smoking in practically the same breath as her initial full-frontal fumbling with Dale was a sign of self-hatred. She was ready to buy the argument—after all, it was her argument, not Berman's—but that didn't explain why canceling the Dale situation had upped her cigarette intake. She clicked the remote control and a

274

pinpoint of light flared in the middle of the ancient TV screen. Last night, the local public television station rebroadcast a Keith Sommerstone documentary on the Korean War, and she'd watched an hour of it, mesmerized by the footage he'd gathered, his seamless editing, his ability to humanize even the most complicated political information, and the sheer scope of his project. He had vision. He was a genius. If she was going to have to go through life *not* being a genius—and at forty, the dream of being a prodigy had pretty much dried up—then she could at least appreciate someone else's brilliance.

Maybe her ambition for this project had been too narrow. Pauline Anderton and Great American Nobodies. She should have recognized the difficulty of selling the idea. She should have expanded her ambition. She shouldn't have let Dale fill her with optimism. The television screen finally sizzled to life. The public TV station was broadcasting one of those chipper children's shows which everyone raved about and which Gerald, at age four, had declared "moronic." Watching a pack of blobby creatures roll down a green and purple hill while mumbling nonsense syllables, she had to agree. Yet, at the time, his rejection of the show had felt like one more rejection of her. She hit the channel button a few more times until she landed on a morning news show and killed the sound. The screen was filled with maps with graphics of clouds and weather fronts swirling above them. It used to be that she saw these reports as mere predictions of temperature and precipitation; now she regarded them as diagnostic reports on the health of the planet.

She dialed her home number. Gerald picked up on the first ring, a cranky "Hel*lo*," as if she'd interrupted him at an important chore.

"Hi, honey," she said. "It's me."

"Hi . . . mom."

He was getting better at avoiding her first name, but there was still this slight hesitation.

"You and daddy weren't home when I called last night. Did you go out to dinner?"

"We went to the Cambodian place."

She could picture the two of them, sitting at one of the small corner tables in the restaurant's basement, quietly discussing food or computers or some book Thomas had given Gerald to read, as serious and engaged as a couple of grad students.

"Did you have a good day at school yesterday, sweetie?"

"Yes, except I wasn't sure who was going to pick me up, since you weren't here, and then I got sick and couldn't go to my piano lesson after all."

"Gerald! That's not like you. What happened?" Gerald had the most amazing constitution his pediatrician had ever seen. So far, he'd avoided all the major childhood illnesses, along with colds, flus, and ear and throat infections.

"I don't know. I just felt funny. So I went to the nurse's office and took a nap and then Thomas told me I didn't have to go to the lesson."

"I'm sorry, sweetie. Are you all right now?"

"I woke up a little iffy, but I think I'm starting to feel better."

Jane stubbed out the cigarette in the glass ashtray by the bed and sat up against the puffy, vinyl headboard, clutching the blankets against her chest. He missed her. What he was really saying, without saying it, of course, was that he missed her and had been worried that she was out of town. He had been anxious and depressed, had felt cut off from her, and now that she had called, now that they were talking, he was starting to feel better. Tell me more, Gerald, she longed to say. Tell me how you hated to see me leave and you wished I'd been at the restaurant last night, even if my presence would have dumbed down your conversation with Thomas. But no, she'd take what she'd been handed already and quit while she was ahead.

"Gerald, do me a favor, sweetie, and ask your father to pick up."

"I would like to, but he left early to visit Aunt Joyce and the baby. What's the baby's name again?"

"I think they decided on Clara." The name had been Brian's choice—God knows why—and wisely, Joyce had accepted it. Not the most attractive name, but unusual and interesting, and surely it was a good sign that Brian cared enough about his child's future to have an opinion about her name. "Is Sarah there? Is she making you breakfast?"

"I'm making it for her."

"I hope it's delicious. I'll talk to you later today."

"That would be nice."

"Nice," she thought as she got out of bed. He thought it would be nice for her to call. At this moment, coming from Gerald, it sounded like a declaration of love.

Tricked into believing it was as cold outside as it was in the room, she put on a sweater over her jersey. She opened her door and walked into a wall of wet heat. If she'd known it was going to be this humid, she wouldn't have bothered to get the disastrous haircut. The climate would have done it all for her and she could have saved the hundred and ten bucks. All this ferocious heat and it wasn't even eight o'clock. As she walked toward the coffee shop, a door opened in one of the motel rooms ahead—Chloe's room, if she remembered correctly—and Tim came out, bare-chested, his T-shirt clutched in one hand, his sneakers in the other. She stood beside the ice machine and watched as he made his way along the concrete walkway, fumbled with a key, and entered what had to be his room. If that meant what it appeared to mean, it more than made up for dragging unpaid-intern Tim down here and sticking him in one of these grim rooms. She couldn't imagine Chloe continuing this after the plane touched down in Boston, but at least for the moment, skinny little Tim had definitely scored. Good for him. Maybe he should head up to Desmond's room next and try his luck there.

The booths and counter stools in the coffee shop were upholstered in veiny red vinyl, and there was a plastic case on the counter filled with what appeared to be honest-to-God pies. Context was everything. In Boston or New York, this would be the hippest spot in town, all these coffee-shop-chic accoutrements, but here, in this place, it was just a tad too real. The waitress behind the counter motioned with a pot of coffee and said, "Sit wherever, I'll be right over."

Jane slid into a booth. The window offered a spectacular view of the parking lot and the road beyond, clogged with rush-hour traffic. Three men were on stools at the counter, cradling cups of coffee as if they were in no rush to get anywhere, casting disinterested glances at a television suspended from the ceiling. More clouds swirling over weather maps and shots of a rain-lashed island somewhere in the Caribbean.

The waitress came to her booth, adjusted her silverware, flipped her coffee cup and filled it, all with a show of nimble professionalism Jane admired. It isn't what you do in life that matters, it's how well you do it. She was a big, square woman with straight, dark hair that hung like a curtain to the middle of her back and was cut in long, rounded bangs in front, as if they'd been rolled in a can. Lucy, according to her name tag. No doubt younger than she looked, as this type of woman always seemed to be.

"Not too busy here this morning," Jane said.

"No. The storm probably scared them off. I just hope we don't get a rush at the last minute." Her accent sounded less Southern than country-western: I jest hope.

"Which storm is that?"

She shifted her weight onto one foot and nodded toward the television. "Another darned tropical storm. They all come up here from Mexico, blow up along the coast. I wish they'd go somewhere else for a change. My youngest's got to be at the hospital in Pensacola by two, so I don't have time for another storm."

"Nothing serious, I hope."

"Kidneys. But he's a tough little bastard. Six years old and he says to the doctor, 'I'm gonna kick this thing.' Can you imagine that?"

"I hope it goes well today."

"It will or it won't. Not up to me to decide. You know what you want?"

She'd decided on toast and a poached egg, but after listening to this tragic story, those items sounded so self-indulgently calorie-conscious, she couldn't bring herself to order them. "Buttermilk pancakes," she said. "With bacon."

There was a rack of postcards beside the cash register on the counter, and when the waitress had gone back into the kitchen, she went over to it and picked out three. One for Gerald, one for Thomas. One—why not admit it?—for Dale. Dear Dale, she'd write. Thank you for the loan. Thank you for not calling me.

She slid back into her booth and took a pen from her purse. "Dear Dr. Berman," she wrote, in tiny script, surprising herself. "Everything I haven't told you—about Thomas, about *Dale*—it isn't that I don't trust you, it isn't that I don't believe you could help, it's just that there's so much I don't want to know about myself. Can we start from scratch?"

Lucy delivered her pancakes, each nearly as wide across as the plate itself. If you were going to eat this kind of slop, you damn well better enjoy it. She smeared them with butter and poured a stream of syrup over the top until the whole mess was swimming, bacon included. As she was trying to fit a forkful into her mouth, she realized that she wasn't alone. Tim was standing next to her booth, looking down at her with his silent, goofy grin. She pointed to the banquette opposite her with her fork.

He was one of those skinny boys with shoulder-length hippie hair and the soft, scraggly facial hair of an adolescent. He had a long, pale face, and pale arms that stuck out shapelessly from his yellow T-shirt. It was odd how many of the people who worked on the technical side of the crew at the station were some variation on this physical type, proof, perhaps, that genetics had determined his career choice. He picked up a spoon and started to drum at the back of his hand with it.

"Sleep well?" she asked.

"I guess so," he said, unable to meet her eye.

"The air conditioner in my room was broken, so I spent the night huddled under a stack of blankets. Frankly, I was so exhausted, I probably would have fallen asleep if it had been snowing in there." He nodded, apparently as confused as she was as to why she was telling him this. She cut off another forkful of pancakes and put them into her mouth. "There's been too much going on lately—at work, at home."

He was beginning to look a little nervous, a sure sign that she was talking too much. "How's the pancakes?" he asked.

"Buttery. You should have some. You should have some of mine, in fact. You need them more than I do."

He ordered a bowl of corn flakes, a piece of pie, and a large Diet Pepsi. Her immediate impulse was to scold him for his diet, but hers wasn't much better this morning. "You're ready for the taping today?"

"I guess so." He hooked his stringy hair behind his ears. "I mean everything's more or less ready."

When his food arrived, she sat back and watched him shovel in the cereal and wash it down with soda. This was one way to suppress her own rampaging appetite.

"Have you enjoyed working on this project?" she asked.

"I'm getting credit," he said. "At school."

"Credit. Basically, that's all anyone wants in life, credit; not quite as good as appreciation, but a reasonable alternative." She reached back among the salt and pepper shakers and the ketchup and mustard bottles and slid the ashtray across the table. She lit a cigarette, blew the smoke above his head, and asked him if he minded her smoking, embarrassed by the realization that she was probably trying to be seductive. "You must be learning a lot from Chloe."

"I guess. Yeah, I am. She says she learned a lot from *you.*"

Jane was touched by this. Chloe often thanked her for her help, was generous with her appreciation, but compliments always count for more when they come through a third party.

"She likes you a lot," he went on. "She felt terrible about that dinner show getting canceled."

Jane bristled and ground out her cigarette. It wasn't that she expected Chloe wouldn't talk about it, but it was the first time anyone outside the station had mentioned it, and it made the loss of the show more real; the story of the cancellation had a life of its own, and she couldn't control it. "I appreciate her sympathy, but obviously, it had nothing to do with her."

Tim took another big swallow of his Diet Pepsi, bobbed his head, and said, "Yeah, that's what I told her. I told her they must have had the whole cancellation planned way before they accepted her proposal for a show."

Jane felt her face flush. At the counter, one of the men got up and walked toward the door while the remaining two advised him to board up his windows, assuming he'd taken down the boards from the last storm. The butter and syrup and grease from the bacon were starting to congeal on her plate, and the sight of the hardening puddles of slime made her feel queasy. The subject of Chloe's contrition seemed to have broken through Tim's wall of silence; he was talking, or his lips were moving anyway, although Jane was having a difficult time hearing the words that were coming out. She was bargaining with herself, trying to talk herself out of this hot, senseless rage she felt toward Chloe, all tangled up with the sick feeling in her stomach. Jane hadn't had any long-term hopes for *Dinner Conversation,* and some tiny piece of her—carefully tucked into a far corner of her body—was happy for Chloe. But for Christ's sake, the least she could have done was tell her she was actually setting up meetings, writing proposals, and pitching some of the ideas she had tossed around with Jane. She could have been adult about the whole thing and come to talk with her after David had broken the bad news about *Dinner Conversation.* Jane motioned the waitress over to their table. "I'm done with this," she said, indicating the mess on her plate.

She watched the waitress gather up the dish and her silverware. For her own sake, someone should sit Chloe down and have a talk with her, tell her how to behave, how to avoid burning bridges, how to take advantage of her advantages without burying a lot of people in the process. Maybe this afternoon when they got back from Anderton's daughter's house, Jane would take her out for a drink and a heart-to-heart.

The door to the coffee shop opened, and Chloe walked in.

And then maybe, on the way home, she'd drown her. All right, so she was young, smart, beautiful; Jane had no resentment about that, or none that she couldn't control. But Jane had considered herself Chloe's mentor, had spent what undoubtedly amounted to *hours* helping her shape and refine some of her ideas.

Waitress Lucy leaned over the table to retrieve Tim's empty cereal bowl. "What gets me," she said, "is that they come in and ruin Miami so you can't even live there, and then they start marching up this way, as if we don't have enough problems with crowding already."

Tim was trying to get an ice cube unstuck from the bottom of his glass, pounding the bottom of it with the side of his fist. And which of the generally shallow ideas of Chloe's had the station grabbed at? "I'm sorry?" Jane asked the waitress. "What did you say?"

"They don't want to learn English, so we've got to spend millions putting up signs in Spanish." Lucy had the plates and silverware expertly stacked on her arm. Jane didn't know what crucial piece of her non sequiturial monologue she'd missed, but it sounded like some narrow-minded rant. The waitress motioned with her shoulder toward the cash register where Chloe was slowly turning the rack of postcards. "And look at her," she said, "all done up in that costume, like a spic whore."

The angry diatribe Jane was composing in her head came to a screeching halt. Had she heard correctly? She couldn't remember when or where she'd last heard a slur of this kind tossed off in what she'd assumed to be polite conversation, and the naked ugliness of it was like a blow. The last minute fell into place: ruin Miami, learning English, overcrowding. Nausea again gripped her stomach. Tim turned and waved at Chloe.

"Sorry," the waitress said. "I didn't know she was a friend of yours."

"That isn't the point," Jane said.

Tim started to jiggle his skinny legs; Jane could feel the floor under her feet shaking. "Yeah, and she's not Puerto Rican."

"And *that* isn't the point either!" Jane said. "Assuming it's all right to say that in front of us, whether we know her or not! As if we were as racist as you are."

"Yeah. Whatever." Lucy picked up Tim's dirty napkin and walked off.

Chloe clomped to the booth on her big, thick sandals and shooed Tim over on the banquette. "Have you guys heard about the storm? They might get something like half a foot of rain here."

Jane tossed her cigarettes and matches into her purse. She couldn't even look Chloe directly in the face. She felt such a confusing mix of anger—for obvious reasons—and apology—for not taking her claims of discrimination more seriously, for not defending her more loudly, probably for being white—she didn't dare open her mouth. She pulled a twenty dollar bill out of her purse and slapped it onto the table. Let Lucy keep the change or give it to her sick kid, assuming she really had one. "You're not eating here," Jane said, and slid out of the booth.

"That's okay. I only want coffee."

"You don't want anything here. Believe me."

"I just want—"

She took hold of Chloe's upper arm—narrower than her own wrist—and gave it a tug. "I said we're leaving. All of us. Right now. We're not giving this coffee shop another penny."

She practically dragged Chloe out the door with Tim trailing behind them like a child embarrassed by his parents. "Did someone say something?" Chloe asked.

"Yes," Jane said. The heat and humidity slammed into her again as they walked outside. She let go of Chloe's arm and leaned against the hot glass of the door to stabilize herself. "Someone said something. And I'm sorry, I'm very, very sorry." Chloe opened her pretty mouth, outlined in subtle pink lipstick, about to speak some brave and wise words. "But how could you *do* this to me, Chloe? How?"

"I just came in for coffee, Jane. It isn't my fault."

"No," Jane said. "It isn't. It absolutely is not. And I know it, but I'm pissed off anyway." She walked toward her room, digging in her bag for her keys.

"You forgot this," Tim called after her. "On the table."

She ignored him and made it to her door just in time. She needed ten minutes of privacy, that was all, ten minutes for a good, humiliating, poor-forty-year-old-me cry. Then she'd be ready to put it behind her and face the rest of the day.

Twenty-two
Desperate Hair

1.

All in all, it had not been a good day.

Desmond collapsed back onto the orange bedspread in his room at the Gulf City Hotel. He'd complained about the broken air conditioner at the front desk this morning, and the clerk had told him, cheerfully, as if offering a solution to the problem, that the air conditioners were broken in almost *all* the rooms. Infuriating as the response was, it did make him feel marginally better to know he hadn't been singled out for frostbite. It was late afternoon and the air outside was steam-bath wet and hot, but it couldn't be above fifty in this chamber of horrors. He kicked off his shoes and folded himself, mummylike, into the bedspread.

Things had gone wrong from the moment he woke up and turned on the television. Almost every local channel had reports of a tropical storm—a rogue storm, an anomaly for this time of year—zigzagging its way through the Gulf. The chances of it hitting Gulf City full force were slim—thirty percent, if he averaged out the conflicting predictions—but it was being discussed by newscasters as a near apocalyptic event. Between stock footage of rain-lashed palm trees, they were broadcasting shots of people pushing around shopping carts full to overflowing with bottled water and toilet paper. One religious channel was presenting it as yet another manifestation of divine retribution for the opening of a gay strip club, the address of which they unfortunately had not revealed.

As they were driving out to Lorna's house, everyone was strangely quiet, Jane staring out the passenger window, Tim and Chloe pressed against the doors on either side of the back seat. Worried about the storm, Desmond had thought initially, but then he'd asked what he assumed was a perfectly innocuous question about breakfast and there had been a mumbled chorus of disapproving voices: "Don't ask." "What breakfast?" "Who knows!" There had been a fight over breakfast, he conjectured, the specifics of which he would undoubtedly rather not know. So why, if they were all at each other's throats, did he feel like the one being shut out?

Lorna had greeted them at her door with a disingenuous look of surprise, as if he hadn't confirmed their arrival yesterday afternoon. "I thought you might have turned around and gone north again, once you heard about all this tropical rain they're predicting."

"It's silly, isn't it?" Jane had said, doing her best to sound knowing and conspiratorial. "We have a similar problem in New England—dire warnings about snowstorms that never materialize. You get exhausted from all the hype."

Lorna was in her mid-fifties and had been teaching fourth grade for more than twenty years. She had a way of looking at you with disapproving condescension, as if she were about to slap you with a detention or take away your hall pass. "You get a lot more exhausted from cleaning up after the storms that *do* materialize. *I* certainly do, anyway."

Jane obviously felt she was being judged harshly and had backed into a defensive stance, and any hope of rapport between the two women was dashed. Lorna discerned that Chloe and Tim were there for the technical side of things and demoted them to the bottom rung of the hierarchy. "Please don't put that tripod there," she said, as if she were talking to two disrespectful ten-year-olds. "Can't you see what the legs are doing to my carpet? Would you like me to come into *your* home and do that to *your* carpets? No, I didn't think so."

Lorna looked like some of the earlier pictures of her mother—broad-shouldered and thick-waisted with an impressively large head. But while

Pauline had gone for the bouffant hairstyles of the 1960s, usually colored with flat brown, do-it-yourself dyes, Lorna had her graying hair cut into a mannish bob, parted on one side and close-cropped in the back. She had big square eyeglasses she was in the habit of yanking off her face and staring at, as if to say, "How did *those* get there?"

The house had been redecorated since Desmond's last visit. Lorna's youngest daughter had started up an interior decorating business in Pensacola and had used Lorna's house as a testing ground and showroom. The living room was a mad, overgrown garden of floral chintz slipcovers, floral curtains, floral swags over the window frames and doors, and big, ceramic vases stuffed with silk peonies and roses and lilacs and magnolias and irises. There were so many clashing patterns and colors, the overall effect was similar to one of those op art pieces so popular during the LSD craze of the 1960s.

"I love what she did in here," Desmond said, trying to focus his eyes.

"Yes," Lorna barked. "It's very feminine."

"I see you've moved your collection of memorabilia," he said.

"It clashed with the new decor, so we stuck it out here." She led them out to a glassed-in sunporch on the side of the house. There was a ceiling fan spinning at the far end, but with the windows cranked shut and the sun beating on the roof, the room must have been over a hundred degrees. Two long tables were set up under the windows along one wall, and on them, Lorna had stacked up, in no discernible order, album covers, newspaper clippings, photo albums, and plastic bags of Pauline Anderton's stage outfits. Desmond stood in the intense heat, gazing down at the collection. Much of it had been bleached or rotted by the sun, some of the dresses appeared to have mildew stains on them, and everything was covered with dust. Even if there was something marginally appropriate about it, it was still heartbreaking.

Lorna must have been able to read the disapproval on Desmond's face. "My mother wasn't the least bit sentimental about her career or anything else," she said, enunciating every word with her careful, schoolteacher diction. " 'Hit the high C and get the hell out of there.' That was one of her mottos. She wouldn't approve of me keeping any of this stuff in the first place, so I'm not worried she wouldn't approve if some of it is getting a little worn. It isn't a museum, you know."

In retrospect, it seemed as if all the disappointments of the day were preparing him for the biggest let-down of all—his interview with Lorna. Sitting in an overstuffed armchair with a sunflower slipcover, arms folded over her chest, yanking her glasses off and on, Lorna had alternated between crisp, vague, and evasive answers.

Had her mother been discouraged by her husband, Michael's, dismissal of her talent?

"She never listened to what he said."

Had she been hurt by his criticism of her singing?

"She wasn't easily hurt."

Why had her mother given up singing after her husband died?

"She wanted to."

Why had she turned down so many offers?

"She felt like it."

As for the information supplied to them by the Walshes, about Pauline's last rowdy days, her fights with her sister, her tendency to throw furniture around—Lorna tossed that off as meaningless.

"I didn't know those two were still alive. You couldn't trust anything they said even before they lost their minds."

She broke off the interview after two hours, claiming she had to go out and stock up on supplies for the storm. Desmond had managed to secure a promise from her that she'd let them come back tomorrow. "Come if you want," she said, and then qualified the invitation with: "Assuming we haven't all blown out to sea." They could rearrange some of the memorabilia if they wanted to, lay it out so it would be easier to photograph. Tim had packed up the video equipment and stacked it all in neat piles in a shady corner of the sunporch. Chloe didn't want to part with it overnight, but leaving it there was like a security deposit. Lorna couldn't change her mind about letting them in, and Desmond had discovered over the years that you never knew what you were going to find once you got your foot in the door.

Although really, he thought, lying on the thin, uneven mattress, wrapping the orange bedspread around his body more tightly, listening to the relentless clatter of the broken air conditioner, he didn't hold out too many hopes for this one. Lorna would offer nothing tomorrow she hadn't offered today. The collected junk would look just as badly deteriorated. He wasn't going to find a missing key to Pauline's story. Jane had said little on the ride home, obviously as discouraged as he was about this project. When he finally asked her what she'd thought, she said, "That Lorna's not exactly great TV material."

As he was showering this morning, he'd had a fantasy that he'd walk into

Lorna's house and feel an inner vibration, the kind of thing some people report feeling when they hallucinate a ghostly presence. He'd sit down with Lorna and, armed with the insight he'd gained while on sabbatical from his relationship with Russell, he'd wrest from her the essential truth about the end of Pauline Anderton's life. His understanding of Anderton would be complete, the disparate pieces of her life would connect neatly, he'd go back to Boston and wrap up the whole package. And no matter how unfortunate the effects of his Boston sabbatical had been on his relationship with Russell, he would at least know that he'd been right about taking it; it was something he'd had to do to reclaim his identity and clear his mind.

2.

Desmond and Jane decided to have dinner together and set out from the hotel on foot. The wind was up tonight, and as they walked along the promenade, the powdery white sand blew up from the beach and across the road like a dusting of fine, dry snow. The water and the sky were a matching shade of golf-course green. Weather reports were as inconclusive this evening as they'd been all day. The traffic had disappeared, and many of the bars and restaurants were closed—for the season or the storm, Desmond wasn't sure which. For all the threats of violent rain and wind, there was something relaxing about the thought of a large, loud weather system coming to knock down a few trees and set right the disordered pattern of the jet stream.

Jane stopped to read the menu posted outside a white stucco steak house. "We did a show on mad cow disease a few months ago," she said. "They think it can incubate in the body for up to twenty-five years."

"Frightening thought." And yet, what was life but one big incubation period for all the miseries and indignities that would eventually kill you? "Beef might not be the best choice in this area anyway."

"I suppose we should look for something fishy."

"That's probably the sensible way to go. Something alcoholic might be another sensible way to go."

It was still hot, despite the wind, and the farther they got from the hotel, the more slowly they walked. They stopped at a place on the beach, a small brown clapboard building with a sign that flashed the word: "Co ktails" in blue neon. The Brown Room, the long-defunct lounge where Pauline Anderton had been discovered, was probably similar to this. It was nearly empty, and the air smelled of stale alcohol and cigarettes, but there was something about the giddy melancholy of the blue Christmas lights behind the bar and the purple fluorescent glow from a murky fish tank that appealed to Desmond's current mood. To Jane's, too, apparently, for she said, "Exactly what I had in mind."

When their drinks arrived, they clinked glasses despondently. After a few sips, Desmond said: "I couldn't think of anything to toast, could you?"

"Not really. I wouldn't call it an auspicious day. It started out badly and kept moving in that direction. Maybe tomorrow will be better."

"Tomorrow will be windier," Desmond said. "Apart from that . . ."

Halfway through her second drink, Jane leaned forward in her chair and lit a cigarette from the candle in the middle of the table, exhaled a mushroom cloud of smoke, and began confessing.

They hadn't received the money from the station, she said. She'd lied about that. Why? To please him and to make herself feel good, important, productive. They weren't going to receive money from the station. As far as the station was concerned, their project was not viable. These drinks, that hotel, this whole trip was being funded by a loan, money she'd borrowed from a friend. And that was just for starters. Did he want to hear more? Her show, *Dinner Conversation,* had been canceled. She'd stay on at the station, but she'd be shuffled into some humiliatingly minor position working on *DC*'s replacement, a show based on a concept proposed by pretty, perfect Chloe, whom, by the way, she couldn't even be angry at anymore because this morning, over breakfast, in the coffee shop at their swell auberge, she'd witnessed, firsthand, the kind of racist insults that Chloe, pretty and perfect or not, occasionally had to put up with. And, just in case he was wondering, the "friend" she'd borrowed the money from—all very hush-hush and under-the-table—was her ex-husband. Dale. Maybe he'd heard her mention the name once or twice?

"It has a way of popping up in conversation," Desmond said.

"He has a way of popping up in my life."

The bartender was standing in the back of the cocktail lounge, discussing the Gulf-facing windows with a man in overalls. Probably making plans to board them up. It might be fun to ride out a storm in this seedy dive, windows shuttered and Christmas lights blinking, an unlimited supply of potable liquid within easy reach.

When they'd returned to the hotel from Lorna's house earlier in the afternoon, Tim had pulled Desmond aside and handed him a postcard which, he said, Jane had left on the table at the coffee shop this morning. "I meant to give it to her, but I forgot." Too intimidated was more to the point. The picture on the front was supposedly of the beach, but the photographer had obviously fallen in love with the road. The beach was relegated to the background where it appeared as a blur of white. On the back, she'd written a note to her shrink, a touching admission of guilt, but it wasn't clear to him—probably it wasn't clear to Jane, either—if she had intended to send it or not. He didn't know what to do with it himself; tossing it out might be the simplest course.

"You remember when we were at the Ritz," Desmond said, "the day you told me the station had almost certainly okayed the money? You also told me that day that your marriage was in the WASH cycle. Do you remember that? Warm Affection mixed with . . . something else I'm not sure of."

"Oh, yes. That was my wishful thinking du jour."

"I have the feeling it might be more a matter of Wondering About Second Husband. Choice of, to be more specific."

"I had an affair with him, Desmond. With Dale. Which is like going back for seconds to the buffet table where you got food poisoning." She let her head fall into her hands and gave a tug at her hair. "Ugh. I *hate* this perm. Despise it. Don't you?"

"Yes, it's horrible. It makes you look older and, to be even more blunt, it makes you look a little desperate."

"I am desperate. Isn't that obvious? I couldn't *be* any more desperate. Who else but a desperate person would do such a thing?"

"Maybe you're still in love with him."

"I don't know," she said. "All I know is, he understands me, and when I'm with him, I know he sees me for who I am."

In the flickering light of the candle, it was clear to Desmond that Jane, in her desperate hair, was wearing a costume. There's always something exhilarating and awful about seeing people clearly, and most often, especially if you like them, you have to look away. So he couldn't tell her that it seemed obvious she had it backward, that it was Thomas who understood her and saw her for who she was, while Dale merely saw her for who she wanted to be.

"I suppose we should be moving on to dinner soon," he said.

"We should," she said.

They ordered another round of drinks. Dinner was not on the menu tonight.

Twenty-three
Margo?

1.

He opened his eyes, stared up at the ceiling over the bed for a moment, and then turned on his side. Where was he? He was freezing. Florida, that was it. He could hear sand, that fine white quartz sand for which the area was famous, blowing against the window. He tried to get up, but his head was spinning. It had been years since he'd had a genuine hangover. He got himself upright, sat on the edge of the bed facing the window until he found his balance, then stood and opened the drapes. It was after seven, but so cloudy, there wasn't much more light out there than there had been at midnight when he and Jane had finished the last of their drinks and somehow—he wasn't yet clear on the specifics—made it back to the Gulf City Hotel. The chairs and tables and umbrellas had been removed from the patio, and the sand was rising in swirling clouds that looked like ghosts, dancing above the beach.

In the bathroom, he decided having a hangover wasn't so bad. There was something about the dazed, muffled way his mind was functioning that was restful. True, his life was rapidly becoming an empty shell, but in his current condition, he could appreciate how much more free time that would leave him.

As he was returning from the bathroom, he noticed that Jane was sleeping in the other double bed, wrapped up in blankets against the chill of the broken air conditioner. It came back to him then, the way they'd crawled back into the room and she'd collapsed on the bed, and asked if he minded if she slept there. "I don't think I can move," she'd said, and then immediately added, "In other words, I don't want to be alone."

He was beginning to fall back into unconsciousness when the phone rang. Jane groaned and draped an arm over her eyes. "Gerald?" she asked. "Is everything all right?"

It was Chloe, clipped and wide awake, clearly not hungover at all. "I tried calling Jane," she said, "but she isn't in her room."

"I know," Desmond told her. "She's here. What's up?"

"She's there? Well, whatever." Her mother had called her an hour ago to tell her that she'd been watching the Weather Channel and thought she should get on a plane before they closed down the airport. There was a chance of flooding. There were high wind warnings. She paused and waited for Desmond to respond, and when he didn't, she said, "And I'm just not convinced this project is worth the risk, Desmond. I'd recommend you rethink your plans."

The rats were leaving the ship, wise creatures. "I'll take it under advisement," he said.

"I called the airline and got two seats on a flight that's leaving this morning. There are a few more spaces available, if you want to change your reservation. We have to leave for the airport in ten minutes."

"Can you be ready to leave town in ten minutes?" he asked Jane. She was lying on her back, her eyes and mouth wide open, and didn't move. "We'll be staying."

"Oh, well, since you are, I'll stop by your room and give you a list of all the video equipment, just so you won't forget anything. And I've written up a little contract for you to sign, saying you take full responsibility for getting it all back to Boston."

"What if we'd decided to come back with you?" he asked her.

"You didn't," she said. "Also I've got your airline tickets, the paperwork on the van, the receipts for the deposit on the rooms . . ."

A few minutes later, she knocked on his door, handed him a fat manila envelope of paperwork, her handwritten contract, and a pen. "I'll have to have my lawyer check this over first," he said.

"Very funny. The main thing is, don't check the equipment at the curb. Flag down a skycap—make sure he's a real one; you can tell by the photo ID and the shoes. If they're all beat up, get someone else—and follow him to the counter."

"I will. Anything else?"

"I'm just trying to be helpful, Desmond."

"I know that, and you are. In fact, you've been extremely helpful all along, and both Jane and I appreciate it."

Tim was standing at the edge of the curb, and when a taxi pulled into the parking lot of the hotel, he waved his scrawny arm to flag it down.

"And we appreciate Tim's help, too."

Chloe had an efficient black suitcase, a little canvas sarcophagus on wheels. So far, he'd seen her in three different outfits. How she managed to fit them all into such a tiny case was a mystery. She passed the suitcase to Tim. "Load it in the trunk," she told him. "And make sure there's nothing on top of it because my PalmPilot's in there." She peered over his shoulder, into the room. "Is Jane still there?"

"I think she's in the bathroom."

"Tell her I'll see her back at the station." She leaned in and gave Desmond a soft kiss on the cheek, almost as if she were bestowing a gift. She smelled of bergamot and orange oil, and her lips were warm, and watching her walk to the taxi, toss her lush black curls, and step into the back seat, Desmond felt as if a gift had been bestowed upon him.

2.

As they drove through the swampy, overgrown back streets on the outskirts of Gulf City, Jane noticed that many of the houses had their windows shuttered. She ought to be concerned about the storm, she knew, but this hateful, selfish part of her had to take into consideration the fact that no matter how many roofs leaked and how many houses suffered damage from water or wind, not one of them would be hers. Her house, she supposed, was suffering damage of a different sort. Tropical storm Jane had blown through and thrown life there into disarray, and she didn't know how to start the cleanup. Make a resolution, that was usually the way she began. Except that now she was beyond resolutions. She'd broken too many. She no longer believed herself. This project was rapidly spinning toward disaster, and she was spinning right beside it. She'd bared her soul to Desmond, revealed every piece of information she could think to reveal, until finally she'd ended up feeling shredded. And she still didn't have a clue what to do to put her life back together. *I'd be happier if you were my wife.* But what if now, after her transgressions this fall, she didn't know how to be his wife?

They stopped at a light, and off to the right she saw a low, stucco house with an overgrown lawn, and an immense satellite dish off to one side. Three children in bathing suits were chasing each other with buckets of water, while their mother, hair in curlers, cigarette in mouth, washed the car. That was the sign of either reckless optimism or stupidity, washing your car as a drenching tropical storm bore down on the Gulf. The woman looked up at the car, and Jane waved at her. Good job, she wanted to tell her. The car looks great. When you're done, want me to help you wash your windows?

Outside Lorna's house, a thin man was standing on a stepladder, adjusting the shutters over the big windows of the living room. "That's Frank," Desmond said, "Lorna's husband. He's the principal at the school where she teaches. I imagine that's how they met. Not a bad guy, but he's used to having the last word, so it's best not to contradict him."

"In that case, I'd better keep my mouth shut."

Desmond pulled into the drive, shut off the engine, and they stepped out into the hot, soupy air. The sky was a deep, dark green, a lovely color for a ginger ale bottle, but a little disconcerting for the usually cerulean heavens.

"Can I help you?" Frank asked as they approached the house.

"We have an appointment to see Lorna," Desmond said. "Although we might be a few minutes early. I don't know if you remember me. I interviewed you a couple of years ago about your mother-in-law."

"I remember you," Frank said. "I just can't believe you'd come out here with this storm on its way. Lorna's not going to want to talk to you today. Don't you listen to the weather?"

Principal or not, Jane didn't see the point in merely caving in. "It's terrible the way they report things, isn't it?" she said. "The media is completely out of control."

He looked down at her disdainfully from his perch on the third step of the ladder. "As I understand it, you're both from the media, one way or another."

The wind blew Jane's hair into her face. Maybe she should have taken her own advice and kept her mouth shut.

"We left some equipment here yesterday," Desmond said. "We'll just pick it up and be on our way."

"Well, you'll have to check that out with Lorna first."

He, no doubt, was as terrified of litigation as everyone else in the country. Personally, Jane loathed the kind of people who reach for a lawsuit at the first signs of damage or disappointment. One of the women who worked at the station had discussed, with astonishing sincerity, the possibility of suing her son's school for not giving him a passing grade in biology. Even if she'd never consider actually filing a lawsuit, it was certainly handy having them around as loose threats.

"The equipment is worth hundreds of thousands of dollars," she said, "and we'd hate to burden you with the responsibility of having to shelter it and make sure nothing happened to it during a storm."

When Lorna finally came to the door, she told them they'd have to postpone the interview. "You don't think I'm going to sit in there and talk about mother with the house washing away, do you? I've got too many storm preparations. You can come back tomorrow if you like."

"The fact is," Desmond said, "I think we've got as much information as we need. We want to pick up the equipment and go."

"You're giving up," Lorna said, triumphantly, as if she'd known all along her dead mother would ultimately prove too much for weak-willed people like them.

"We haven't decided yet," Desmond said. "Right now, we need to get the equipment. You agreed to let us in and we're not leaving without it."

Lorna finally stepped aside and opened the door for them. "Ten minutes," she said. "That's it."

As Jane was stepping into the house, she looked up to the green sky. They were all overreacting. It was nice, for once, to be the person who was taking things in stride. A drop of rain hit her on the side of the nose and exploded against her skin, cold and wet.

3.

Almost all the windows in the house had been shuttered and the rooms were dark and cool. There was something comforting about the way the house felt, lit in this dim way by a few lamps in the suffocatingly floral living room. Judging from the smell, Lorna's storm preparations included baking; Desmond was almost overwhelmed by the smell of cookies and chocolate. How worried could she be about the weather if she'd spent most of the morning whipping up a batch of toll house cookies?

"Everything's out there," Lorna said, pointing to the sunporch. "Right where you left it. What happened to your young helpers?"

As Desmond wandered out to the sunporch, he heard Jane telling Lorna something about Chloe's and Tim's return to Boston on the last flight out. The light filtering through the cracks in the shutters did little to illuminate the sunporch. It was much cooler in here than it had been yesterday, but the humidity was still stifling. This was a room for storing exotic tropical plants or cigars, not a collection of perishable paper and vinyl. Tim had arranged the black canvas bags and the metal suitcases and the lights and the tripods in a neat pile by the door. It would take several trips to get it all out to the van. He picked up two heavy cases, carried them into the living room and set them beside the front door. From the kitchen, he heard Jane say, "Coffee would be fine, if you're making it. They're very good. Mine always come out dry. My son is trying to teach me how to bake, but I'm hopeless."

He stepped back into the hot air of the porch. It had started to rain. He could hear it drumming loudly against the roof, but nothing out of the ordinary, certainly not the predicted apocalyptic deluge. He heard a rustling at the far end of the room, near the tables stacked with the Pauline Anderton collection. Probably an animal, come inside to take shelter from the rain, eating its way through the stacks of old clippings. Too bad they hadn't been able to film that—mice munching on the last remains—a perfect shot to begin the documentary. The documentary that wasn't to be. He gathered up an armload of cases.

A branch scraped against one of the shutters, and then, from the far end of the room, he heard a rustling of fabric and what sounded like a fart. Desmond peered down the narrow room to the shadowy far end where Lorna had dumped the furniture ousted from the living room during the floral makeover. He set down the cases and flipped a switch by the door. A cone-shaped wall lamp cast a beam of faint, yellow light into the gloom and lit up the abandoned chairs and end tables. He heard another sound—a groan, he was almost certain. He adjusted the lamp so the light shone first on one of the windows and then on a high-backed chair. There, hunched over and mumbling, sat an old woman in a floral housedress. She straightened up, shielded her eyes against the light, and barked out two or three unintelligible words.

"Excuse me?" he said, hoping he didn't sound as stunned as he felt.

"Lower it," she commanded.

He readjusted the light and maneuvered his way to the back of the room. "I'm sorry," he said, squatting down until they were at eye level. "I didn't see you sitting here."

She gazed at him through a pair of square eyeglasses. "Who?" she asked. "Who did?"

"Who did . . . what?"

Perhaps he'd woken her up. One of her hands was wrapped around a coffee mug she had resting on the arm of the chair. She lifted it to her mouth and took a sip. "What noise?" she asked.

"Noise?"

"What is it?"

"Ah. It's rain," he said. "There's a storm on the way, and it's started to rain."

She nodded, and her whole body bobbed forward from the waist. "Oh, yeah. Sophia."

Sophia? And then he remembered: the name of the storm.

"Same crap," she said. "Can't trust anyone."

Whatever that meant. "No, you can't. You know, you might be more comfortable in the house. I think Lorna's baked some cookies for you."

Margo—for surely this was Pauline Anderton's senile sister—scoffed at this comment and stuck out her tongue. "She makes lousy cookies. I wanted pie, but she wasn't in the mood for pie."

There was a wooden folding chair leaning against the wall. Desmond opened it up and set it on the floor across from Margo. She would be in the neighborhood of eighty-three now. She looked tiny, sunk into the cushions of the chair, but her face was so smooth, her skin so pink and translucent, she appeared to have entered a second infancy. She was wearing a faded white and blue flowered housedress with a smock over it. Although "wearing" didn't seem the most apt word, since it looked as if the clothes had been buttoned onto her with little thought as to whether or not they fit.

"We visited your old house," Desmond said.

She opened her eyes a bit wider. "What old house?"

"Your old house in Waugborn. Massachusetts."

"I never had any old house in any *Waug*born."

"Well, yes, as a matter of fact, you did. You and your husband had a little ranch. Raised ranch, might be the right term." He gave the street address and described the neighborhood as he imagined it had been when she lived there.

"That was a new house," Margo said, "not old."

"Good point. These days it's starting to show its age."

"I hated that house. Always smelled of bananas."

"From what I've read, it sounds as if you and your husband were quite happy there." And then because he wanted to wedge the name into the conversation, he added, "Until Pauline showed up. Then I gather things got rocky."

"Hah." Margo knocked back the rest of whatever was in her coffee mug. "Don't talk to me about *Pauline*. I'm sick of hearing about *Pauline*. They ought to let *Pauline* rot in peace."

"I'm beginning to think I should have done just that. I'm writing a book about her. A biography. I'm afraid I'm not doing a very good job of it."

Margo pressed the boxy glasses against her face and peered at him. "You're the one. Lorna said something. I can't remember anymore. That's why they stuck me in the loony bin."

"You don't live here?"

"I'm on a day pass. Listen, who do you think's gonna read a book like that about *Pauline*?"

It was a reasonable question, one his nonsenile editor had asked him years ago. "At the moment," he said, "I'm more concerned about finishing it. There are too many questions I haven't been able to find answers to."

"You know what I say: don't know the answer, make it up."

At least there was a consensus on this point.

"Down at the loony bin," she went on, "they ask me a question—'Did you eat your dinny-dinny tonighty-night?' How the hell am I supposed to remember? And who gives a crap anyway? 'Oh, yes, nursey, I ate it all up.

Yummy yummy.' " Her body shook with silent laughter. "What do you want to know? Did I eat my dinny-dinny?"

Desmond wasn't sure if she was talking to him or performing a monologue for an imaginary audience, but he decided to give it a try—probably an indication that he was on the verge of senility. "I can't figure out what happened after Michael died," he said. "Pauline's husband. I can't figure out why she just stopped singing."

Margo began laughing at this, so hard Desmond was afraid she might rock herself right out of her chair. When she finally quieted down a bit, she roared, "*Pauline* never *could* sing. You didn't know? Loud and raw, that was it. All heart, no talent."

"I don't agree with you there," Desmond said. "Her records were brilliant. Some of them, anyway. It took talent to express all that heart."

Margo handed him her coffee mug and told him to set it on the floor. Milk! she sneered. What did they think she was, a g.d. baby? "*Pauline* had no training, couldn't control her voice. No technique."

"Yes," Desmond said, "but she had—"

"Come here, buster. Your ears don't work. She had nothing. Except . . . Michael. That lousy son of a bitch was the inspiration for everything. How come you don't know that?"

"I've read all of her letters," he said.

"Every song was about loving *Michael*. He dies—no talent, no technique, no inspiration, no nothing. So why bother? Some things you can't fake."

"But they didn't have a close marriage," Desmond said. "Michael didn't encourage her. Michael wasn't—"

She leaned forward in her chair and swatted her hand at him. "Michael . . . was the key . . . to *every*thing. What kind of biographer are you? Go get me some more milk and those cookies, before the wind blows the roof off this crate. Are we in a house?"

Are we in a house?

The overhead lights went on. "What on earth are you doing out here?"

Desmond leapt up from his chair. "The cameras," he started to explain, and then realized Lorna wasn't talking to him.

"You told me you were going to stay in the bedroom. This room isn't air-conditioned, there's a storm out there, and there's a live oak right over the roof of this porch."

Jane was standing in the doorway, holding a glass of milk in one hand and a cookie in the other. She was looking at Desmond for explanation, but all he could do was shrug. He didn't want to irritate Lorna, and have her cut off the conversation. "I was suggesting she move into the house," he said. "She told me she was more comfortable out here."

"We were talking about *Pauline*," the old woman laughed. "He liked her records. Dummy."

Lorna took the old woman's arm and lifted her up out of the chair. The two of them shuffled to the end of the porch, up over the doorstep, and into the living room. Jane offered him a piece of her cookie. "Is that the sister?" she asked. They could hear bickering in the other room, something about tuna-fish sandwiches.

"I'm not so sure."

Lorna reappeared in the doorway and told them, pointing to the pile of equipment, that she'd given them ten minutes and they'd been there for twenty already. It was time for them to go.

In the living room, the old woman had been planted on the big puffy sofa with all the other flowers and was contentedly munching her way through a plate of fresh cookies. "I don't mean to spoil your snack," Desmond said to her. "I just have one more question."

"The interview is over," Lorna said. "I made that clear. Period."

"Oh, let him ask," the old woman said. "He's harmless enough." She winked at Desmond. "Did you put sugar in these cookies, Lorna Doone?"

"It's a simple, factual point. I've never been certain of the year your husband died."

The old woman stuffed half a cookie into her mouth. "Which husband?"

"You had more than one?" Jane asked.

"Obviously," Lorna said softly, "she's confused."

"Who wouldn't be confused?" the old woman said. "First I've got this life, then I've got the other one, then I'm stuck in the loony bin. I've got my husband, her husband. Who wouldn't be confused? It's easier being nuts."

Jane nudged Desmond, as if she wanted to tell him something surreptitiously. She probably wanted to tell him what he already knew. "One more question," he said. "That's all. I know you don't want to anymore, but if you had to, could you still sing?"

She shook with one of her silent laughs. "I already told you, I never could sing. Just hit the high C and get the hell out of there. Sometimes, to piss off those g.d. nurses in the loony bin, I get up in the middle of the night and belt out a few bars of 'Cry Me a River.' You want to hear?"

Twenty-four
The Key to Everything

"I moaned about my husband all the time, but I loved him to death. Then he died. I never much cared for the second guy I lived with. My brother-in-law. But he was crazy about me. So I figured, 'If you can't have the person you love, you might as well take the booby prize and have the person who's in love with you.'"

From *Cry Me a River:*
The Lives of Pauline Anderton by Desmond Sullivan

1.

By the time they pulled into the parking lot of the Gulf City Hotel, the rain was coming down so hard, they seemed to be driving underwater. All Jane could see through the windshield were the vague shapes of buildings and trees. Fortunately, she wasn't behind the wheel. The roads were deserted— that helped—and Desmond assured her that leaving the windshield wipers off made it easier to see. It was all too beautiful—the dark curtain of rain washing the afternoon sky, the green Gulf waters roiling beyond the seawall, the trees bent over in thirsty delight. Water, water, water.

Nothing had gone the way she'd expected it to today, and for once, that was happy news. Pauline Anderton was alive. However it affected their project, the mere fact of it was, at this moment, exhilarating. It showed that it was never too late for things to turn around, that it was never pointless to hope for a shift in wind direction and a change in the weather. All it took was patience, conviction, and commitment to pursuing the real story instead of inventing the missing pieces. Luck didn't hurt, either.

Desmond shut off the engine. "Are you ready to run?" he asked.

They dashed through the wall of water, ran into his room, and collapsed onto the beds, dripping. Miraculously, the air conditioner was turned off, and the room was blessedly warm. "What's your best guess," he said, "about the impact of this little discovery on our pilot?"

She mulled this over for a moment. "With TV, you never know. But my best guess is: feeding frenzy."

He got towels from the bathroom and tossed her one, then stood at the window, gazing out at the storm and drying his hair. Considering what had happened this morning, he seemed remarkably quiet, almost subdued. He looked gawky and frail with his wet clothes stuck to his body.

"Desmond?" she said. "Are you all right?"

He turned away from the window and faced her, the towel draped over his wet head. "I missed it," he said finally.

"What?"

"The key to everything. Michael. The whole unfinished piece of the biography."

"It probably wasn't as obvious as it now seems."

He shook his head. "It's right there—in the cards she sent, the letters she wrote, the sarcastic interviews she gave. It was all there, and I was looking at it, but I still missed it."

There was a useful cliché for this attitude, something about a gift horse. "You know it now," she said. "That's what matters, isn't it?"

"You know why I missed it, Jane? Why I wasn't seeing the key to everything in her life? Because I wasn't seeing what it was in mine."

"I imagine you're talking about Russell."

"I wasn't looking for the missing piece, I was running away from it."

The key to everything. What a great luxury to believe in the simple efficiency of a thing like that. If she were handed such a magic tool, she'd know where to go from here; how to forget Dale, how to feel like a real mother to Gerald, how to be Thomas's wife.

Desmond finished drying his hair and dropped the towel onto the bed. He opened the drawer of the bedside table. "I have something for you," he said.

If he pulled a Bible out of there, she was going to have to rethink this friendship. Fortunately, it wasn't that. He handed her a postcard. "Tim picked this up in the coffee shop yesterday morning. He asked me to give it to you."

She turned it over. *Dear Dr. Berman—Everything I haven't told you . . .* After all the confessing she'd done in the past forty-eight hours, after baring so much of her heart to Desmond, after letting him read her fictionalized appointment books, you'd think she'd be immune to shame. And yet, looking over what she'd written—*it's just that there's so much I don't want to know about myself*—she felt humiliation squeezing her chest.

"I suppose you read this?" she asked.

"Who could resist?"

She fanned herself with the card and turned it over a few more times. Her handwriting on the back was cramped and tight, a sign, no doubt, of stray obsessive-compulsive tendencies. Something else to be ashamed of. "What do I do with it, Desmond? Do I rip it up, stick it in the mail, slip it under the doctor's door?"

He sat beside her on the bed and read the message with her one more time. He opened his mouth to tell her something, stopped himself, then sighed, and began again. "It's just my opinion," he said, "but I think you addressed this to the wrong person. I think you should cross out the doctor's name and deliver it to your husband."

Jane looked at the picture on the front: a beach, water, a road to somewhere. Deliver it to Thomas. *Can we start from scratch?* That was a question she could answer herself: No, they couldn't start from scratch. They'd been married too long, and there had been too many disappointments and betrayals. They were both too damned old. But what if she, like Desmond, had been missing something all along? *There's so much I don't want to know about myself.* Not the key to everything, that was too much to hope for, not a whole new life, a concept that was too exhausting to even consider at this stage, but the starting point of a life that was a little better, a little more truthful. She really would have to give this some serious consideration. It didn't look as if the storm was about to blow over, and there wasn't anything else to do in the orange room.

2.

They left Florida two days later. They boarded a plane and lifted off into a sky so clear and blue and clean you wanted to drink it. The plane circled out over the sparkling waters of the Gulf and swung north.

They changed planes in Atlanta, and at the gate, Desmond kissed Jane goodbye and waited for his connection to New York. This detour meant he'd miss a class or two at Deerforth, but someone who'd been hired to teach a course called Creative Nonfiction surely ought to be able to come up with a convincing excuse to tell his students.

An outer edge of the storm that had battered Gulf City had pushed up the coast, wrung the heat and humidity out of the New York air, and opened the door for autumn. Or a reasonable facsimile of autumn. In the taxi from JFK, the sky looked ocean blue, and the buildings of the city were gleaming.

The door to Morning in America was locked. At two in the afternoon? That was a first. He rapped on the glass and pulled at the handle. As he was trying to peer through the window, the carpenter from next door came up to him, sandwich in one hand, coffee in the other. "They asked me to put in a buzzer," he said.

"Oh? Were they having problems?"

"Nothing like that. The neighborhood's safer than ever." He was a good-looking man with dark hair and a long, lean torso. He was wearing glasses, big brown ones, Desmond noted. Well, the world was full of eyeglasses. "If you don't have a lock on the door, people assume there's nothing inside worth buying."

"I get it. And this is the bell?"

"Ring it," he said, "and they buzz you in."

The store was tidier than usual, and there was a Bruce Springsteen album playing on the vintage 1980s stereo near the cash register. He walked to the back of the store, and then down into the basement. The walls were covered with photos of Bill and Hillary Clinton. One Formica-topped table was labeled "'90s version of '50s dining set." A door to some dark recess of the decade opened, and Russell and Melanie pushed into the room, carrying a sofa.

"Desmond!" Melanie said. "You didn't tell me he was coming in today, Russell."

"I didn't know," Russell said. "I thought you were in Florida. That's what your letter said, anyway."

"Forget the letter," Desmond said. "It wasn't honest, it wasn't truthful. I shouldn't have sent it."

They set down the sofa and Melanie pulled a pack of cigarettes out of her back pocket. "Time for me to go for a smoke. How long you staying around?" she asked.

"It depends."

"Yeah, well, I won't ask on what." She patted his shoulder on her way up the stairs.

Desmond and Russell stared at each other for a moment as the silence of the dank basement gathered around them.

"Look, Desmond," Russell finally said, "I don't know what you're doing here, but there are a few things I have to tell you."

"Don't tell me anything," Desmond said. "Please. Don't confess or apologize or blame me or tell me your plans. Just sit down and listen while I tell you how much I love you."

3.

There was a strong, unfamiliar smell in the house, so powerful it almost brought tears to Jane's eyes when she walked in the door. She followed it into the kitchen. Gerald was standing on his stool at the counter, pounding down a puffy lump of dough.

"Hi . . . mom."

"Gerald," she said. "What's that smell?"

"Fresh bread. There's a loaf in the oven, and this here is for a batch of pecan rolls."

"Oh, sweetie," she said. She went up behind him and wrapped her arms around his body as tightly as she could. "I'm so happy to see you. I missed you so much."

"I can't breathe," he said.

She let him go and kissed the back of his head. "Pecan rolls are my favorite food in the world."

"Yes, Jane, I know. That's why I'm making them."

It wasn't exactly a hello kiss, a big, warm welcome, but it was his version of the same. "Where's your father, sweetie?"

"I believe he's up in your bedroom."

By the time she got to the staircase, Thomas was standing on the landing, grinning benevolently. "Well, well," he said. "You made it. What an adventure!"

"It was that," she said. "From start to finish."

Her pulse was racing, and despite the fact that the house was cool, she could feel sweat trickling down the sides of her body. Now or never, she told herself. Just dive right in. She reached out and wrapped her fingers around the newel post to steady herself. "I don't know why anyone would want to live in a climate . . ." That wasn't a promising start. It was best to try again. "Thomas. I have to talk to you."

"I hope it's not as serious as it sounds."

"Remember the night Joyce had her baby? You told me you'd coached a soccer team, and I said I didn't know? There are a couple of things you don't know about me."

He looked so ridiculously tall, standing up there on the landing, gazing down at her. After a moment, he said, "Are you sure I don't know, Jody?"

"No, I'm not. But it doesn't matter whether you know or not, I want to tell you, anyway."

She began to feel clearer as she walked up the stairs. She'd always imagined she'd lead a tumultuous love life, full of money, passion, and painless tragedies. Oh well. Her marriage to Thomas wasn't a passionate love story or a tragic love story. It wasn't a great love story. But maybe, in the end, it was her love story.

Twenty-five
The Man I Love

1.

Rosemary Boyle clicked off the television set and rearranged the stack of pillows on the bed in her New York sublet. This wasn't the most spacious apartment she'd rented over the years, and the light was barely adequate; but whoever had furnished it had a pillow obsession. The place looked like a harem and was a sprawler's paradise. Too bad she preferred sitting upright in a stiff chair. The one thing she couldn't argue with was the location. It took her fifteen minutes to walk to the class she was teaching at Columbia, and she'd been told it was only a block and a half to the Hudson. One of these days she'd stroll in a westerly direction and glance at the river. The sight of it might inspire a poem. On second thought, maybe she wouldn't walk that way; she didn't like paeans to nature, those limpid sonnets that were supposed to make you applaud the writer's sensitivity to lower forms of life and scenic vistas. She'd take an old-fashioned versified transcription of a therapy session—full of anger, self-pity, and blame—any day. Those were always good for a laugh.

She tossed the remote control onto the night table. She'd paid for a whole month of cable just so she could watch Jane's big documentary project and prove what a good, devoted friend she was, but good friend or not, she didn't intend to lie here and listen to Pauline Anderton howling her way through "Over the Rainbow" as the end credits rolled. At this very moment, people all over the country were probably tripping over their feet in a mad dash for their mute buttons.

In one hour, she was heading out to a party a friend of Desmond Sullivan's was throwing for him and Jane. Prior to watching the documentary, Rosemary had been dreading the event, assuming she'd have to control her drinking so she wouldn't end up in a dark corner, three sips past sober, telling someone what she really thought of the thing. Now that she'd seen it, she could drink herself into a stupor without worry; *Cry Me a River* was actually not horrible. Jane had produced an odd, interesting film that not only told the story of a (boring) life, but also had something—not much, but something—to say about the music business, the fleeting nature of celebrity, and even, God forbid, about love. Hats off to Jane Cody and the sentimental Mr. Sullivan.

Rosemary shoved the plump, orange cat off one of the pillows. He hissed and took a swipe at her. "Just try it," she said. She picked him up and dropped him onto the floor. She'd been with Fuddy for almost three years now, ever since that Boston teaching stint. Aside from Charlie, this was the longest live-in relationship of her adult life. The woman from whom she'd been subletting the Boston apartment had called her in May of that year—two weeks before she was due to return from wherever she'd been—and told Rosemary she'd suddenly developed an allergy to cats, and that if Rosemary didn't agree to take Fuddy with her when she moved out, he would most likely have to be "put down."

"I've had him for eight years," the woman had said, "and I'd just *hate* to have to do that to him."

Rosemary didn't mind being manipulated as long as the person was clever about it—had a plan they'd thought through and used a shred of imagination. This gal was making so little effort, it was insulting. Who developed allergies after eight years of living with an animal?

"Don't worry about Fuddy," Rosemary had told the woman.

"You'll take him?"

"I'll kill him."

She and the cat were a good couple. They respected each other's turf and never gave in to cuddly mawkishness. She didn't like to think that she'd turned into one of those cat people she loathed—smelling of kitty litter and covered with clumps of fur—but even if she had, it was her little secret. The only visitors she had these days were a couple of students she'd talked into doing her housecleaning once a week, and they were too young and too eager to boost their grades to notice anything.

Jane Cody's biggest character flaw was that she didn't realize how incredibly lucky she'd always been. The documentary was a perfect example. She hooked up with Desmond Sullivan on a dubious project to profile the life of a woman who was of absolutely no interest to anyone. Then it turned out that even if no one cared that Pauline Anderton had *lived*, everyone cared that she *hadn't* died. She stopped singing after her husband's death—they should have given her the Nobel Peace Prize for that—and went to live with her sister and brother-in-law in some hellish suburb with a name that sounded like a skin disease. When the sister dropped dead, everyone mistakenly thought it was Pauline who had kicked the bucket. So off she goes to Florida with the brother-in-law, who—hard to imagine, but there's no accounting for taste—had always had a yearning for her. She would have stayed there in Gulf City, yet another of the planet's garden spots, and lived out her days in happy, senile obscurity, if only Jane and Desmond hadn't tripped over her and blown her cover.

Rosemary had to admit that Jane had had the good sense to spot the story's sideshow appeal and exploit its potential. She ran with it—ran right out of public television, for starters—and panhandled some money from one of those cable stations that are desperate for anything they can market as a World Premiere. If you believed what Jane had told her, they'd finished filming the next biography in the series she was producing. Desmond Sullivan's Anderton book had been published six months ago. Rosemary had stumbled over a couple of respectful reviews, but so far, judging from its rank on Amazon.com, it was far behind *Dead Husband* in sales. She wasn't going to gloat over that fact—not in public, anyway. Too bad for Desmond's sales figures he and Jane hadn't discovered that Pauline Anderton had murdered a few people or was really a man. Even Jane Cody couldn't guarantee that much luck.

Ever since college, Rosemary had felt competitive with Jane. She wasn't sure why that was, although she suspected it had something to do with the similarities in their personalities. People talked about competition between friends as something shameful, but what greater compliment is there to someone you love than to want to rise to her level of accomplishment—and then leave her in the dust as you climb past her?

Pretty soon she was going to have to hoist herself up from this mountain of pillows and get ready for the party. Out of respect for Jane and Desmond, she'd make an effort with her clothes. It was a cloudy spring night with the promise of showers. There was a faint whiff of floral sweetness in the air, even in Manhattan. She'd wear heels and maybe a black dress she'd bought the other day. It was much too short for someone over forty, but that was part of its appeal. She didn't dance, eat, speak, or write gracefully, so why should she attempt to age gracefully? Her goal was to get more offensively outrageous with each passing year.

When she got to the party, she'd plant herself in a poorly lit spot in the room, and applaud Jane and Desmond heartily. They deserved it. They'd raised the dead. Poor Charlie. She'd tried to raise him from the dead, but all she'd done was raise a few hundred grand. And now, the final indignity: after six and a half years, his death barely stung her at all. There were days when she had only the most fleeting thoughts of him, and other days when she actually believed it might be nice to have the love and companionship of another human being. Fortunately, there weren't many of those latter days. She was happy with the cat and the occasional bottle of Chianti.

She closed her eyes and settled back on the pillows. If she fell asleep and woke up at dawn, having missed the champagne and small talk, she wouldn't exactly drown in regret. Given her current problems with sleep, that didn't seem likely. It was time to face the music, time to dig out her party clothes and her public persona.

2.

Rosemary took one last glance around the room, set her empty glass on a windowsill, and began to slither through the crowd as unobtrusively as she could. It was nearly midnight, long past her bedtime, and the party was just beginning to get its second wind. She'd been holding up her corner of the overdecorated living room for two hours, and now, at last, it was time to go home.

She'd guessed right about this party from start to finish: the toasts for Jane and Desmond, the applause, the delicate finger food, the delicate waiters. It was all very merry and fitting, but she'd lost her taste for cheerful celebrations like this—unless they were organized to celebrate her accomplishments. And unless she figured out a follow-up to *Dead Husband,* that wasn't going to happen anytime soon. There were too many couples drifting around the apartment for any real fun: the married academics, bored senseless with each other but inseparable; the hosts, cooing and clingy, but obviously trawling the party for an *amuse-bouche* or two to spend the night with them; all those inscrutable pairs of well-scrubbed men who might be anything from lovers to fraternal twins. Desmond and his garrulous little lover had barely parted company once all evening, a dead giveaway that neither one trusted the other. And then there was Jane and Thomas, down from Boston and both flushed with Jane's newfound semisuccess. The two of them seemed to have discovered a fresh level of compatibility in recent years, something Rosemary had envied, right up to an hour ago when Jane had introduced her to a dark, handsome co-producer. "Andrew," she'd said, and then let her hand linger on his arm in a proprietary way, as if she wanted Rosemary to know— or assume—there was more to their relationship than business. Lock up your sons and lovers, ladies, a happily married wife and mother was on the loose.

Couples were so smug, so self-satisfied, even when unfaithful and miserable. The worst of it was when people approached her in tandem, trying to make polite conversation, silently saying: Too bad the ark is a couples-only resort and you singles are going to be left here to drown.

She found the bedroom where the coats had been stashed and pulled her sweater from the middle of the pile on the bed. As she was putting it on, she heard a giggle come from the bathroom. She peered in and saw Jane's son and the equally unappealing friend he'd dragged down from Boston—a girl named Schenectady or Newburgh or something—going through the medicine cabinet. Gerald would be eight now and was even larger than the last time she'd seen him, and he was wearing a red corduroy jumpsuit with a zipper up the front. Poor Jane.

"What are you children doing in there?" she asked.

Both turned, the girl frightened and embarrassed. Gerald was holding a box of condoms. In that terrifying adult voice of his, he said, "Plattsburgh has a headache and I was trying to find her an aspirin."

"Likely story," Rosemary said. She took the condoms from Gerald and put the box on the top shelf of the medicine chest. There were several bottles of prescription pills in there, but all of them were safely out of even Gerald's reach. As she was closing the cabinet, she noticed one on the bottom shelf. She read the label as she moved it to higher ground: Valium. It had been years since she'd felt the sweet leveling of Valium. Everyone was taking Xanax these days, a more sophisticated but less satisfying drug. There were only about three pills left in the bottle. She casually slipped it into the pocket of her sweater.

"I saw that!" Gerald said.

She sighed and turned to him. "Yes? And what are you going to do about it?"

"I'm going to tell."

"Please do," she said.

But as she was leaving the bathroom, she thought better of her actions. She went back, opened the medicine chest and handed Gerald the box of condoms. "Just don't say anything until I've left the building."

One feature of the party she hadn't guessed at was that the hosts would have the nerve to use Pauline Anderton for background music. Throughout the night, her voice had been braying in the distance, as appropriate for atmosphere as a construction worker with a jackhammer. When she stepped out of the bedroom, she heard a surprisingly calm and subtle version of "The Man I Love" oozing out of the speakers in the next room. Guitar and piano and maybe a cello somewhere behind them. *Someday he'll come aloooong.* Tears started to well up behind Rosemary's eyes. That raspy, awful, honest voice was touching a raw nerve. She absolutely would not cry in public.

She made it to the entryway of the apartment in one piece, but Anderton was barely through the first verse, and the thing was getting more emotional every second. She buttoned her sweater and grabbed the doorknob.

"Leaving so soon?"

It was one of the hosts, the willowy one with the pretty skin and the cheekbones, the one who'd obviously had some work done around his eyes. Velan, Vegan—something along those lines.

"I'm afraid so," she said. "Tomorrow's a school day."

"Tomorrow's Sunday, darling."

"I teach Sunday school. *Darling.*" But no, she wasn't going to leave on a bitter note. "I had a wonderful time. Thank Paul for me."

"Peter."

"Him too."

He opened the door for her and leaned in the doorway, watching as she walked down the hall. "May I tell you something?"

She stopped. "What is it?"

"You have got gorgeous legs."

If she turned around and looked right at him, she really was going to burst into tears. "Thank you," she said.

It was raining, one of those soft, spring rains that wash down the streets and refresh the trees and flowers, and make you think, for a few minutes anyway, the whole planet is a wondrous, self-sustaining garden. Rosemary loved rain like this, unless, of course, she was trying to hail a cab. She stood in the gutter with her arm out as taxi after taxi sped past her. Her hair was wet and her sweater and dress were clinging to her back. Self-pity was sneaking up on her, getting ready to grab her by the throat. She couldn't get Pauline Anderton's voice out of her head—*Someday someday someday someday.* She didn't understand how a rocky and raw and unruly sound like that could spark in her so much strong, uninvited longing.

Some creep on the street let out a piercing whistle and—of course—a cab appeared from nowhere, drove right past her, and stopped halfway down the block. She ought to run down there and start a fight. When she looked closer, she saw it was Melanie, that little dyke business partner of Russell's who'd paid so much attention to her at the party. Can I get you another drink? Would you like to try one of these hors d'oeuvres? I'll bet your students are all in love with you. Was that guy bothering you? Well, if she had the balls to whistle like that, she'd earned the cab. Except she wasn't getting in; she was holding the door open and beckoning Rosemary.

"Come on," she called out.

What chivalry! Rosemary brushed the rain off her hair, straightened out her dress, and walked down the street. Slowly. She had gorgeous legs.

"Thank you," she told Melanie. "You're a real gentleman."

Judging from the grin, she'd taken it as a compliment. "I try my best," she said.

Rosemary got in and Melanie shut the door behind her. She leaned her head into the open window. "Have a good trip, Rosemary Boyle."

Rosemary was surprised by her own disappointment. "I assumed we'd be sharing," she said.

"I'm going downtown."

"What a shame." *Still I'm sure to meet him one day . . . maybe . . .* "Why don't you come along for the ride? My treat."

"You mean it?" Melanie asked, already opening the door.

Rosemary gave her address and the driver pulled out into the speeding traffic, windshield wipers flapping. Through the rain-washed windows, the street was a blur of pretty, garish lights, and the city looked like a carnival. Melanie took off her jacket, some leather, military thing, and draped it over Rosemary's shoulders. Maybe inviting Melanie along had been a bad idea— if only she'd left before that goddamned song had come on. But the jacket was warm, and Melanie, who couldn't seem to stop grinning, had insanely beautiful teeth. And after all, if you didn't take a few chances in life, you'd never discover anything new about yourself, you'd never have a fresh source of inspiration, and you'd end up dragging around your dead husband for eternity.

The driver was a genius at navigating the lights, and in no time at all they were gliding up Broadway, a mere few minutes from her building. Now or never, Rosemary thought. If the whole thing was a complete bust, she could take a Valium. She reached out and touched the gold stud in Melanie's earlobe. "What do you say we stop and pick up a bottle of cheap Chianti?" she asked. "You're not allergic to cats, are you?"

Acknowledgments

My thanks to the Ragdale Foundation, the Writers' Room of Boston, the Dorset Colony House, and Chuck Adams.